One More Sunrise

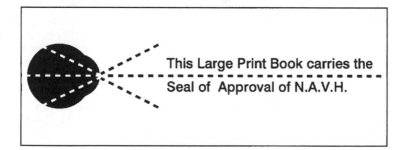

This Large Print Book carries the
Seal of Approval of N.A.V.H.

Frontier Doctor Trilogy
Book One

One More
Sunrise

Al & JoAnna Lacy

Thorndike Press • Waterville, Maine

Published in 2006 by arrangement with
Multnomah Publishers, Inc.

Thorndike Press® Large Print Christian Historical Fiction.

The tree indicium is a trademark of Thorndike Press.

The text of this Large Print edition is unabridged.
Other aspects of the book may vary from the original edition.

Set in 16 pt. Plantin by Elena Picard.

Printed in the United States on permanent paper.

Library of Congress Cataloging-in-Publication Data

Lacy, Al.
    One more sunrise : frontier doctor trilogy /
by Al & JoAnna Lacy. — Large print ed.
        p. cm.
    ISBN 0-7862-8250-9 (lg. print : hc : alk. paper)
    1. Women physicians — Fiction. 2. Denver (Colo.) —
Fiction. 3. Orphan trains — Fiction. 4. Physicians —
Fiction. 5. Large type books. I. Title.
PS3562.A256O54 2005
813'.54—dc22   2005027022

This book is
affectionately dedicated
to our dear friend, faithful fan,
and brother in Christ, Art Rempel
of Camrose, Alberta, Canada.
God bless you, Art! We love you.

As the Founder/CEO of NAVH, the only national health agency solely devoted to those who, although not totally blind, have an eye disease which could lead to serious visual impairment, I am pleased to recognize Thorndike Press★ as one of the leading publishers in the large print field.

Founded in 1954 in San Francisco to prepare large print textbooks for partially seeing children, NAVH became the pioneer and standard setting agency in the preparation of large type.

Today, those publishers who meet our standards carry the prestigious "Seal of Approval" indicating high quality large print. We are delighted that Thorndike Press is one of the publishers whose titles meet these standards. We are also pleased to recognize the significant contribution Thorndike Press is making in this important and growing field.

Lorraine H. Marchi, L.H.D.
Founder/CEO
NAVH

★ Thorndike Press encompasses the following imprints: Thorndike, Wheeler, Walker and Large Print Press.

Prologue

When the challenge of the Western frontier began luring men and women westward from the eastern, northern, southern, and midwestern states in the middle of the nineteenth century, they found a land that was beyond what they had imagined. From the wide Missouri River to the white-foamed shore of the Pacific Ocean, wherever they settled, they clung to the hope of a bright new beginning for their lives.

Often their hopes were dashed by fierce opposition from the Indians who had inhabited the land before them. At other times there was also struggle for survival against the hard winters and the loneliness of the vast frontier.

Those determined pioneers who braved the elements, the loneliness, and the attacks of the Indians, proved themselves to be a hardy lot and were unknowingly entering upon a struggle that would ultimately give their descendants control of half a continent.

In his book *The Winning of the West*, Theodore Roosevelt said, "The borderers who thronged across the mountains, the restless hunters, the hard, dogged frontier ranchers and farmers, were led by no one commander. They were not carrying out the plans of any far-sighted leader. In obedience to the instincts working half-blindly within their hearts, they made in the wilderness homes for their children."

These commendable accomplishments, however, were not without tremendous cost of life for the first twenty to thirty years. Of all the perils confronting the settlers of the Wild West, serious illness, injuries from mishaps of countless number, and wounds from battles with Indians and outlaws were the most dreaded. The lack of proper medical care resulted in thousands of deaths.

The scarcity of medical doctors on the frontier in those early years made life extremely difficult and sometimes unbearable. As towns were being established in the West, little by little, medical practitioners east of the wide Missouri caught the challenge of the frontier.

Communities that grew around army

posts and forts had the military doctors to care for them. But many towns had no doctors at all. However, as time passed, this improved. By the mid-1870s, towns of any size at all had at least one doctor. The larger towns had clinics, and a few even had hospitals.

Often the frontier doctor had to travel long distances at any hour — by day or night — in all kinds of weather. Time and again the doctor's own life was in jeopardy. He might ride on horseback or drive his buggy thirty miles or more to a distant home in the mountains, to a home in a small settlement on the prairie, or to a ranch or farm where he would care for a patient. He would perform surgery when needed, set broken bones, deliver a baby, or administer necessary medicines. Most of the time, he would sit with his patient for hours before leaving his or her side, then sleep on the return trip while his horse found the way home.

Quite often the frontier doctor's only remuneration consisted of fresh vegetables from a garden, maybe a jar or two of canned corn or beans, a plucked chicken, or a chunk of beef cut from a recently slaughtered steer.

The successful frontier doctor was not

only a hardy man, but was obviously dedicated to his profession.

In this Frontier Doctor series, we will tell our readers three stories involving just such a physician.

One

The lone rider bent low in the saddle as he kept his sleek, muscular gray roan gelding at a full gallop on the rolling prairie, leaving small clouds of dust in his wake. Riding due east toward Cheyenne in the bright morning sunshine, his angular jaw was set in a grim line.

Beyond the scattered cattle ranches and the foothills behind him were the towering Rocky Mountains, the lofty peaks taking their magnificent jagged bite out of the azure Wyoming sky.

Rancher Earl Monroe squinted against the wind produced by the speed of his horse and said aloud, "You've just got to be in your office, Dr. Logan. You've just got to be."

At the office of Dr. Jacob Logan on Main Street in Cheyenne, the doctor's wife — who served as receptionist — busied herself freshening up the waiting

11

room. At the moment, there were no patients in the chairs, so she was taking advantage of the lull in appointments to do a little dusting.

Although she was in her early fifties, lovely Naomi Logan could easily pass for a woman in her forties. While using the feather duster adeptly, she was humming a lilting gospel tune. When the waiting room had been cleaned and adjusted to her satisfaction, Naomi moved behind her desk and placed the feather duster in the cabinet behind it. When she started to sit down, the desk calendar caught her eye and she realized that she hadn't flipped it to the new month since coming to work an hour earlier.

She turned the calendar's small page and sighed as she looked at it. "Tuesday, June 1, 1880. Where does the time go?"

Suddenly her attention was drawn out the large front window to a gray roan horse skidding to a stop at the hitch rail in front of the white clapboard building. The rider hurriedly left the saddle and dashed across the boardwalk, heading for the door.

Naomi immediately recognized rancher Earl Monroe and remained standing behind the desk as he came in, an anxious look on his face. She brushed a stray wisp of hair from her forehead and smiled.

"Hello, Earl. You look worried. What's wrong?"

The rancher wiped a palm over his mouth. "It's an emergency, ma'am. Is Dr. Logan in?"

"My husband is delivering a baby on a ranch about twenty miles east of town, Earl, but my son is here. He's taking care of a patient in the examining room with Nurse Ella Dover's help."

Monroe's brow furrowed. "You have a son that's a doctor?"

"Yes. Dane is an M.D. He just joined his father as partner in the practice a week ago. He's been doing his internship right here at Memorial Hospital for the past two years. He's a good doctor. What's your emergency, Earl?"

"It's really not *my* emergency, Mrs. Logan. You are aware that our nearest neighbors are Abel and Betty Donaldson, who are also your patients."

"Yes. They own the *Rocking D Ranch.* What is it?"

"You know their twelve-year-old son, Joshua."

"Yes."

"He got bucked off a horse about half an hour ago and landed on his shoulder. It's hurt bad. The boy's in extreme pain, and they were afraid to try to put him in a wagon to bring him to town. I happened to be visiting the Donaldsons at the time, and since I had to come into town anyway, I told them I'd ride like the wind and come tell Dr. Logan about Joshua, and ask him to get out to the ranch as soon as possible. Could — could your son go out there right away?"

Naomi was used to seeing frantic people in the office. She told him to sit down and she would be back shortly. Earl Monroe watched her hurry through the door at the rear of the office and then sat down on the designated chair.

Less than a minute had passed when Naomi reentered the office. Earl stood up. Naomi said, "Dane — ah, the young Dr. Logan is almost done with his patient, Earl. He will head to the *Rocking D* immediately. Can you write down the directions to the ranch?"

"If you'll give me a pencil and a piece of paper, I'll draw him a little map."

Naomi quickly produced the items from the top of her desk and handed them to him. Earl sketched the map for young Dr. Logan to use, and thanking Naomi, excused himself, saying he had to go tend to his other errand.

At the *Rocking D Ranch,* Joshua Donaldson was sitting up on his bed with a pile of pillows at his back. His parents were sitting on wooden chairs beside the bed, with their other two children — ten-year-old Sarah and eight-year-old Ruth — standing between them. Both girls were looking at their brother with compassion as he cradled the arm of the injured shoulder up tight against his chest.

Blinking rapidly, Joshua was determined not to cry as he bit his lips in an effort to keep the tears from forming. His pain-filled blue eyes stared at his parents. Ever so slowly, though, his eyes began to fill up, and one lonely tear slipped from the corner of his left eye.

Betty patted his arm. "Son, it's all right to cry. Don't worry. There's no one here but us, and we certainly understand."

As she spoke, the mother rose to her feet and gently brushed back the blond hair that had tumbled onto his forehead.

She glanced at the clock on the nearby dresser, noting that it was almost ten o'clock. "Dr. Logan should be here soon, honey. Earl's horse is a fast one. Dr. Logan will have medicine to ease your pain, and he'll fix you up good as new."

The tears were now flowing from both eyes, making twin streams down Joshua's pallid cheeks.

"Your mama is right, son," said Abel, laying a hand gently on the boy's leg. "There's nothing wrong with crying when you're in pain."

Joshua wiped the tears away with the back of his hand, then quickly returned it to support the arm of his injured shoulder.

"I love you, Josh," said Sarah, tears in her eyes.

"Me, too," put in her little sister. "I would take the pain for you if I could."

Joshua let a tight smile curve his lips. "Thank you, Ruthie. I love you both very much."

Suddenly through the open window of Joshua's room, they heard pounding hooves and the sound of a bouncing buggy approaching the house.

Rising from the chair and heading for the bedroom door, Abel said, "That's gotta be Doc Logan. Be back with him in a minute."

Breathing a prayer for his son as he dashed through the house to the front door, Abel thanked the Lord that Dr. Logan had arrived. When he opened the door, he was surprised to see a young man

16

alighting from a buggy with a medical bag in his hand.

He stepped out on the porch. "We were expecting Dr. Logan. Who are you, sir?"

Dr. Dane Logan was twenty-four years of age, tall, slender, and dark-headed. Hurrying up to the rancher, he said, "I'm Dr. Jacob Logan's son, Dane, Mr. Donaldson. I just became his partner a week ago. Dad is delivering a baby on a ranch east of Cheyenne, so when Earl Monroe came to the office and told Mom about Joshua having been bucked off the horse and suffering a shoulder injury, I headed this way as soon as I could."

Abel smiled, extended his hand, and Dr. Dane grasped it. "Thank you for coming, Doctor. Follow me."

Seconds later, as Abel and the young physician hurried into Joshua's room, surprise showed on the faces of Betty, the girls, and the patient.

"Mama, children," said Abel, "this is Dr. Dane Logan. He's Dr. Jacob Logan's son. Dr. Dane just became his father's partner a week ago. When Earl got to the office, Mrs. Logan told him her husband was delivering a baby out of town, but this fine young doctor came in his father's place."

"Thank you for coming, Doctor," said

Betty, affording him a gentle smile. "We'll stay out of the way while you examine Josh."

Dr. Dane moved up to the bed, glanced at the girls, then looked down at the boy. "I'll do my best not to hurt you any more than necessary, Josh, but it will have to hurt some in order for me to determine the extent of your injury."

Joshua bit his lower lip and nodded. "Yes, sir."

The boy winced and sucked air through his teeth a few times while the doctor made a careful examination of the damaged shoulder.

When he finished, Dr. Dane ran his gaze to the parents. "It is definitely dislocated. I'll have to put the shoulder back in place." Then he said to his patient, "Josh, I'm going to give you a strong dose of laudanum. It will take about thirty minutes for it to take full effect. It's going to hurt when I put your shoulder back in place, but the laudanum will make the pain much easier to withstand."

Joshua looked up at the doctor solemnly. "Yes, sir."

Dr. Dane opened his medical bag and took out a bottle of syrupy liquid.

When the heavy dose of laudanum had

been administered, Betty said, "Since it will take about half an hour for the laudanum to do its job, Doctor, how about some hot coffee? I have some on the stove that I was going to offer your father."

Dr. Dane smiled. "Sounds good, ma'am."

Betty hurried from the room.

Dr. Dane stepped up close to his patient and took hold of the pillows at his back. "Let's get you in a horizontal position, Josh."

Abel stepped up and offered his assistance. With the father's help, Dr. Dane carefully eased the boy down on the bed and placed one of the pillows under his injured shoulder. Gently squeezing Joshua's hand, the doctor said, "Just try to relax, Josh, and let the medicine do its work."

Dr. Dane noticed that the evidence of the pain Joshua was experiencing in his shoulder was already beginning to ease from his face.

Moments later, Betty, Abel, and the doctor were sitting at a small table in the corner of the room, sipping coffee, while the girls remained beside their brother.

Betty looked toward her son. "He seems to be in less pain already, Doctor."

Dr. Dane nodded. "We'll get that

19

shoulder put back in place, and we'll have him all well in a few weeks, ma'am."

Abel took a sip and set the cup down. "I wasn't aware that Dr. and Mrs. Logan had a son. Do you have brothers and sisters?"

"No, sir. I need to explain that I'm adopted. They adopted me several years ago."

"Oh. Have you been elsewhere until now?"

"Well, the past two years, I've been doing my internship at Memorial Hospital here in town."

Betty's eyes showed keen interest. "So when did the Logans adopt you?"

Dane grinned. "Nine years ago. You see, I was born and raised on Manhattan Island in New York City. Just before my fifteenth birthday, a street gang murdered my parents, Craig and Fay Weston, and my twelve-year-old sister, Diane, and my nine-year-old brother, Ronnie."

Betty's eyes widened and her hand went to her mouth. "Oh, how terrible. I'm so sorry."

"That *is* terrible," said Abel. "So how did you end up being adopted by the Logans?"

Dane glanced toward Joshua, then looked back at the Donaldsons. "It's a long story, but I'll shorten it so I can start on Joshua's shoulder in another twenty minutes. I had a burning desire inside me to be a physician and surgeon since I was very small. While I was living on the streets, I was befriended by a doctor and his wife. My relationship with Dr. Lee Harris and his dear wife, Maude, whetted my appetite even more to become a medical doctor." He pointed to his medical bag where it sat beside Joshua's bed. "That medical bag used to belong to Dr. Harris. He gave it to me as a keepsake to remember him by."

Both the Donaldsons smiled and nodded.

Dane went on. "Well, eventually I ended up with the Children's Aid Society in New York and was put on an orphan train. On my way west, the train stopped in Chicago. Dr. Logan had been doing a series of lectures at Northwestern University Medical College, and Mom — Mrs. Logan — was with him. They boarded the train to go home to Cheyenne. We got acquainted along the way, and before the train reached Cheyenne, they told me they wanted to adopt me. I was overjoyed and quickly accepted their offer."

Abel shook his head in wonderment. "Isn't that something?"

"Wonderful!" said Betty.

"That's for sure. Well, I finished high school here in Cheyenne, then Dad and Mom sent me to Northwestern University Medical College in Chicago. I graduated in May 1878."

Abel nodded. "This is why we didn't know the Logans had a son. We moved here from Nebraska in 1875. You were away at college. And, of course, since you were interning at Memorial Hospital, and none of us have had to be hospitalized in the past two years, we had no way of meeting you. Well, Dr. Dane Logan, we're sure happy that you're working with your father!"

"We sure are," said Betty. "I'm so glad you were able to fulfill your desire to become a medical doctor. And you must be thrilled to be partner to your adoptive father."

A smile spread over the young doctor's handsome face. "Words can't even describe it, ma'am. Of course, someday I want to have a practice of my own, but until then, I'll relish every moment working with Dad."

Dane then looked at the clock on the dresser and glanced to Joshua's bed where his sisters stood beside him. "Well, I'll finish this cup of coffee and go to work on my patient."

When the doctor drained his coffee cup and headed toward the bed, Betty sent Sarah and Ruth to their room, knowing that Joshua was still going to experience some pain.

A drowsy Joshua opened his eyes and looked up at the doctor when he felt him touch his arm. He gave him a searching, uneasy stare.

Dr. Dane squeezed the boy's arm. "Son, I know this is still going to be painful for you, but I'll do it as quickly and gently as possible."

Joshua licked his lips and nodded. "Okay." His voice cracked.

The parents moved up close to the bed and looked on, wincing, as they watched the doctor set the shoulder. As was expected, Joshua experienced some pain, especially at the instant the shoulder was snapped back in place.

Dr. Dane commended him for being such a brave boy, then wrapped the shoulder and put Joshua's arm in a sling, keeping it close to his body. When he had finished, Joshua set dull eyes on the doctor and said with a slurring tongue, "Th-thank you, Dogtor. Thad wasn' as bad as I thoud id would b-be."

"You're welcome, Joshua. Now, I want

you to lie here quietly and let the laudanum relax you so you can go to sleep. And, Joshua?"

"Yes, sir?"

"No physical activities until I say so. And *no* horseback riding!"

A lazy, lopsided grin formed on Joshua's lips. "Yez, zir."

"I'll be back to check on you soon. You are a very good patient, and you're a brave boy. I'm sure your parents are proud of you."

Abel and Betty smiled at each other, then at their son. Abel said, "We sure are, Josh."

Joshua let another crooked grin curve his lips, then closed his heavy eyelids.

Dr. Dane stayed at the boy's side until the laudanum took effect more heavily, and Joshua finally slipped into a deep sleep.

The doctor turned to the parents. "He'll be fine. I'll leave you some powders to give him when he awakes. They'll keep his pain to a minimum. I'll be back in three days to check on him."

Betty glanced at the clock on the dresser. "Dr. Logan, it's past noon. Would you like some lunch before you head back to town?"

The doctor grinned. "I'll just take you up on it, ma'am."

Checking his sleeping patient one more time, Dr. Dane followed the couple toward the kitchen. Betty paused at the door of the girls' room to tell them Dr. Logan was staying for lunch, and she needed their help.

Earlier that morning, Betty had put a large kettle of navy bean soup on the kitchen stove, and while going after the coffee before Joshua's shoulder was set by the doctor, she stirred up the fire under the kettle. When they entered the kitchen, the tantalizing aroma made the doctor's mouth water.

The two men were ordered by Betty to sit down, and as Dr. Dane sat on the chair assigned him by Betty, he looked up and saw two picture frames on the walls that had Scripture verses printed on white paper. One read:

> For the wages of sin is death;
> but the gift of God is eternal life
> through Jesus Christ our Lord.
> — Romans 6:23

The other one read:

> Jesus saith unto him,
> I am the way, the truth, and the life:

no man cometh unto the Father,
but by me.
— John 14:6

A smile spread over the doctor's face.
"Hey, I love those Scriptures you have up
there! Looks to me like I'm in a Christian
home."

Sarah and Ruth were standing at the
cupboard. They looked at each other and
grinned.

Abel matched the doctor's smile. "You
sure are, my friend. And since Dr. Jacob
Logan and his wife are Christians, it
doesn't surprise me that their adopted son
is!"

Dr. Dane laughed. "Well, I guess I'd
better come clean. Mom told me you were
Christians when she gave me the map Earl
Monroe had drawn so I could find this
place. I knew what kind of home I was
coming to all along."

"In a couple minutes, we'll be ready to
eat," said Betty, "and we'll see if our new
doctor knows how to pray over a meal!"

Two

While Abel Donaldson was laughing over Dr. Dane Logan's touch of humor, Sarah placed a plate of hot cornbread on the table and Ruth set a small crock of butter next to it.

Betty ladled up the navy bean soup, sliced an onion to go with it, then poured milk for the girls and coffee for the rest of them. Smiling shyly at the young physician, she said, "This isn't much, Doctor, but we're happy to share it with you."

"It looks and smells like a feast to me, ma'am. Breakfast was a long time ago."

Abel scooted his chair a little closer to the table. "Well then, let's eat! As Betty suggested, Doctor, will you pray over the meal?"

Dr. Dane smiled. "I think I can handle that."

Heads were bowed, and the doctor thanked the Lord for the food, asking Him to bless it to the nourishment of their bodies. He also prayed for Joshua's shoulder to heal quickly.

When the amen was said and they started eating, Abel said, "So you like our Scripture verses in the frames, eh, Doctor?"

Dr. Dane swallowed a mouthful of soup. "Sure do. Those exact same verses were on the walls of Dr. Lee Harris's home in Manhattan. It was Dr. and Mrs. Harris who led me to the Lord."

"They have to be special people to you," said Betty.

Dr. Dane nodded. "They're both in heaven now. But I'm sure looking forward to seeing them one day over there when we'll never part again."

"It's wonderful to have that assurance, isn't it?" said Abel.

Dr. Dane picked up a slice of buttered cornbread. "That it is, my brother. That it is."

It was quiet for a minute or so while everyone worked at devouring the meal. Then Betty set her eyes on the young man. "Dr. Dane, you didn't mention a wife when you were telling us your story. Are you married?"

Dane shook his head and swallowed more soup. "No, ma'am. I'm just waiting for the Lord to bring the right young lady into my life."

Abel nodded. "Well, it'll happen in God's time, I assure you."

"Yes, sir. Sometimes I get a little impatient, but I know you're right. When the Lord is ready to bring her into my life, He will do it."

"Well, it sure worked that way with me," said Abel. "Someday when we have more time, I'll tell you how God brought Betty and me together."

"I'd like to hear about it."

"Believe me, Doctor, the Lord has marvelous ways of working this kind of thing out in our lives. He has that special young lady all picked out for you, and when it's time, He will bring her to you so you'll have no doubt that she is the one He has chosen to be Mrs. Dr. Dane Logan."

"That is encouraging, Mr. Donaldson. I can hardly wait for that banner day when the Lord brings her to me."

As the meal went on, they talked about their churches. The Donaldsons explained that they belonged to a small country church a couple of miles south of their ranch, and that they loved it.

Dane told them he belonged to the same church in Cheyenne where his parents had belonged for over twenty years. He loved the pastor, and taught a teenage boys' class.

When lunch was over, Dr. Dane went back to Joshua's room and checked on him. He was still in a deep sleep.

Turning to the parents, Dr. Dane said, "Well, I'll be going now. Thank you for the good lunch. I'll be back on Friday to see how Joshua's doing."

Abel pulled his wallet from his hip pocket. "How much do I owe you, Doctor?"

Dr. Dane smiled. "You can wait till the house calls are no longer necessary to pay me, if you wish."

"I'd rather pay you as you make each call."

"All right." He touched fingers to his temple. "Let's see. You owe me three dollars."

Betty looked surprised, as did her husband.

"Now wait a minute, Doctor," Abel said. "Three dollars can't be right."

Dr. Dane's brow furrowed. "Oh. Well, let's just make it two dollars."

Abel chuckled. "Doctor, I didn't mean three dollars was too much. I meant it wasn't enough. C'mon now. You've had to ride all the way out here, and you've spent well over three hours in this house."

"But a half hour of that time was spent sitting at your table eating Mrs. Donaldson's fabulous cooking. Three dollars is plenty."

Abel pulled out a ten-dollar bill and pressed into the doctor's hand. "You take this with our thanks for taking such good care of Josh."

Dane looked at the ten-dollar bill. "Mr. Donaldson, I can't take this much for just one house call. I —"

"All right," Abel said, grinning. "Let's allow it to cover your house call on Friday too."

"That's better."

Abel looked him square in the eye. "And I mean *just* Friday's house call. Any more house calls after that will be paid by me when you're here. Understand?"

The doctor looked at Abel, but before he could reply, Abel said, "I happen to know that you doctors on this frontier often treat patients who can't pay you a nickel. Others pay you with beans, eggs, and dead chickens. God has blessed this ranch, and we'd like to make up for some of the calls you make when you don't get much. Okay?"

"Thank you, and may the Lord bless you for it."

The Donaldsons and their daughters walked out onto the front porch with the doctor and watched him climb in his buggy. He waved as he drove away, saying he would see them on Friday. They waved back, smiling.

As he drove toward the road that would take him back to town, Dr. Dane noted the great number of *Rocking D* cattle that were grazing as they were spread in clusters over the vast acres of the ranch. "I can see that you've blessed them, Lord. And I know one of the reasons why. Please bless them in a special way for what they did for me."

It was then that Dane noticed the afternoon had turned warm. He pulled the horse to a halt, shrugged out of his suit coat, and laid it on the seat beside him. Taking up the reins, he thought about his father having been called to the ranch east of Cheyenne to deliver a baby. If Dad wasn't back yet, there might be a waiting room full of people back at the office. He put the horse to a comfortable trot, with a warm breeze blowing on his face.

He looked up at the clear cobalt blue sky, and thought of his childhood in New York and his years at Northwestern University in Chicago. He told himself the sky was never as clear back there as it was here in the West. So much of the time it was overcast and gray.

A contented smile spread over his face. "Thank You, Lord, for letting me make this part of the country my home. Being a much-needed physician here in frontier America is great. It couldn't possibly be better."

He snapped the reins and put his steed to a faster trot. Easing back on the seat, he let his mind wander back to the conversation at the Donaldson table about the young lady the Lord had already chosen and would one day send into his life to be his bride.

With the warm breeze touching his face and the sound of the horse's hooves pounding the soft surface of the road, Dane's thoughts trailed back to lovely Tharyn Myers — the girl who had stirred his heart like none other.

Memories flooded his mind, and suddenly he was reliving how he met her and saved her life . . .

While living on the streets of Manhattan as an orphan, fifteen-year-old Dane Weston was hired at Clarkson Pharmacy by Bryce Clarkson as janitor and general hired man. Dane's friend, Dr. Lee Harris, had persuaded Clarkson to hire him when Clarkson's previous hired man had quit and moved away.

Dane's first day on the job was a Saturday. He began his work at eight o'clock that day by mopping the floor while pharmacist Bryce Clarkson was behind the counter filling prescriptions his customers had brought in and left with him late in the afternoon the day before.

The pharmacy's opening time was nine o'clock. At five minutes before opening time, Dane was wiping dust off the medicine bottles on the shelf behind the counter with a damp cloth.

Bryce Clarkson looked out the front window and saw a mother and her daughter waiting at the door. He told Dane he was going to open early for Mrs. Myers and her daughter. The Myerses were good customers.

From his place behind the counter, Dane observed as his employer opened the door and greeted Erline Myers and her daughter, Tharyn. Tharyn was very pretty, and had long auburn hair and sky blue eyes. Clarkson mentioned that he hadn't seen Tharyn since her birthday in March and jokingly asked her how it felt to be thirteen years old. She giggled and said it felt good.

The pharmacist introduced mother and daughter to Dane, explaining that he was his new hired man. When they had shaken Dane's hand, Clarkson told them how Dane recently became an orphan.

Erline and Tharyn both expressed their sympathy, and as Erline handed Clarkson two prescriptions, she asked Dane where he was living now. He replied that he was living among the thousands of other orphans on the streets and told her the location of the alley where he and nine other orphans in the colony had their cardboard boxes.

Dane told them the owner of the grocery store always made sure that the colony had plenty of water to drink and that they sometimes ate food that had been thrown in the garbage cans behind the café.

While holding the reins and keeping his horse to a trot on the rolling prairie, Dane smiled to himself. He could remember the sour look that came over Tharyn's pretty face at his mention of eating garbage. She did not comment, however.

Bryce Clarkson looked at the prescriptions Erline had placed in his hand and told her he was out of the medicine required for one of them, but that the supplier was due later that morning. He was sure he could have the prescription ready by eleven o'clock.

Erline responded by saying she would send Tharyn and a neighbor girl just before noon to pick it up. The family was going to Grand Central Station to meet her husband's sister, who was coming from Boston to spend a few days with them. They should be back home by 11:45.

Dane spoke up and told Clarkson if it was all right with him, he would deliver the medicine to the Myerses' home and save Tharyn from having to come and pick it up. Clark told him that would be fine. Mother and daughter both thanked Dane for his kindness.

As Clarkson was taking the medicine from the shelf to prepare the other prescription, he told Erline and Tharyn that Dane's goal in life was to become a physician and surgeon. Both of them commended him for wanting to be a doctor.

Dane knew they must be wondering how an orphan boy living on the streets of Manhattan could ever realize that dream. He brought this up to them, and said at that point he didn't know how he would ever do it, but somehow he would.

Erline paid Clarkson for both prescriptions, and as he handed her the medicine he had just prepared, she told Tharyn they must hurry. As mother and daughter headed toward the door, Erline told Dane they would look forward to seeing him at the apartment.

As Dane held the reins, guiding the buggy toward Cheyenne, he smiled to himself once again as he thought of how excited he was when he left the pharmacy late that morning. He could hardly wait to see Tharyn again.

The tenement where the Myers family lived was less than three blocks from the pharmacy. At 11:40, Dane entered the block where the Myerses' tenement was located, with a paper bag in his hand. He looked on with interest at a tenement where two workers were standing on a scaffold, pulling ropes through pulleys which were anchored at the top of the building. They were slowly nearing the fifth-floor balcony, which was partially finished.

As Dane passed the tenement, he glanced at a wagon parked in the street, which was loaded with building materials. His attention then went to the two big husky horses that were hitched to the wagon.

Just as Dane passed the team and wagon, he heard hoofbeats and buggy wheels in the street coming up behind him. As the buggy passed him, he saw Tharyn Myers sticking her head out the window. She called to him and waved. Dane waved back and quickened his pace.

The hired buggy rolled to a stop in front of the tenement where the Myers family lived. A man, whom Dane figured was Tharyn's father, jumped out and helped Tharyn from the buggy first. She moved back a couple of steps toward the sidewalk while the man was helping her mother out.

Suddenly two wild cries were heard, and Dane turned to look over his shoulder. He saw the two workers who had been on the scaffold at the building's fifth floor helplessly falling toward the ground. The scaffold was also falling.

The two men hit the ground not more than two seconds before the scaffold hit it a few feet away with a loud bang and clattering noise. The loud, sharp noise startled the team of horses hitched to the wagon loaded with building materials, and they bolted in blind terror.

For an instant, both Dane and Tharyn were frozen in place as they saw the wild-eyed team bolt. Erline Myers was suddenly looking that direction, eyes wide, face pale. At the same time, her husband was helping his sister out of the buggy, and the horse hitched to the buggy bolted. This sent Tharyn's aunt flying. She fell on top of Tharyn's father, knocking him down, and they both rolled against Erline's legs, toppling her.

The blindly charging team was bearing down on them at full speed with the heavily loaded wagon fish-tailing behind them.

Frozen in place, Tharyn was also directly in line with the charging team. Dane's reflexes suddenly came alive. He dropped the paper sack containing the medicine and dashed to the spot in time to grasp Tharyn and yank her out of the path of danger. The swift movement caused them both to fall on the sidewalk.

The charging horses and wagon slammed into Tharyn's parents and her aunt, leaving them in a battered, bloody heap, and headed on down the street.

Dr. Dane found himself gripping the reins so hard, pain was lancing through his fingers. He took a deep breath, relaxed his grip on the reins, and let the breath out slowly.

He thought of how Tharyn's father and aunt were killed instantly, and recalled how Erline lived a short time in a nearby hospital, then died.

Since Tharyn had no other relatives, she had no home. Dane took her to the alley where he and the small colony of orphans lived, and she became a part of the colony. Over and over, she thanked Dane for risking his own life to save hers, and in a short time, they became very close. They called each other big brother and little sister.

A ranch wagon was coming toward Dane on the road, and when the two vehicles came close, the rancher and his wife raised hands of greeting to him. Dane smiled and waved at them.

When the vehicles had met and passed each other, Dane put his mind back on Tharyn and relived the day he had the joy of seeing the sweet girl open her heart to Jesus as a result of his witnessing to her, and thought of how this drew them even closer to each other.

The buggy hit a bump and bounced Dane on the seat. He righted himself, and at the same time his mind went to that horrible day when police officers James Thornton and Fred Collins, whom he knew well, turned into the alley off the sidewalk and headed toward the group of orphans, their eyes fixed on him and their faces grim.

As the buggy maintained its course toward Cheyenne, Dane felt as if his stomach were pulled back harshly against his spine. He shuddered as he relived the nightmare of being arrested for stabbing an eleven-year-old boy named Benny Jackson to death in a nearby alley. Several people had observed the incident, and when they gave Officers Thornton and Collins the description of the teenage killer, it fit Dane perfectly. Dane's protests that he was innocent fell on deaf ears.

His thoughts then raced to the day when he stood before the judge in the courtroom after the eyewitnesses to the murder had sworn under oath that he was the one they saw kill Benny Jackson.

Bouncing on the buggy seat with the horrid memory burning into his brain, Dane's throat constricted as he relived the ghastly moment when the jury pronounced him guilty and the judge sentenced him to life in Manhattan's city prison.

Next in his recollection were the times that Tharyn came to the prison to visit him. On the heels of these memories came the reminiscence of the last time he ever saw her.

Led by a guard to the prison's visiting room, Dane looked at the pretty thirteen-year-old girl through the barred window, and he could tell by the look on her face that something was bothering her.

Tears filled Tharyn's eyes as she told him about the entire colony being picked up by Charles Loring Brace, the director of the Children's Aid Society, and taken to the Society's headquarters. She explained that they were all going to be put on an orphan train in a few days and be taken out West so they could find families who would take them in as foster children.

What was bothering her was her fear that she would never see Dane again. Not in this life.

Dane recalled reaching through the bars and taking hold of Tharyn's trembling hands. His voice quivered as he told her how glad he was that she and the other orphans in the colony were off the streets and had food and shelter. He was also glad that she and the others were going to have homes out West.

Dr. Dane's eyes misted with tears as he recalled telling Tharyn the Lord knew he was innocent, and one day would see that he was cleared of the crime and was freed from the prison. He then told Tharyn that he would want to come to wherever she had found a home in the West and see her. He asked if she would write to him there in the prison and let him know where she ended up. That way they could stay in touch by mail, and when the Lord saw to it that he was cleared of the crime and released from prison, they could see each other again.

Tharyn's voice echoed through Dane's mind as he held the buggy's reins. She said she would write him when she got settled in whatever new home she was taken into out West. And then, she said there was something else she wanted to tell him. He recalls how thrilled he was when she told him that because of his love for the field of medicine, it had rubbed off on her. She wanted to become a nurse. He encouraged her to pursue her dream.

When it was time for Tharyn to leave, the good-bye was a very emotional one, and they agreed that if they never saw each other again on earth, they knew they would meet in heaven.

Tears were in Dane's eyes as he guided the buggy closer to Cheyenne. The uneven rooftops of the town were now outlined against the distant sky.

His thoughts went to Charles Loring Brace, who visited him occasionally at the prison, believing that he indeed was innocent, and that one day God would see that he was cleared of the crime and released from prison.

Dane then happily thought of the day when the teenage boy named Monte Smalz — who strongly resembled him and had murdered Benny Jackson — was caught by the police. When Dane was released from the prison, he immediately went to the Children's Aid Society, and in a matter of weeks, was put on the orphan train that eventually took him through Chicago. There he met Dr. and Mrs. Jacob Logan, who took him home to Cheyenne with them and adopted him.

Tears filled Dane's eyes as the buggy drew near Cheyenne. "Thank you, Lord," he said with a quavering voice. "Thank You for bringing me to Cheyenne almost ten years ago and for letting me realize my dream of becoming a doctor."

Three

As Dr. Dane Logan was pulling into Cheyenne on Main Street, his thoughts went to Tharyn Myers once more. There was an ache in his heart. "Little sis, where did you end up? I never received a letter from you. There may have been some good reason why you didn't write me like you promised, but I sure wish I knew where you are."

Dane thought about the fact that not one day had passed since the last time he saw Tharyn over nine years ago, that she hadn't come to mind. He wondered again if she ever became a nurse, and if she had married by now.

He swallowed the lump that had risen in his throat. "Lord, You know the status of her life, and where she is. Please take care of her, wherever that might be."

At that moment, Dane was passing Memorial Hospital. Two nurses were coming out the lobby door. They spotted him and waved. He waved back. "Hello, ladies! Is it time to change shifts already?"

"It sure is, Doctor," called one of them. "Time to go home and get supper started pretty soon so we can have the food on the tables when our hungry husbands come home from work."

"Tell them hello for me, will you?"

"Sure will, Doctor," said one of them, and the other one nodded.

Dr. Dane was within two blocks of the office when he noticed a group of people gathered in the street in front of the Lone Pine Saloon, forming a circle around two angry men. The pair was facing each other in the center of the circle, shouting loudly. One of them was much larger than the other. Dane recognized the smaller man. He had done surgery on Ernie Piper several months ago at Memorial Hospital to remove a tumor from behind his right ear. Ernie was known for spending an hour or so almost every day at the saloon, and Dr. Dane had warned him about the dangers of drinking.

As the angry men spat out their harsh words at each other, it was obvious that they had been drinking. Dane looked around to see if Sheriff Jack Polson was on the street. There was no sign of him. He quickly pulled the buggy to a halt.

Suddenly the big man's fist lashed out and connected solidly with Ernie's jaw. Ernie staggered backward, then charged his opponent with both fists pumping. The big man hit him again, and Ernie went down.

The young doctor rushed up to the circle of onlookers and asked one of the men if someone had gone for the sheriff.

The man shook his head. "He's out of town at the moment, Doc. Both deputies are with him."

Dane focused on the combatants again. Ernie was still down, and the big man was kicking him savagely in the midsection.

Anger welled up in the doctor. He pushed his way through the crowd. "Hey! That's enough! Stop kicking him!"

The big man turned and gave him a heated glare. "You shut up, mister! I'll kick him if I want to! He's got it comin'!" With that, he sent another kick into Ernie's ribs. Ernie let out a pained howl.

Sudden antagonism surged to the surface in Dane Logan. The heat of anger turned his cheeks red. Instantly, he moved into the center of the circle. "Get away from him!"

The big man set his jaw and swung at the intruder. Dane avoided the punch and retaliated by lashing a right to his mouth. The punch popped the big man's head back, surprising him. Before he could set himself, Dane whipped a cracking left hook to the chin, and crossed a smashing right to the man's temple. As he staggered backward, shaking his head, the people in the crowd back-stepped, trying to get out of the way.

On the ground, Ernie Piper sat up, blinking in unbelief as he saw who was defending him.

The big man planted his feet, and with wrath blazing from his eyes, charged Dane like a mad bull. His lips were bleeding, and as he swung at Dane's face, he roared, "I'll getcha!"

Again, Dane dodged the meaty fist. This time he drove a piston-style punch to the man's solar plexus. The breath gushed from his mouth, spraying blood, and Dane followed with a powerful blow to his jaw.

The big man's legs wobbled and his eyes glazed slightly. Dane rushed in and chopped him again with another punch to the jaw, whipping his head to one side, then as the man was righting himself, Dane hit him with another left, then followed with another right, putting him down.

When the big man hit the ground, people cheered. Ernie Piper was on his feet now, holding a hand to his midsection, his eyes bulging. He couldn't believe what he was seeing.

The man was gasping for breath on the ground and rolled on to his knees, staring up through a blue haze at the lithe man who had put him down. There was a roaring inside his skull. He shook his head to clear it, but the roaring continued. His wrath was hot. He clenched his blood-stained teeth and struggled to his feet.

"Haven't you had enough?" asked Dane. "Best thing for you to do is to move on and forget whatever was going on between you and Ernie. You outweigh him by at least eighty pounds."

The man let out an animal-like roar and charged, fists pumping. His legs were un-steady, but it was obvious that he intended to destroy this adept young man who had put him down.

Dane ducked both hissing fists and drove another powerful blow to his solar plexus that bent him over. A whistling left hook cracked on his jaw, and he hit the ground facedown, out cold.

The crowd roared its approval while Dr. Dane turned to Ernie. "You hurt?"

Ernie shook his head. "Nothing serious, Doc. Just some sore ribs. I'm okay."

At that moment, pounding hooves were heard, and three riders skidded to a halt. Immediately men in the crowd began telling Sheriff Jack Polson and his two deputies what had happened.

Looking puzzled, Ernie said, "Dr. Logan, did you used to be a professional boxer?"

Dane grinned. "No. Nothing like that."

"Well, where'd you learn to fight like that?"

"On the streets of New York City," responded the doctor. "And for recreation while I was in medical college, I used to go to a gym in Chicago and do some boxing."

By this time, Sheriff Polson — who was in his late forties — moved up to the pair and glanced down at the unconscious man on the ground. "Doc, we've had trouble with T. J. Finnegan before. Every time he comes to town, he starts trouble of some kind. And it's always after he's been drinking in the saloon for a while." Then to the small man he said, "Ernie, are you all right?"

"I'm a little sore in the ribs, Sheriff, but I'm okay. Personally, I think you ought to talk young Dr. Logan into being one of your deputies. He's really good with his fists."

Polson grinned. "So I was just told." He set his eyes on the doctor, who had T. J. Finnegan's blood sprayed on his white shirt. "You want to give up doctoring and put on a badge?"

Dane chuckled. "No, thanks, Sheriff. I'll stick to doctoring. In fact, I'd better get to the office. I've been out at the *Rocking D Ranch* patching up young Josh Donaldson. He got bucked off a horse and landed on his shoulder, dislocating it. I had to set it and put his arm in a sling. Dad was delivering a baby on a ranch east of town. He may not be back yet, and Mom may have an office full of patients waiting to be taken care of. I need to get there right away."

By this time, the big man was conscious. He groped his way to his feet, blood running from his split lips. The sheriff faced him and said, "Looks like your lips are split pretty bad, T.J. Maybe you'd better let Dr. Logan stitch them up."

Finnegan's eyes widened as he set them on Dane. "You're not Dr. Logan."

"Yes, he is," spoke up one of the deputies. "He's Dr. Jacob Logan's son. Dr. Dane is his partner now."

Finnegan looked Dane up and down. "You a boxer?"

"No. I just don't like to see someone bullied. And you were bullying Ernie."

The sheriff said, "Why don't you go with Dr. Logan to his office, T.J., and let him stitch up those lips."

Finnegan's eyes flashed with anger. "I ain't lettin' him touch me!" With that, he wheeled and staggered toward his horse, which was tied to the hitch rail close by.

Ernie thanked the young physician for coming to his rescue, then walked away, his hand pressed to his midsection.

The sheriff chuckled. "You sure you don't want to wear a badge and help me keep this town safe, Doc?"

Dane gave him a lopsided grin. "No, thanks."

T. J. Finnegan put his horse to a trot and headed out of town, holding a hand to his bleeding mouth. As Dr. Dane climbed back in his buggy, people in the crowd called to him, thanking him for what he had done to help Ernie. The lowering sun was casting long shadows across the wide street.

Moments later, Dane pulled up in front of the doctor's office, noticing that his father's horse and buggy were there. Grabbing his suit coat and the medical bag, he hopped out, tied the reins to the hitch rail, and entered the office. He knew that by now, Nurse Ella Dover and his mother had already gone home.

Dr. Jacob Logan was just escorting a middle-aged woman from the waiting area toward the door of the examining room. He looked over his shoulder and stopped at the door. "Mrs. Williams, you go on into the examining room and sit down. I'll be with you shortly. I need to talk to my son for a moment."

The woman gave Dr. Dane a petulant glance, nodded, and moved on through the door.

Dr. Jacob closed the door behind her, then moved toward his son. "Your mother told me you had gone to the Donaldson ranch. Is Joshua —" His eyes were suddenly fastened on Dane's blood-speckled shirt. "How'd you get that blood on you? Certainly not from Joshua."

Dane's features tinted. "Of course not. I had to stop a bully from beating up on Ernie Piper. I guess you know the guy. Name's T. J. Finnegan."

"Oh, sure. T.J. gets his belly full of whiskey, then becomes Mr. Troublemaker.

So today, it was pound on poor little Ernie, eh?"

"Uh-huh. Trouble started right in front of the Lone Pine. I had to knock him out. Took several punches, so I split his lips. Got some of his blood on me."

"Sheriff and deputies weren't in on it?"

"No. They were out of town. Came back just after T.J. went down for the count."

"Ernie okay?"

"Mm-hmm. Just some sore ribs."

Jacob nodded. "I started to ask you if Joshua is all right."

"He's fine, Dad. It was a fairly simple dislocation of the shoulder. I guess Mom told you he got bucked off a horse."

"Yes. I'm glad he'll be all right."

"Oh yeah. He was a brave boy. He'll be back to normal in a few weeks. With that houseful of females to tend to his every need, he'll enjoy his recuperation time."

Jacob smiled. "I'm sure you're right about that."

"The Donaldsons were surprised to learn that you had an adopted son. They had never heard about me."

"Well, now they know."

"Yeah. So how did the delivery go? Everyone okay?"

"Mm-hmm. Mother and husky son are

both doing great. The father . . . well, you know how fathers are. He sure was frantic when he banged on our door early this morning. The sun wasn't even up yet." He yawned. "So I'm sort of tuckered out."

"Tell you what, Dad . . ."

"Yes?"

"Mrs. Williams has to be our last patient for the day. Let me tend to her and you go on home. I'll be there shortly. I'm sure Mom has supper on the stove."

"Okay, son. But . . . ah . . . Mrs. Williams can be pretty cantankerous. And since you're new to her, just be prepared for lots of questions and some argument."

Dane grinned. "Don't worry, Dad. Believe me, I've had my share of cantankerous people. I'll just turn on my irresistible charm, and Mrs. Williams and I will get along fine."

His father laughed and shook his head. "Well, enjoy yourself, son." Jacob picked up his medical bag and headed for the front door. "See you at supper."

"Right. Tell Mom I'll be there shortly."

When Jacob went out the door, Dane turned, squared his shoulders, and headed toward the examining room.

By September 1880, Dr. Dane Logan

was getting quite well known by the people of Cheyenne and the farmers and ranchers in a thirty-to forty-mile radius. Like his adoptive father, he put his patients in the Cheyenne Memorial Hospital and performed surgeries there whenever possible. Sometimes — like with his father — emergency surgeries had to be done in the homes of the patients, especially those on farms and ranches.

As time continued to pass, Dane thought of Tharyn Myers daily, and prayed for her, wishing he knew where she was and if she was well and happy.

Though Dane lived in a boardinghouse a half-block from his parents' home, he ate nearly all of his evening meals with them.

One evening in mid-September, while the Logans and their son were enjoying supper together, father and son were talking about a new farm family named Jones who had brought their twelve-year-old daughter to the office with a rash on her face. Both doctors had looked at her.

Dane chuckled. "You know what, Dad?"

Jacob looked at him from across the table while chewing a piece of Naomi's delicious fried chicken. "What?"

"I was just coming out of the examining room into the office as Mr. and Mrs. Jones were standing with the girl at Mom's desk, and when I heard Mrs. Jones tell Mom her daughter's name was Sharon, at first I thought she said Tharyn. It sort of gave me a start. And then when Mom repeated it while writing the girl's name down, I realized I had heard wrong."

Naomi set soft eyes on her son. "Honey, it seems to me that you must carry Tharyn in your heart twenty-four hours a day, seven days a week, three hundred sixty-five days a year, and three hundred sixty-six days every leap year."

Dane smiled at her. "You're right, Mom. She's still 'little sis' to me, and I suppose she always will be. If I just knew she was well and happy, it sure would relieve my mind."

Jacob took a sip of hot tea, and set the cup down. "Son, your mama and I have told you this before, but I'll say it again. Tharyn belongs to the Lord. I have no doubt that He led her to a good Christian family when she was on that orphan train. From what she told you about wanting to become a nurse, I have a feeling she achieved her goal."

"Yes," said Naomi. "You've talked about her so much all these years, I feel like I know her. From what you told us about her personality, I'd say since she is now twenty-two years of age, she is an excellent nurse at some good doctor's side, or in some clinic or hospital. And she is probably married to a good Christian man."

Dane's face pinched at those last words.

"Son, I know you think a lot of that girl, but it seems to me the feelings you have go deeper than just thinking of her as the sweet girl you adopted as your little sister in that Manhattan alley," Jacob said. "You were fifteen and she was thirteen when you met, and you haven't seen each other since. You were both too young to be in love at that time, but you sure seem to feel that way about her now, even though you haven't seen her in over nine years. The Lord has a young lady all picked out for you, and when He is ready to cross your paths, He will do it, and you'll *really* fall in love."

Dane drew in a deep breath and let it out slowly through his nostrils. "I know you're right, Dad. Tharyn is the only girl who ever captured my heart. I've just never met anyone like her. But, of course, we were too young to be in love back then. No doubt when I meet that special gal the Lord has chosen for me, my thoughts of Tharyn will fade."

"That's right, honey," said Naomi. "They will."

That night when Dane was in his bed at the boardinghouse and trying to get to sleep, he found Tharyn once again on his mind.

He rolled from one side to the other, then flopped on to his back, staring up at the ceiling in the dim light that came through the window from a half-moon.

Once again, he tried to imagine where Tharyn might be in the vast expanse of the West. Was she indeed a nurse? And was she married?

He thought of how she depended on him to take care of her when her parents were killed, and how lost and afraid she was when he was arrested and put in prison.

He closed his eyes. "Lord, as I've asked You so many times before, take care of her, wherever she is. And — and please bring the young lady You have chosen to be my wife into my life very soon."

The next day, Dr. Jacob Logan was with a patient in one of the curtained sections of the examining room while Dr. Dane was with a small boy in another section, being assisted by Nurse Ella Dover while the boy's mother looked on.

At the desk in the front office, Naomi Logan looked up to see a white-faced farmer named Clyde Ballard come in. The Ballards had long been Dr. Jacob's patients.

Naomi smiled up at the farmer. "Good morning, Clyde. Do you need to see the doctor?"

Clyde removed his hat. "Not this time, ma'am. You know that my seventy-two-year-old mother lives with us."

"Yes."

"Well, Mama fell down the stairs in our house about a half hour ago, all the way from the second floor to the bottom floor. She's in a great deal of pain and her legs are numb. Can your husband or your son come and look at her?"

Naomi rose to her feet. "They're both with patients in the back room. Let me go see which one will be free first to go with you."

Clyde Ballard paced the floor, wringing his hands while waiting for Naomi to return.

After three or four minutes, she returned. "Dr. Jacob will be ready to go first, Clyde. He'll be through with his patient in just a few minutes."

Less than ten minutes later, Dr. Jacob came through the examining room door with a middle-aged man who was wearing a bandage over his left eye. Jacob had his medical bag in hand.

He told Naomi to make an appointment for the man in two days so he could examine his eye, then looked at Clyde. "Let's go."

Naomi glanced out the big window and watched her husband jump into his buggy while Clyde swung aboard his horse. As they hurried away, she looked up at the man with the bandage over his eye. She opened the appointment book and they agreed on the time for him to come in on Wednesday.

The man moved out the door, and at the same time, a man and his wife came in. Naomi knew they had an appointment. She told them to be seated, and Dr. Dane would be with them shortly.

Naomi went into the examining room to see how it was going with the four-year-old boy who had fallen out of a tree and broken his collarbone. She stepped up and said, "Well, Dr. Logan, how's Bobby doing?"

Dr. Dane spoke without taking his eyes off his work. "Bobby will be all right once I get him trussed up, Mom. He will heal up in a few weeks. I heard you talking to Dad a few minutes ago. Was that Bertha Ballard who fell down some stairs?"

Naomi knew her son had helped care for Clyde Ballard's mother when she was in Memorial Hospital a few months ago. "Yes. Your father is on his way to the Ballard farm right now, following Clyde."

"I sure hope she isn't seriously hurt."

"Me too. Well, I have to get back to the office. Mr. and Mrs. Wakefield are here."

Dane nodded. "I'll be ready to see them in about ten minutes."

Four

It was early morning, Tuesday, September 14. In Fort Collins, Colorado — some forty miles south of Cheyenne, Wyoming — a stagecoach and its six horses waited in front of the Wells Fargo office. The air was cool as the sun began to flush the sky over the eastern plains, casting a faint scarlet hue on the towering, jagged Rockies to the west.

Inside the Wells Fargo office, driver Buck Cummons had his stalwart young shotgunner, Doke Veatch, at his side as he ran his gaze over the five passengers who would soon board the stage for its trip north. Crew and passengers had eaten breakfast together and had become somewhat acquainted.

Four of the five would be staying aboard to Casper, Wyoming — the stage's final destination before turning around. There were only three stops between Fort Collins and Casper: Cheyenne, Wheatland, and

Douglas. Passenger Vern Stanton would be getting off at Douglas.

Stanton was a huge, hard-faced man in his midforties. At breakfast, everyone learned that he had been a sergeant in the Union Army during the Civil War, and though none had shared their impressions of the man with the others, they felt he would have been a typical sergeant with his crusty, no-nonsense personality.

The other two male passengers were Clayton Jubb, who was a Casper hardware store clerk in his midthirties, and Wayne Hoover, Casper's forty-six-year-old mayor.

One of the female passengers was Stella Yoder, a widow in her early sixties. She wore a calico dress on her ample frame, and her silver hair was pulled into a tight bun atop her head. Her face was crisscrossed with deep lines on her leathery skin.

At the breakfast table, Stella told the others that she had spent most of her life on the rugged Wyoming prairie. She still lived on the six-hundred-acre ranch just north of Casper, where she was taken from Missouri as a very young bride and still ran the ranch with the help of a handful of ranch hands. She told the others that her husband and two sons died in a blizzard ten years before while driving cattle home that they had purchased from a ranch near Powder River, Wyoming.

The other female passenger was twenty-year-old Anna Devries, from Rochester, New York. She was on her way to Casper to become a mail order bride and had stopped in Fort Collins to spend a day with a friend from school who had come to Colorado a year ago to become a mail order bride. The young man Anna was planning to marry worked a ranch with his father a few miles west of Casper.

Anna was wearing a simple dress of deep apple red broadcloth. The only trimming was a double row of navy blue rickrack around the collar and cuffs. A navy crochet shawl covered her slim shoulders, meant to ward off the slight chill of the September day.

Anna's honey blond hair was pulled back from the sides of her pretty face and tied at the crown with a dark blue ribbon. The rest of her blond tresses fell down her back in soft waves almost reaching her waist.

Driver Buck Cummons, who recently turned fifty, smiled at his passengers. "Well, folks, we're ready to board." He looked at his shotgunner, giving him an eye signal, and Veatch nodded that he understood.

Vern Stanton hurried to the door and held it open for the ladies to pass through. They both smiled and thanked him, then he preceded them to the stagecoach while Jubb and Hoover followed, with the driver on their heels.

When Stanton reached the coach, he opened the door, then offered his hand to Stella and helped her aboard. While he was doing this, four young men who stood in front of the livery stable next to the Fargo office began calling to Anna with flirtatious words, calling her "blondie" and smiling.

Suddenly, Stanton turned and looked at them, his motion like the swift cut of a knife and his eyes like coals of fire. His attention stayed fixed on them until they went silent and their smiles faded away.

"Thank you, Mr. Stanton," said Anna and took his hand.

Stanton helped her into the coach, and she sat down beside Stella on the seat that faced the rear of the coach. The bulky former army sergeant climbed in and sat down facing them, and Jubb and Hoover followed, crowding onto the seat with Stanton. Driver Buck Cummons closed the door, then looked back toward the office and nodded. At the door, Doke Veatch nodded in return, then pivoted and moved into the office.

"Okay," said Doke to the Fargo agent who stood behind the counter.

The agent reached under the counter, lifted an oblong metal box by its handle and extended it to Doke. He then lifted up a folded piece of canvas and handed it to him. Doke smiled, took the canvas, shook it open, and wrapped it around the metal box. "See you in a few days." He left the office.

By the time Doke reached the stage, Buck was up on the seat with the reins in his hands and one foot teetering on the brake. Doke reached up, set the canvas-covered metal box on the seat, shoved it toward Buck, then climbed up and sat down. He placed the metal box beneath the seat and picked up his shotgun. "Okay, Buck. Let's go."

The Wyoming sun was halfway down the afternoon sky. In a patch of forest just south of a small settlement known as Chugwater some forty-five miles north of Cheyenne and twenty miles south of Wheatland, the six men who made up the

Tag Moran gang sat on the ground, each one of them with his back against a tree. Their saddled horses stood close by, swishing their tails at the flies that were pestering them.

Four of the gang members were brothers. The oldest, at twenty-eight, was Tag Moran, who was also known to be the toughest. Bart Moran was twenty-six, Jason was twenty-four, and Darryl was twenty-one. The other two gang members were twenty-seven-year-old Gib Tully and twenty-three-year-old Tony Chacone.

Tag took a pocket watch from his vest pocket, looked at it, and returned it to its place. "Stage should be along in about forty minutes."

Gib Tully grinned at Tag. "I'm sure glad you ran onto your old pal, Harry Eads, in Wheatland, Tag. You didn't know he worked for Wells Fargo until you ran into him there on the street this mornin', did you?"

"Sure didn't. He's lived in Wheatland for a long time, but from what he told me, he's only been with Fargo a few months. When he gave me the information this morning about the stage carrying the fifty thousand dollars from the Bank of Fort Collins to its subsidiary bank in Casper, all he asked for telling me about it was a couple hundred dollars, so I went ahead and gave it to him."

"Wow! Fifty thousand dollars!" said Tony Chacone. "Maybe we should have started robbing stagecoaches a long time ago. We've robbed banks in western Nebraska, all over Wyoming, and in northern Colorado, and done well, but it sounds to me like we've been missing something."

Tag shook his head. "Just robbing stagecoaches at random isn't worth the effort, Tony. All you get is what the crew and passengers might have in their wallets and purses. But when you get a tip on big money being transported by a stage — like I got from Harry — it's plenty worth the effort."

"Opportunities like this with stagecoaches don't come along very often, big brother," said Bart, "but we've sure been successful robbing banks these past two years. We've been living well on our loot, plus we've got forty-five thousand in the kitty at the hideout. That's seventy-five hundred for each man. This fifty thousand will sure add to the kitty — over eight thousand apiece. That'll sure make my darling Lucinda happy."

Gib laughed. "Yeah, it'll make my sweet

Kathryn happy too."

Tag chuckled. "It ought to. When I came up with the idea of forming this gang, those wives of yours weren't too happy about you guys becoming outlaws. But they've sure changed their tune since we've come home to the hideout these past two years with all that money."

"Yep, Tag," said Gib, "they sure have. Kathryn has her hopes up high because of the goal you've set for each member of the gang to have a quarter-million dollars so we can all head for California and live like kings the rest of our lives."

"So does Lucinda," said Bart. "Maybe the rest of you guys will find gals to marry in California so you can share your wealth with them like Gib and I are doing with our wives."

Darryl Moran spoke up. "Well, before we reach that goal, we've got a lot more banks to rob."

Tag nodded. "You're right, baby brother, and I've got big plans. I'll tell all of you about banks we'll be hitting in the future when we get back to the hideout." He looked toward the south. "Right now, we've got to concentrate on the stage that's coming our way with the fifty thousand."

Some twelve miles south of Chugwater, Buck Cummons pulled back on the reins, slowing the six-up team. A few seconds later, he veered the stage off the road and guided the team toward the gurgling stream of water known as Horse Creek. When Buck drew the team to a halt, Doke Veatch laid his double-barreled shotgun at his feet, then hopped down from the box and grasped a bucket from where it hung on a wire hook on the side of the coach.

Buck climbed down while his shotgunner was dipping the bucket in the creek, stepped up to the door, and pulled it open. "Doke's gonna water the horses here, folks. It's quite a stretch from Cheyenne to Wheatland, so we always stop here at Horse Creek and give the team a drink. If you'd like to step out and stretch your legs, you're welcome to do so."

Vern Stanton stepped out, adjusted the gun belt on his waist, glanced at the shotgunner as he was carrying the full bucket toward the horses, and said, "How about me helping Doke, Buck? I'm really eager to get to Douglas as soon as possible. I've been gone for over a month. My wife —"

"We only have one bucket, Mr. Stanton,"

cut in Buck. "It won't take Doke long to water the horses. We'll be on our way shortly."

Stanton sighed and nodded. "Okay."

The others told Buck they would just stay in the coach. Stanton waited impatiently, pacing back and forth near the team while watching the shotgunner hurrying between the creek and the team, giving each horse a full bucket to drink.

The stop lasted a total of twenty minutes. The stage then pulled away from the creek bank and headed up the road.

In the patch of forest just south of Chugwater, the gang members were now on their feet in anticipation of the stage showing up. Jason Moran was telling his brother Tag how excited he was about becoming filthy rich and spending the rest of his life in California, living high on the hog, when suddenly Darryl pointed south down the road. "Here comes the stage!"

Every eye turned that way, and they saw the cloud of dust on the road, preceded by the fast-moving stagecoach.

Tag ran his gaze over the exuberant faces of the other five. "Okay, boys. You know what to do."

In the driver's box on the stagecoach, Buck Cummons slowed the team as they drew near a narrow spot that was sided by huge boulders, each some fifteen feet in height.

As the stage entered the narrow passage, suddenly a large length of broken tree came tumbling down from the boulder on the right and blocked the coach's path. "Whoa!" Cummons cried and quickly pulled rein, stopping the frightened horses.

The passengers were pushing their faces out the windows, and at the same instant, they and the crew saw five men, guns drawn, surrounding the stage.

Some of the horses whinnied nervously.

Gib Tully stood facing driver and shotgunner, and snapped loudly, "You first, driver! Throw your guns down on the ground. Your revolver *and* your rifle!"

Buck licked his lips, pulled his revolver from its holster, tossed it earthward, then leaned over and picked up the rifle that lay at his feet. From the corner of his eye, he saw the anger on Doke's reddened features and whispered, "Don't try anything. They'll kill you." With that, he tossed the rifle down.

On Doke's side, Tony Chacone aimed

his revolver at him. "Now you, mister shotgunner! Your scatter-gun *and* that gun on your hip!"

The expression on Doke's face hardened. He felt his blood heat up as he threw the shotgun to the ground. As he reached for his sidearm, he looked at the other robbers, and shock showed in his eyes.

Buck noticed it and frowned. Just as Doke was tossing his revolver earthward, a sixth man stepped around one of the boulders in front of the stage, gun in hand. When Doke saw him, his head bobbed. Buck's frown deepened as he saw Doke and the sixth man stare at each other for a few seconds. The outlaw stepped up to the side of the coach, eyed the passengers through the windows, and barked, "All right! Everybody out!"

A tiny gasp escaped Anna Devries's lips, and fear etched itself on her face. Stella patted her hand. "It'll be all right, honey. They won't hurt you. Let's you and I go out first."

"Bring your purses, ladies!" commanded Tag Moran.

As the women started out of the coach, Clayton Jubb and Wayne Hoover noticed Vern Stanton quickly reach down inside his right boot, take out a small revolver that was strapped to his leg, and stash it under the seat.

While the three men were climbing out of the coach, the Moran brothers held their guns on them. Chacone and Tully were still holding their guns pointed at the driver and shotgunner.

Tag stepped up to the men. "Get your hands in the air."

All three obeyed. The outlaws noticed the mean look they were getting from the big, beefy man. Tag pointed his revolver straight at Vern Stanton's face. "If you're thinking about resisting, big boy, you'd better forget it."

Vern did not reply, but burned Tag's face with hot eyes. Tag relieved the big man of the gun in his holster and handed it to Jason.

He then patted Vern's suit coat at the sides, making sure he was not also wearing a shoulder holster. He then relieved Jubb and Hoover of the small revolvers they wore in their shoulder holsters, and also handed them to Jason.

Tag grinned at the three men. "Next . . . your wallets."

He took the wallets from their pockets and handed them to Darryl. "Okay, you guys get back in the coach."

Vern Stanton glowered at the gang leader, struggling to keep his temper in check.

Through clenched teeth, Tag hissed, "Just do as I say, big boy, or you'll be sorry."

Stanton held Tag's gaze for a few seconds, then turned slowly and moved toward the coach door.

When Stanton, Jubb, and Hoover had obeyed, and were seated in the coach as before, Tag stepped up to the two women. Anna was trembling.

Tag snatched the purse from her hand. "Get back in the coach."

Anna bit her lower lip, blinked at the tears that had filled her eyes, glanced at a stern-faced Stella, and climbed back inside the coach.

When Tag faced Stella, who showed no fear of him, she set her jaw and said in her rough, croaky voice, "It takes a real coward to hold a gun on a woman."

Tag sneered at her. "Keep your mouth shut, old woman! Gimme that purse."

"You want my purse? Well, here it is!" Suddenly Stella swung the purse and hit him across the face with it.

Her sudden unexpected move took Tag off guard, and the impact of the blow caused him to stagger back a few steps. Rage filled his eyes and he lunged at her, fist swinging. He caught her on the cheek and she went down.

Tag grabbed the purse and tossed it to Darryl. He gave Stella a hard stare, then moved toward the front of the coach and looked up at driver and shotgunner.

At that instant, Anna stepped out of the coach, concern for Stella having replaced the look of fear on her face, and leaned over, offering her hand. "Come on, dear, I'll help you up."

Stella shook her head again, in attempt to clear the cobwebs from her brain. She mumbled something indistinguishable, lifted her hand toward Anna, who grasped it and helped her to her feet.

A dazed look was in Stella's eyes as she gingerly ran a shaky palm over the red welt that was forming on her pale cheek.

The Moran brothers looked on until the women were back inside the coach. Chacone and Tully still held their guns trained on driver and shotgunner.

Tag looked back up at the crew of two, and before he could speak, Buck said thinly, "You didn't have to hit her. She's an old woman."

"Shut up, or I'll drag you down here and

beat you to a pulp. Now both of you toss down your wallets."

Reluctantly, both men complied. Tag caught both wallets, handed them to Darryl, then set cold eyes on Buck. "Now I want the money box."

Buck put a blank look on his face. "Money box? What're you talking about? We don't have a money box."

Tag looked at Doke, then back at Buck. "Don't lie to me, mister! You're carrying money to the Bank of Casper from their affiliate bank in Fort Collins. Now produce it! You've got ten seconds! Refuse and you get a bullet in your thick head!"

Doke said, "You'd best give them the box. It isn't worth getting killed over."

Buck sighed, leaned over, and reluctantly reached under the seat.

He brought up the canvas-covered metal box, removed the canvas, and handed the box down to Tag.

Grasping the handle of the box, Tag smiled at Doke. "You gave him good advice, pal."

Buck noticed that the gang's leader held Doke's gaze for a few seconds, then turned and said to his fellow outlaws, "Okay, boys, let's go. We got the box."

Passengers and crew watched while three

78

of the gang members went behind the boulder to the right and led six horses into view. The gang placed the male passengers' and the crew's handguns in their saddlebags, along with the purses and wallets.

Tony then went to Doke's double-barreled shotgun, picked it up off the ground, snapped it open, and took out the two shells. He threw the shells into the forest as far as he could, then tossed the shotgun into a nearby patch of weeds.

At the same time, Gib was emptying Buck's rifle. He threw the cartridges over the top of the boulder, then flung the rifle toward its base. It landed in the dust, sliding, then clattered as it struck the hard surface of the boulder.

The gang mounted their horses, and just before Tag led them away, he gave Buck a hard look. "Thanks for the cash box, *pal.*"

He focused on Doke's face for a second or two, then spurred his horse. The six outlaws galloped away in a cloud of dust, heading south.

Buck grabbed a handful of spare cartridges from a cloth sack at his feet, started out of the box, and said to Doke, "Let's get to our guns!" Suddenly Vern Stanton jumped out of the coach, his spare revolver in hand, took aim at the fleeing outlaws, and fired. The last man in the line of galloping horses stiffened and peeled out of the saddle.

By this time, Buck and Doke were on the ground, picking up their weapons and loading them with the extra ammunition they carried up on the box.

The outlaws pulled rein and saw Darryl Moran lying on the ground, writhing in pain some twenty yards behind them. His riderless horse had left him behind and had joined the others.

Tag and the rest of his men looked beyond Darryl and saw the big man with the revolver in his hand taking aim at them. They also saw driver and shotgunner on the ground reloading their weapons.

"That big guy had that gun stashed somewhere on the stage!" exclaimed Bart Moran.

Vern Stanton fired his second shot, and the bullet hissed within inches of Gib Tully's head. Gib whipped out his revolver and fired back, but missed Stanton completely. The rest of the outlaws were pulling their guns when Stanton fired another shot, and the slug ripped through Tag's hat, sending it flying. Tag's eyes bulged as he put his hand to his bare head.

At the same time, Buck Cummons

shouldered his rifle and fired. The bullet tore through the flesh of Gib's shoulder. He jerked from the impact. The outlaws were trying to take aim at the three men at the stagecoach, but their horses were dancing about fearfully and whinnying, spoiling any chance of getting off effective shots.

More bullets were coming from the driver and the big man.

Tony Chacone finally got his horse stilled long enough to fire a shot. The slug chewed dirt a few feet from Stanton, and the big man fired again. His bullet barely missed Tony's left ear.

Anxiety framed Tag Moran's face. "Gib, are you hurt bad?"

"It's only a flesh wound, Tag," gasped Tully, gripping his wounded shoulder. "The bullet went on through."

Another slug whistled past them from the driver's rifle.

Tag looked back at his youngest brother writhing on the ground. "Guys, Darryl's hurt bad. We'll only get shot up ourselves if we try to pick him up and take him with us. Doke will take him to a doctor, I'm sure. Let's go!"

Five

As the outlaws galloped away and disappeared over a rise, Vern Stanton looked at Buck Cummons and Doke Veatch, breathing heavily with anger. "I wish I had a way to follow 'em and get our guns and money back. I'd like to put 'em down like I did that one that's lying on the ground out there."

Clayton Jubb and Wayne Hoover left the coach and stepped up to the spot where the other three men stood, looking at the outlaw who lay flat on his back some fifty yards away. Inside the coach, Anna Devries had an arm around the dazed Stella Yoder and was looking at the men through the open door.

Buck turned to Stanton. "Where did you have that gun hidden?"

The man still had his gaze fixed on the fallen outlaw. Slowly he looked around at Cummons. "I had it in my boot, strapped to my leg. Never hurts a man to have a spare gun on him. I knew those rotten out-laws would make us give up our guns, so I took this one out of my boot while the women were leaving the coach and slipped it under the seat."

Wayne Hoover said, "I knew you'd use it if you had the opportunity, Vern. Too bad Clayton and I didn't have guns hidden on us too. Maybe we could have put some more of those dirty skunks down."

Clayton Jubb grinned at Buck. "I'm sure you hit one of them, even though he stayed on his horse."

Buck nodded. "I got him, all right. He'll lose some blood."

Stanton glanced at the fallen outlaw again, then turned to the driver. "How much money is in that metal box?"

"I was told by the Fargo agent in Fort Collins it was fifty thousand dollars."

"Hey, look!" exclaimed Doke, pointing to the rise where the outlaws had disap-peared from view.

"Well, lookee there," said Stanton. "That guy's horse is coming back to him!"

They watched as the black horse trotted down the slope and drew up to the outlaw on the ground, looking down at him and bobbing his head.

Still gripping his shotgun, Doke said, "I

wonder if he's still alive."

"Well, if he is, we'll just leave him there to die," Vern Stanton said gruffly.

Doke shook his head. "We can't do that. If the man's alive, we have to get him to a doctor."

"The closest doctor is back in Cheyenne," said Buck. "Chugwater doesn't have one, and the doctor who used to be in Wheatland died a couple years ago. They haven't gotten a new one, yet. But we're already behind in schedule, Doke. Even if that guy out there is still alive, we can't take him to Cheyenne. We need to keep moving. We've got another passenger booked to get on the stage at Wheatland, and he and these people need to get to Casper."

Doke nodded. "I understand that, but if he's still alive, we can't just let him die. I'll take him to a doctor in Cheyenne on his horse, if you'll let me do it and go on without me. I'll ride his horse to Casper and meet you there."

Buck sighed. "All right. Let's all get on the stage, and we'll take a few minutes to drive out there and see if he's dead or alive."

Vern Stanton shook his head. "I don't understand you, Veatch. Why do you care if that no-good outlaw out there *is* still alive? He's got my bullet in him because he robbed us. I say let him die!"

Buck sighed again. "Mr. Stanton, I tend to have the same feelings you do about this, but you were in the Civil War. I've read about how men on the battlefields saved the lives of wounded enemies because it was the decent thing to do. Right?"

Stanton's bitter eyes played across the driver's face. "Yeah. I guess so."

"Let's go," said Buck, and headed for the front of the coach.

The trio climbed back inside the coach, and the crew mounted the box.

While Buck was driving the stage toward the fallen outlaw and the horse which was still standing over him, he looked at his shotgunner. "Doke, I couldn't help but notice the way you and some of those robbers looked at each other, especially the leader. Do you know them?"

"Yeah. I know 'em."

"I thought so. Well, who are they?"

"They're the Tag Moran gang, who've been written up in the newspapers all over this part of the country for the past two years. They've robbed banks in Nebraska, Colorado, and Wyoming, and successfully eluded the law."

"I've read about them. So how do you know them?"

"The four Moran brothers and I have known each other since we were boys over in Scottsbluff, Nebraska. We grew up together. I haven't seen them since they went on the outlaw trail." He squinted at the man lying on the ground as they drew near. "Looks to me like Darryl Moran lying there."

Seconds later, when Buck pulled rein, Doke jumped down and hurried to the fallen man. All five passengers were watching him from inside the coach, then Vern Stanton opened the door and stepped out.

The outlaw's horse whinnied at Doke as if to ask for help for his master when he knelt down beside him. Doke looked over his shoulder at Buck, who was still up on the box. "He's unconscious, but still alive. And I was right. It's Darryl Moran."

Stanton moved up, stood over Doke, and ran his gaze between Doke and Buck. "I heard you two talking while we were driving up here. Doke, I still don't agree with what you're planning to do. Just because you and this outlaw used to be friends is no reason to go to the trouble of taking him all the way back to Cheyenne to a doctor. You oughtta let him die."

Doke was checking the blood flow from the wound in Darryl's back. He looked up at Stanton. "I can't just let him die. Even though Darryl went bad like his brothers, I still have to try to save his life."

"Okay, Doke," said Buck from up on the seat, "I'll take the stage on and let you take that guy to one of the doctors in Cheyenne. You will turn him over to the Laramie County sheriff, won't you?"

"Of course. I'll tell the doctor who he is, how he got shot, and once he's patched Darryl up, the doctor can turn him over to the sheriff. But I just can't let him die."

While Vern Stanton scowled at him, Doke picked up the limp, wounded outlaw, cradling him in his arms. He turned to the big man. "Mr. Stanton, will you take Darryl and boost him up to me after I get in the saddle?"

At first, big Vern looked as if he would refuse, but he clenched his teeth and nodded. Doke placed the bleeding outlaw in Stanton's arms, moved to the horse, took hold of the pommel, stepped into the stirrup, and swung into the saddle.

Stanton hoisted Darryl up to him, placing his limp form in a sitting position on the saddle in front of Doke. With the unconscious outlaw leaning against him, Doke looked up at Buck. "I'll do my best to catch up with you by the time you get to Casper. If not, I'll run into you while you're heading back south."

Buck nodded. "I'll be looking for you."

Doke then wheeled the horse southward and headed toward Cheyenne.

Tag Moran and his gang rode hard for several miles, then Tag slowed his mount and motioned toward a small stream. "Let's water the horses and ourselves, boys."

As they moved at a slow walk toward the stream, Tag looked at Gib Tully, who was still holding his wounded shoulder. "We need to wrap that wound, Gib."

"Yeah," breathed Tully. "It's not bleeding bad, but if we can stop the bleeding altogether, I'll be all right till we get to the hideout. Kathryn can patch me up then."

They drew up to the stream and dismounted. While the others were leading the horses into the slow-moving current to let them drink, Tony Chacone helped Gib sit down on a fallen tree trunk with Tag walking beside them. Tag ripped the sleeve of his good arm from Gib's shirt and went to work to make a bandage for his shoulder wound.

While he was doing so, Tony said, "Wasn't that something, Darryl's horse leaving us and heading back to him."

Gib nodded. "Doesn't surprise me. Ol' Blackie kept running when Darryl fell off him 'cause guns were roaring. He was scared. But when we were riding hard with no guns going off, it didn't take ol' Blackie long to decide to go back to his master."

"I sure hope that guy you called Doke will take Darryl to a doctor, Tag," said Gib. "Where do you know him from?"

"Doke Veatch is from Scottsbluff, Gib. We all grew up together. We were good friends. I know him well. He'll take care of Darryl, all right. Little brother will end up in jail, I'm sure, but at least he'll still be alive."

Tony grinned. "Well, maybe someday we can bust him out of jail, Tag."

"We'll just do that, my friend."

When the horses and their riders had all had their fill of water, Tag said, "Let's open this cash box and see if we've really got fifty thousand."

Gib was still sitting on the fallen tree trunk. His wounded shoulder was no longer bleeding. Tag carried the box to the spot and sat down beside Gib. The others gathered around and watched as their leader opened the box and took out a wad of currency in small denominations. Tag counted it, and they all were pleased to find that it was exactly fifty thousand dollars.

Tag placed the money back in the box and closed the lid. "We'll put most of this in our retirement fund, boys."

"That's really gonna help," said Bart.

They all laughed and agreed.

Tag stood up, box in hand. "Fellas, now that we've got Gib's wound bandaged up so it isn't bleeding, I want to delay our return to the hideout long enough to find out about Darryl. I'm not sure where Doke will take him on the stagecoach to get him to a doctor, but I want to talk to him and find out how little brother's doing. Wherever he takes Darryl, Doke will have to be back on that stage as soon as possible, I'm sure. How about we go back to that patch of woods near Chugwater and buy some groceries at that little store there? You boys can hide in the woods while I track Doke down and find out about Darryl."

Everyone was in agreement. Gib was hoisted into his saddle, and the gang rode back northward toward Chugwater.

Dr. Dane Logan was occupied in one of the curtained sections of the examining room at the office in Cheyenne, removing dirt particles from a farmer's eye. The usual stethoscope hung around his neck.

Dr. Jacob Logan had been awakened by a loud knock on his door before daylight to find a frantic rancher whose wife had gone into labor just after midnight. Dressing quickly, he had hitched his horse to the buggy and speedily followed the rancher and had not yet returned.

While dripping water into the farmer's eye and carefully clearing away dark little specks of dirt with a cotton swab, Dr. Dane heard the door between the office and the examining room open, and footsteps moving to another part of the room. There were low voices, one of which was his mother, and another which was that of Nurse Ella Dover. There was also a low-toned male voice.

Then footsteps the doctor recognized turned in his direction.

Naomi Logan pulled back the curtain. "How's it going, son?"

"Just fine, Mom. Mr. Webber's eye will be fine."

"Good. We . . . ah . . . have an emergency."

Dane glanced over his shoulder. "What is it, Mom?"

"An outlaw was just brought in with a bullet in his back. He's part of a gang who held up a stagecoach over by Chugwater a little while ago. Got himself shot while they were pulling the robbery. Rest of them got away. He is bleeding profusely. I had the man who brought him in put him on the examining table in section three. Ella is with him, and doing what she can to stop the blood flow."

"Okay, Mom. I'm almost through here. Tell Ella I'll be there in two minutes or less."

Dr. Dane finished cleaning the farmer's eye within another minute, sent him on his way, and hurried toward section three. He saw a young man standing just outside the curtain, watching him as he approached.

The doctor paused. "You're the one who brought the wounded man in, I assume."

"Yes, Doctor."

"And he's an outlaw."

"Yes, sir. Got shot like your mother just told you. I explained it to her while I was carrying him in here."

Dr. Dane nodded. "You can tell me all about it later. Right now I've got to go to work on him. You can come inside the curtain if you want. Just don't get close to the table."

"All right."

When Dr. Dane stepped through the curtain, he saw the unconscious young man lying facedown and Ella Dover working furiously to cut the fabric away from the bullet hole. She was also pressing a clean cloth on the gaping wound, trying desperately to stem the flow. The sickening coppery smell of blood was strong.

Dr. Dane moved to the opposite side of the table from Ella and pressed his fingers on the side of the patient's neck. "Pulse is very weak."

Ella glanced at him. "I don't think he's going to make it, Doctor. He's in bad shape. He's obviously lost a lot of blood."

"I've got to get that slug out," said Dr. Dane, picking up a metal probe from a small cart next to the table.

Ella wiped blood from around the wound, then watched as the doctor went after the slug.

Suddenly the patient jerked, stiffened, then went limp.

Dr. Dane quickly turned him over and attempted to get him breathing again by massaging his chest.

Ella looked at the young man standing close by and shook her head.

After a minute or so, Dr. Dane ceased massaging the chest, placed the earpieces of the stethoscope in his ears and pressed the microphone over the heart, listening intently. After a brief moment, he sighed, shook his head, and looked at Ella. "He's dead."

He turned to the pallid-faced young man. "I'd guess by the size of the hole in his back that it was a thirty-eight caliber bullet. You can tell me the story now."

"My name is Doke Veatch, Doctor. I'm the shotgunner on the Wells Fargo stage that runs between Fort Collins and Casper. We were on our way north. A gang of robbers forced us to stop just south of Chugwater and robbed us. Not only took our money, but also our handguns. Left me with an empty shotgun and the driver with an empty rifle. When they were riding away, one of the male passengers — who had managed to hide his spare revolver inside the stage — grabbed it and opened fire on them. He hit this one, dropping him from his horse. The others didn't stop. Just kept on riding."

Dr. Dane nodded. "You ever see any of the robbers before?"

Doke felt his spine stiffen. "No, sir. I have no idea who they were."

Ella was covering the body with a sheet.

Dr. Dane said, "Doke, I need to have our sheriff come and see if he knows who this outlaw is. He will want to know about the incident and he will want to talk to you."

Doke shrugged. "Sure."

The doctor excused himself, went through the office and stepped out onto the boardwalk. He called to a man walking by and asked him to go tell Sheriff Jack Polson he needed him to come to the office right away.

Dane was talking to his mother at her desk when the sheriff came through the door. "What have we got, Doctor?"

"A corpse, Sheriff. One you need to know about."

The doctor led Sheriff Polson to the examining room where Ella Dover was cleaning blood off the table next to the lifeless form that was covered with the sheet.

Dr. Dane introduced the sheriff to Doke Veatch, explaining that Doke was shotgunner on the Wells Fargo stage that ran the route from Fort Collins to Casper.

Polson shook Doke's hand. "Sure. Your

face is familiar. I've seen you on the stage several times when it's been here in Cheyenne."

Doke smiled. "I've seen you too, Sheriff."

"I've met your driver, but I can't think of his name."

"Buck Cummons."

Polson snapped his fingers. "Yes! Buck Cummons. He's been with Wells Fargo for quite a while, hasn't he?"

"Yes, sir. Over twenty years."

Dr. Dane pulled the sheet down, exposing the face of the dead man. "I'll let Doke tell you the story, Sheriff."

Doke told the story, exactly as he had told it to the doctor, adding that they were carrying the metal cash box containing fifty thousand dollars from the Bank of Fort Collins to the Bank of Casper, which the robbers somehow knew was aboard.

The sheriff rubbed his chin, leaned close to the lifeless form, and studied the facial features. He turned to Doke. "How many robbers were there?"

"Six, including this one."

Polson rubbed his chin again and looked down once more at the face of the corpse. "Sounds like the Tag Moran gang to me. They're the only gang of six that are robbing banks in the territory. Though I have no photographs of any of the gang's members, I feel certain from the descriptions sent to me by lawmen in Colorado and Nebraska that this is indeed one of the Moran brothers."

Doke felt his stomach roll over.

Polson rubbed his chin thoughtfully once more. "Strange."

Doke frowned. "What do you mean, Sheriff?"

"As far as I know, the Moran gang has never held up a stagecoach before. They concentrate on banks." He paused and shook his head. "But of course, as you explained, you were carrying the metal box containing fifty thousand dollars that somehow they had found out about. This is no doubt why they held up the stage."

"I would say so, sir."

"I'll wire the bank of Fort Collins about the robbery, even though I know Wells Fargo will do so as soon as they learn about it in Wheatland."

"Yes, sir," said Doke. "Well, if it's all right with you, I'll take this dead outlaw's horse and ride north. I need to catch up to the stagecoach by dawn tomorrow morning before Buck has to head back south from Casper."

"Sure," said the sheriff. "Just let Wells Fargo have the horse."

Doke nodded. "Fine."

Dr. Dane laid a hand on Doke's shoulder. "I want to commend you, Doke, for the compassion you showed this outlaw. Most men wouldn't have bothered with him. They'd just have let him die and said good riddance."

Doke rubbed the back of his neck. "I just couldn't go off and leave the man lying on the ground, bleeding, Doctor. I had to try to save his life."

"Well, indeed you are to be commended," said Polson. "It was a genuine act of mercy."

Doke smiled. "I guess there's enough callousness in this world, Sheriff. Well, I'd better get going."

Doke bid good-bye to Ella Dover, then the doctor and the sheriff followed him into the office, where he also bid good-bye to Naomi Logan.

Both men stepped out onto the boardwalk and waved to the Wells Fargo shotgunner as he rode away, riding north out of town.

Dr. Dane turned to the sheriff. "I've read a lot about this Moran gang. They seem to be quite elusive. Not one of them has ever been in jail."

"Right. They're slick for sure. But one of these days they'll make a mistake and get themselves caught. Not too long ago, I was in contact with Chief U.S. Marshal John Brockman in Denver about all the banks the Moran gang have robbed right here in Laramie County. He is aware of every one of their robberies in Wyoming, Nebraska, and Colorado. He told me if the gang isn't caught soon by lawmen and posses in the towns where they hold up banks, he will have to form his own posse of deputy U.S. marshals and go after them."

Dr. Dane nodded. "Do I understand correctly that in the two years this Moran gang has been holding up banks, they have not yet killed anyone?"

"Yes. Truly amazing, isn't it? But sooner or later, someone will resist them during a robbery, and the gang will kill them."

"I'm sure you're right about that."

"Well," said the sheriff, "I've got to get back to the office. I'll send a couple of my deputies to pick up the outlaw's body and take it to the undertaker for burial. The county will foot the bill."

Just before the sun lifted its fiery rim above the eastern horizon the next morning, Buck Cummons was boarding his passengers in Casper for the trip south when he noticed a rider galloping his horse down the street.

He recognized the horse first, then seconds later, he was able to make out the face of the rider.

Doke Veatch skidded the horse to a halt close to the stage and swung down from the saddle. Moving toward the driver, he said, "Morning, Buck. I'm glad I made it before you pulled out. The sheriff in Cheyenne told me to give this horse to Wells Fargo, so I'll just run in and tell our friendly agent that he's got a new horse."

Buck studied Doke's face. "You look pretty tired."

"I'm that all right. Darryl Moran died at the doctor's office in Cheyenne, Buck. I had to ride all night in order to get here in time."

Buck chuckled. "Well, I have a hard time feeling sorry for an outlaw when he gets himself killed. Anyway, you can sleep sitting up there beside me in the box while we head south."

Doke led Darryl Moran's horse into the Fargo corral, then went inside and informed the agent that he had a new horse.

Soon the stagecoach — with six passengers aboard — pulled out of Casper and headed toward Douglas, which was some sixty miles away. Doke slouched on the seat next to Buck and dozed for a while, then sat up, yawning.

Buck looked at him and grinned. "Feel better?"

Doke yawned again. "Yep. Think I can stay awake now."

Buck brought up the Tag Moran gang, commenting on how people all over Wyoming were talking about them, and that all the banks in the territory were tense because they never knew where the gang would strike next.

Doke yawned once more and nodded.

Buck said, "Tell me more about your childhood and your acquaintance with the Moran brothers."

"Well, we were neighbors in Scottsbluff. As I told you, we grew up together. We were schoolmates and spent a lot of time together. I haven't seen them in about four years. I don't know who the other two men in the gang are."

The stage hit a bump, causing both men to have to adjust their position on the seat. Buck lifted his hat and ran splayed fingers through his hair. "So you and the Moran brothers were pretty close friends, I take it."

"Mm-hmm. Especially me and Tag. He saved my life once."

"Oh?"

"Mm-hmm. When we were boys, we used to swim in the North Platte River together in the summertime a lot. One day Tag, his three brothers, and I were swimming in the North Platte. Tag was seventeen and I was twelve. There had been a lengthy, severe rainstorm in southeast Wyoming and northwest Nebraska the day before, and there was a lot of debris floating in the river. All of us had been swimming for about an hour when we decided to crawl up on the bank and rest."

Buck frowned. "Swimming with debris in the river?"

"Well, up to that point it wasn't too bad, but I'm about to tell you of the change that came."

"Okay."

"After a while, I decided to go in again, but at that moment, heavy debris was floating on the river's surface. Tag told me I should wait till the heavy stuff passed. But you know how twelve-year-old boys are. I laughed and told Tag I could swim around the debris. So I ran and dived in. I didn't know it, but there was a log floating just under the choppy, foam-covered surface. When I dived in, I struck my head on the log and it knocked me cold."

Buck shook his head. "Oh, boy."

"Well, the Moran brothers saw what happened, and it was Tag who dived in to rescue me in spite of the debris that was coming down the river. They told me later that I kept going under the surface, then bobbing to the top. Tag had to risk his own life to finally get his hands on me. He pulled me out and pumped water from my lungs. When I came to, Bart, Jason, and Darryl told me how Tag risked his life to save me from drowning. I hugged him and thanked him for it."

"I can see why you were close to him."

"Very close, even though he's five years older than me. It grieves me, Buck, that Tag has become an outlaw, but I still owe him for laying his own life on the line to save mine. This was one reason why I wanted to try to save Darryl's life yesterday. He was Tag's brother, and I'll always feel a debt to Tag."

"I can see that," said Buck. "It's just too bad Tag and his brothers became outlaws."

"Yeah. It puts a wall between us, for sure."

At just after nine o'clock, the stage pulled into Douglas, and after a half-hour layover, it was rolling swiftly along the road southward toward Wheatland.

Though he tried to stay awake, Doke slumped down on the seat next to Buck.

Six

Wheatland's Main Street was busy with traffic as the brilliant Wyoming sun edged its way toward its apex in the awesome blue sky.

Wagons, buggies, and carriages moved both directions, stirring up dust. People moved up and down the boardwalks, some stopping to talk to each other. Amid the creaking vehicles in the dusty street were riders on horseback.

Tag Moran stood in the shadow of the slanted wooden roof that hovered over the boardwalk several doors down from the Wells Fargo office. He leaned against one of the supporting posts, his hat pulled low, and kept his line of sight trained on the wide, dusty street toward the north.

The outlaw leader had moseyed past the Fargo office a few minutes earlier and noted the chalkboard by the front door, which gave the arrival and departure times of the stagecoaches.

The stage from Casper, which Tag knew had a regular stop in Douglas, was scheduled to arrive at noon.

For a moment, Tag ran his gaze the other direction along the street, noting the town's two banks that stood catercornered from each other at Wheatland's main intersection. He and his gang had held up Wheatland National Bank six months ago and made a clean getaway, even though the sheriff came after them with a posse of twelve men. One day soon he would bring the gang back and rob the Bank of Wyoming across the street.

He thought of the fifty thousand dollars they had gained by robbing the Wells Fargo stagecoach yesterday and smiled. Looking north once more, he said in a whisper, "Doke, ol' pal, if I could talk you into tying in with us, you'd be invaluable. You could let us in on more money shipments like the one yesterday when the affiliated banks send cash to each other."

Tag rubbed his jaw. *If I could have some time with you, Doke, I think I could convince you it could be done without endangering yourself with the law, or with Wells Fargo. And when we cut you your share, you'd have money to make your life much more enjoyable than it is on shotgunner's pay.*

Suddenly Tag's attention was drawn up the street where he saw the stagecoach coming toward Main Street ahead of its cloud of dust.

Up in the box on the stage, Buck Cummons tugged on the reins as the stage drew into town. While they were moving slowly down the street, Doke yawned and laid his shotgun at his feet. Then, rubbing his belly, he said, "I've got a hungry on, Buck. I'm glad it's time to stop for lunch."

Buck chortled. "We both like the food at the Meadowlark, pal. I'm gonna get me a big T-bone steak."

"Sounds good to me."

Moments later, Buck drew the stage to a stop in front of the Wells Fargo office. He and Doke left the box and moved earthward. At the same time, the six passengers climbed out of the coach, looking across the street at the Meadowlark Café. One of the men was telling the others how good the food was there.

The same man looked at Buck and Doke with a smile. "You gentlemen going to join us across the street?"

"We sure are," replied Buck. "You all go ahead. We have to let our agent know we're here, in case he hasn't seen us. Doke and I will be with you shortly."

The group of four men and two women hurried across the street between traffic while Buck told Doke to wait there; he would be right back. Buck dashed into the office, greeted the agent, and advised him that all was well.

While Buck was in the office, Doke stood at the edge of the street, looking first to the north, then to the south. Suddenly he caught sight of a man standing in the shade of the boardwalk's slanted roof, waving his hat and motioning to him. Doke focused on him.

It was Tag Moran!

Doke nodded to Tag that he saw him, then heard Buck coming out of the office.

Buck drew up beside him. "Okay, hungry man, let's get over there where the food is!"

Doke noticed Tag step back between two buildings. "Ah . . . tell you what, Buck," he said gesturing southward. "I just saw somebody I know down there a ways. I really should at least go say howdy. You go on, and I'll be there in a few minutes. Order me a sixteen-ounce steak medium well with all the trimmings."

Buck glanced the direction Doke had pointed, seeing people moving up and down the boardwalk. "Okay. Medium well. Coffee black and steaming hot."

"You got it."

As Buck weaved his way between vehicles and riders on horseback toward the café, Doke stepped into the street so he could hurry toward Tag without interruption. Tag moved back into sight and waved.

When Doke reached him, he excused himself as he crossed the boardwalk in front of an elderly couple, and joined Tag between the buildings.

Smiling, Doke said, "I didn't expect to see you, Tag."

"I had to find out about Darryl."

Doke felt the mask of gloom come over his face. "He — he didn't make it, Tag. I'm sorry."

Tag's features slacked. "He's dead?"

"Yeah. I talked to Buck Cummons, my driver, into letting me take Darryl's horse and hurry him to the nearest doctor, which was in Cheyenne."

Tag nodded silently, pain showing in his eyes.

"I asked on the street in Cheyenne which doctor I should take my wounded friend to, and they told me about a father-son practice, so I went there. The father wasn't there, but the son, Dr. Dane Logan, was in the office. Darryl died shortly after the doctor went to work on him."

Tag's jaw stiffened. "You didn't tell that doc Darryl was an outlaw, did you?"

"I had to, Tag. With that slug in his back, the doctor wanted to know how it happened. My face is known in Cheyenne from being on the stage that stops there. I didn't dare lie about it, so I told him, explaining that I was the shotgunner on the stage, but I didn't let on that I knew Darryl."

Tag's cheeks were now dead white and his eyes had turned the color of slate. "Maybe that doc let Darryl die because he was an outlaw."

"Oh no, Tag. Darryl was almost dead when I carried him into Dr. Logan's office. He had lost a lot of blood. The doctor was starting to dig the slug out when Darryl died."

Tag ground his teeth, wondering if the doctor was really putting on an act by starting to go after the slug, and would have let Darryl die in order to rid the world of one more outlaw.

But he said no more.

Tag let the sadness he felt over Darryl's death surface. "Well, thank you, Doke, for trying to save my baby brother's life."

Doke laid a hand on Tag's shoulder. "May I remind you of that day when you dived into the dangerous North Platte River and risked your life to save mine?"

A smile tugged at the corners of Tag's mouth, and he nodded.

Squeezing his shoulder, Doke said, "Tag, I owe you for that. I'll never forget it. It was for you that I tried to save Darryl's life."

Though Tag Moran's two years as an outlaw had hardened him a great deal, a soft look came into his eyes. He blinked at the tears that had welled up. "Thanks again, Doke, for trying to save Darryl."

"I'd do it again."

Tag's earlier thoughts concerning his desire to bring Doke into play came to mind. "I know you would. Doke, ol' pal, I imagine you don't approve of me and my brothers being outlaws, but you would never turn us into the law if you had a chance, would you?"

Doke chuckled dryly. "Absolutely not. My debt to you for saving my life will always be at the forefront of my mind. I would never do anything to help the law catch you."

Tag smiled. "I believe you, ol' pal. I was

really surprised when I saw you up on the seat of that stagecoach. I had no idea you were employed as a shotgunner for Wells Fargo. I had lost all track of you. Are you married?"

"No. I live in Fort Collins and have dated some nice girls, but nothing serious has developed yet. How about you? Is there a Mrs. Tag Moran?"

"No."

"Was Darryl married?"

"No."

"How about your other brothers?"

"The only one that's married is Bart. Doke, I'd like to have a talk with you. I suppose you're in a hurry right now?"

"Well, yeah. Buck's expecting me at the Meadowlark Café right away. The stage is supposed to leave in just under an hour."

"Well, listen. I'd like to have you come to our hideout so we could talk. You said you live in Fort Collins."

"Yes."

"Well, our hideout is in the mountains about thirty miles west of Fort Collins. It's a large old cabin situated close to the Cache La Poudre River high in the Rockies. It's at ten thousand five hundred feet above sea level, hidden in dense forest. If I drew you a map, would you come and see me sometime soon so we could talk?"

"Sure. I'd like that."

Tag grinned, took a slip of paper out of a shirt pocket and a pencil out of a pants pocket. Holding the paper against the clapboard wall of the closest building, he began drawing a map. "Here's how it works, Doke. Me and my boys make plans to hold up four or five banks somewhere in Colorado, Wyoming, or Nebraska. Of course, in a particular area. When we've held up the banks as planned, we head back to the hideout. We always use roundabout routes to get to the cabin to throw off the posses. Then we stay at the cabin for a few weeks to let things cool down. I'd sure like to have you come so we can have a good talk."

Doke nodded. "I'll do that as soon as I can get a few days off."

Tag finished the map and held it in his hand. "I realize there's no way to contact me to let me know just when that might be, so you'll just have to ride on up. Even if me and the boys happen to be gone on another bank-robbing spree when you arrive, Bart's wife, Lucinda, will be there. One of the other two that you saw when we robbed you is Gib Tully. His wife, Kathryn, will also be there. Once a month or so, Kathryn and Lucinda take the wagon into Fort Collins to buy food and supplies. No one in Fort Collins knows who they are, so they don't know they're outlaws' wives. They always make the trip to Fort Collins and back within about half a day. If we're not at the cabin when you arrive, the gals can tell you when they expect us back. Since we stay at the cabin more than we travel and hit banks, your chances of finding us there are good."

"All right. I'll sure come as soon as I can."

"Let me show you the map."

When Tag had gone over the map with Doke to make sure he understood how to find the cabin, he handed the map to him.

Doke folded the paper and placed it in his shirt pocket. "I'll sure come as soon as I can," he repeated. "Well, I'd better get over there to the café before Buck comes looking for me."

Tag Moran stood at the corner of the building and watched his old friend head for the Meadowlark Café. When Doke entered the café, Tag wheeled and dashed between the buildings to the alley, where he had his horse tied. He rode south out of town and headed for the patch of forest just outside of Chugwater, where he and the gang had waited to rob the stage the day before.

In the shade of the trees at the patch of forest, Bart Moran was pacing impatiently while the others sat on the ground, their backs resting against the trees.

Jason looked up at his brother and shook his head. "Bart, you're a worrywart. If Tag doesn't find Doke in Wheatland, he'll come on back and let us know."

Bart sighed and nodded. "Yeah, that's the plan. But seems to me he's had time to make his contact and get back here. I —"

"Hey!" blurted Tony Chacone, jumping to his feet and pointing north. "Here he comes now!"

Jason and Gib quickly rose to their feet, and all four were standing in a row as Tag rode in. They didn't like the pallor of his face nor the look in his eyes.

Tag dismounted before them. "I was able to make contact with Doke in Wheatland, boys. I was right about him. He had taken Darryl to a doctor in Cheyenne on Darryl's own horse to save his life. But — but —" His eyes filled with tears, and he choked as he added, "Darryl's dead. He died shortly after Doke got him to the doctor's office."

Jason burst into tears, burying his face in his hands. Bart put an arm around him, struggling with his own emotions. Tag joined them and they wept together. While they were weeping, both Tony and Gib spoke their condolences.

When the Moran brothers had gained control of their emotions, Tag took a deep breath. "Fellas, Doke told me that doc in Cheyenne pressed him about Darryl's having the bullet in his back and wanted to know the details. Doke said because his face is known in Cheyenne, since the stage stops there every few days, he had to tell him the truth so as not to get himself in trouble. So he explained to the doc about the holdup, and Darryl getting shot when we were riding away. He didn't let on that he knew Darryl, of course. So the doc did find out that Darryl was an outlaw."

"I guess we can't blame Doke for telling the truth," said Bart. "At least he sure tried to save Darryl's life."

"Yes," said Tag. "But I've got a feeling that doctor in Cheyenne might just have let Darryl die because he was an outlaw."

"You really think he'd do that?" queried Tony.

"Why not? If he let Darryl die, that would be one less outlaw in the West."

There was dead silence for a moment, then Gib said, "You know, Tag, you may be right. What's that doc's name?"

"Dane Logan."

Jason swung a fist through the air. "Well, if Logan did let Darryl die because he was an outlaw, he oughtta be strung up on one of these trees!"

"There ain't never gonna be any way to prove that," said Bart.

Tag brushed the back of his hand across his nose. "No, but if we *could* prove it, I'd be the guy to put the noose around his neck."

There was another silent moment, then Jason turned to Tag. "So we're going to the hideout, aren't we?"

"We sure are. With the money we have from the last five banks we robbed, along with the fifty thousand we got off the stage, we'll take a few extra days off. I hate to have to go and tell Lucinda and Kathryn that Darryl got killed, but they have to know. It'll help, though, when I can also tell them about the big money we have from the stage robbery to fatten up the kitty, as well as stuff our pockets for living expenses. We'll take an extra couple of weeks off to let things cool down with the law."

Tony headed toward his horse. "Well, then, let's get going."

As the others moved toward their mounts, Tag said, "While we're riding, fellas, I want to tell you about something I have in mind to talk to Doke about. He's gonna come to the hideout soon so he and I can talk."

Bart swung into his saddle and set his red-rimmed eyes on Tag. "You told Doke how to find the hideout?"

"Mm-hmm."

"Are you sure you can trust him? I mean, if he knows where we're hiding, he could bring the law on us if he decided to do it."

"Nothing to worry about, Bart. I asked him if he would ever turn us over to the law. He said no. That because I saved his life that day at the North Platte River, he would never do anything to help the law catch us. And I believe him. He's a true friend."

"I feel the same way," said Jason. "After all, he didn't have to go to all the trouble he did to try to save Darryl's life."

The others agreed that Doke could be trusted, and they rode out of the patch of forest, heading south.

The following afternoon at the gang's

cabin high in the Rocky Mountains, Lucinda Moran stood on the front porch with a hand on Kathryn Tully's shoulder. Kathryn was seated on a wooden chair.

"Honey," said Lucinda, "you're fretting over nothing."

Kathryn sniffed and wiped tears. "I hope you're right, but they should have been back by now. I'm just afraid something has happened to them."

"You've got to get a grip on yourself. It'll be all right. Tag said they had some really good banks to hit this time. Maybe they had to take special care in just when they hit each bank and needed more time than they had planned."

Kathryn patted Lucinda's hand. "I hope you're right. I hope they did extra well so it will put us a lot closer to the day when we can all head for California and leave this outlaw life behind forever."

Lucinda let her eyes trail a bald eagle that was circling above the towering pine trees that surrounded the cabin. "Honey, even if they did extra well, you have to realize it's going to be a few more years before each man in the gang has a quarter of a million dollars. You know this is Tag's goal, and he's not going to change his mind. You must learn to be patient."

"I know you're right, Lucinda. Patience isn't my long suit. But — but if I had known back when I married Gib that he would choose to be an outlaw, I would never have married him. This just isn't the plan I had for my life. I don't need a quarter of a million dollars to be happy. A small house and a husband with an honest job is all I want. I don't care how hard we might have to work. It would be far better to have just enough money to live on than to have large sums of ill-gotten gain."

Tears continued to fill Kathryn's emerald green eyes and to trickle down her cheeks.

"But the big money is Gib's dream too, Kathryn. You're his wife, so you're in it now and you'll just have to make the best of it."

Kathryn sniffed and wiped tears. "Yes, you're right about that. But it's so hard to live this way. Every time Gib rides away for another series of bank robberies, I never know if I'll ever see him again. Not only that, but if my family back home knew that I was now the wife of an outlaw, they would be so ashamed of me."

Lucinda leaned over, put an arm around her neck and hugged her tight. "I understand how you feel, honey, but this is the life both of our husbands have chosen, so we'll just have to live with it."

At that moment, they heard horses blowing. Kathryn rose from the chair, and they both moved to the porch railing, searching among the dense forest for sign of movement.

Kathryn's heart was beating wildly.

Soon they saw horses and riders weaving their way among the trees. Kathryn's line of sight focused on the face of her husband. "Oh, Gib's all right," she said with elation. "He's home again. And Bart's home safe, Lucinda."

"Yes," said Lucinda, a smile spreading over her face.

Kathryn frowned as she ran her eyes over the other riders. "Something's wrong. There are only five of them. Darryl's not with them."

"I see that," said Lucinda. "I — I hope nothing has happened to him."

In her heart, Kathryn was grateful that the missing man was not Gib. A tingle of fear and dread went through her at the thought that one day it could be Gib who didn't come home.

When the five riders drew up to the porch and started dismounting, Kathryn dashed off the porch and ran to Gib.

Lucinda followed and made a beeline to Bart.

While the two women were embracing their husbands, Kathryn asked of the group, "Where's Darryl?"

Tag said, "Let's go sit down on the porch and we'll tell you about Darryl."

When they were all seated on the wooden chairs on the porch with Kathryn and Lucinda holding their husbands' hands, Tag choked up as he announced to the women that Darryl had been killed when they robbed a stagecoach two days ago in Wyoming. He told the story of the robbery and Darryl's death in detail, including why they had to ride away, leaving Darryl on the ground with a bullet in his back.

Tag went on to tell the women about Doke Veatch, their old friend from childhood being the shotgunner on the stage, and how he told the rest of the gang as they rode away that he was sure Doke would pick Darryl up and take him to a doctor. He then explained about his meeting Doke in Wheatland yesterday morning and learning that he had taken Darryl to a doctor in Cheyenne, but that Darryl had died shortly after they arrived at the doctor's office.

When the impact of the bad news had eased, Tag went to his horse, took the metal money box from where it was tied to the saddlebag, and showed the women the fifty thousand dollars. He went on to explain how he learned the large sum of money would be on the stage, and how they had forced the stage to stop so they could rob it.

Lucinda showed more pleasure as she observed the fifty thousand dollars than did Kathryn.

Tag went on to tell the women that the bank robberies on this trip garnered them over twenty thousand dollars. He went on to say that of course they would have to put some of the money in their pockets, but still, a good amount could be added to the kitty, along with the fifty thousand dollars.

Tag then wiped the tears from his eyes. "Since Darryl is gone, and the money is going to be split five ways instead of six, we'll reach our goal even sooner."

Still holding onto Gib's hand, Kathryn said, "What happened to Darryl could happen to any one of you next time you pull a robbery. I would rather have less luxury and have my husband. Tag, with what has happened to Darryl, I think you should set your sights lower. Please . . . isn't what we already have in the kitty plus this money enough for us? We don't have to live like kings and queens. Let's take what we have and go to California, leave the outlaw life forever, and make do with what we have."

Tag set his jaw and shook his head. "No way, Kathryn. We deserve to live like royalty for the rest of our lives, but we can't do it on what we have."

Kathryn turned and looked at her husband, her face pinched.

"Gib, you made it back alive and unharmed. Let's take our share and head to California. It's too much of a risk every time you ride out of here to rob more banks. Our share of the money the gang now has is enough for me."

Gib smiled, shaking his head. "Honey, nothing's going to happen to me. I promise. We've stuck with Tag this far. Let's go all the way with him. Just think of what it would be like to have two hundred and fifty thousand dollars in our pockets."

The others watched as Kathryn laid her head against Gib's shoulder. Knowing that her husband could not actually make such a promise, she wanted to insist that he leave the gang right now, but it would be useless. Gib was as determined to reach the goal as was Tag.

She sighed and looked up at the face that she loved so much. "All right, darling, I'll do whatever you say."

Gib smiled broadly. "Good girl."

Tag then brought up Doke Veatch and said that sometime soon Doke would be coming to the cabin to see them. He explained his thoughts about the possibility of getting information from Doke about future Wells Fargo shipments of money between banks, so they could make big hauls like they did the day before yesterday. No one would ever know Doke was the inside informant, and of course, he would be given his cut of the money when they robbed the stagecoaches.

Tag explained that there was no time yesterday morning to discuss it with Doke, but that he told him he had something important to talk to him about, and asked if he would come to the hideout sometime soon so they could talk. Doke agreed, which prompted Tag to draw him a map so he could find the place easily.

Lucinda's features darkened. "Tag, I don't know this Doke Veatch. Can he be trusted? He could bring the law up here."

Tag chuckled. "He's not gonna do anything like that. My brothers and I have known Doke since all of us were very young, back in our Scottsbluff days. Bart and Jason could tell you about the day when we went swimming in the North Platte River and I saved Doke from drowning. He has a loyalty to me for saving his life that will never go away. He talked to me about it in Wheatland in our short conversation. He would never turn on me and lead the law to us."

"I can testify to Doke's loyalty toward Tag, Lucinda," said Bart. "There's nothing to worry about."

"That's right," put in Jason. "Absolutely nothing to worry about."

Lucinda nodded and gave her husband a thin smile.

"Hey!" said Gib. "I don't know about the rest of you guys, but I could use some of that home cooking we always get in this place!"

Tag, Tony, Bart, and Jason all agreed wholeheartedly.

Lucinda laughed. "Well, Kathryn, let's you and me head for the kitchen and fix up some good eats for these hungry men."

As the two women made their way into the cabin and toward the kitchen, Kathryn was trying to still the fears running through her mind as expressed to the group earlier.

Lucinda was secretly having her own fear. Learning that Doke Veatch had been given a map to the hideout left her with a strange feeling of trepidation. *Call it woman's intuition,* she thought, *but I don't like it.*

Seven

In Denver, Colorado, Chief United States Marshal John Brockman was doing paperwork at his desk in his office. The morning sun shone through the large window, brightening the room.

There was a tap on the door. The chief looked up as it came open and Deputy U.S. Marshal Charlie Wesson stepped in with a yellow envelope in his hand. "Chief, a telegram just came for you from Sheriff Jack Polson in Cheyenne. From what the Western Union delivery boy said, it has something to do with the Tag Moran gang."

Brockman's eyes widened as the deputy handed him the envelope. Looking at it, he said, "Charlie, you don't suppose this is going to be good news, telling me that some lawman and his posse have managed to capture that nefarious bunch."

Wesson grinned. "Hey, that *would* be good news!"

Brockman opened the envelope, took out the telegram, and read it while Charlie waited to hear its contents. When he saw disappointment frame the chief's rugged features, Charlie's grin faded.

Brockman looked up at him. "Sheriff Polson wanted to let me know that Moran and his gang held up a stagecoach near Chugwater. They got a cash box containing fifty thousand dollars being sent to the Bank of Casper from the Bank of Fort Collins."

"Oh no. So now they're going after stagecoaches as well as banks."

"Yep. Polson says Darryl Moran was shot by a passenger on the stage while the gang was riding away. He was taken to Dr. Jacob Logan's office in Cheyenne, but died on the operating table. The rest of them are still at large."

Charlie pulled at an ear. "Well, sir, at least there's one less member in the gang."

Brockman nodded. "Yes, but if Tag Moran and the rest of them aren't caught soon, I'm going to have to take some deputies and go after them."

"Well, if you do, Chief, I'd sure like to be one of those deputies."

"We'll see."

Wesson returned to the desk in the outer

office, and Brockman went back to the paperwork.

Nearly an hour had passed when Charlie Wesson tapped on the door and stuck his head in. "Chief, there's a man out here who would like to see you. His name is Wally Talbot. He says he met you once in Kansas, and he just wants to see you for a few minutes before leaving for home."

Brockman pushed his desk chair back and rose to his feet. "Please bring him in." As he spoke, he stepped around in front of the desk.

When Wally Talbot, who was in his late thirties, entered the office, he stopped and looked at the smiling chief with admiring eyes.

Behind him, Charlie Wesson closed the door to give the two men privacy.

Brockman, who was a little older than Talbot, had coal black hair with just a touch of silver at the temples. He was square-jawed and had a pair of identical white-ridged scars on his right cheekbone. His eyes were pools of gray that seemed to look through a person rather than at him.

Talbot moved up to him and extended his right hand. As they met each other's grip, he said, "Chief Brockman, you and I met in Wichita back in May 1868. I was —"

"You were about to be forced into drawing against a gunfighter named Hatch Wasserman."

Surprise showed in Talbot's eyes. He chuckled as they let go of each other's hands. "I didn't think you'd remember me! You saved my hide by taking out Wasserman. Then you led me to the Lord."

"I remember it well, Wally. How are you doing?"

"Just great, sir."

"You still living on that farm just outside of Wichita?"

"Sure am. When you led me to Jesus that day, you told me of a good Bible-believing church in town and strongly advised me to go there. I did that very next Sunday and got baptized. I met the lady who is now my wife in that church and now we have three children — all who have come to know Jesus as their Saviour."

"Wonderful! Come on over here and sit down."

Before either man could move, there was another tap on the door. Charlie Wesson opened it and stuck his head in. "Chief, Mrs. Brockman and the children are here to see you. I told Mrs. Brockman that you were busy at the moment, but I just

131

wanted to let you know they're here."

"Bring them in, Charlie. I'd like for them to meet Mr. Talbot."

Wesson nodded and hurried away.

Wally looked at the tall man. "This will be an honor, sir."

He then saw the beautiful blonde enter, smiling at her husband. Her two children were beside her.

"Breanna, I want you to meet an old friend of mine from Wichita, Wally Talbot."

Breanna offered her hand, and as Talbot took it gently, she said, "I'm happy to meet you, Mr. Talbot."

Talbot did a slight bow. "The pleasure is mine, ma'am."

John smiled down at his son and daughter. "Paul, this is Mr. Wally Talbot."

Paul extended his hand. "Glad to meet you, Mr. Talbot."

"You too, Paul," said Talbot, shaking his hand. "How old are you?"

"Eight years old, sir."

Talbot smiled warmly, then turned to the chief. "Fine young gentleman, he is." Then he set his eyes on the pretty little girl. "And who is this?"

"Her name is Ginny. Ginny, say hello to Mr. Talbot."

Taking hold of the sides of her skirt, Ginny curtsied and smiled. "Hello, Mr. Talbot. I'm very happy to meet you. I'm six years old."

"And a fine young lady," said Talbot, doing a slight bow.

Ginny then turned to her father and embraced him. Paul joined in and John hugged them both. When they let go of him, Breanna said, "We just finished our grocery shopping, so we're ready to have our company for dinner tonight. As long as we were this close to the office, we decided to come in and see you."

John smiled. "Well, it's always good to see my little family. And I'm glad to know we'll be able to feed our company tonight."

Breanna laughed at his dry humor.

Talbot was looking at the children as they stood beside their father, thinking how amazingly Paul's features resembled his father's and Ginny's resembled her mother's.

Breanna ran her gaze between her husband and the man from Kansas. "So how do you two know each other?"

John grinned. "Well, it goes back to May 1868."

"When he was known only as The Stranger, ma'am," added Talbot. "We only met once, but he certainly proved to be my friend."

Paul's eyes lit up. He always loved to hear about his father's past life and hoped to be just like him one day. He grinned from ear to ear, looking up at him. John caught the beam on his son's upturned face and laid his hand on Paul's shoulder, giving it a squeeze.

Talbot spoke again. "Your husband saved my life, Mrs. Brockman. I was in town that particular day and a well-known gunfighter by the name of Hatch Wasserman purposely stepped up to me on Main Street and started talking rough to me. I didn't know who he was, but I knew he was a gunfighter by the way he wore his gun low on his hip and tied down. He was looking for a fight, for sure. I was just a farmer and wore a gun for protection, not because I wanted to get into a gunfight with the likes of him. Your husband happened to be close by, and he could tell by the looks of me I was a farmer, not a gunfighter.

"When I told Wasserman to go away and leave me alone, he took the gunfighter's stance and challenged me to draw against him. It was then that this man in black moved up, called Wasserman by name, and told him to back off and leave me alone. Then Wasserman drew against your husband, ma'am, and he put him down. Just before Wasserman died there in the dust, he identified this man as the one people called 'The Stranger.' "

Paul looked up and grinned at his father.

Talbot set his eyes on the tall man. "I'd heard of this fella called 'The Stranger' who rode all over the West helping people who were in trouble and putting outlaws where they belonged, but I'd never seen him before that day."

Talbot reached in his pocket and drew out a silver medallion the size of a silver dollar. "Do you remember giving this to me that day?"

Breanna and the children looked at the medallion, then Ginny smiled at her mother. Breanna winked at her.

"I sure do, Wally," said John.

The medallion was centered with a five-point star, and around the circular edge were inscribed the words: THE STRANGER THAT SHALL COME FROM A FAR LAND. — *Deuteronomy 29:22.*

Wally turned the medallion toward Breanna. "Did you know he gave medallions like this to people he helped out of trouble, ma'am?"

Breanna nodded. "Oh yes. I have one of my own that he gave to me the first time we met. God sent John to me when I needed him."

Wally arched his eyebrows. "Really?"

"Yes, sir. Really."

Wally looked back at the tall man. "Something's been eating at me all these years."

"What's that?"

"This 'far country' you're from, Mr. John Stranger — what country is it?"

John smiled. "Oh, that's a secret, Wally. Only Breanna knows what country it is."

Wally looked back at Breanna. "Would you let me in on the secret, Mrs. Stranger — er, uh — I mean, Mrs. Brockman?"

Breanna's blue eyes flashed as she looked from the medallion to her husband with a teasing smile on her face, then turned back to Talbot. "Sorry, sir. That's a well-guarded secret."

Wally playfully swung a fist through the air. "Phooey! Well, you can't blame a guy for trying."

The Brockman family laughed.

Wally looked at the medallion with affection. "Well, I'll always treasure this, Chief." He slipped it back into his pocket. Then he turned to Breanna. "There was something else this husband of yours did that day he saved my life, ma'am."

"Mm-hmm?"

"Right after Wichita's sheriff and two of his deputies carried Hatch Wasserman's body away, this John Stranger fella asked me where I'd be right then if Wasserman had killed me — heaven or hell. I told him I hoped I'd be in heaven, but I didn't know for sure. He told me I could know for sure I was going to heaven when I die, and he would show me from the Bible if I'd let him. I said I would. He went and got his Bible from his saddlebag, sat me down on a bench in front of the general store, and led me to Jesus. I can tell you right now, ma'am, I know for sure and positive when I take my last breath in this world, I'll be in heaven with my Saviour."

"Wonderful, isn't it?" said Breanna.

"It sure is."

John spoke up. "Wally told me just before you and the children arrived, Breanna, that he got baptized in the church I recommended there in Wichita, met the lady who is now his wife in that church, and all three of their children are Christians."

Breanna nodded with a wide smile. "Praise the Lord!"

John's brow furrowed slightly. "I'm curious, Wally. What brought you here to Denver?"

"I have a friend named Bill Altman from Wichita who now lives up there in the mountains some thirty miles west of Denver in Central City. You know where it is?"

"Oh yes. I've been there several times."

"Well, my friend Bill is dying with consumption, Chief. We knew each other as boys in Kansas, and have kept in touch by mail since Bill moved to Central City about twenty years ago. I've been witnessing to him in my letters the past twelve years, giving him Scripture and trying to get him to open his heart to Jesus, but he hadn't done it yet when I received the letter about his consumption. He's had it for about four years, but hadn't told me about it until recently. So I came last week to talk to him, and I had the joy of leading both Bill and his wife to the Lord."

"That's great!"

"Yes, sir. Do you know Central City's physician, Chief?"

"Sure do. Dr. Robert Fraser. He and his wife are both fine Christians."

"For sure. Well, Dr. Fraser told me that Bill won't live more than a few weeks. So — so the next time Bill and I meet, it will be in heaven."

"Well, praise the Lord, Wally. You and Bill will have all eternity together in heaven — no more parting."

"Yes, we talked about that. And just think, Chief . . ."

"Mm-hmm?"

"Since you cared enough about me to lead me to the Lord twelve years ago in Wichita, you have a hand in Bill and Darlene Altman's salvation."

"Hallelujah!" said John.

Paul looked up at the man from Wichita. "Mr. Talbot, how did you know Papa was now a lawman here in Denver?"

"Well, Paul, about a year ago Wichita's sheriff told me that the man they called John Stranger was now Chief U.S. Marshal here in Denver, and that his real name was John Brockman. I wasn't sure your papa would remember me, but since I was planning to come to see Bill Altman, I decided to also see the man who saved my life and led me to the Lord."

"I'm very glad you did, Wally," said John.

"The children and I are too," said Breanna.

"We sure are, Mr. Talbot," spoke up Paul. "I always like to meet people my papa helped out back when he was known as 'The Stranger.' "

Breanna asked, "When are you leaving for home?"

"I'm scheduled on the eastbound train that leaves Denver at nine-thirty tomorrow morning, ma'am."

"So you'll be here in town till tomorrow morning."

"Yes, ma'am."

"Good. Since you're going to be here this evening, I would like to have you come for supper and be an added guest."

John nodded. "Yes. We'd love to have you, Wally."

Paul jumped up and down. "Yes! Then we could tell Mr. and Mrs. Tabor and Miss Tharyn about Papa taking out that no-good gunfighter and saving your life, Mr. Talbot!"

Ginny jumped in rhythm with her brother. "And we could tell them about Papa leading you to Jesus too, Mr. Talbot! They'll really be glad to meet you!"

Wally's features tinted slightly. He shook his head slowly. "Folks, I really appreciate your invitation, but I wouldn't want to interfere with you and your guests."

Breanna shook her head emphatically. "You would *not* be interfering, Mr. Talbot. David and Kitty Tabor and their daughter, Tharyn, are very dear friends of ours. They

140

are sweet and dedicated Christians. I know they would love to meet one of John's friends from his John Stranger days. My husband has quite a colorful past, and everyone is always fascinated with tales of his travels. They would also enjoy hearing the details of how this led to John bringing you to the Lord. Please say you will have supper with us tonight."

John laid his hand on Wally's shoulder. "Yes, Wally. That way you and I can have more time to talk and catch up on more details of each other's lives since 1868."

A smile spread over Wally's face from ear to ear. "Well, okay! Sounds great to me!"

"Good!" exclaimed Breanna. "Well, Paul, Ginny — we'd better head for home."

"And I'd best be letting you get back to your work, Chief," said Wally. "I'll go get me a room at one of the hotels. I have a horse I rented at the Black Saddle Stable here in town. What time would you want me to show up here at the office again so I can go to your house with you?"

"Tell you what, Wally. The hotel room isn't necessary. You can stay in one of our guest rooms tonight. We live about six miles out of town in the country. If you can occupy yourself until five o'clock this afternoon, be here then and I'll lead you to our place. I keep my horse in the stable out back."

Wally grinned. "I can occupy myself, all right. I want to look this town over good before I head for home. So you live in the country, eh? Good! Then this ol' farmer will really feel at home!"

Wally thanked all of the Brockman family for their kindness, then left, saying he would be back at the office a few minutes before five o'clock.

Breanna moved to her husband with a sweet smile on her lips. "Well, Mr. John Stranger, Mrs. Stranger and these little Strangers need to get home so we can prepare for our big evening."

Raising up on her tiptoes, she planted a kiss on John's lips. He hugged her. Ginny was next to get a hug, then Paul did the same.

As they started for the office door with John following, Paul said, "I really like that, Mama! I think it's neat being a 'Little Stranger'!"

Eight

꧁꧂

Breanna Brockman guided the trotting team south along Broadway with Ginny sitting on the wagon seat between her and Paul. The children were talking about Wally Talbot and all the other people their father helped out of trouble when he rode the West as The Stranger.

Breanna smiled. Paul, especially, was intrigued with his father's mysterious past and talked about it often. He was fascinated with all the stories he had heard from his father's admirers how John Stranger faced so many of the West's fastest gunslingers who found themselves compelled by their egos to challenge him to a quick draw. Only a few months ago, Breanna had heard her son comment when he had heard one of the stories from an old former lawman from Arizona: "Yep! All those gunslingers thought they could outdraw my papa. They're gone and Papa is still here. Guess we know who was the fastest!"

When they were past the residential area, Paul was telling his little sister what she had heard so many times before; he was going to grow up to be a lawman just like Papa.

The wagon came to a fork in the road, and Breanna took the fork to the right, heading southwest toward the foothills of the Rockies. They had gone some two miles from the edge of town when they saw a wagon coming toward them with the team at a full gallop, leaving a cloud of dust behind.

"Isn't that the Fordhams, Mama?" said Paul. "It looks like their horses."

Breanna focused on the two people sitting in the seat of the fishtailing wagon. The man was slumped on the seat, holding what appeared to be a bloody towel to his head. His face was covered. The woman was driving the team.

"Yes it is, honey," responded Breanna. "And it looks like Mr. Fordham is hurt."

"Look, Mama!" exclaimed Ginny, pointing. "Mrs. Fordham has spotted us and is waving for us to stop."

Breanna put the team to a gallop for a few seconds to close the gap between them as quickly as possible, then pulled back on the reins.

The two wagons quickly drew abreast and came to a halt. Gayle Fordham's horror-stricken eyes were fixed on Breanna as she cried, "Bob got kicked in the head by one of our draft horses! He's bleeding badly, Breanna. I'm taking him to the hospital, but when I saw you coming toward us, I told him maybe we should stop you and see if you could slow down his bleeding. I remember you told me once that just like any doctor, as a nurse, you always carry your medical bag with you."

Breanna was already climbing down from the wagon seat. "Yes, Gayle, I have it right here." She reached into the wagon bed just behind the seat, grasped the handle of her medical bag, and headed around the rear of the Fordham vehicle.

Gayle tried to help Bob climb from the seat into the bed of their wagon. He pressed the bloody towel to the right side of his head as he struggled weakly to accomplish the task.

Paul jumped down. "I'll help you get him back there, Mrs. Fordham." He ran to the rear of the Fordham wagon, pulled the lever to drop the tailgate, then bounded into the bed and hurried to Gayle's side to assist her.

Ginny was looking on from her place on

the Brockman wagon seat, eyes wide.

Breanna set her medical bag in the wagon bed, climbed in, and made her way to the spot where Gayle and Paul were helping Bob lie down.

As Breanna knelt beside the injured rancher, pulled the towel from his fingers, and began examining his bleeding head, Gayle said, "He was unconscious when I found him in the barn. I threw a bucketful of water in his face, and he came to. He insisted on climbing up onto the seat."

"Well, we've got him where we need him now," said Breanna, opening her medical bag.

Bob's eyes were closed, and he was gritting his teeth in obvious pain.

"How bad is it, Breanna?" asked the rancher's wife. "I couldn't tell exactly where he was hit; there was so much blood."

The nurse was taking out needle and thread. "The sharp-shod toe calk of the horse's shoe struck him just above the right temple at his hairline, Gayle. Pretty bad gash, here. Didn't crack the skull, but there's a three-inch split in the scalp I'll have to stitch up."

She reached back into the medical bag and drew out a bottle of wood alcohol.

"Bob, brace yourself. I've got to put alcohol on it before I start the stitching process. It's going to burn like fire."

Bob jerked and howled when the liquid touched the open gash, then settled back down. Working adeptly, Breanna stitched up the gash in a matter of ten minutes, then took a roll of bandage from the bag and wrapped it around his head. As she cinched it with a tight knot, she sighed. "There! The bleeding is stopped. You need to take him on into the hospital, Gayle. Be best if one of the doctors looks him over, and I'm sure they'll want to keep him for observation for a day or two. He's had a pretty bad blow to his head."

"Thank you so much, Breanna," said Gayle while scraping some straw from the floor of the wagon bed and placing it under her husband's head. "Send me your bill, okay?"

Breanna smiled. "Oh yes. And it'll be a big one too."

Bob looked up with dull eyes. "Breanna, we're not kidding. How much do we owe you for this?"

Breanna shook her head. "No money. Both of you promised John and me a month ago that you'd visit our church services. You haven't come yet. Please think about the Scriptures we showed you on the subject of salvation that evening we visited you, and please come to church as soon as you're feeling better, Bob. Okay? Okay, Gayle?"

Bob nodded. "We'll do it."

"Yes, we will," said Gayle.

Moments later, the Fordhams were on their way toward Denver, and Breanna and her children were headed toward home.

At the same time at Cheyenne's Memorial Hospital, Drs. Jacob and Dane Logan were standing over seventy-two-year-old Bertha Ballard, who lay on her bed in a private room. She was sleeping under the influence of a heavy dose of laudanum.

Dr. Dane was carefully examining Bertha's broken hip while his father looked on. When he finished, he covered her up and said, "Well, Dad, if Bertha and her son will give consent, I'll do it. I know I can help her."

Jacob smiled. "All right, son. Let's go talk to Clyde."

Both doctors entered the corridor and walked to a nearby waiting room. Clyde Ballard and his wife, Frances, both rose to their feet as the doctors entered the waiting room.

"So what's the verdict?" Clyde set his gaze on the older man.

Dr. Jacob took a step closer to the couple. "I didn't want to comment on Bertha's condition till I had talked with Dane and he had the opportunity to examine her hip. I'll let him give you his prognosis of the situation."

Frances took hold of her husband's hand, fearful that they were going to hear bad news.

Dr. Dane gestured toward the group of straight-backed wooden chairs that stood in one corner of the room. "Let's sit down."

Clyde and Frances exchanged apprehensive glances as they moved toward the chairs.

When the four of them were seated so the doctors were facing the nervous couple, Dr. Dane said, "Clyde, your mother is going to be crippled the rest of her life and be confined to a bed and a wheelchair unless she has a hip replacement."

Frances frowned. "I didn't know this could be done. I've never heard of a hip being replaced."

"I haven't either," put in Clyde.

"It's relatively new, yes," said Dr. Dane,

"but it is being done, and I can do it, I'm sure."

Clyde's brow furrowed. "Have you done this before?"

"No, but let me explain why I'm sure I can."

"All right."

Dr. Dane cleared his throat gently. "There is an eminent surgeon in France named Dr. Louis Ollier who began doing elbow replacements some ten years ago."

Clyde's eyebrows arched. "Really? Actually replacing elbows?"

"Yes. About five years ago, a German surgeon, Dr. Theodore Gluck, spent a full month in Paris with Dr. Ollier, learning his elbow replacement technique. Dr. Gluck returned to Germany, and applying this knowledge to what he already knew about orthopedics, he worked at developing a technique to replace hips in older people with arthritic hips, and people of any age who have bad hips from accidents of various kinds."

"And I assume he has been successful," said Clyde.

"Yes, sir."

Frances's eyes widened. "Oh, that's wonderful! Tell us more."

"Well, at first, Dr. Gluck began to replace hips with an iron ball, which was attached to the femur with a screw. However —"

"Pardon my ignorance, Doctor," cut in Clyde, "but what's the femur?"

"Oh. I'm sorry. The femur is the long bone of the thigh."

"Oh, of course. I've heard that. A long time ago. I'm sorry, Doctor. Please go on."

Dr. Dane smiled. "As I was saying, at first Dr. Gluck began by replacing hips with an iron ball, which was attached to the femur with a screw. However, when the patient began walking, the weight of the ball on the femur caused more breakdown of the bone tissue, so that when it rubbed against the hip socket, even the slightest pressure was extremely painful. Dr. Gluck knew he would have to come up with something different than the iron ball.

"He soon came up with the idea of replacing a hip with an ivory ball-and-socket joint that he cemented and screwed into place. The ivory, being so much lighter than an iron ball, made it a success."

Frances smiled and patted her husband's arm.

Clyde smiled back.

Dr. Dane said, "The reason I know I can do the hip replacement for your mother,

Clyde, is because during my last year at Northwestern University Medical School, Dr. Theodore Gluck came to lecture on the subject. He had been there in previous years to lecture on other medical subjects.

"In his first lecture, he gave us some history about orthopedics. The first orthopedic procedure — which dates back over four thousand years — involved placing wooden splints of bark, held in place with heavy cloth, on opposing sides of a broken bone. It was really interesting. Dr. Gluck told us that doctors who treated bones were held in low esteem for centuries by others in the medical profession. Orthopedists were called 'gorillas with shaven arms.' "

"Oh, that's terrible," said Frances. "They don't feel that way any more, do they?"

"No. And Dr. Gluck's successes have been the main reason for this change. The quality of life today for people with bone problems has been emphatically improved. And now, with Dr. Gluck's hip replacement technique, so many people with arthritic hips who would have spent the last years of their lives bedridden and in terrible pain now can walk again, and because of the ivory balls, can do it without pain."

"This is marvelous, Dr. Dane," said Clyde. "And you feel certain that even though you have never done a replacement, you can do it on my mother?"

"Yes. Dr. Gluck taught us about his ivory hip replacement technique, then actually did one on a man in his sixties while we students looked on. I took notes at the time, wrote down the exact procedure of sizing the ivory ball for the individual, and precisely what Dr. Gluck did from start to finish in the surgery. I'm sure I can do it for your mother, but I will need her consent as well as yours."

"You can obtain the ivory?"

"Yes. They have quite a supply at Northwestern because the school is having Dr. Gluck come from Germany once a year to teach this procedure. I can get the ivory without a problem."

Clyde and Frances looked at each other.

"Give your consent, dear," said Frances. "Give Mother this opportunity to walk again."

Clyde turned to Dr. Dane. "If Mom will give her consent, I will too."

The older Dr. Logan stood up. "She's probably awake by now. Let's go see."

The four of them moved down the corridor, and when they entered the room, a nurse was standing over Bertha, giving her water with a teaspoon.

"How's she doing?" Dr. Dane asked the nurse.

The nurse smiled. "As well as can be expected, Doctor. I'm almost through."

The nurse dipped the spoon into the cup of water she held in one hand, and gave Bertha several more sips. When she had all she wanted, the nurse excused herself and left the room.

Clyde and Frances stood on one side of the bed, and the doctors stood on the other.

Clyde looked down at his mother, who was running her dull gaze back and forth between her family members and the physicians. "Mom, Frances and I have been in conversation with Dr. Dane Logan and his father. Dr. Dane tells us he can do surgery on your hip and make it so you can walk again."

Bertha's eyes sharpened slightly. "Really?"

"Yes. I'll let him explain it to you."

Dr. Dane leaned over Bertha. "Can you hear me all right, Mrs. Ballard?"

She nodded and licked her dry lips.

Although still groggy with the aftereffects of the laudanum, Bertha attempted to pay close attention as the young doctor carefully explained the new hip replacement procedure.

When he finished, she licked her lips again and looked up into his eyes. "Will it take the pain away, Doctor?" she asked, grimacing as she tried to change her position in the bed.

"Yes, it will. Once the healing of the surgery is complete, then you will need to literally learn to walk again. This will be done gradually, but in a matter of time, you should be pain free and be able to live a normal life with your new hip."

"Oh, that sounds so wonderful, Doctor!" She looked at the older physician. "I really am glad your son joined you in your practice, Dr. Jacob."

Dr. Jacob smiled. "Me too, ma'am."

Bertha set her gaze on her son and daughter-in-law. "Do you children agree that I should have this done?"

"Absolutely," said Clyde.

"Yes!" said Frances.

Bertha looked back at Dr. Dane. "Well, when do we start?"

The doctors exchanged glances and smiled at each other. They were pleased with Bertha's quick and firm decision.

Dr. Dane squeezed her hand. "Mrs. Ballard, I'll wire Northwestern University and ask them to send the ivory. As soon as it arrives, I'll do the surgery. It will probably take four or five days to get it here."

She managed a smile. "Oh, Doctor, I'm so thrilled with the prospect of being able to walk again. It will be so wonderful! Just think, I won't be confined to a wheelchair and a bed for the rest of my life."

Frances leaned down and planted a kiss on Bertha's cheek. "I'm so glad for you, Mother."

Dr. Jacob spoke up. "My son and I will go to the hospital superintendent's office right now and let him know that Dr. Dane is going to do the hip replacement."

As the doctors started toward the door, Clyde said, "I want to thank both of you for your earnest desire to help Mom."

They both smiled, nodded, and moved toward the door. Dr. Dane said over his shoulder, "I'll keep in touch about the ivory."

As father and son headed down the corridor, they saw two young women coming toward them, talking to each other. When Dane's line of sight riveted on the one with long auburn hair, tiny, tingling currents scintillated through his chest.

Dr. Jacob noticed his son stiffen and his eyes widen as he focused on one of the young women just before they entered one of the rooms. He frowned. "Son, what's wrong?"

Dane stopped and wiped a palm over his face. "I . . . uh . . . well, that lovely young lady with the long auburn hair very much resembled Tharyn Myers."

Dr. Jacob laid a hand on his shoulder. "Son, I'm wondering if you will ever get Tharyn out of your heart."

Dane shook his head. "I'm wondering the same thing, Dad. If — if I just knew —"

"I understand, son, but there's no way to know."

Dane sighed and started walking again. "Yeah. That's the worst part."

They descended the stairs to the first floor and soon entered the office of hospital superintendent, Dr. Wiley Chamberlain.

They were welcomed warmly and sat down in front of Chamberlain's desk. Dr. Dane informed him that he was going to do the hip replacement on Bertha Ballard.

Chamberlain instantly showed interest, asking the young doctor if he had ever done a hip replacement before. Dr. Dane replied that he had not, but when he explained how he had learned by personally observing Dr. Theodore Gluck perform one at Northwestern University Medical College, Chamberlain was all for it.

"I've read about Dr. Gluck's ivory ball, gentlemen. And Dr. Dane, I'd sure like to be at your side when you do the surgery."

"I'd be honored to have you there, sir," said Dane.

Dr. Jacob laughed. "I'll be on this boy's other side, Dr. Chamberlain!"

When father and son were riding toward their office in Dane's buggy down Cheyenne's wide Main Street, Dane said, "You know, Dad, you and I talked that day when I completed my internship at the hospital about the fact that I would only plan to stay on as partner in the practice for a short time, then I would seek my own practice somewhere."

"Yes, son. Don't tell me you've already got plans in the making."

Dane chuckled. "No, but I just want to make sure you will back me when that day comes."

"Well, of course I will, Dane. I told you that the day you joined me in the practice. Sure, I'd like to keep you for a long, long time, but I understand your desire to have your own practice. Your mother and I have prayed about it a lot, and we've left it in

God's hands. Until the Lord leads you to establish your own practice or take over some retiring doctor's practice, I want to keep you right where you are."

Dane put an arm around his father and hugged him close. "God so blessed me when He put it on your heart and Mom's to adopt me."

Jacob looked at him with tears glistening in his eyes. "You weren't the only one who got blessed, son. The Lord blessed your mother and me when He brought you into our lives. We've praised Him every day since the moment we adopted you. We couldn't have a better son."

Suddenly they saw a man jump off the boardwalk and come running down the street, waving his arms and calling to them. They both recognized Harry Fisher, one of Cheyenne's residents. Harry and his wife were their patients.

Dane pulled the buggy over.

Fisher drew up and said breathlessly, "Dr. Jacob! Dr. Dane! I was just at your office. Ella Dover told me you were both at the hospital."

"What's wrong, Harry?" asked Dr. Jacob.

"Walt Minard just collapsed while waiting on customers at his store! Mrs. Minard asked me to come and find at least one of you in a hurry!"

"Climb on the running board, Harry," said Dr. Dane.

Harry jumped on and Dane put the horse to a gallop. Minard's General Store was at the far end of the next block.

Moments later when Dane brought his horse to a halt in front of the store, they saw a crowd gathered on the boardwalk, trying to see through the large front window.

Both doctors were picking up their medical bags from the floor of the buggy as Dr. Dane said, "Harry, will you tie my horse to the hitch rail for me?"

"Sure, Doc. You get on in there."

Dr. Dane led the way, elbowing his way through the crowd. When father and son entered the store, they also found a crowd pressed around the fallen man and his wife, who knelt beside him on the floor.

"Please, folks," said Dr. Jacob, "stand back and give us room."

The people obeyed, pressing back to give the doctors more room to work.

Loretta Minard set fear-filled eyes on the younger doctor as he knelt beside her. "I'm so glad you're here! Please, please, don't let him die!"

At the same time, Dr. Jacob knelt on Walt's other side.

Dr. Dane took one look at Walt's gray color and whipped the stethoscope out of his medical bag. The man was conscious, but having a hard time breathing.

Dr. Jacob was unbuttoning Walt's shirt.

Dr. Dane put the earpieces in his ears and quickly placed the microphone against Walt's bare chest. After moving the microphone around on Walt's chest for several minutes while listening closely, he looked into Loretta's worried eyes. "He is in heart failure, ma'am. We need to get him to the hospital immediately after I give him a dose of nitroglycerin. We'll take him in my buggy." He looked up at the crowd. "Will one of you go out and tell Harry Fisher to have my buggy ready, please?"

"I'll do it, Doctor," a young man said, and quickly made an exit.

Dr. Dane took a small bottle of nitroglycerin from his medical bag and administered it to Walt, talking to him in a low, comforting voice.

While he was doing so, Dr. Jacob said, "Son, you won't have room for me in the buggy. Patients are waiting at the office. As soon as we've got Walt in the buggy, I'll go on and take care of them." Then he said to

161

Loretta, "Walt's in the best of hands, Mrs. Minard. My son will take good care of him."

She nodded. "Yes, Doctor. I'll ride with Dr. Dane and Walt to the hospital. My two clerks can watch over the store."

When Dr. Dane finished administering the nitroglycerin, he placed the bottle and the stethoscope in the bag and looked at Loretta. "Will you carry the bag for me please, ma'am?"

"Of course."

Dr. Dane picked the stricken man up in his arms and rose to his feet. Loretta was already on her feet and following Dr. Jacob, who was asking people to clear the way.

When they reached the street, Harry Fisher had the horse and buggy prepared, already pointed in the direction of the hospital.

Dr. Dane told Loretta to place his medical bag on the floor of the buggy, then allowed her to climb in ahead of him. He then placed Walt's limp form on the seat, laying his upper body in Loretta's lap. She quickly cradled his head in her arms, trying desperately to keep her composure.

As Dr. Dane was climbing in beside them, Loretta stroked her dear husband's

162

gray face. "You'll be fine, sweetheart." Her voice cracked with emotion as she added, "Dr. Dane will take good care of you."

Big tears filled her eyes. She wiped them away with the palm of her hand, and while Dr. Dane put the horse to a fast trot, Loretta continued speaking comforting words to her husband.

One of the men in the crowd stepped up to Dr. Jacob Logan and said, "Do you doctors ever have a day of rest?"

Jacob managed a weak smile. "Once in a while, Ralph."

Ralph shook his head while others looked on. "I don't know how you do it. There isn't enough money in the world to make me want to be a doctor."

Jacob's smile widened. "It isn't money, Ralph. It's a certain something the Lord puts in a man's makeup that drives him to be a physician. There is a deep-seated desire to save lives and help people who are sick or injured to be cured. Our satisfaction comes when we accomplish this."

A middle-aged woman in the crowd said, "God bless you, Dr. Logan. Somehow I have a feeling that your son is going to save Walt Minard's life."

Dr. Jacob grinned and nodded. "My son has already saved many a life in the few months he has been my partner, Mrs. Scully."

In a matter of a few minutes, Dr. Dane Logan pulled the wagon to a halt near the front door of Cheyenne's Memorial Hospital. He hopped out and lifted Walt into his arms.

Loretta climbed down quickly and was on the doctor's heels as he headed for the front door.

When they moved into the lobby, he turned and said over his shoulder, "The receptionist over there at the desk will need to get some information from you. Then please sit down here in the waiting area. I'll check back with you as soon as possible."

Loretta nodded. "Yes, Doctor. Thank you."

She then looked at her husband's colorless face and stroked it. "I love you, sweetheart."

"I love you too," breathed Walt.

Dr. Dane adjusted Walt in his arms and gave Loretta an assuring look. "Talk to you soon." With that, he hurried across the lobby, moved through the double doors that led into the corridor, and disappeared.

Nine

The sun had just set over the towering Rocky Mountains west of Denver as Chief U.S. Marshal John Brockman and Wally Talbot rode south on Broadway side by side. John was riding his faithful black gelding, Ebony, and Wally was riding the bay gelding he had rented at Denver's Black Saddle Stable for the ride to Central City.

"Wally," said John, "I'm sorry about the delay at the office. I didn't mean to keep you waiting, but the deputy who came in at the last minute with the outlaw he had been trailing needed to give me his verbal report."

Wally smiled at him. "Hey, Chief, it's all right. I understand. I didn't mind waiting."

They were nearing the edge of town. John adjusted himself in the saddle. "I hope Breanna has gone ahead and started supper. She's used to my being late like this. In my business, I never know what will happen next."

Wally chuckled. "I can imagine that, Chief."

Soon they were out of town and approaching the fork in the road. As John took the fork to the right, Wally said, "Pretty country out here. How much land do you have on your place?"

"Six acres. Just enough to give us some open space around the house and barn. Let's pick up the pace a bit." As he spoke, he put Ebony to a fast trot, and Wally made his horse keep up.

Moments later, they were riding alongside a small creek that was lined with cottonwood trees. The creek ran all the way into the mountains, sided by a trail on its other side. John thought of the many times he and Breanna had ridden their horses together into the mountains, following the trail and the creek.

The valley in front of them widened toward the foothills, and farther beyond was lost in a vast sweep of pines and aspens beneath the fading light of the western sky that lifted the dark peaks of the rugged Rockies into bold relief.

As John guided Ebony off the road to the right and led Wally down the tree-lined lane of the Brockman place, he pointed toward the beautiful white two-story house that stood in a grove of cottonwood and weeping willow trees. "Well, there's your hotel for the night, my friend."

Wally smiled. "Looks good to me!" He let his eyes roam over the place in the fading light. A small barn and other outbuildings could be seen behind the house, all painted white. A split-rail fence formed a corral around the barn. The house had a wrap-around porch and black shutters adorning all its windows. "Beautiful place, Chief."

"Thank you," said John as they rode past the house, where the guests' horse and carriage stood near the front porch.

As they drew near the barn and corral, another big black gelding trotted up to the corral gate, whinnying.

Ebony whinnied back.

Pulling rein, Wally looked at him behind the corral gate. "Wow! What a magnificent animal! You must like black horses."

"I like all colors of horses, Wally," said John as they drew their mounts to a halt. "But this is Breanna's horse. His name is Chance. I saved your life once in Kansas —"

Wally regarded him quizzically.

"Well, Chance saved my life once in Montana when he was a wild stallion. I brought him home and gave him to

Breanna. He will always be something special to me."

Wally chuckled. "And, Chief Brockman, you will always be something special to me." John's face flushed as they dismounted. They removed the saddles and bridles from their horses, put them in the corral with Chance, and headed toward the house.

It was a warm September evening. The doors and windows of the house were open. The warm glow of lantern light spilled out across the wide porch and on to Breanna's flower beds.

Wally drew in a long breath through his nostrils. "Something sure smells good, Chief."

John had already noted the sweet scent in the air. "Yes, that's my wife's famous fried chicken and biscuits. I keep telling her she should open her own restaurant, but she insists she is already busy enough."

Wally laughed, and just as they were drawing up to the back porch, Breanna appeared in the open doorway. "Welcome, Wally," she said as the two men mounted the steps.

"Thank you, ma'am. It sure does smell good!"

Breanna smiled at him, then took hold of

her husband's hand. "I've been keeping supper hot on the stove."

"I'm sorry for being late, sweetheart. Deputy Dan Lynch came in with an outlaw he'd been trailing, and —"

"You don't have to explain, darling. I know how it is at the chief U.S. marshal's office."

When they stepped into the kitchen, Ginny was there. She smiled at Wally and curtsied. "Hello, Mr. Talbot," she said, then rushed into her father's arms.

As John lifted her up, he kissed her cheek. "I love you, sweet baby."

She then kissed his cheek with a big smack. "I love you too, sweet Papa."

Breanna said to John, "Take Wally into the parlor, honey, and introduce him to the Tabors. Ginny and I will have supper on the table in a few minutes. Kitty and Tharyn insisted on helping us, but I won out."

John chuckled. "Don't you always?"

Breanna punched him playfully in the midsection. "We won't talk about my argumentative prowess right now."

John chuckled again. "Come on, Wally. Let's go into the parlor."

When the two men entered the parlor, Paul dashed to his father, and after they had hugged, John introduced Wally to David and Kitty Tabor, who were in their midfifties. He then introduced him to beautiful twenty-two-year-old Tharyn, who had long auburn hair and expressive blue eyes.

As everyone sat down, John said, "Wally, David is president of Denver's First National Bank. I believe we told you that these people go to the same church we do."

"Yes," Wally said. "It's quite obvious that the Brockmans think an awful lot of you folks."

"That works both ways, Mr. Talbot," said Kitty.

David set kind eyes on Wally. "Breanna has filled us in on you, Mr. Talbot. You must —"

"You can call me Wally, Mr. Tabor."

The banker laughed. "Then you can call me David."

A broad smile spread over the farmer's face. "Okay, David. You were saying . . ."

"I was going to say that you must have deep feelings toward this man who saved you from being gunned down by a professional gunfighter, then led you to Christ."

Wally nodded, glanced at John, then looked back to David. "The English language doesn't have the words to say how I feel about Chief John Stranger Brockman, sir."

At that moment, Breanna appeared with Ginny at her side. "Okay, folks, supper's on the table."

As they were all walking toward the dining room, David sniffed the delightful aromas that were filling the house. "Mm-mmm! I can hardly wait, Breanna. If it tastes half as good as it smells all of us are in for a real treat."

Kitty patted his arm. "You know Breanna always fixes your favorite food, dear. That's because anything to eat is always your favorite food!"

As they passed through the dining room door, David patted his slight paunch. "Well, it's true, Kitty darlin'. Eating is one of my favorite activities!"

Everyone laughed.

Candlelight in the chandelier above the table gleamed onto a lovely yellow damask tablecloth. Yellow napkins were folded and lying on each blue and white plate. Breanna had made a captivating centerpiece of white and yellow daisies, and their fragrance filled the air.

David rubbed his stomach. "Boy, am I hungry!"

Breanna laughed. "Well, there's plenty,

David. I want you to fill up."

Kitty said, "You needn't tell him that, Breanna. He always does fill up when we eat at your house!"

Breanna directed her guests where to sit at the table.

When everyone was seated, John set his gray eyes on his friend from Kansas. "Wally, would you ask the blessing on the food, please?"

Wally smiled. "I would be honored to do so, Chief."

Heads were bowed, and eyes were closed.

Wally thanked the Lord for the food, asking Him to bless it to the nourishment of their bodies, then said, "And, Lord, thank You for sending the Stranger to me that day in Wichita twelve years ago, when —" He choked up, cleared his throat, and wiped at the tears that were filling the corners of his closed eyes.

No one opened their eyes as Wally wept for a few seconds, then finally got his amen out.

Wally set his gaze on John. "I'll never be able to thank you properly for saving my life, and for leading me to the Lord."

John smiled. "Wally, you have already thanked me sufficiently. Let's eat!"

During the meal, the conversation led to Tharyn, and the fact that the Tabors had chosen her off an orphan train nine years ago, took her home, and adopted her immediately.

This caught Wally's interest. He looked across the table at Tharyn. "I've heard a lot about the orphan trains, Miss Tharyn. I've read some stories in the *Wichita Herald* about some of the orphans that have been chosen there over the years. Would you mind telling me your story?"

Tharyn smiled. "All right, sir. I was born and raised in New York City — Manhattan, to be specific."

"Mm-hmm."

"When I was thirteen years old, my parents were killed when a team of frightened horses hitched to a wagon full of building materials ran them down in front of our tenement."

Wally's brow furrowed. "Oh my. I'm so sorry, dear."

Tharyn smiled thinly and nodded. "You see, Mr. Talbot, like you I know what it is to have someone save my life. I would have been trampled to death like my parents were if a fifteen-year-old boy named Dane Weston, whom I had just met that morning, hadn't dashed up and removed me from the path of the charging horses just before they hit my parents."

Wally moved his head back and forth slowly. "This Dane Weston must have become a real hero in your eyes."

"He really did. Especially because he risked his own life to save mine. Dane could have been trampled to death too, had his timing been off just slightly."

"Some young man, I'll say."

"Yes, sir. You see, Dane was an orphan who lived on the streets in downtown Manhattan. He just happened to be in our neighborhood at the time. Since I had become an orphan, Dane took me under his wing, so to speak, and made a place for me with his colony of orphans in an alley. And — and it was Dane who witnessed to me about salvation and was responsible for me becoming a Christian."

"I'll say it again. Some young man! Did Dane come west on the orphan train too?"

Tharyn felt a pain lance her heart. A lump formed in her throat. She managed to swallow it, and said, "No, sir. He . . . ah . . . he stayed in New York."

To change the subject, David said, "Breanna told us about your family, Wally. How about some details?"

Wally was happy to tell the Tabors about

his family, and did so through the rest of the meal.

When everyone had finished eating, John, David, Wally, and Paul went to the parlor while Breanna, Kitty, Tharyn, and Ginny cleaned up the dining room table and went to the kitchen to wash and dry the dishes.

For the next half hour, amid much giggling and laughter, the ladies had an enjoyable time talking as they worked together. When they were finished, Breanna looked around to make sure the kitchen was spick and span, then excused herself. "I'll be right back. Kitty, would you mind getting some dessert plates and cups and saucers down from the cupboard? You know where they are."

Kitty smiled. "Sure."

In a few minutes, Breanna was back, carrying a three-tiered white cake that was smothered with fresh strawberries and mounded with whipped cream. "I had this stashed in the ice house to keep it cool."

Kitty looked at the cake, then at Breanna. "Honey, that looks scrumptious. Just wait till David sees this. You're really spoiling him!"

Breanna giggled. "I love to spoil people. It gives me so much joy."

"Well, then, go right ahead," said Kitty as she and the others watched Breanna cut a large piece of cake.

A big smile graced her features as Breanna said, "This piece is for David."

Later while everyone was enjoying the delicious dessert, John explained to the Tabors about Wally coming from Wichita to visit his old friend Bill Altman and his wife in Central City, and how he had the joy of leading Bill and Darlene Altman to the Lord.

The Tabors expressed their joy in the salvation of Wally's friends, then John said solemnly, "This is a special blessing because Bill Altman has consumption. Dr. Robert Fraser in Central City is estimating that Bill will die within a few weeks."

"Oh my," said Kitty.

"There's no hope that he could have a turn for the better, Wally?" asked Tharyn.

"No, Miss Tharyn. I asked Dr. Fraser the same question, but he assured me that Bill won't be here long. The consumption is just too far advanced."

Breanna set her soft gaze on Wally. "But, praise the Lord, isn't it wonderful to know that you will be with your friend Bill forever in heaven?"

Wally brushed a tear from the corner of

his eye. "It sure is, Mrs. Brockman. It sure is."

The conversation turned to other things, then gradually began to wane. Finding a silence in the group, Tharyn said, "I had an interesting day today. I got to assist Dr. Lyle Goodwin on an abdominal tumor surgery. This was my first time ever to assist in this kind of a surgery, and I learned a lot."

"That's good, honey," said Breanna. "And it's always good to work with Dr. Goodwin, isn't it?"

"Oh yes. You must have thoroughly enjoyed all those years you worked for him at his clinic."

"I sure did. He's such a precious man, and a fine Christian too."

"Yes. I sure wish he wasn't about to retire."

Breanna nodded. "He doesn't want to, but his age is making it more and more difficult to keep up with the workload."

Wally's eyebrows arched. "I didn't realize you were a nurse, Miss Tharyn."

"That she is," spoke up Breanna, "and an excellent one too. In fact, she's one of the best in the business. In just over two years, Tharyn has now become the top surgical nurse at Mile High Hospital. She is in demand more than any other surgical nurse on the staff."

Tharyn blushed.

Breanna went on. "You see, Wally, when Tharyn and I first got acquainted, she was thirteen years old. She told me she wanted to be a nurse one day, so I spent time with her, teaching her about the medical profession. I saw immediately that she had a genuine aptitude toward nursing. She finished her schooling and entered the Denver School of Nursing at the age of seventeen. When she graduated three years later, with her certified medical nurse's degree, she was at the top of her class. My brother-in-law, Dr. Matt Carroll, is superintendent of Mile High Hospital. He hired her the day after she graduated."

Wally nodded. "So the head man at the hospital is your brother-in-law."

"Mm-hmm. He is married to my sister, Dottie."

"Mr. Talbot," said Tharyn, "Breanna was a marvelous help to me when we worked together, which was often. She taught me so much."

Wally looked at Breanna. "So you worked for the hospital too?"

"Yes."

"But you're not working now?"

"I worked full-time at the hospital until five months before Paul was born. And now having Ginny too, I want to spend as much time with my children as possible. Periodically, however, whenever my brother-in-law needs help at the hospital, I do that. This gives Tharyn and me time to work together some, which we enjoy very much."

A smile spread across Tharyn's lovely face. "That's for sure!"

Wally placed the tips of his fingers to his temple. "I just thought of something. In my conversation with Dr. Fraser in Central City, he said something in passing about bringing patients here to Mile High Hospital when he has to do serious surgery on them."

"He sure does," said Breanna. "We all know him well. He is a fine, dedicated Christian, as is his dear wife."

"I haven't met Mrs. Fraser," put in Tharyn, "but I've done some surgeries with Dr. Fraser, and I like him very much."

Breanna smiled. "When I was working at the hospital a couple of weeks ago, I had the privilege of being his surgical nurse for gall bladder surgery. When we were washing up after surgery, Dr. Fraser and I were talking about Dr. Goodwin making plans to retire, and he told me he is doing the same thing."

"Really?" said John. "I wasn't aware of that."

"I meant to tell you, honey, but it slipped my mind. Dr. Fraser told me he will be turning seventy-five in November, and like Dr. Goodwin, he feels he is just not capable of carrying the load any longer."

"It must be quite a load too," said John. "He's the only doctor in a thirty-mile radius up there in the mountains. So how soon does he plan to retire?"

"Just as soon as he can find the right young doctor to take over his practice."

"Mmm. That could take a while. This part of the country isn't running over with them."

"You're right about that. Dr. Fraser said he is leaving it in God's hands. He said he is praying that the Lord will send him a young doctor who will let him fill in for him when he has to come to Denver to do surgery, or has to be away from the Central City office periodically."

John chuckled. "Just can't quite let go altogether. I hope the Lord does that very thing for him."

Tharyn said, "I heard recently that Dr. Faulkner in Colorado Springs and Dr.

Berryman in Fort Collins are both planning to retire soon. With these good doctors in the area retiring, I sure hope there are young doctors who will want to come west and take over their practices."

"I heard about them too," said Breanna. "With the way people are coming to the West from back east, certainly there will be more young doctors who will want to come."

"I would think so," said Kitty. "As the West becomes more populated, the opportunities become greater for both men and women in the medical profession."

There was a lull in the conversation. Breanna turned to Tharyn. "Honey, I wish Scott could have been here for the evening, too."

Tharyn smiled. "Me too. I really miss him."

Wally turned to Tharyn. "Is this Scott your young man?"

"Yes, he is. His last name is Hubbard. Scott is from Pueblo, Colorado, some one hundred miles south of Denver. He is presently visiting his parents and old friends there. He'll be back on September 24. Scott is employed at Denver's other bank, the Rocky Mountain Bank."

David chuckled. "Well, since Scott's getting serious about my daughter, one of these days I'm going to persuade him to come to work at First National Bank. He's a fine Christian young man, and is also a member of our church."

Wally grinned at the lovely redhead. "Well, I hope it works out between you and Scott, Miss Tharyn."

"It's looking good," put in Kitty. "From some statements Scott has made to David and me recently, I expect him to ask Tharyn to marry him just any time now."

Tharyn's features tinted.

Kitty frowned. "Well, don't *you,* honey?"

Tharyn cleared her throat softly and nodded. "Yes, Mother. I . . . ah . . . I have a feeling Scott is going to propose as soon as he gets back."

The conversation went another direction for a few minutes, including the upcoming visit of President Rutherford B. Hayes to Denver. He and Vice President William A. Wheeler were at a Republican Convention in San Francisco and planned to spend a day in Denver on their way back to Washington, D.C.

When that subject had been exhausted, David said, "Well, Kitty and Tharyn, it's time for us to be heading home."

The Brockmans and Wally Talbot

walked the Tabors to the front porch, and Wally said, "I sure am glad I got to meet you folks. God bless you."

The Tabors expressed the same feelings toward Wally, and when they were riding away in their carriage, John ushered Paul and Ginny through the door. "Okay, kiddies, time for Papa's little babies to get to bed."

Paul made a mock scowl. "Papa, we're not babies anymore."

John laughed as he closed the door behind the small group. "Son, you and Ginny will always be my babies."

Breanna put an arm around each of them and smiled as she looked into their young eyes. "You will always be Mama's babies too!"

Ten

While the Tabor family rode back toward Denver, Kitty sat between David and Tharyn, thinking about the day in the not-so-distant future when she would watch her daughter walk down the aisle of the church auditorium on David's arm.

A lump rose in Kitty's throat as she pictured the scene in her mind.

Scott would be waiting on the floor at the base of the platform, his eyes fixed on his beautiful bride in her fancy white wedding dress. When David and Tharyn would reach the end of the aisle, from the platform, Pastor Nathan Blandford would say, "Who gives this woman to be married to this man?"

With a quiver in his voice, David would reply, "Her mother and I." He would then place Tharyn's hand in Scott's hand, and the bride and groom would mount the platform steps to take their vows.

Kitty felt a tingle slither down her back-bone.

Both David and Tharyn felt the sudden movement of Kitty's body.

"You cold, honey?" asked David.

"No. I just had a little tingle run down my spine. I'm fine."

Tharyn patted her mother's hand, then let her eyes take in the magnificence of the heavens above her. The sky was a deep velvet black, blazing with millions of twin-kling stars.

As Tharyn felt the sway of the carriage and the bumps of the road, her mind went back to the conversation that evening, when she told Wally Talbot about Dane Weston having saved her life and how he had been the one responsible for her be-coming a Christian.

Her heart was heavy as she thought about Dane's request that she write him at the prison as soon as she had been taken into a foster home out West. He wanted to know that she was all right, and when she had an address, he was looking forward to them corresponding with each other.

The carriage hit a large bump, and after the Tabors had adjusted themselves on the seat, Tharyn bit her lip as she thought about the letter she wrote to Dane shortly after being taken into the Tabor home. She told him all about her new parents — that they were born-again Christians and how happy she was with them. She had explained that David and Kitty Tabor had adopted her, and now her name was Tharyn Tabor. She gave him the address of the Tabor home, explained that her new father was a banker in Denver, and that she and her new parents were praying for him. She asked him to write back to her. As she closed off the letter, she called Dane her big brother and signed it: "Love, Your Little Sis."

After sending her first letter to Dane, Tharyn's hopes had been high, and after about ten days, she began making her way to the post office daily to see if he had written back to her. She recalled how each day as she entered the post office, her heart beat wildly with anticipation.

But each time, there was no letter from Dane. As the days dragged on with no response, her heart grew heavy. Would she never hear from him?

The carriage rounded a bend in the road beneath the shimmering heavens. David and Kitty were talking about something which didn't register in Tharyn's mind as she remembered thinking that maybe —

for some reason — Dane had not received her letter. Prisons being what they were, most anything could have happened to that letter. So she resolved to write him again, which she did. When there was no response to that letter, she wrote again and again. Still there was no response.

Finally, Tharyn decided that the boy she called her big brother had elected not to keep in touch with her since it appeared he was going to spend the rest of his life in prison. Though he was innocent of the crime for which he had been given a life sentence, he apparently felt it was better for her if she didn't have contact with a young man who had been convicted of murder and would never see the free world again.

Soon the carriage was moving into Denver on Broadway, with its flickering street lamps. Moments later, David turned on to a side street, drove half a block, and swung into the driveway of the Tabor home.

David drove past the house, parked the carriage at the back porch, and hopped out. He helped his wife and daughter from the carriage seat, then led the horse and carriage toward the small barn as the two women entered the house.

In the kitchen, Tharyn lit a lantern while her mother was lighting one in the hall. Kitty waited for Tharyn to catch up to her so they could climb the stairs together.

Kitty touched Tharyn's arm. "Sweetie, is something wrong?"

Tharyn gave her a quizzical glance. "No, Mama. Why do you ask?"

"Well, you just seem — ah — preoccupied. You hardly said anything on the way home."

"Oh. I was just thinking about the things we talked about at the Brockmans' this evening."

"I see. Well, let's get into our robes so we'll be ready for Bible reading and prayer with your father."

Some twenty minutes later, the Tabors sat down in the parlor with a bright coal oil lantern burning on the end table at the sofa. Mother and daughter sat together on the sofa, and David sat in an overstuffed chair, facing them.

"Well," said David, flipping the pages of his Bible, "tonight we'll pick up where we left off last night, in Matthew 25."

Kitty and Tharyn opened their Bibles and found the designated passage.

"Okay," said David, "we left off in verse 30 last night. Tonight we'll read through the end of the chapter, then discuss what Jesus said."

As was the custom, they would each read a verse aloud, covering the designated passage, then go back and discuss it. The order was always David first, Kitty second, and Tharyn third.

David said, "Listen to Jesus now. Verse 31. 'When the Son of man shall come in his glory, and all the holy angels with him, then shall he sit upon the throne of his glory:' "

Kitty picked it up in verse 32. " 'And before him shall be gathered all nations: and he shall separate them one from another, as a shepherd divideth his sheep from the goats:' "

Tharyn followed, reading verse 33. " 'And he shall set the sheep on his right hand, but the goats on the left.' "

David read verse 34. " 'Then shall the King say unto them on his right hand, Come, ye blessed of my Father, inherit the kingdom prepared for you from the foundation of the world:' "

Kitty read verse 35. " 'For I was an hungred, and ye gave me meat: I was thirsty, and ye gave me drink: I was a stranger, and ye took me in:' "

Tharyn read verse 36. " 'Naked, and ye

189

clothed me: I was sick, and ye visited me: I was in —' " She swallowed hard. " 'I was in p-prison — and — and ye c-came unto me.' " Her eyes filled with tears.

Suddenly her slender body was rigid.

Kitty took hold of her arm. "Tharyn, what's wrong?"

Tharyn laid her Bible on the sofa, stood up, and the look she gave her mother was vague and unfocused.

David could see Tharyn's face clearly. He left his chair and took hold of her hands. "*Prison,* Tharyn. In prison, and ye came to me. It's Dane, isn't it? That verse made you think of Dane."

She set her tear-dimmed eyes on her father. "Yes, Papa. I've had him heavily on my mind since I told Wally Talbot tonight about his saving my life." She pulled her hands free. "Please excuse me." With that, she broke into sobs and ran from the room.

David started after her, but Kitty grasped his arm. "I'll take care of it, honey. I think she needs a female to talk to."

He nodded. "Sure."

Kitty hurried out of the parlor. She rushed up the stairs and moved down the hall to Tharyn's room. The door was closed, but she could hear her sobbing inside.

Kitty tapped on the door and opened it. Tharyn was stretched across her bed, facedown. As she moved toward the bed, Kitty said softly, "Sweetheart, can we talk?"

Tharyn rolled onto her side, wiped tears from her eyes, and sniffed.

"S-sure, Mama."

Kitty sat down on the edge of the bed and Tharyn sat up, facing her. Once again she wiped tears.

Kitty took hold of her hand. "Honey, I thought maybe by now you were getting Dane out of your heart. Especially since you and Scott are getting serious about each other."

Tharyn's features pinched. "I thought so too, Mama. I — I guess a girl can't always know her own heart, can she?"

"I'm sure that's true, honey, but you can't let your memories of Dane interfere with what you have with Scott. Dane's out of your life. He has been for nine years. You wrote to him several times, but he didn't care enough to answer you. Honey, you've got to let him go and concentrate on your future with Scott."

Tharyn nodded. "You're right, Mama. There's no way I can ever forget Dane. I mean, just wipe him out of my memory.

But I'll focus on Scott. He *is* my future."

Kitty patted her arm. "Good girl. Now let's pray together, then you can go to bed."

As Tharyn lay in bed in the darkness after her mother had been with her, she closed her eyes. "Dear Lord, thank You for my wonderful parents. They have been so good to me. And thank You for bringing Scott into my life."

She paused and swallowed with difficulty. "Lord, I pray once again for Dane as I have for these many years. Please free him from the prison. You know he didn't commit that murder."

Abruptly, a new thought worked its way into Tharyn's mind. *Maybe new evidence has been found that proved him innocent. Maybe he's out of prison now.* "Oh, I hope that's the case. If so, I hope he's pursuing his dream of being a doctor."

Then another thought edged its way in. *Then why hasn't he written me or come to see me?*

Fresh pain filled her heart.

She took a deep breath. "Well, enough of this self-pity. The Lord has brought Scott into my life, and my thoughts should be on him and our future together."

Anticipating Scott Hubbard's return from Pueblo, she fell asleep with her mind on him.

In Cheyenne on Tuesday, September 21, Dr. Dane Logan stood with Loretta Minard in her husband's hospital room as a male attendant helped Walt into a wheelchair from a straight-backed wooden chair. He was dressed and excited about being able to go home.

Loretta smiled as she saw the contented look on her husband's face. "Thank you, Dr. Logan, for what you've done to help Walt's heart come back to normal."

"Yes, Doctor," said Walt, as he settled on the wheelchair. "Your dad was right. He told me I was in good hands."

Dr. Dane grinned. "Well, that's my job. I'm just so glad to see you doing so well. Now don't forget to stay on the medicine I gave you. And don't do anything strenuous until I say you can. We have an appointment set for you to come to the office so I can check your heart in a week, remember?"

"Yes, sir."

"I'll make sure he gets there, Doctor," said Loretta.

As the attendant wheeled Walt out of the

room, Loretta and the doctor followed into the corridor. Loretta paused, raised up on her tiptoes, and kissed Dane's cheek. "God bless you, Dr. Logan. The Lord truly has given you much wisdom." With that, she hurried after her husband.

Dr. Dane stood and watched as the Minards made their way down the corridor, the wheels of the wheelchair squeaking. When they reached the corner, Loretta stopped and looked back. Seeing Dr. Dane still standing there, she waved. He returned the gesture, then watched her disappear around the corner.

"Thank You, Lord," he said softly. "Thank You for giving this country doctor the wisdom, guidance, and skill I've prayed for."

In one of the operating rooms at Cheyenne Memorial Hospital on Friday morning, September 24, Dr. Jacob Logan and Dr. Wiley Chamberlain looked at each other and smiled as Dr. Dane Logan put the last stitch in the incision of Bertha Ballard's hip. Nurse Laura Connally was assisting him.

Laura noticed the two older doctors smiling at each other. She smiled, looked at the younger doctor, and said, "Dr.

Logan, that was some kind of surgery. I have no doubt Mrs. Ballard is going to walk again."

"Sure she will!" exclaimed Dr. Chamberlain. "That ivory ball-and-socket joint is definitely the answer. Dr. Logan, I'm proud of you."

"Me too!" said the other Dr. Logan. "You did a beautiful job, son."

Dane smiled. "I couldn't have done it if Dr. Theodore Gluck hadn't shown me how to do it, and the Lord hadn't guided my hands."

"It's plain to see that God meant you to be a physician and surgeon, my boy." Dr. Jacob turned to the hospital superintendent. "Well, Dr. Chamberlain, you have a meeting to attend, and I have patients waiting for treatment at my office."

When the two older doctors had gone, Dr. Dane looked down at Bertha for a long moment, then turned to the nurse. "I'll go tell her son and daughter-in-law how the surgery went, Laura. I'll let them know that you are at her side, and that you'll come and get them when she awakens, so they can talk to her."

"Yes, Doctor."

He walked to the door, paused, and looked over his shoulder. "I'll be back in the morning to check on her. Thank you for assisting me. You did a good job."

"Working with you is a pleasure, Doctor," she said with a warm smile. "You are so dedicated to your profession."

Dr. Dane walked down the corridor a few steps and entered the waiting room. Clyde and Frances Ballard rose to their feet instantly, waiting for the doctor to speak.

"She's doing fine," Dr. Dane said with a smile. "Everything went well, and both doctors who were with me agreed that the hip replacement was a success. Bertha will walk again after a few months of therapy."

"Wonderful!" said Frances.

"Yes!" exclaimed Clyde, wrapping his arms around Frances.

They held on to each other for a moment, then Clyde said, "Dr. Logan, how can we ever thank you?"

"No need. Seeing your mother walk again will be thanks enough."

"How soon can we see her?" queried Frances.

"It'll probably be at least another hour before she comes out of it and can talk to you. The nurse with her is Laura Connally. She will come and let you know when you can see Bertha."

"We'll be right here," said Clyde. "And thanks again for making it so she can walk again."

While driving his buggy toward the office, Dane praised the Lord for His help in doing Bertha's surgery. "There's so much satisfaction in this profession, Lord. That dear woman would have been a cripple the rest of her life, but because of what I learned from Dr. Gluck, and because You have given me the ability to perform surgery, she will walk again. Thank You."

Two men on the boardwalk caught his eye and waved to him. Dr. Dane smiled and waved back. Soon he was reading the shingle that swung in the breeze:

Cheyenne Medical Office
Dr. Jacob Logan
Dr. Dane Logan

As he guided the buggy up to a hitching post in front of the office, his head bobbed at the sight of the two young women on the boardwalk whom he had seen in the hospital a few days before. When he focused on the one with the long auburn hair, the same tiny, tingling currents scintillated through his chest as before.

Though there were some differences in the young lady's facial features from Tharyn's, she had the same shade of blue eyes and resembled her amazingly in size and stature.

The young ladies passed on by, totally unaware of the effect that the redhead had on him.

Dr. Dane hopped out of the buggy, picked up his medical bag, tied the horse's reins to the post, and headed toward the office door. "Lord," he said in a half-whisper, "You know where Tharyn is and how she is doing. Please take care of her and bless her."

High in the Rocky Mountains west of Fort Collins, Colorado, Tag Moran, his brothers Bart and Jason, along with Gib Tully and Tony Chacone were sitting on the front porch of the large log cabin. The roar of the Cache La Poudre River several hundred feet below was music to their ears.

Each man was in a wool mackinaw with his hat pulled down tight against the stiff, cool breeze that was whistling through the surrounding pine and aspen trees. The aspen leaves had recently turned gold and were fluttering in the breeze. The sun was shining down from a clear azure sky. It was almost noon, and although the cabin windows and doors were closed because of the fall chill in the air, they caught some of the aroma of lunch cooking.

Tony Chacone made a slurping sound. "Sure smells good. I'm plenty hungry."

Bart Moran nodded. "Me too. It's been a long time since breakfast."

Jason sighed. "I sure hope I can find a gal to marry who can cook like Lucinda and Kathryn. Do you guys suppose I'll have to wait till we've each got our quarter of a million and are living in California before I find her?"

Tag chuckled. "Probably so, little brother. Looks like it's gonna be that way for me too. But I'll tell you this much: When we strut around San Francisco — or wherever we decide to settle — in our fancy duds with diamond rings on our fingers, we won't have any problem finding gals who want to marry us."

In the kitchen of the cabin, Lucinda Moran and Kathryn Tully were busily preparing to feed the men. Kathryn was putting plates and eating utensils on the table as she looked at Lucinda, who was stirring a pot of beans at the stove. "I sure wish Tag would listen to me and just lead us and the men to California before winter hits these mountains."

Lucinda looked down at the pot of beans, then lifted her gaze to Kathryn. "I understand the fear you have that if they keep on holding up banks for as long as Tag has planned, Gib could get killed like Darryl did. And I know Bart could get killed too, but since Bart and Gib are both in agreement with Tag that all five of them will not quit the robbery trail until each has a quarter of a million dollars, I have to go along with Bart."

"Yes, but —"

"You mustn't nag Gib about it, Kathryn. Just go along with it because it's his big dream."

Kathryn laid down the last fork and bit her lips. "It could go another way. So far, the gang hasn't killed anybody during their robberies, but it could happen. Someone could offer resistance with a gun, and bullets would fly. If the gang kills someone, the law will be even hotter on their trail, and whoever did the killing will be hanged. Either way, Lucinda, one or both of us could lose our husbands."

Suddenly, Kathryn broke into tears and dashed from the room.

Lucinda sighed, slid the pot of beans and

the coffeepot to the side of the stove, and hurried after her.

When Lucinda entered the den, Kathryn was sitting on the small sofa, her face buried in her hands, and tears streaming between her fingers.

Lucinda sat down beside her and put a hand on her shoulder. "Look, Kathryn, I understand your feelings about all of this, but you've got to get a grip on yourself. As I see it, you've got the same two choices that I have — stick by your husband in spite of your fears . . . or leave him."

Kathryn drew a shuddering breath, lifted her head, and looked at her friend through a wall of tears. "It — it really comes down to that, doesn't it?"

"Yes."

Kathryn ran a sleeve across her nose and mouth. "Then there's only one answer. I love Gib too much to leave him. So — so I'll just have to learn to live with this horrible, torturous fear inside me."

"That's right."

There was a quivering in the pit of Kathryn's stomach that ran right through her flesh to her bones. She drew another shuddering breath. Several seconds passed. She palmed tears from her face. "Then I'll do it, Lucinda."

"Good," said Lucinda, rising to her feet. "Come on. Let's feed those hungry outlaws."

Outside on the porch, Tag and his men were discussing their next round of bank robberies.

"I read in a newspaper not long ago," said Tag, "about a very substantial bank over in Vernal, Utah. We haven't ever hit a bank in Utah. On this next round, I want to hit it. Then we'll head into southwestern Wyoming, where we've never hit a bank before. I figure we'll hit the banks in Evanston, Green River, and Rock Springs."

"Sounds good to me," said Bart."

The others spoke their agreement.

Tag grinned. "One day I want to hit both banks in Salt Lake City simultaneously. Sometime next year. I guarantee you, boys, we'll come out a whole lot richer then!"

"Keep talking, man," spoke up Tony. "This is sounding better all the time!"

The others laughed, including Tag, who then said, "And of course, since we did so well when we hit both banks in Cheyenne simultaneously a year and a half ago, I want to go back there and do it again. They will have let their guard down by then."

"Good thinking, Tag," said Jason. "So

you're figuring to hit the banks in Vernal, Evanston, Green River, and Rock Springs in October, right?"

"Right. Then we'll hibernate for the winter here at the cabin. Come spring, we'll —"

Tag was interrupted when Tony jumped off his chair, whipped out his revolver, and snapped back the hammer.

The others stood up, looking around.

"What is it, Tony?" asked Tag.

"I saw movement in the timber down there toward the river. We've got company."

Tag wondered if it was Doke Veatch.

With their hearts pounding, Tag and the others grabbed their rifles, which were leaning against the front wall of the cabin near the door.

As the gang flattened themselves on the floor of the porch, looking down the side of the mountain, Lucinda opened the cabin door. She called loudly, "Hey, you hungry outlaws! Lunch is on!"

From his prostrate position, Tag hissed, "Sh-h-h!"

Lucinda blinked as she saw all five of them on their bellies, rifles in hand.

In a hoarse whisper, Tag said, "Get back in the cabin! Someone is coming!"

At that instant, Tony pointed to movement in the deep shadows of the timber. "Oh! It's only a cougar!"

Every eye was immediately fixed on the tawny male mountain lion as he threaded his way among the trees some three hundred feet downslope from the cabin.

"Whew!" gasped Jason. "I'd rather face one of those cats any day than a lawman and his posse!"

Relieved, the others agreed, rising to their feet.

"Lunch is ready, boys," Kathryn said.

Eleven

While Tag and the others were eating lunch, he was telling the women about his plan to rob the bank in Vernal, Utah, next. He explained why it was such a prosperous bank, according to the newspaper article he had read.

Kathryn Tully felt her nerves tighten. *If it's that prosperous,* she thought, *it will be well-guarded.*

When Tag went on to say that sometime next year, he wanted to rob Salt Lake City's two banks simultaneously, Kathryn's stomach began to wrench. Try as she might, she was still having a horrible time giving in to living like this indefinitely.

She thought about Darryl Moran being killed as a result of the stagecoach robbery, and in her mind, she kept picturing Gib lying dead on a slab after he had been gunned down during a bank robbery. This was so real that it made her clench her fists underneath the table. She bit down hard in an effort to hide her feelings and shook away the panic that had bubbled up like acid in her chest.

While Tag was giving the details of his plan to rob the two Salt Lake City banks to the group, he ran his gaze to Kathryn's face, and she did her best to disguise the turmoil that was going on inside her.

Tag could see that Kathryn was uncomfortable with the subject at hand, but said nothing to her.

Tag went on. "As I was telling the boys before the cougar showed up, since we haven't hit any banks in southwest Wyoming, we'll go there after the Vernal holdup. We'll hit the banks in Evanston, Green River, and Rock Springs. We'll do this next month, then hibernate here at the cabin for the winter."

Tony Chacone was draining his coffee cup. Kathryn left the table, saying she would get him some more coffee. As she moved toward the stove where the coffeepot sat over the fire, she glanced out the kitchen window. What she saw made her heart bang her ribs. She stopped, looked back at the others. "There's movement out there in the trees! Someone's coming!"

Tony chuckled. "Aw, it's just an ol' mountain lion, Kathryn. He's prowling around down there in the forest."

Kathryn's face was white with fear. She shook her head. "It's no mountain lion. It's a man on horseback, and he's heading straight for the cabin. There's got to be more men with him. It's a posse as sure as anything!"

Suddenly all five men were on their feet, pulling their revolvers, and charging toward the window.

Lucinda followed, her own face almost as pale as Kathryn's.

Tag reached the window first and pressed his face close to the glass. "Hey! It's no posse, Kathryn. It's Doke Veatch! All of you remember that I told you he'd be coming up here to see us."

Bart looked past Tag's shoulder. "Whew! It's Doke, all right. I'm sure glad it's not a posse."

Tag slid his gun back in its holster and hurried to the door. He stepped out on the porch, with the others on his heels, just as Doke drew up and pulled rein. He smiled. "Howdy, Tag. Howdy, Bart. Howdy, Jason."

The Moran brothers bounded off the porch while Doke was dismounting, and each one shook his hand, saying how good it was to see him.

Tag took Doke by the arm, led him up the steps, and said, "Doke, I want you to meet Bart's wife, Lucinda."

Lucinda offered her hand. Doke took it, saying what a pleasure it was to meet her.

Tag then introduced him to Gib and Kathryn Tully, and to Tony Chacone.

When Doke had shaken hands with them, Tag said, "We were eating lunch when we saw you coming, Doke. You hungry?"

The Wells Fargo shotgunner patted his stomach. "Sure am."

Moments later, they were seated at the table with fresh, hot coffee in their cups, and while the hungry Doke Veatch wolfed down his food, he and the Moran brothers talked about old times in their childhood.

When Darryl's name came up, there was sadness on their faces.

Tag said, "Doke, I've been thinking about that doctor in Cheyenne."

Doke swallowed a mouthful of chewed beans. "Uh-huh?"

"I still wonder if he let Darryl die because you told him Darryl was an outlaw."

Doke shook his head. "I don't think so. Darryl was already close to death when I carried him into the doctor's office."

Tag frowned. "Lots of men with a bullet

in them have been close to death, but good doctors have been able to save them. I think he saw a chance to rid the world of an outlaw."

Doke didn't like the look in Tag's eyes. "I — I really don't see it that way, Tag."

The frown deepened. "What's his name? Wayne Brogan? Something like that."

"Dane Logan. Dr. Dane Logan."

"Oh yeah. Dane Logan. I won't forget it again. I think Darryl would still be alive right now if Logan hadn't asked you about the circumstances when he was shot."

Doke's face pinched. "Tag, I hope you understand why I had to tell Dr. Logan that Darryl was shot while holding up the stage. If I'd lied about how Darryl was shot, and for some reason the doctor called in the law to investigate, I could have been found a liar. This could have led to an investigation that might prove that the Moran brothers and I grew up together in Scottsbluff. You remember I told you I didn't let the doctor know that I knew Darryl."

"Yeah. I'm not blaming you for anything, Doke. It means a lot to me that you tried to save his life."

"Right," spoke up Bart. "We really appreciate it."

Jason smiled. "We sure do, Doke. And let me say, it sure is good to see you again. Boy, were we surprised when we stopped that stage and saw you sitting up there in the shotgunner's seat."

Tag laughed. "That's for sure!" He leaned his elbows on the table and looked Doke in the eye. "Did your driver give you a problem when you said you wanted to pick up that wounded outlaw and take him to a doctor?"

Doke shook his head. "No. The passenger who shot Darryl wanted to just let him lie there and die, but the driver went along with me wanting to take Darryl's horse and get him to a doctor in Cheyenne. He told me to go ahead and do it."

There was a quiet moment. Kathryn broke the silence by saying, "Doke, Tag has told us a little bit about saving your life when you were both just boys. We're about finished with lunch here, but after lunch, will you tell us about it?"

Doke grinned, looked at Tag, then back at Kathryn. "Sure. I'll tell you all about it."

After lunch, Lucinda and Kathryn told the men they would do the dishes after they had heard Doke's story, and everyone gathered in the parlor and sat down.

As requested, Doke told the story so

Kathryn, Lucinda, Gib, and Tony could hear the details of how Tag saved his life at the North Platte River when they were teenagers.

When he finished, Doke said, "So you can understand how I feel about Tag. He risked his life to save mine in that debris-filled river." He blinked at the excess moisture gathering in his eyes and cleared his throat. "I owe my life to Tag. I will always be his friend."

Kathryn stood up. "That's quite a story, Doke. Well, Lucinda, the dirty dishes await us."

The women excused themselves and headed for the kitchen.

Doke looked at Tag, then ran his gaze over the faces of the other men. "I've read about you guys and your bank robberies in the newspapers. I know there are lawmen all over these parts who would love to catch you and put you in prison. How is it that you are able to evade the law when you've had so many posses on your trail after you've held up bank after bank?"

Tag grinned at him. "Well, Doke ol' pal, the main reason we established our hideout high up here in the Rockies is because it's so much harder to track us in the mountains. If we were hiding out somewhere on the plains, it would be much simpler to catch us. Some other time, I'll tell how we found this old cabin and claimed it for ourselves. Anyway, you noticed in your ride up here that there are many streams flowing down the mountains."

"That's for sure."

"Well, when we're running from a posse, we take advantage of those numerous streams by riding our horses in them. None of them are more than four feet deep." He paused. "I'm not talking about the Cache La Poudre River. In some places, it's ten and twelve feet deep. I mean those small streams."

Doke nodded.

"You see, Doke," Tag went on, "there is no way to track someone who's riding his horse in a stream. So we ride those streams. We always find a rocky place to enter them, so the horses leave no tracks. When we come out of the streams, usually after several miles, we always pick a rocky place to do it."

Doke nodded. "Smart."

"Yeah," put in Jason, "and often we switch streams to further throw those relentless posses off. This makes it virtually impossible for the law to find us."

Doke shook his head in wonderment.

"That's good thinking, guys. I hope they never catch you."

Tag set his gaze on Doke. "Tell you what, my friend, I think it's time for you and me to have that private talk I told you about."

"Sure," said Doke, slipping his pocket watch from his vest pocket. He glanced at it and put it back. "I have to leave by around four o'clock and head back to Fort Collins so I can get a good night's rest. I have to be at the Wells Fargo office early in the morning. My stage will be heading north just after sunup. Four o'clock will give us enough time, won't it?"

"Sure," said Tag, rising to his feet. "Let's put on our jackets and go outside. We'll talk out there on the porch."

Moments later, the two friends sat down on wooden chairs on the front porch. The late September breeze made them button their jackets all the way to their necks. The roar of the river below filled the clear mountain air.

Tag adjusted his chair so he could look at Doke, then leaned forward, putting his elbows on his knees. "As you know, we really made a good haul when we robbed your stage of that cash box from the Fort Collins bank."

"Yeah. Fifty thousand."

"We like that kind of money, Doke. I understand Wells Fargo carries those cash boxes quite often for the banks."

Doke nodded, feeling a tightness forming in his chest.

"I won't tell you how I found out about the fifty thousand you were carrying that day, Doke, but I got to thinking about it. As shotgunner, you always know when you're going to have a cash box, don't you?"

Doke's mouth was going dry. "Well, yeah."

"How about we work out a way you can let us know in advance? We'll rob the stage, and we'll give you a cut of the take. Nobody ever has to know that you're the one who gives us the information."

Doke looked around, his mind racing. The pressure he was feeling from Tag made his flesh crawl. "Tag, I'd like to help you because of what you did for me that day at the North Platte River. But — but —"

Tag's brow furrowed. "But what?"

Doke took a deep breath. His voice came out in a quiver. "Tag, the people at Wells Fargo have been very good to me. I — I have a sense of loyalty to them like I have toward you in a different way. I — I just can't do it to them. Whenever they are robbed of a cash box, just like when you and your gang robbed my stage, Wells Fargo has to make it up to the banks. They trust me. I just can't betray that trust. Do you understand?"

Tag Moran studied his old friend's nervous features for a long moment, then eased back on the chair. "Yeah. I understand. I'm an outlaw, Doke, but I still have to admire a man who has principles about him." He extended his open right hand. When Doke took it and they gripped one another's hands, Tag said, "Still friends?"

A grin curved Doke's mouth. "You bet. Still friends."

Tag stood up, pulled a pocket watch from his pants pocket, and looked at it. "It'll be four o'clock in twenty minutes. Let's go back inside for a few minutes, okay?"

"Sure."

When they entered the parlor, Lucinda and Kathryn had returned from the kitchen.

Jason looked up from his chair and smiled. "Well, Tag, did you two get whatever it was all talked out?"

Tag nodded. "We did. As Doke told us

215

earlier, he has to leave by four o'clock. Anything else you want to say to him, Jason? Bart?"

Everyone stood up.

"Just that it sure was good seeing you, ol' pal," said Bart.

They shook hands, then Jason stuck out his hand. "Come back and see us again, okay?"

"Sure," said Doke as they shook hands. He ran his gaze over the other faces, then looked at Tag. "I'll say it again. I hope the law never catches up to you."

Kathryn was standing next to her husband. She smiled at Doke. "I hope they don't either."

Gib took hold of her hand and squeezed it.

Everyone put on jackets so they could walk Doke out to his horse. As they stepped out onto the porch, Tag laid a hand on Doke's shoulder.

"Like Jason said, Doke, come back and see us again."

"I'll do it, Tag."

With that, Doke moved down the porch steps, untied his horse, and swung into the saddle. He smiled, gave a wave, wheeled the horse about, and rode down the steep slope through the trees. Everyone called

216

out their good-byes. Doke turned around in the saddle and gave them a friendly wave.

Seconds later, he and his horse passed from view.

As Lucinda held her gaze on the spot where Doke was last seen, a cold dread took hold of her heart. She looked at Tag. "What's to keep some lawman from following him up here?"

Tag's brow furrowed. "No one even suspects that he knows us, so why would they follow him?"

Lucinda shrugged, a worried frown creasing her brow. "I don't know. I only know I have a strong, uneasy feeling about him. Maybe you shouldn't be so open with him about things, Tag."

Bart took hold of her hand. "You worry too much, sweetheart. Doke isn't going to do anything to bring harm to the man who saved his life. His loyalty to Tag is steadfast and strong."

Lucinda shrugged her shoulders again. "I hope you're right about him. All I can do is tell you how I feel."

Kathryn shivered and rubbed her hands together. "I don't know about the rest of you, but with that sun going down behind those peaks over there, this breeze is getting colder. I'm going inside."

"Us boys are gonna go feed and water the horses," said Tag. "You ladies go back in the cabin."

As Lucinda moved inside on Kathryn's heels, a heaviness about Doke Veatch still pervaded her senses.

While the men were walking around the side of the cabin toward the barn, Jason said, "Tag, I wish we could invite Doke to join the gang, but I have a feeling he would never become an outlaw."

"I agree," said Tag. "He just isn't the type."

As Doke Veatch rode down the steep slopes of the mountains along the bank of the Cache La Poudre River toward Fort Collins, he let his eyes roam about him, taking in the beauty of the Rockies. All around him lay a vast sweep of towering peaks and sunken gorges. The peaks were timber-clad up to timberline, which in the Rockies was about 11,200 feet. Above that rose the jagged peaks of rock that reached toward the sky.

A magnificent golden light showed upon the western firmament — the afterglow of sunset. The highest peaks wore crowns of gold. All the lower tips of ranges were purpling in shadow. The marvelous light from the setting sun magnified the rocky cliffs on every side, and the winding ranges took on a look of unreality.

Doke lowered his gaze down along the bank of the foamy river and put his mind back on Tag Moran and his gang. He wondered actually how long they could elude the law. It seemed to him that sooner or later, some posse would finally catch up to them, and they would end up behind bars for a long stretch. He shook his head and told himself if he had the opportunity to gain a million dollars by being an outlaw and robber, it wouldn't be worth the risk of getting caught and going to prison for it.

Suddenly the gelding stopped, bobbed his head, and stared across the river. Doke looked to the opposite bank and saw two male mountain lions staring at him and snarling. He shivered as he peered into their eyes. "Boys, I'm sure glad you're on *that* side of the river. I wouldn't want to tangle with you, and neither would this horse."

Doke urged the gelding onward, and soon they were out of sight from the cougars. He put his mind on his job with the Wells Fargo Stagelines and concentrated on getting back to Fort Collins.

★ ★ ★

In Denver, at Mile High Hospital, Tharyn Tabor was assisting Dr. Lyle Goodwin in an appendectomy on a ten-year-old boy.

When they had finished and were in the surgical washroom cleaning up, a nurse came in. "Tharyn, a certain handsome young man is here to see you. He's just outside the door." She giggled. "I think you might know him."

Tharyn's heart leaped in her chest. Scott's train from Pueblo was due to arrive at Denver's Union Station some thirty minutes ago. She had had a hard time concentrating on her work, knowing he no doubt would stop by the hospital to see her before he went home.

She smiled at the nurse. "Alice, do his initials happen to be S.H.?"

Alice giggled again. "How'd you guess?"

"Oh, I'm just so supremely intelligent!"

"I'm sure Dr. Goodwin will agree with that!"

"Absolutely!" said the silver-haired physician, while drying his hands on a towel.

"What can I say? Tell Scott I'll be out in just a few minutes."

"Will do," said Alice, and moved out the door.

Dr. Goodwin dropped the towel in a

220

basket provided for used linens and looked at Tharyn. "Do you think Scott is going to propose to you soon?"

She smiled. "It just might happen tonight."

She then looked at her reflection in the mirror, dabbed at her hair to make it just right, and headed for the door. "I'll see you later, Dr. Goodwin." With that, she opened the door and stepped out into the corridor.

The instant Tharyn closed the door behind her and caught sight of Scott, she sensed that something was amiss. There was a strange look in his eyes, and she could tell he had been raking his fingers through his unruly hair.

He pressed a smile on his lips and stepped up to her. "Hello, Tharyn."

"Hello, Scott. I'm glad to see you back."

Tharyn started to lift her arms to embrace him, but at the same moment, two nurses came walking by. The nurses smiled at the young couple and kept their attention on them, though keeping their stride. Tharyn took a step back. Showing affection for the man whom she was sure was about to become her fiancé was a private matter. She didn't want a gawking audience.

A few seconds passed. Though the nurses now were no longer looking at them, Scott made no move to embrace her, which was unusual for him.

When the nurses were farther yet down the corridor, Tharyn looked deeply into Scott's eyes, moved close to him again, and took hold of his hand. "Scott, is something wrong?"

Scott was about to reply when Dr. Albert Parker — who was one of the hospital's prominent surgeons — rushed up. "Tharyn, we have an emergency. Dr. Goodwin just told me that you're free right now, as far as he knows. I must do a lithotomy on a very sick woman. I need your help immediately. All the other surgical nurses are busy. Can you help me?"

"Of course, Doctor." Looking at Scott, Tharyn said, "I'm sorry, but I must go with Dr. Parker right now." She noticed a look of relief come over his face.

"It's all right, Tharyn. I understand."

"Can you come to the house and see me this evening?"

Scott nodded. "I'd take you out to dinner, but I have some things to do right away. I'll be tied up till about seven-thirty. I'll come as soon as I can. Probably by eight o'clock."

"All right. I'll be watching for you."

As Tharyn hurried away with Dr. Parker, she was puzzled by Scott's demeanor. Not only was there a strange look in his eyes, but his voice also told her something was wrong.

Dr. Parker and Tharyn were soon in one of the surgical rooms hovering over a woman in her early fifties who was suffering severely with a bladder stone. The doctor discussed the impending operation with the patient and learned that this would be her first surgery ever.

While Dr. Parker made preparations to perform the lithotomy, Tharyn poured ether into a cloth and said to the patient, "Mrs. Kraft, I know you've never had surgery before, so you've never had an anesthetic. Listen to me now. It will seem like I'm smothering you when I place this cloth over your face. Don't let it frighten you. Just inhale the fumes as quickly as you can, and you'll be under the anesthetic in no time. When you come to, it'll all be over."

Helen Kraft looked up at her with pain-filled eyes and nodded slightly. "You're so sweet, dear," she said weakly. "You're a born nurse. God bless you."

Tharyn smiled down at her. "God bless you too, ma'am. Here comes the ether."

She pressed the moist cloth to the patient's nose and mouth and held it there.

Helen fought it, gasping for breath.

"Don't be afraid," Tharyn said softly. "You'll be fine. Just breathe in the fumes deeply."

Helen closed her eyes and did as instructed. In less than two minutes, she relaxed and went limp.

The surgeon was ready to begin, holding the scalpel close to the skin.

Tharyn bent low over the woman, lifted an eyelid, and studied the pupil and the iris. "She's completely under, Doctor."

The doctor nodded and went to work to remove the bladder stone. While Tharyn was wiping blood away from the incision and periodically applying more ether to keep the patient under, her mind went to Scott. She wondered if a problem had developed between him and his parents. Or was it possible that one of them was seriously ill? Or — *Well, it could be one of many things. I'll just have to wait until this evening to find out.*

Twelve

At Denver's First National Bank, President David Tabor was at his desk in the enclosed area at the rear of the building, talking to a customer.

The area had a waist-high wooden fence around it, and two swinging gates to allow employees and customers to enter and exit the area. There were three other desks in the enclosed area. Two were occupied by vice presidents, and the third was occupied by middle-aged Arla Yunker, who served as secretary to all three executives.

Tabor also had a private office adjacent to the enclosed area where he could meet with employees and customers when their business required privacy. Besides his desk in that office, there was also a large table where he held regular meetings with the bank directors.

Both vice presidents were away from their desks in another part of the building as David Tabor's customer walked away.

He looked up at the clock on a nearby wall and saw that it was almost five o'clock. He ran his gaze around the interior of the bank and noted that there were still several customers in the place. Some were at the tellers' windows, and others were at the counter in the center of the lobby, making out deposit slips or doing paperwork that related to the business they would have with the tellers.

It was then that he noticed Arla standing at one of the area's small gates, talking to a well-dressed man. David did not recognize him. He figured the man might be new in town and possibly had come in to open an account.

Arla said something to the man that David could not distinguish, then turned and headed toward him. As she approached the desk, she said, "Mr. Tabor, I have a gentleman here who says he would like to talk to you about a loan. I told him it's only a few minutes till closing time and asked if he could come back tomorrow. He said it is very important that he discuss the loan with you now."

David thought of Tharyn and knew that she would be expecting him at about five-twenty. He always picked her up on weekdays at that time. The hospital staff shift change was at five o'clock.

He glanced past Arla and looked at the well-dressed man. "Since it's important to him that we discuss the loan right now, tell him I'll see him."

Arla turned and went back to the man. "Mr. Tabor will see you."

The man smiled broadly and followed Arla as she led him to the bank president's desk.

David rose to his feet behind the desk and smiled at the man.

"Mr. Tabor," said Arla, "this is Mr. Edward Fremont."

David extended his right hand across the desk. As they shook hands, he said, "Glad to meet you, Mr. Fremont."

"Nice to meet you too, sir," said Fremont.

"Please sit down."

Fremont sat down on one of the two chairs that stood in front of the desk, and the bank president sat down in his desk chair facing him.

Arla said, "Mr. Tabor, would you like for me to stay in case you need me to help with the loan papers?"

David shook his head. "That won't be necessary, Arla. It's eight minutes to closing time. You go on home as soon as you need to."

"All right, Mr. Tabor," Arla said, and returned to her desk.

"I'm sorry to come in so close to closing time, Mr. Tabor," said Fremont, "but this really won't take long."

David adjusted himself on his chair. "All right. Tell me how much you need to borrow, then we'll get into the information I will need." From the corner of his eye, he saw Arla leave her desk and head for a nearby supply room.

Fremont's features went stonelike as he leaned forward, keeping his voice low. "I want to borrow all the cash you have in the bank. I mean in every teller's cash drawer and in the vault. I won't be signing any loan papers, of course, and I will never pay the loan back."

David felt a flutter in his stomach as he leaned toward the man. His right hand was already in his lap and he kept it out of the man's sight. "So this is a robbery."

"You guessed it. Now I want you to look over there at the counter in the middle of the place."

David shifted slightly on his chair and looked at the counter, and the man and two women who stood there. The women were busy writing. The man was looking directly at him.

"See the man in the dark hat who's lookin' at you?"

"Yeah."

"He's one of my accomplices. Now look over there by the front door. Do you see that man? He appears to be waiting for someone who is doing business at the tellers' cages."

David eyed the man. "Yeah. I see him."

"Well, if I don't signal them in a moment that all is well, they'll start shootin'. Understand? They'll put bullets in your employees and in your customers. So, let's you and me go into the vault and get the money that's in there. I'll give the signal, and my pals will let people leave unharmed. As soon as the bank is closed, we'll also take the money from the tellers' cash drawers."

David Tabor was filled with rage. There was a thunderous rush of blood in his ears. This slick, polished bank robber was so sure of himself that there was no weapon in either hand.

David's right hand was still beneath the desktop. His own voice was now stonelike. "Tell you what, Fremont, or whatever your name is. I want you to signal your pals that all is well, and motion for them to come over here."

The robber looked at him blankly. "What are you talkin' about? I want them right where they are."

A frown deepened on David's face. "You're not getting what you want."

"Oh? And what's to stop me?"

"This Colt .45 I've got trained on your belly underneath the desk."

The robber's head jerked slightly. He looked at Tabor with wide, incredulous eyes. "You're bluffin'." His face went white when he heard the unmistakable sound of a hammer being cocked.

"Am I?"

The robber swallowed hard, but did not reply.

"Now, you signal your pals to come over here this instant, or you'll have a belly full of hot lead."

At that moment, Arla Yunker was returning to her desk from the nearby supply room. She frowned when she observed the scene before her. She could tell by the way her boss had his hand underneath the top of the desk that he was holding his revolver trained on the man sitting in front of him. She knew he always kept the Colt .45 in a holster attached to the desk in case he should need it. Both vice presidents' desks were equipped the same way.

When the robber looked like he was going to resist, David hissed, "Right now, mister! I mean it!"

The robber swallowed hard again. Fear showed in his eyes.

He turned slightly and made a hand signal to both of his accomplices, then motioned for them to come to him.

Only the two women who had been at the counter in the center of the lobby were at the tellers' cages. All the other customers had gone.

As the accomplices headed their direction, David said, "When they get here, you tell them to very slowly take those guns out of their holsters, lay the guns on the floor, and get their hands up in the air. Got it?"

The robber licked his lips nervously. "Got it."

When the accomplices came through the nearest gate and approached the desk, they could tell something was wrong. Before either could react, the man in the chair with the pale features said, "Boys, I couldn't work out the loan. He's got a gun trained on me beneath the desktop. Take your guns out real slow and put 'em down on the floor, or he'll kill me."

Both men bristled and started to go for

their holstered weapons.

"No!" blurted their leader. "This guy means business! Do as I tell you and put your hands up over your heads!"

The two men reluctantly placed their guns on the floor.

"Now get those hands in the air!" commanded David.

They obeyed, looking at each other, then at their leader.

A stunned Arla Yunker stood at her desk, gaping at the scene.

Without taking his eyes off the man in the chair, David said, "Arla, will you go explain to one of the tellers that I'm holding these would-be robbers at gunpoint, please? Tell him to run down to the federal building and bring back a couple of deputy U.S. marshals."

It was almost six o'clock when Tharyn Tabor walked into the hospital lobby from the corridor, carrying a light coat.

The receptionist at the desk smiled at her. "Tharyn, dear, you look very tired. Had a pretty heavy day, didn't you?"

Tharyn smiled in return. "That I did, Rosie. I am a bit weary." She ran her gaze to the waiting area. It was empty, so she looked around the lobby, then at the receptionist. "Has my father been here?"

"Not yet. Looks like both of you are running late."

"Well, certainly he'll be here any minute," said Tharyn, and walked to the double glass doors that overlooked the parking lot and the nearby street. Her father's buggy was just pulling into the parking lot.

She looked back at the receptionist. "Here he is now. Good night, Rosie. See you tomorrow."

Rosie waved. "Get some rest, honey."

"I will." With that, Tharyn slipped into her coat and stepped out into the gathering twilight.

David Tabor pulled the buggy to a halt, hopped out, and threw his arms around his adopted daughter.

They embraced. He kissed her on the cheek, then helped her into the buggy.

When he rounded the buggy and climbed in beside her, Tharyn said, "Must have been a busy day for you too. I just came into the lobby about a minute before you got here."

"Ah . . . yes," he replied, putting the buggy in motion. "Very busy day. I'll tell you about it at supper, so I can fill your mother in at the same time. You have a late operation to help on?"

"Mm-hmm. Dr. Albert Parker had to do a lithotomy late this afternoon, and I was the only surgical nurse available. The operation took a little longer than he expected. But I'm glad to say the lady will be fine."

"Good," he said as he guided the buggy out of the parking lot and made a left turn. A lamplighter could be seen on each side of the street. Both men were busy firing up the street lamps.

David patted his daughter's hand. "Did Scott get home as scheduled?"

The uneasiness Tharyn had been feeling concerning Scott Hubbard surfaced once more. She managed a smile. "Sure did. He came by the hospital to see me on his way home from the railroad station. We were just starting to talk when Dr. Parker came along and said he needed me immediately to help him with the lithotomy. Scott said he had some things to take care of that would take a while, so he would be by the house about eight o'clock this evening."

When they arrived home and entered the house through the back door, Kitty was in the kitchen, keeping the food hot.

"Sorry, honey," said David as he moved up and kissed her cheek. "Had an unexpected situation at the bank right at closing time."

"And even if he hadn't," put in Tharyn as she moved up on Kitty's other side, "I would have made us both late. I'll tell you about it during supper." She kissed her mother's cheek.

Kitty smiled. "No harm done. You can both tell me your stories while we're eating."

Tharyn looked to the hot food on the stove. "Yum, yum, Mama! Makes my mouth water!"

Kitty smiled while stirring gravy in a pan. "I hope it tastes as good as it smells, sweet daughter." She squinted at her. "You look awfully tired. Are they piling too much on you at the hospital?"

"Not really, Mama. Just so happened I had to help Dr. Albert Parker on a surgery late this afternoon. I'll explain it while we're eating. I'm a bit weary, but I'll be fine after I eat this good meal and get a good night's sleep."

"All right. You two get washed up, and I'll have supper on the table shortly." She started to turn back to the stove, then looked at Tharyn. "Oh, I almost forgot. Did Scott get home as scheduled?"

"Yes. He came by the hospital to see me,

but we didn't get to talk but a moment. He's coming here to the house about eight o'clock this evening."

"Well, it'll be nice to see Scott again. Hurry up you two, and get your hands washed."

A few minutes later, the Tabor family sat down at the table. David prayed over the food, then they began eating.

Kitty said, "All right, let's hear your stories. I want to hear what happened at the bank first. What was the unexpected situation, darling?"

When David told his story about the attempted robbery, both Kitty and Tharyn spoke their praise to the Lord that no one was hurt, and that the three robbers were now behind bars in the Denver County Jail.

David said, "I was glad that Chief Brockman was still at the U.S. marshal's office when the teller went to get help. He and two deputies came to the bank in a hurry." He chuckled. "Chief Brockman told me that he was hoping those three robbers were part of that nefarious Tag Moran gang. Didn't turn out that way, but at least they will each get a long prison term. Chief Brockman knew who they were. He had wanted posters on them.

They came here from Kansas and have a long criminal history there."

Kitty was buttering her second biscuit. "I have a feeling that one of these days Chief Brockman is going to go after that Moran gang. If he does, their days are numbered."

David smiled. "He will catch them if indeed he concentrates on them. It's just so hard for him, with all the other outlaws running all over this part of the West. He's got his hands full."

"For sure," said Kitty. "Well, Miss Tharyn, let's hear about that surgery in which you assisted Dr. Parker."

Tharyn's mind had gone once again to Scott and the fact that something was bothering him. Though the supper looked and smelled so good, she found that her concern over Scott had stolen her appetite. She sat morosely pushing her food around on the plate.

Looking up at her mother, she explained about Dr. Parker recruiting her to assist him with the lithotomy on a woman named Helen Kraft, and that the operation took longer than the doctor had estimated.

Kitty looked at Tharyn's plate, then met her gaze. "You're just wearing that food out, pushing it around on your plate. I thought you were hungry. Is something bothering you?"

David frowned. "Tharyn, if I upset you by telling you about the attempted robbery, I'm sorry."

Tharyn looked at her father. "No, Papa. Since you came through it all right, I'm not upset about it." She ran her gaze to her mother. "What's bothering me is that when Scott stopped to see me at the hospital, I could tell that he was definitely upset about something. He just wasn't himself. When I asked him about it, he didn't have a chance to answer because that was when Dr. Parker approached me about helping him with the lithotomy."

"Well, honey," said David, "if Scott still seems upset when he comes tonight, I'll offer to listen if he needs to share something."

"All right, Papa," said Tharyn, giving him a thin smile.

When the meal was over, David went to the parlor to read the daily newspaper while Kitty and Tharyn did the dishes and cleaned up the kitchen.

In the parlor a few minutes later, David heard a knock at the front door of the house and walked into the hall to answer it. He found Scott Hubbard there and welcomed him back. He led him into the parlor and told him to sit down, saying he would go to the kitchen and let Tharyn know he was there.

As David moved to the kitchen he told himself that Scott definitely seemed a bit preoccupied.

When David and Kitty entered the parlor with Tharyn, Scott rose to his feet and greeted mother and daughter.

Kitty said, "I'm really glad you're back, Scott." Then she added jokingly, "Tharyn has done nothing but mope around ever since you left."

Scott looked at the lovely redhead and forced a chuckle. "Oh, she did, eh?"

Tharyn worked up a wide smile. "Yes. That's all I did."

"So how are your parents, Scott?" queried David.

Scott turned to him. "Hmm?"

"I said, how are your parents?"

"Oh. They're fine, Mr. Tabor. Just fine."

This eliminated that part of Tharyn's conjecture. Kitty and David exchanged glances, both knowing that something indeed had Scott preoccupied.

David said, "Scott, you don't seem like your usual jovial self. Something seems to be bothering you. Is there anything I can do to help?"

"Thank you, Mr. Tabor. I appreciate your concern, but what I really need is to talk to Tharyn privately."

David looked at Kitty. "Well, honey, you and I should go to the kitchen and let them talk."

Kitty nodded. "All right."

Scott thanked them. They left the parlor and moved down the hall toward the kitchen.

Scott was visibly nervous. "Tharyn, how about you sit over here in this overstuffed chair, and I'll sit in this one, facing you?"

"Fine," she said. "Don't I even get a hug? We haven't seen each other for a long time."

Scott hugged her, but Tharyn could tell his heart wasn't in it. She sat down, and as he dropped into the other chair and looked at her — obviously nervous — she said, "Scott, what is it?"

Trying to keep his voice from wavering, he said, "I need to tell you a story."

Tharyn listened with her pulse pounding as Scott told her about a sweet Christian girl in Pueblo he had known since they were in sixth grade together. Her name was Rachel Simmons. He went on to tell her that he and Rachel were childhood sweet-hearts, but they both thought that's all it was — a childhood thing. When he left Pueblo at twenty-one years of age to take the job at Rocky Mountain Bank three years ago, he and Rachel parted simply as old friends.

At this point, Tharyn's pulse was throbbing and her stomach was churning.

Not wanting to look him in the eye, she stared at the painting on the parlor's far wall. It was an outdoor scene with children running through an open field of wild-flowers. There was a dense forest in the distance and snowcapped mountain peaks beyond the forest.

Scott rubbed the back of his neck. "The first three or four times I went back to see my parents in Pueblo after coming to Denver, Rachel and I spent some time together, but still felt simply like old friends. And . . . and then here in Denver last year, you and I began to notice each other at church, and after dating several times, we felt that we were meant for each other."

Tharyn let her eyes leave the painting for a second or two, met his gaze, then looked at the painting again.

Scott cleared his throat. "Tharyn, I fully intended one day soon to ask you to marry me. But — but when I first got to Pueblo on this trip, Rachel and I spent some time together. And, well, something clicked between us. We both realized that we had been in love since our teen years and that the Lord had meant us for each other."

Tharyn went slack, as though her bones had turned to water. Her cheeks turned pale.

Hastening to get it over with, Scott said, "I asked Rachel to marry me, and she accepted my proposal."

Tharyn's heart felt crushed. It was all she could do to keep from bursting into sobs.

Scott leaned toward her. "Tharyn, I'm sorry for leading you on all this time, but I didn't know my own heart until I made this trip, and Rachel and I came to the realization that we were in love. I — I didn't mean to hurt you, but I can't go on pretending. This wouldn't be right before the Lord. And just as the Lord had planned for Rachel and me to be husband and wife, He also has a fine Christian young man that He has chosen for you to marry."

Tharyn was now looking at the floor, blinking at the tears that were filling her eyes.

Scott inched closer to her. "Certainly

you want to have the man God has picked out for you."

Tharyn drew a shuddering breath. She felt numb all over and her throat was constricted. She could only stare at him blankly through her tears.

Scott sighed. "The reason I had to be this late getting here was that I first had to go to the bank and resign my position as of right now. I already have a good job lined up in a Pueblo bank, and I'm leaving for Pueblo on the 7:45 train in the morning. The — the second place I had to go was to the parsonage. I wanted to tell Pastor Blandford that I was leaving Denver and why."

Tharyn's mind went to an orphan boy she met on the streets of New York named Russell Mims. While she lived in the colony of orphans in an alley off Broadway, Russell had always shown her kindness and affection. After Dane Weston had been arrested and put in prison, Russell told Tharyn that though he was two years older than she, he knew he was in love with her and wanted to marry her one day.

Russell was on the same orphan train as Tharyn, and when she was chosen by the Tabors in Denver, Russell told her that wherever he ended up farther down the line, he would write to her and keep in touch because he loved her and still wanted to marry her when they were both old enough for marriage.

Russell was chosen by foster parents in San Francisco, and after he and Tharyn had exchanged a couple of letters, he wrote and told her that he had fallen in love with a girl in his church in San Francisco and they planned one day to marry.

Tharyn never heard from Russell again.

This surprise had hurt her, but not nearly as much as Scott had just hurt her.

Still struggling to keep her composure, she found her voice, though it was strained and weak. "Scott, I hope it works out for you." As she spoke, she rose from the chair and said levelly, "Good-bye."

With that, she hurried from the room. Just as she reached the hall, she burst into sobs and let out a loud wail as she rushed up the stairs. She reached the second floor of the house and was still wailing as she darted down the hall toward her bedroom.

In the kitchen, the Tabors heard Tharyn's shrill wail and rushed up the hall toward the front of the house. They found Scott in the foyer, heading for the front door, his features pinched.

"Scott," said David, "what happened?"

As Kitty looked toward the stairs that led up to the second floor, Scott said, "Tharyn went up to her room. She'll tell you about it."

While they looked at him dumbfounded, Scott rushed out the door and closed it gently behind him.

David and Kitty moved up the stairs and entered Tharyn's room without knocking.

Tharyn was on her bed, sobbing as if her heart would shatter in her chest at any moment. They both sat down on the same side of the bed and gathered her into their arms.

Before either of the parents could ask a question, they heard a loud knock downstairs at the front door.

Leaving Kitty holding the sobbing Tharyn in her arms, David said, "I'll get it."

When David reached the bottom of the stairs and opened the door, to his surprise, he found Pastor Blandford and his wife standing on the porch.

Thirteen

David Tabor smiled at Pastor Nathan Blandford and his wife, Nellie. "Well, good evening! Please come in."

As the Blandfords stepped inside, the pastor said, "David, I can tell you are surprised to see us on your doorstep at this time of night. It has to do with Scott Hubbard having just been here. We know Tharyn has to be very upset, and we're here to try to be of comfort to her."

"Well, Pastor," said David, "Kitty and I were just trying to find out from Tharyn what happened when you knocked on the door. Kitty is up in Tharyn's room with her. We were in the kitchen because Scott asked us to let him have a private talk with Tharyn in the parlor. The next thing we know we hear Tharyn wailing and sobbing while running up the stairs. When we came out of the kitchen, Scott was about to go out our front door. He told us Tharyn would explain what happened. Come into the parlor and sit down. I'll go upstairs and bring Tharyn and Kitty down."

David hurried out of the parlor. When he entered Tharyn's room, Kitty was still holding the weeping Tharyn in her arms.

David said to Kitty, "Did she tell you what happened between her and Scott?"

Kitty shook her head and looked at her daughter.

Tharyn sniffed and drew a shuddering breath. "No, Papa. I was waiting for you to come back so I could tell you and Mama at the same time."

"Who was at the door?" queried Kitty.

"Pastor Blandford and Nellie. They seem to know all about this Scott thing and came to try to be a comfort to Tharyn. They're waiting in the parlor."

Tharyn wiped tears from her face. "It was sweet of them to come. I understand why they already know about Scott leaving. Let's go down and talk to them. Then both of you can get the whole story at the same time."

Moments later, the Tabors and their daughter entered the parlor. Tharyn's eyes were red and swollen from weeping.

Nellie rushed to Tharyn and put her arms around her. "Oh, sweetie, I'm so sorry you're hurting."

Tharyn clung to her without comment.

Pastor Blandford laid a hand on Tharyn's shoulder.

"We came because we love you, Tharyn, and want to help you in this time of heartache."

Kitty said, "Tharyn was waiting till her papa came back to tell us together what happened, Pastor. So we still don't know."

"Let's sit down," said the pastor. "I'll tell you what Nellie and I know, then Tharyn can take it from there."

"The rest of you get seated," said Kitty. "Excuse me for a moment. I think we could all use a strong cup of tea. The stove is still hot. I'll only be a few minutes." With that, she hurried out the parlor door.

As she had promised, Kitty was back shortly, carrying a tray that bore a steaming teapot, cups, and saucers. "My grandmother always said that a cup of strong tea never failed to help in any kind of stressful situation."

Her hands shook slightly as she set the tray down on a small table, poured the tea, and passed it around.

Kitty sat down on the sofa. Tharyn was seated between Kitty and Nellie. David and the pastor sat in chairs, facing them.

The pastor had his Bible in hand.

Keeping it on his lap for the moment, he said, "Scott came to the parsonage earlier this evening and told us that he was leaving Denver on the 7:45 train for Pueblo in the morning, and that he wouldn't be back. He explained that upon this latest visit to Pueblo, he and his old childhood sweetheart got together and realized that they actually had been in love since they were teenagers, and they were sure the Lord had meant them for each other. Her name is Rachel Simmons. Scott asked Rachel to marry him, and she accepted his proposal. They are going to get married soon. Scott expressed to Nellie and me the sorrow he felt, because this news was going to shock Tharyn and hurt her."

Blandford set his soft gaze on the broken-hearted young woman. "Nellie and I have been waiting a half block down the street in our buggy, Tharyn. We didn't want to interfere while Scott was here. When we saw him come out of the house, we waited till he was out of sight, then drove the buggy up to the house and knocked on the door."

Tharyn wiped at the tears that were filling her eyes. "Pastor and Mrs. Blandford, I very much appreciate your coming to me at this very difficult time. Scott told me that he had been to your house before coming here to let you know he was leaving Denver."

"Kitty and I appreciate your coming, too," said David.

Kitty nodded. "More than we can tell you."

The pastor let a smile curve his lips. "Tharyn, I'm sorry for your broken heart, but believe me, it's for the best. The Lord knew what was going to happen between Scott and Rachel, but He already had other plans for you. He has someone very special for you to marry, and when the time is right, He will bring that special young man into your life."

Tharyn stared at the pastor blankly, trying to absorb his words and accept what he was saying, but her parents and the Blandfords could see that she was having a hard time with it.

Kitty was about to add her own thoughts to the pastor's when Tharyn suddenly blurted, "What's wrong with me?" Her voice was strangled with tears. "This is the second time someone has told me he loved me and wanted to marry me, and then it all blew up in my face!"

Blandford frowned. "The *second* time, Tharyn?"

She wiped away more tears. "There was

a young man who was in the same orphan colony I was in Manhattan, Pastor. His name was Russell Mims. He was two years older than I. He told me he loved me and one day wanted to marry me when we were old enough to get married. He was on the same orphan train as I, but he wasn't chosen by foster parents till he got to San Francisco. We wrote back and forth for a while, then one day I got a letter from him saying he had met a nice girl there, and was going to marry her."

The Blandfords exchanged glances.

Tharyn threw her hands to her face. "Do I do something that drives these men into another's arms?"

Pastor Blandford shook his head. "No, my dear. That's not it. As I said, God has a plan for your life, and He has a very special young man already reserved for you. I want to show you some things in the Scriptures."

David left his chair, picked up a Bible from the same table that held the tray, and handed it to Tharyn. "You use this Bible, honey. I'll run upstairs and get Mama's and mine."

While David was upstairs, Nellie took a small Bible from her purse.

David was back quickly. He handed

Kitty her Bible, then returned to his chair.

Tharyn looked at her pastor with misty eyes and waited for him to continue.

"First," said the pastor, "I want us to look at something in Genesis chapter 2. Let's turn there."

Each Bible was opened to the designated chapter.

"Now let's read about God's creation of the first man, Adam. Verse 7. 'And the LORD God formed man of the dust of the ground, and breathed into his nostrils the breath of life; and man became a living soul.' It goes on to say that God planted a garden eastward in Eden. And He put the man in the garden. Verse 15 tells us that the Lord put the man in the garden of Eden to dress it and to keep it. Now, look at verse eighteen. 'And the LORD God said, It is not good that the man should be alone; I will make him an help meet for him.' "

Blandford looked at Tharyn. "See that? God said it is not good that the man should be alone. He was going to give him a mate. He did just that in verses 21 and 22. He made a woman from one of Adam's ribs. He then brought her unto Adam, and then and there, God performed the first marriage ceremony. Verse 25 says they were now man and wife. Later, in chapter 3 and verse 20, Adam gives her the name Eve."

Each person was looking at Genesis 3:20 in their Bible.

The pastor said, "Now, Tharyn, look at chapter 2, verse 18 again."

Tharyn flipped back a page, set her eyes on Genesis 2:18, and nodded.

"Look at what God spoke: 'It is not good that the man should be alone.' "

"Yes."

"Repeat them to me."

She looked up at him. "It is not good that the man should be alone."

Blandford smiled. "That young man that I said the Lord has all picked out for you . . ."

"Yes, sir?"

"It is not good that he should be alone, so the Lord is going to give him his mate — *you!* He will bring the two of you together when in His plan for both of your lives, it is that perfect time. And then when the two of you have fallen in love, as you walk with God, He will show you when it is time for you to marry. Understand?"

Tharyn nodded slowly. "It's beginning to sink in, Pastor."

"Good. So you see, the Lord had not chosen you to be Russell Mims's mate nor

Scott Hubbard's mate. He has not yet brought His chosen man to you and let you fall in love. Just think how awful it would have been if you married Mims or Hubbard but missed the one man God had already chosen for you."

Tharyn licked her lips and nodded again. "That would be awful, wouldn't it?"

"Absolutely. Your life would be miserable, and whichever man you married outside of God's will would be as miserable as you. It wouldn't work. Do you see that?"

"Yes, sir."

"Good. Now I want to ask you something. Later in the book of Genesis, we meet a man named Jacob. Who was Jacob? Do you know?"

"Yes, sir. Jacob was the son of Isaac and Rebekah, and it was Jacob whom God named 'Israel.' It was Jacob's twelve sons who formed the twelve tribes of Israel."

The pastor smiled. "You are absolutely correct."

"This girl knows her Bible, Pastor," spoke up Kitty.

"So it seems." He set his attention again on Tharyn. "Do you remember how God brought Isaac and Rebekah together?"

Tharyn nodded. "He put it on Abraham's heart to have his servant Eliezer go to his home country, Mesopotamia, to seek out a wife for Isaac."

"Correct. God had it in His perfect plan that Eliezer would find Rebekah and take her to Isaac. The two of them would marry and bring Jacob into the world. Now let's all turn to Genesis chapter 24."

When everyone had found the page, the pastor said, "To begin with, I'm going to read the first four verses. 'And Abraham was old, and well stricken in age: and the LORD had blessed Abraham in all things. And Abraham said unto his eldest servant of his house, that ruled over all that he had, Put, I pray thee, thy hand under my thigh: And I will make thee swear by the LORD, the God of heaven, and the God of earth, that thou shalt not take a wife unto my son of the daughters of the Canaanites, among whom I dwell: But thou shalt go unto my country, and to my kindred, and take a wife unto my son Isaac.' Genesis 15:2 identifies Eliezer as this servant — who was also called the steward of Abraham's house. So the story goes on how Eliezer went to the city of Nahor in Mesopotamia. It tells how God guided Eliezer to Rebekah, and how both she and her family knew Eliezer was sent from God. Her family encouraged her to go with Eliezer to meet the man God had chosen for her."

Tharyn nodded. "I remember it clearly, Pastor. In my daily Bible reading, I went through Genesis just last month."

He smiled. "Now, dear young lady, don't you suppose that once Rebekah became old enough to marry, that she began wondering who the man was that God had chosen to be her husband?"

"Oh yes. I'm sure this is so."

"What if Rebekah had married some other man before Eliezer came to take her to Isaac? She would have been out of God's will and would have married the wrong man."

Tharyn nodded silently, her eyes showing that she was getting the point.

Blandford smiled. "Tharyn, being in the center of God's will as Isaac's wife, Rebekah gave birth to Jacob, the child who grew up to be the man whom God gave the name Israel. Rebekah's twelve grandsons — Jacob's sons — were the children of Israel.

"Scripture reveals," proceeded Blandford, "that Judah was the fourth son of Jacob, and that God sent His only begotten Son to be the Saviour of the world through the tribe of Judah. If Rebekah had not waited for God to send His chosen husband for her into her life, she would never have been the mother of Jacob, the grandmother of Jacob's twelve sons, and had the distinction of being an ancestor of Jesus Christ on His earthly side. Do you see that?"

"Yes, Pastor. I see it."

"All right. God has the right man picked out for you. It obviously wasn't Russell Mims. And it obviously wasn't Scott Hubbard. Right?"

A smile tugged at the corners of Tharyn's mouth. "Yes."

"Good. So, honey, you cheer up and let the Lord bring you His chosen man for you in His own time."

The smile spread over her lovely face. "Pastor, your wisdom with the Word of God has been a great help and a wonderful blessing to me. Thank you."

He grinned. "I'm your pastor, Tharyn. It is my responsibility, privilege, and pleasure to be of help to you."

She took a deep breath. "Pastor, Scott's jilting left some wounds that will need to heal, but I will leave my future in my heavenly Father's hands." She turned to Nellie, then ran her gaze between the Blandfords. "I want to thank both of you for coming to help me."

"Let's pray before Nellie and I leave," said the pastor.

The five of them joined hands as Pastor Blandford led in prayer, asking God to heal Tharyn's wounded heart and give her the faith and patience to wait for that man He had chosen to be her husband to come into her life.

That night in her bed, Tharyn wept because of the wounds Scott had left in her heart. She remembered how when she lived in the Manhattan alley it was Dane Weston who was always so kind to her and comforted her when she needed it.

"Lord, You are my great Comforter, and I thank You for that. I know You also understand that we humans need other humans to lean on. I wish I still had Dane to lean on."

Finding that sleep eluded her, Tharyn left her bed and sat down on the chair by her window. She gazed out at the full moon and the winking stars. Again, she prayed, seeking God's comfort and consolation. She told the Lord she knew that what Pastor Blandford had shown her in the Scriptures about His will in a believer's life was true, and she thanked Him for giving the pastor the wisdom he needed to apply it to her life.

As she continued to pray, God's peace filled her heart and mind, and she thanked Him for it. Tharyn placed her life and her future in the Lord's capable hands. She went back to her bed, slipped between the covers, and found rest in the everlasting arms of the one who had shed His blood, died for her on the cross, and had come back from the dead so He could save her and one day take her to heaven.

The next day, Breanna Brockman was working at Mile High Hospital, filling in for a nurse who had to be out of town. During the morning, Breanna was walking through the surgical wing on her way to another part of the hospital when Tharyn happened to come out the door of one of the operating rooms.

They stopped to speak to each other, and Breanna could tell that Tharyn was not quite her usual jovial self.

"Honey, is something wrong? You don't seem quite like yourself."

Tharyn smiled. "I'm all right, Breanna. I just went through a very difficult time last night. It's going to take a little time to shake off its effects."

"Do you mind sharing it with me?"

"Of course not. It's simply that Scott came to the house last night to tell me he is going back to Pueblo to live and is going to marry his childhood sweetheart."

Stunned, Breanna took hold of Tharyn's hand. "Oh, honey, I'm so sorry."

"It hurt me deeply, Breanna, but Pastor and Mrs. Blandford came to see me after Scott was gone last night and helped me."

Tharyn went on to tell Breanna of the pastor's talk on Rebekah and Isaac.

"Good," said Breanna. "And Pastor Blandford was right, Tharyn. The Lord will definitely guide your life, and when it is His chosen time, He will bring that knight in shining armor into your life. He certainly did that for me when He sent John into my life."

Tharyn hugged her tight. "Thank you for the encouragement, Breanna. I love you."

Breanna kissed her cheek. "I love you too, honey."

Chief U.S. Marshal John Brockman emerged from Denver's gun shop, having purchased a box of cartridges.

As usual, Brockman was clad in a black broadcloth coat with black trousers, white shirt, black string tie, shiny black boots, and black flat-crowned hat. Slung on his right hip was a tied-down Colt .45 revolver in a black-belted holster. The handle grips on the .45 were bone white.

He stepped off the boardwalk, patted the long neck of his black horse, and placed the cartridge box in one of his saddlebags.

At that moment, Brockman noticed three mangy-looking men coming across the broad street toward him. Each one had a mean look on his unshaven face and dirty hair sticking out from under his sweat-stained hat. All three wore guns, but the one in the middle had his gun belt slung low and his holster tied to his thigh.

The one in the middle stepped ahead of the others. "I've been lookin' for you, Stranger. You *are* the hotshot John Stranger, right?"

Brockman turned to face him squarely. "I was known as John Stranger for a long time, yes."

A sneer formed on the man's face as he looked Brockman up and down with disdain. "I'm challengin' you, Stranger. Take that badge off and face me man to man."

Brockman shook his head. "You don't want to do that, mister. Just move on now."

"Hah! I've heard so much talk about this hotshot John Stranger bein' so fast with his gun. One of my pals saw you face off with some slow, so-called gunfighter in Dodge City, Kansas, a few years ago. He said you put the man down, but you were only able to do it because the guy was so slow."

John flicked his cool gray eyes to the other two men with him, then set them on his challenger. "I'm telling you to take your pals and ride out of town right now, mister, or I'll arrest you for loitering."

People were gathering around.

"My name's Cal Dudley, Stranger. You folks hear that? *Cal Dudley.* I want all of you to remember my name, 'cause I'm about to outdraw the famous John Stranger!"

Brockman set his jaw sternly. "That's enough, Dudley. Get on your horse and ride, and take your chums with you."

Dudley backed into the street a few steps, then stopped and went into a gunfighter's crouch with his gun hand hovering over his revolver.

The growing crowd removed themselves from the line of fire.

Brockman spoke in a soft voice. "Don't be a fool and go for that gun. I don't want to have to put you down."

Dudley bit down hard, his breath hissing through his nostrils. His hand snaked downward, but froze before it even touched the butt of the gun. In less than a heartbeat, Brockman's gun was in his hand, cocked, and aimed at Dudley's chest.

Dudley's eyes bulged and his jaw slacked. He stood up straight, removing his hand from its position above his gun handle. "Okay, Mr. Stranger. You win."

Brockman holstered his gun. "Mount up and ride. Right now."

Both of Dudley's friends wheeled and headed across the street where their horses were tied.

Dudley started to turn, but instead of following his cohorts, he whipped out his gun and was bringing it to bear on Brockman.

But John's gun was out and spitting fire before Dudley could drop the hammer. The slug struck him in the upper arm of his gun hand, its impact twisting him sideways. The gun dropped from his hand. He went down on his knees, then collapsed in a heap, breathing hard.

Brockman looked at the other two, who had stopped in the middle of the street and were looking at him. "You two get out of town right now and don't come back. I'll be taking your pal to the hospital."

Without hesitation, Dudley's friends hurried toward their horses.

While two Denver County sheriff's deputies came running up, a man in the crowd stepped close to the fallen Dudley. "You'd better be thankful, mister! You're still alive only because Chief Brockman willed it so. He could've killed you easily."

"That's right!" said another man in the crowd.

Brockman turned toward a townsman who was sitting in his wagon a few feet away, looking on. "Hey, Melvin. Will you help me get this man to the hospital?"

"Sure, Chief. Load him in and we'll go."

The sheriff's deputies picked the bleeding Dudley up and put him in the bed of the wagon. Leaving Ebony tied to the hitch rail, John jumped in beside Dudley.

As the wagon rolled down the street toward the hospital, Dudley gripped his bleeding upper arm and looked up at Brockman.

"You just ruined my gun arm!"

Brockman grinned. "Good. Now you won't be challenging someone who'll aim for your heart instead of your arm. When the slug is out and you're feeling better, I want you out of town in a hurry. Got it?"

Dudley's voice was barely audible. "I got . . . it. I'll be gone as soon as I can ride." He paused. "Uh . . . Stranger?"

"Mm-hmm?"

"Thanks for not killin' me."

Breanna Brockman was at the front desk in the hospital lobby, talking to receptionist Rosie O'Brien, when she saw her husband come in, carrying a bleeding man in his arms.

Excusing herself to Rosie, Breanna dashed to John. "What happened? Who's this man?"

"Stay beside me, sweetheart, and I'll answer your questions."

While they walked toward the surgical wing, John told Breanna the story.

Just as they reached the surgical wing, Tharyn Tabor was coming out of one of the operating rooms. Her eyes widened as Breanna told her John had been forced to shoot this man he was carrying because he tried to force him into a gunfight.

Moments later, when Cal Dudley was in one of the surgical rooms on an operating table, John stood in the corridor with Breanna and Tharyn.

Breanna slid an arm around her husband's slender waist. "Tharyn, I wouldn't change a thing about this man God picked out for me, but I hope the one He has picked out for you doesn't wear a badge."

John looked down at Breanna and frowned. "Honey, Scott doesn't wear a badge. What are you talking about?"

Breanna smiled. "I'll tell you all about it over supper tonight, sweetheart."

John looked at Tharyn. "Has something happened between you and Scott?"

Tharyn flicked a glance at a clock on the wall. "I have to be back to the room I just came out of in three minutes, Chief. Breanna will tell you all about it tonight over supper."

Fourteen

On Monday, October 4, at the hideout in the mountains, Tag Moran and his gang were eating breakfast with Lucinda and Kathryn. The horses had already been watered, fed, bridled, and saddled, and were tied at the hitching posts by the front porch of the old cabin.

Tag swallowed a mouthful of scrambled eggs and smacked his lips. "Well, gals, I'm gonna miss your cooking as usual while we're gone."

"Me too," piped up Jason Moran, "but it'll be worth it when we come back with lots of money bags chock-full of the green stuff!"

"Sure will!" agreed Tony Chacone.

Lucinda took a sip of hot coffee, set her cup down, and looked at Tag. "So you're going to hit the bank in Vernal, Utah, first, right?"

Tag nodded. "Yep. Then as usual, we'll have to hide from the law for a few days.

267

After that, we'll head into Wyoming. As you gals know, after each bank robbery, we have to hide out a while to let things cool down. Whenever we hit a bank, word spreads fast to lawmen in nearby towns that we're in the area. They also alert the banks in their towns."

Lucinda nodded. "But when things cool down after the Vernal holdup, you'll hit the bank in Evanston first."

"Right. Then after another cooling-down time, we'll hit the bank in Green River. The bank in Rock Springs will be next, then we'll head for home. We should be back here in about three weeks with lots of money."

Kathryn had barely touched her breakfast. She seemed drained of her strength, and her stomach felt nauseous. She knew when she watched Gib ride away she may never see him again.

Sitting beside her at the table, Gib saw the look of dread in her eyes. He patted her arm. "Honey, don't get upset now."

This drew everyone else's attention to Kathryn.

She swallowed heavily, blinking back hot tears that sprang to her eyes and burned like the bile that was pushing into her throat. She grabbed Gib's hand. "Darling,

I — I'm afraid you're going to get killed like Darryl did."

Gib sighed and laid his palm on her cheek. "Kathryn, you're borrowing trouble needlessly. Don't be afraid. I'll be fine."

The others saw Kathryn's eyes roam his features as though committing them to memory. "But you don't know that, Gib. We all thought Darryl would come home from that stagecoach robbery — but now he lies in a cold grave at Cheyenne."

Gib lifted the hand that she held, and with both hands, cupped her face tenderly. "Honey, you have to keep your mind on the fortune we're building toward our retirement in sunny California in just a few years."

She closed her eyes and the tears spilled freely onto his hands. He kept them there and dropped his head, biting his lips.

The others could see that Kathryn's attitude was weighing on Gib.

He wiped away tears from both her cheeks and kissed her lips. "Honey, all of us will be back in three weeks, richer than ever."

Kathryn struggled to keep her composure while the men were filing out the door to mount up and ride away. When Bart was kissing Lucinda good-bye on the porch, Gib took Kathryn into his arms and said, "Remember, now. Keep your chin up and just keep dreaming about our retirement in California with all that money."

With her throat tight, Kathryn nodded, then kissed him.

After the men had ridden out of sight, Lucinda turned from the porch railing. "Kathryn, you shouldn't act this way. It can only hinder Gib, not help him. It bothers the other men too. I could see it in their eyes."

Kathryn blinked at the tears that were still forming and looked at Lucinda. "I'm sorry. I'll try to do better. I really will."

"Good. You'll help all of us if you do."

That same morning in Cheyenne, Dr. Dane Logan was at the Minard home. Walt was doing quite well, which made his doctor very happy. Loretta tearfully looked at Dr. Dane and said, "How can I ever thank you sufficiently for saving Walt's life? I'll be forever grateful."

Dr. Dane smiled. "Loretta, I already have all the thanks I need just seeing Walt alive and doing so well."

Walt said, "Doctor, I deeply appreciate your dedication to your work. If you hadn't acted as wisely as you did, I would have died."

Dr. Dane smiled and laid a hand on Walt's shoulder. "If the Lord hadn't given me the wisdom, I couldn't have saved your life, Walt."

Moments later, Dr. Dane drove away from the Minard home and headed out of town. His next stop was the Ballard farm. "Lord," he said, "thank You for allowing me to fulfill my lifelong dream to be a physician and surgeon."

Some twenty minutes later, Dr. Dane guided the buggy onto the Ballard place, and when he pulled up in front of the house, the door came open. Clyde and Frances stood at the open door and welcomed him.

As he stepped into the house, he looked at both of them. "So how's Bertha doing?"

"She's napping right now, Doctor," said Frances, "but I'll go wake her up."

"Oh no. I don't want to disturb her nap. She needs the rest. Is she doing all right, though?"

"She's doing very well," said Clyde. "She's walking with her cane, and as you prescribed, she is walking a little more each day."

At that moment, they saw Bertha come out of her room down the hall, and she smiled as she walked slowly toward them.

The doctor smiled back as he watched her move their direction. "She *is* doing well, isn't she?"

When Bertha drew up, she looked into the doctor's eyes. "I'm doing well because my surgeon did such a beautiful job in replacing my hip with the ivory ball. It's given me a new lease on life."

"Well, praise the Lord," said Dr. Dane. "He is the one who made it possible for me to become a surgeon, Bertha. Well, I'd better be going. I just wanted to stop by and check on my patient."

The Ballards stood on the porch and waved as the doctor put his horse in motion and headed up the lane toward the country road that led to Cheyenne.

As the buggy reached the end of the lane and Dr. Dane guided it onto the road, he said, "Thank You once again, dear Lord, for allowing me to do this work that I love so much. I'll enjoy it even more when someday I have my own practice."

A moment later, with the sound of the horse's hooves pounding the surface of the road, Dane Logan let his mind go back to the dismal days when he was orphaned at the age of fifteen. His parents had been so encouraging to him as he contemplated his future as a physician and surgeon. When they were murdered by the street gang, not only was he devastated by this horrendous loss, but the hope of having a medical career was lost too.

He had a few medical books that his parents had bought him and a dream in his heart, but when he had to take up residence in one of Manhattan's back alleys with a colony of other orphans, it seemed impossible that he would ever have the funds to cover the cost of medical school.

As Dane was guiding the buggy on a turn in the road, a smile curved his lips. He thought of dear Dr. Lee Harris, and how Dr. Harris had taught him how to treat the injuries and mild illnesses of the other children in the colony. And then, Dr. Harris got him the job at Clarkson Pharmacy. This put him in touch with medicine, which brightened his life.

Then came that dreadful day when he was arrested for murdering Benny Jackson. A few days later, he was sentenced to life in prison. All hope for ever becoming a doctor was gone.

He thought of the long, hopeless months he spent in the Manhattan prison, then, a smile curved his lips again when he remembered that wonderful day when he was released from the prison because the real killer had been caught.

Romans 8:28 came to mind. *"And we know that all things work together for good to them that love God, to them who are the called according to his purpose."*

God had used Dane Weston, even in the bleak days of his imprisonment, to lead precious souls to the Saviour. His heart thrilled anew at the thought of God's faithfulness, even though he had despaired at times. God had a purpose for him being in the prison, and that purpose had eternal results.

Cheyenne lay ahead of Dane in the beautiful autumn sunshine. "Thank You, Lord, for working out Your purpose in my life. Look where I am today! My dream has been realized. Thank You, precious Lord, for Your faithfulness and Your wonderful blessings. Here I am doing the work I love so much. Great is Thy faithfulness, Lord, unto me!"

When Dane arrived in Cheyenne, he stopped at the hospital to look in on a couple of patients. Just as he was coming out of the second patient's room, he met up with Dr. Jeremy Winstad.

Dane's face brightened at the sight of his friend. "How was your trip to Denver last week?"

Winstad smiled warmly. "It was fine, Doc Dane. I've been wanting to talk to you ever since I got back yesterday. While I was in Denver, I visited Dr. Matt Carroll. You know who he is, don't you?"

"Uh-huh. Head man at Mile High Hospital."

"Right. You've mentioned to me several times that someday you'd like to have your own practice."

Dane let a grin form on his face. "Yes, I have."

"Well, Dr. Carroll told me that Dr. Robert Fraser in Central City is looking for a young doctor to come and take over his practice. Central City is in the mountains some thirty miles west of Denver. There are several towns in that area that have no doctor. He's the only doctor in a thirty-mile radius. Dr. Carroll says it is a good solid practice. Dr. Fraser will turn seventy-five next month and is finding it more difficult all the time to keep up with the workload."

Dane's pulse throbbed. "Sounds good! Thanks for giving me the information. I'll look into it right away."

"Let me know how it turns out."

"I sure will. See you later."

When Dane arrived back at the office,

his parents were looking over a patient's file at his mother's desk.

They asked how it went with the house calls and with the two patients in the hospital. Dane gave them the details, then said, "And something else happened when I was at the hospital."

They both listened intently as he told them of his conversation with Dr. Jeremy Winstad about the pending sale of the practice in Central City.

"I've heard of Dr. Robert Fraser, son," said Jacob, "but I've never had the opportunity to meet him. Since Dr. Carroll thinks so much of him, I'm sure it is indeed a solid practice. So I assume you're going to be making a trip to Central City."

"I really feel I should, Dad. You . . . ah . . . you told me that you understood my wanting to have my own practice."

Jacob and Naomi looked at each other, then Jacob said, "Of course I do. Your mother and I have been praying that the Lord would guide you about it when it was His time."

Naomi smiled at her son. "Of course your father and I have mixed emotions, Dane. We will miss having you close to us, and we will miss having you here in this practice. But we both understand."

"Especially me," said Jacob. "I well remember how very much I looked forward to having my own practice when I finished my internship. You go talk to Dr. Fraser. And don't fret about my having the extra workload here. I'm not an old man yet, and I'm sure I won't have a problem finding a new partner. Memorial Hospital has several young doctors doing their internship, and I know of two or three who are just about finished."

"Okay if I go tomorrow?"

"Sure. I'll look after your patients."

The next day, Dr. Dane took the early train to Denver and rented a horse from a stable near the railroad station.

It was a glorious autumn day. As he rode west into the Rockies and moved up into the high country, he drew in a deep breath of the clean, fresh air and ran his gaze in a panorama. The aspen and birch trees were brilliant with their shimmering golden leaves and the dark green pines towered over them as majestic sentinels. All around were the lofty peaks reaching toward the pale blue sky, some with white caps of snow that had not melted in the relative warmth of the summer.

Drawing in another deep breath, Dane

said, "It's just a great day to be alive."

The sight of the wide-open sky and the sun casting its deep shadows in the canyons filled him with wonder at God's handiwork.

"I could be very happy living in this marvelous mountain country. Lord, if it's Your will, I'd love for it to work out with Dr. Fraser."

Riding through the high country was a slow process. It was just after four o'clock in the afternoon when Dane drew near Central City. The town's setting was beautiful. By reading signs at the edge of town, he learned that there were gold and silver mines nearby. The Holton Coal Mine, he learned, was just two miles west of town.

As he rode into Central City, he let his eyes roam from side to side. The town was laid out in an attractive manner. People were moving about on the boardwalks, and there was steady traffic on Main Street.

Soon Dane spotted the sign that identified the office of Dr. Robert Fraser. He guided the horse to the hitch rail, dismounted, and entered it.

He was greeted by the nurse-receptionist at the desk whose name plate identified her as Nadine Wahl. Dane estimated her to be in her early sixties.

Smiling at her, he said, "I need to see Dr. Fraser if he's in, ma'am."

"Dr. Fraser is with his last scheduled patient for the day at the moment. He should be finished in a few minutes. He will see you, of course. May I tell him your name and your ailment, sir?"

Dane shook his head. "I'm not here as a patient, ma'am. I'm Dr. Dane Logan. I am a partner with my father, Dr. Jacob Logan, in Cheyenne. Yesterday, I was talking to Dr. Jeremy Winstad at Cheyenne Memorial Hospital, and he told me of learning a few days ago from Dr. Matthew Carroll at Mile High Hospital in Denver about Dr. Fraser's plans to retire. I would like to talk to him about taking over his practice."

Nadine's face brightened. "Oh! Well, I can tell you, Dr. Logan, that Dr. Fraser has a wonderful practice here. We —"

Nadine was interrupted by the front door opening. Dane turned to see a sprightly little lady enter. Her hair was as white as the snow on the high peaks that surrounded the town, and her blue eyes were as bright as the wide sky on a sunny day.

"Good afternoon, Nadine," the little lady said to the nurse, then glanced at Dane. "And who might you be, young man?"

Before Dane could reply, Nadine said, "This is Dr. Dane Logan from Cheyenne, Esther. He is here to talk to Dr. Fraser about taking over the practice."

"Oh, really?"

"Yes. Dr. Logan, this is Mrs. Fraser."

Dane smiled warmly. "I'm glad to meet you, ma'am."

Esther extended her hand, and as Dane took it gently, the door to the examining room opened, and the doctor came out with his patient, telling him to be sure and take the medicine he had given him as directed.

The elderly man said he would, and after bidding Esther and Nadine good day, he moved out the front door.

Dr. Fraser smiled at his wife and kissed her cheek. Esther blushed at the kiss as she had for over fifty years. "Dear," she said, turning to the smiling young man, "this is Dr. Dane Logan. Nadine just explained that he is here to talk to you about taking over the practice."

Dr. Robert Fraser's silver eyebrows arched. As they shook hands, Fraser said, "Glad to meet you, Dr. Logan. Where are you from?"

"Cheyenne, sir. I'm partner with my father, Dr. Jacob Logan, there. I'm a graduate of Northwestern University Medical College. I did my two-year internship at Memorial Hospital in Cheyenne, and have been partner with Dad in his practice since last May. Of course, I want a practice of my own."

Fraser smiled. "I understand that."

"Dr. Jeremy Winstad at Memorial Hospital told me yesterday that he had learned from Dr. Matthew Carroll in Denver that you are planning to retire soon and are looking for someone to take over your practice. I came to talk to you about it."

Dr. Fraser removed his spectacles and wiped his hand across his tired eyes. "Son, I am delighted to see you, and we most certainly will talk about it. I have a date for dinner with this lovely wife of mine, but I'm sure she won't mind if you join us so we can talk."

"Of course I won't mind," spoke up Esther. "We'll enjoy having you dine with us, Dr. Logan."

At Central City's finest restaurant, the Frasers and their guest ordered their food, and while they waited, Dane told them his story — including his becoming an orphan at fifteen years of age in Manhattan, New York, his ride on the orphan train, and his

281

adoption by Dr. and Mrs. Jacob Logan of Cheyenne. He went over his education and internship again and told of becoming partner with his father just over four months ago. He then took an envelope from his coat pocket and showed the Frasers his diploma from Northwestern and a certificate of internship completion from Cheyenne's Memorial Hospital.

Dr. Fraser was showing keen interest when the waiter arrived with the food.

As the waiter walked away, Dr. Fraser said, "Dr. Logan, Mrs. Fraser and I are born-again Christians, and we always pray before a meal."

Dane's face beamed as he smiled from ear to ear. "I'm a born-again child of God too. I never eat a meal without thanking the Lord for His wonderful blessings and provisions."

The Frasers smiled at each other. "Wonderful! Dr. Logan, will you lead us in prayer, please?" said Dr. Fraser.

They prayed, then while they enjoyed the meal, Dane told them how he came to know the Lord while an orphan in Manhattan when a medical doctor led him to Christ. He went on to tell them of his desire to be a physician and surgeon from the time of his early childhood. He concluded by explaining the yearning he had in his heart to have his own practice.

Feeling God's leadership in the matter, Dr. Fraser agreed to sell Dane the practice. He would let him buy it by making reasonable monthly payments. Dane offered to give him a check as earnest money before leaving to head back to Cheyenne, and Dr. Fraser accepted it.

Fraser went on to say that he and Esther would be staying in Central City, so he would be available to help young Dr. Logan whenever he was needed. He could fill in when Dr. Logan had to be away — like visiting patients who lived several miles from Central City or when he was doing surgery at Mile High Hospital in Denver.

The Frasers could tell that the young doctor was thrilled with the prospect of taking over the practice.

Dr. Fraser said, "We have an extra bedroom in our house. We would be honored if you would spend the night with us."

Dane smiled and nodded. "I would be even more honored to do so, sir."

"Good! We'll stop by Nadine's house when we leave here, and I'll have her postpone tomorrow's appointments at the office so you and I can go to Denver. I'll introduce you to Dr. Carroll so you can make arrangements with him for hospital privileges. You know — being able to bring your patients there and to do surgery on them when needed."

"I really appreciate that, Dr. Fraser."

"Glad to do it. We'd best get to bed early. We'll have to leave a little before sunup in order to get to Denver at a decent time."

"No problem," said Dane.

Later that night, an excited Dane Logan lay in bed at the Frasers' house and praised the Lord for the way He was working in his life.

Dawn was a slight hint in the eastern sky the next morning when the two physicians rode toward Denver.

They arrived at Mile High Hospital at midmorning and were welcomed by Dr. Matt Carroll.

After learning Dane's background in medicine and that Dr. Fraser was going to sell him his practice, it took only moments for Carroll to happily grant Dr. Dane the desired hospital privileges. When Dr. Fraser followed this by telling Dr. Carroll that Dane was a born-again child of God, Carroll became even happier about giving him the privileges.

Carroll then said to Dane, "I've heard of your adoptive father and that he is a fine doctor, but I've never had the opportunity to meet him. Maybe someday."

Dane grinned. "Well, if not here on earth, Dr. Carroll, the two of you will meet in heaven."

"Praise the Lord for that. Well, Dr. Dane Logan, let me give you a tour of our fine hospital. Would you like to tag along, Dr. Fraser?"

"Well, of course."

Moments later, while the three men were walking down a corridor on the first floor and Carroll was pointing out particulars about the hospital, one of the staff doctors — whose name was Jess White — came out of an examining room. Dr. Carroll stopped him, introduced him to Dr. Dane Logan as the man who would be taking over Dr. Fraser's practice, then said, "So how did your examination of Elsa Johnson go?"

Dr. White rubbed the back of his neck and replied, "Mrs. Johnson is in dire need of a hip replacement."

Dr. Carroll's face showed the concern he felt with this news. "I'll wire the superintendent at Bellevue Hospital in New York and see if they have a doctor who is qualified to do hip replacements. I know two or three of them went to Germany several months ago to study under Dr. Theodore Gluck."

Dr. White shook his head. "I'm sure the Johnsons can't afford to pay a surgeon to come all the way from New York to do the hip replacement, Dr. Carroll."

"May I say something?" spoke up Dr. Dane.

"Certainly," said Dr. Carroll.

Dane told Drs. Carroll and White of his learning about hip replacements from Dr. Theodore Gluck while he was a student at Northwestern University Medical College and that he had done a hip replacement on a seventy-two-year-old woman in Cheyenne recently, who was now doing quite well.

While all three doctors were showing their surprise at this accomplishment by the young doctor, Dane said, "Dr. Carroll, I would be glad to do the surgery on Mrs. Johnson if you, Dr. White, the patient, and her family will allow me to do it."

Dr. Carroll asked, "Did you do the replacement with an ivory ball like Dr. Gluck does?"

"Yes, sir. When I did the surgery on the lady in Cheyenne, I ordered some extra ivory blocks so whenever I was called upon to do more hip replacements, I would have them on hand. If I'm given permission to do the surgery, I'll wire my father immediately and have him take one of the ivory blocks to the railroad station and put it in the hands of the conductor on the evening train. That way, I'll have it yet tonight."

Dr. Jess White said, "Dr. Logan, as far as I'm concerned, you can do the surgery. Mrs. Johnson's son and daughter-in-law are in the room with her right now. You can go talk to all three of them."

"Let's do it," spoke up Dr. Carroll. "I'm behind you on this 100 percent, Dr. Logan."

Dane smiled. "Thank you. How old is Mrs. Johnson?"

"She's sixty-three," said Dr. White. "Dr. Carroll, since you're the head man here, why don't you go in with Dr. Logan? Dr. Fraser and I will wait here."

"All right. Let's go, Dr. Logan."

Dane followed Dr. Carroll into the room, and was introduced to the patient and her family. Dr. Carroll explained to them that Dr. Logan learned how to do hip replacements with ivory balls from the famous German surgeon, Dr. Theodore Gluck, while a student at Northwestern University Medical College in Chicago. He told them that Dr. Dane was in partnership with his father, Dr. Jacob Logan, in Cheyenne, and that Dr. Dane had quite recently done a successful hip replacement on a patient in Cheyenne.

All three were quite impressed, and Dr. Dane was immediately given permission to perform the surgery on Elsa Johnson. He explained how he would get an ivory block from his father yet tonight, then told them he would do an examination on Elsa first thing in the morning so he could carve the ivory ball the proper size, then he would proceed with the surgery. Elsa was filled with hope.

Drs. Carroll and Logan returned to Drs. White and Fraser, and Dr. Fraser then took Dane to the Western Union office where he wired his father.

Dr. Fraser also wired his wife, advised her of what was happening, and asked her to let Nadine know. He would stay until the surgery was done in the morning, then he would head for home.

That night at eleven-thirty, Dr. Dane picked up the ivory block at Denver's Union Station, and he and Dr. Fraser were given rooms to sleep in at the hospital.

At eight o'clock the next morning, Dr.

Dane Logan was scrubbing up in the surgical washroom in preparation to make his examination, carve the ivory ball, and do the surgery.

At the same time, Dr. Matt Carroll moved up to the nurses' station in the surgical wing. There were two nurses behind the counter. They both smiled and greeted him with a friendly good morning.

Returning the smile, he said, "And good morning to you, ladies. Do either of you happen to know where Nurse Tabor is?"

"Yes, sir," said one of them. "Tharyn is in room 212 with a patient."

"Thank you," said Carroll.

Just as he was approaching room 212, Tharyn Tabor came out. "Oh! Good morning, Dr. Carroll."

"Good morning, Tharyn. I need you to assist a doctor who is going to do a hip replacement on Elsa Johnson this morning. You met her yesterday when she was being admitted."

"Yes, sir."

"I'll see that any assignments you have are taken care of by another nurse."

"All right, Doctor." Tharyn's brow furrowed. "I didn't know there was a doctor in Denver who was qualified to do hip replacements. Who is it?"

"He's not a Denver doctor. He is Dr. Logan from Cheyenne, and he definitely is qualified. Dr. Logan is buying Dr. Fraser's practice in Central City. He happens to be here because Dr. Fraser brought him so I could grant him hospital privileges when he takes over his practice. Mrs. Johnson and her family have requested that Dr. Logan do the hip replacement, and I want you to be the one to assist him."

"I'll be glad to. Doctor?"

"Yes?"

"I've heard of Dr. Jacob Logan in Cheyenne and of his very successful practice. I'm wondering why he would sell his practice where he is doing so well and move to Central City."

Carroll grinned. "He isn't. This doctor I want you to assist is Dr. Jacob Logan's son, who at the moment is a partner in the Cheyenne practice."

"Oh, I see. All right. I have a couple of things to take care of. I'll be there in about five or six minutes."

"Good. Mrs. Johnson's in operating room 3. I'll go tell Dr. Logan I'm sending him my best surgical nurse."

Tharyn blushed and smiled modestly. "Thank you for your confidence in me, Doctor." With that, she hurried away.

Dr. Carroll entered operating room 3 and found Dr. Dane Logan preparing to do the surgery.

Elsa Johnson rolled her head on the slender pillow and smiled. "Good morning, Dr. Carroll. I'm so encouraged. I just know Dr. Logan is going to make it so I can walk again."

Carroll smiled down at her. "I have no doubt about it, Mrs. Johnson."

Dr. Carroll noted the ivory ball that lay in a sterilized metal container. "Got it carved, I see."

"Yes," said Dr. Dane. "I'll be ready in a few more minutes. I assume my assisting nurse will be here soon."

"Yes. I'm giving you an experienced surgical nurse to assist you. She is young, but very, very good. In fact, Nurse Tabor is the number one surgical nurse in this hospital. She'll be here in about five minutes. I'll excuse myself now. I have some people waiting to see me in my office. Mrs. Johnson's son and daughter-in-law are in the surgical waiting room."

Dr. Dane nodded. "I'll see them immediately after I'm done with the surgery."

Moments later, Tharyn Tabor hurried down the corridor, entered the surgical wing, and made her way to operating room number 3.

When she entered the room, she saw the young surgeon leaning over his patient. Hearing the door open, he turned and glanced up at her as she moved toward him. "Dr. Logan, I'm Tharyn Tabor. Dr. Carroll sent me to —"

Suddenly their eyes met.

Tiny, tingling currents scintillated through Dane's chest. It had been nine years. The beautiful redhead had matured, but he knew her. "Tharyn!"

Tharyn's eyes were wide, and her mouth was moving. But no sound would come out.

The silence in the room was an almost solid thing, then blinking, she found her voice and choked out, "D-Dane? Is . . . is it really you?"

Fifteen

Their hearts racing, Dane Logan and Tharyn Tabor stood for a timeless moment, looking at each other.

Elsa Johnson observed the scene from the operating table.

Finally, Dane said, "Yes, little sis. It's me. This is like a dream. It *is* really you, isn't it?"

"Yes," Tharyn said, "b-but Dr. Carroll said you're Dr. Jacob Logan's son. I —"

"He and his wife adopted me."

Hardly daring to believe his eyes, Dane moved toward Tharyn, drinking in her loveliness. "I — I want to catch you up on all that has happened to me, and I certainly want to hear your story. But right now we've got Mrs. Johnson on the operating table."

"Dr. Logan?" came Elsa's voice.

He looked at her over his shoulder.

She smiled at him. "It's all right. Take a few minutes. I'm not going anywhere."

Dr. Dane smiled back. "Thank you, ma'am. We'll make it brief."

"Are you two long-lost brother and sister?"

"Not actually. We knew each other when we were teenagers and living as orphans on the streets of New York City. We sort of adopted each other as brother and sister. I was arrested for a crime I did not commit and was put in prison. Tharyn was put on an orphan train shortly thereafter, and we lost track of each other. Over nine years have passed since then."

"Oh, I see."

"We'll take just a few minutes; then we'll get on with your surgery."

Elsa nodded. "That will be fine."

Dane turned back to the lovely young woman with the auburn hair and sky blue eyes. "I was cleared of the crime, Tharyn, when they found the real killer. I was released from the prison on November 16 of that same year: 1871. I left New York on an orphan train in January 1872, and on that trip I met Dr. and Mrs. Jacob Logan on the train. Since I'm making the story short . . . they took me home to Cheyenne and adopted me. They are fine Christian people, and it was a wonderful home in which to finish growing up. My new parents sent me to Northwestern University Medical College in Chicago. After graduation, I did two years' internship at Cheyenne's Memorial Hospital, then back in May of this year I was taken in as partner in my father's practice."

Tharyn nodded. "Dr. Carroll told me that you are taking over Dr. Robert Fraser's practice up in Central City."

"Yes. My parents understand my need to have my own practice. Dr. Fraser has accepted me as buyer of his practice. I'm superbly happy for the way the Lord has worked everything out for me in this."

Tears misted Tharyn's eyes. "I'm so glad, big brother. Let's, ah . . . get on with the surgery. I can tell you my story later."

"All right. Just one quick question . . ."

"Yes?"

"Is — is it *Mrs.* Tharyn Tabor?"

She shook her head. "No. It's *Miss* Tharyn Tabor. Could I ask just one quick question too?"

"Sure."

"Is there a *Mrs.* Dr. Dane Logan?"

He chuckled. "No. The Lord hasn't sent me His chosen young lady to be Mrs. Dr. Dane Logan as yet."

Secretly, both of them were feeling relief. Elsa Johnson had folded her hands over her midsection and was smiling at the reunion.

Dane looked into Tharyn's eyes. "All right, Miss Myers — uh, I mean Miss Tabor — if you will administer the anesthetic, we will provide Mrs. Johnson with a new hip joint."

Two hours later, when the successful surgery was completed, two orderlies came with a gurney to take Elsa Johnson to the recovery room.

Tharyn told Dane she would accompany Elsa to the recovery room and make sure she was coming out from under the anesthetic all right, while Dane went to talk to her son and daughter-in-law. They would meet in the surgical washroom in a little while.

Half an hour later, Dane and Tharyn were alone in the surgical washroom, scrubbing up from the surgery.

"Big brother, I'll fill you in on myself now. I was chosen at Denver's Union Station on November 10, 1871, by David and Kitty Tabor. They are wonderful Christian people. Papa is president of the First National Bank of Denver."

Dane's eyebrows arched. "Wow! The Lord was good to you, wasn't He?"

"That's for sure. I wasn't aware, of course, that you were released from prison on November 16. I clearly remember that I sent you a letter on November 24 to let you know where I was so we could correspond with each other as we agreed. When there was no response from you, I wrote another letter. I still got no response, but I sent several more. When I still didn't hear back from you, I decided that you didn't want to maintain our friendship since you were going to be in prison for life."

Dane was drying his hands on a towel. "I guess the prison officials threw your letters away. Apparently they didn't want to take the time and effort to write you and let you know that I had been released."

Tharyn nodded. "Well, at least now I understand why you never wrote back to me. And, of course, you had no way of knowing where I was."

"Right. I never wrote to the Children's Aid Society to ask where you had been chosen because I learned before they put me on one of their orphan trains that they never gave out any information as to where the orphans were, nor who had taken them in. That information was sealed to the public."

Tharyn shook her head as she dropped

the towel she was using into a laundry basket. She reached out and touched his arm. "This all seems like a dream, Dane. I'm afraid if I close my eyes, you will disappear."

He took hold of her hand. "I know exactly what you mean. I think I'll just keep this grip on your hand so you can't get away. I'm so glad I've found you."

She smiled warmly. "So am I, and I'm not going anywhere. But speaking of going somewhere, how soon are you going back to Central City?"

"Well, it's like this. I want to check on Mrs. Johnson in the morning, and if she's doing all right, I'll turn her over to Dr. White. Then I must return to Cheyenne and wrap things up there. Once that's done, I'll go back to Central City and sign the official papers for the purchase of Dr. Fraser's practice with his attorney and go to work in my new practice. I'll be coming through Denver, of course, to go to Central City. I rented a horse this time and have already returned him to the stable, but next time, I'll have to buy a horse from the stable. I sure would like to see you again when I come back. It'll be about a week."

Tharyn squeezed his hand. "Of course.

We have a lot of catching up to do. I'll look forward to it." She paused for a moment. "I have an idea."

"Mm-hmm?"

"Could you come home with me for dinner this evening and meet my parents? An extra plate on the table won't be a problem at all."

A smile spread from ear to ear. "That would be wonderful. I'd love to meet your parents. And someday soon I want you to meet mine." He chuckled. "You and I could probably talk for weeks trying to catch up, but with my time schedule the way it is right now, I guess we'll have to do it in segments. Once I'm settled in Central City, it'll be much easier to get together, and we won't feel so pressed for time."

"Sounds good to me. I'll look forward to every minute."

Dane sighed. "Well, Dr. Fraser is still here at the hospital. He's probably staying close to Dr. Carroll. I'll let him know my plans and how the hip replacement went, so he can go on back to Central City today."

"I've got to report in to the nurses' station in case I'm needed. How about you meet me in the hospital lobby at five o'clock this afternoon? Papa always comes and picks me up in his buggy about that time on his way home from the bank."

Dane let go of her hand. "Tharyn?"

"Mm-hmm?"

He looked deep into her eyes. "Before I go find Dr. Fraser, could — could I hug you?"

"You sure can!"

They were immediately in each other's arms.

Dane found Dr. Robert Fraser at Dr. Matt Carroll's office and told them both of the successful hip replacement he had done on Elsa Johnson. The doctors were happy to learn that it had gone well. Dr. Dane told Dr. Carroll that if Elsa was doing all right in the morning, he would turn her over to Dr. Jess White. Dr. Carroll agreed.

Dane then explained about his having known Nurse Tharyn Tabor when they were orphans together on the streets of New York, and that she had invited him to dinner at the Tabor home this evening. He told Dr. Fraser that he would head for Cheyenne tomorrow and be back to Central City within a week so they could get the official papers signed and he could take over the practice. Dr. Fraser told him that he would reserve a room for him at one of Central City's boardinghouses. Dane thanked him, then Fraser said he would ride on home. He would expect to see Dane in a week or so.

Dane used the remainder of the morning and the afternoon to walk around Denver and get to know the town. At times he found himself coming face to face with people on the boardwalks. His heart was so filled with joy over all that was taking place in his life, that several times he smiled at them, tipped his hat, and said, "Isn't it a beautiful day?"

At five o'clock, Dane was in the hospital lobby when Tharyn came in from the corridor and greeted him. They waited by the front door, and Dane was telling Tharyn about his walk around Denver when she looked outside and saw her father's buggy coming from the street.

David Tabor's face showed his surprise when he saw Tharyn come through the door with the tall, handsome stranger. As he pulled rein and stopped, Tharyn took Dane by the hand and led him up beside the buggy.

David hopped out as usual to help his daughter climb into the buggy, and noted the light in her eyes and the beam on her face.

"Papa! You will never believe who this is!"

David peered intently at the smiling young man. "Well, sweetheart, I give up. Who is he?"

"You've heard me speak his name hundreds of times over the years, Daddy. This is Dane Weston."

David's mouth sagged. "Dane Weston!"

"Well, now it's Dane Logan, Papa. *Doctor* Dane Logan."

A smile worked its way across the bank president's face. He extended his hand, and as Dane met his grip, David said, "So you're the orphan boy who took such good care of this little girl and are responsible for her being saved. Tharyn, did you say I had heard you speak his name hundreds of times? More like *thousands!*"

Tharyn laughed. "Well, maybe it was."

David looked at his daughter. "So you found him here in the hospital?"

"Uh-huh. Remember me telling you, Papa, how much Dane wanted to be a doctor?"

"Oh yes. But you also told your mother and me about his arrest and imprisonment for a murder that he didn't commit. What happened?"

"Well, Papa, I've invited Dane to come home and have dinner with us this evening. Instead of having him tell the story to you and again to Mama, we'll wait till we get home so he will only have to tell it once."

David smiled. "Okay, honey. Whatever you say. Isn't it incredible that you first found each other on the streets of Manhattan, then lost each other, and have finally found each other again at Mile High Hospital here in Denver?"

"Only the hand of our wonderful heavenly Father could make this happen, Papa. Well, we'd better be going, or Mama's going to wonder what's happened to us."

David allowed Dane to help Tharyn into the buggy, and with her sitting between the two men, the buggy was soon heading down Broadway.

David was shaking his head in wonder at this amazing development.

Dane explained to David that he was from Cheyenne, that he did a hip replacement on a sixty-three-year-old woman with Tharyn assisting him this morning, and that he would be sleeping at the hospital tonight, as he had done last night. David told him he would bring him back to the hospital this evening.

Kitty Tabor was busily taking a succulent glazed ham from the oven when she caught movement at the kitchen door in her peripheral vision. She turned to get a full view, and was surprised to see a handsome young stranger with her husband and daughter.

David rushed to her and helped her set the pan on the countertop.

Tharyn took Dane by the hand and led him to her mother.

Kitty pushed a stray lock of hair from her forehead and wiped her hands on her gingham apron. Her cheeks were rosy from the heat of the stove. She smiled at the stranger, then ran her gaze from David to Tharyn. "Well, who is going to introduce me to this young man?"

Tharyn's voice was quavering a bit. "Mama, I told you about the boy who saved my life and gave me a home with his orphan colony and witnessed to me about Jesus."

Kitty blinked. "This — this is him, honey?"

Tharyn's eyes were wet with tears. "Yes, Mama."

A smile broke over Kitty's face. "Dane? Dane Weston?"

"Yes, ma'am," said Dane. "Only it's Dane Logan now."

Kitty stood looking at Dane, her mouth forming a perfect O.

"Actually, Mama," spoke up Tharyn, "it's *Doctor* Dane Logan. He will tell you and Papa the whole story while we eat supper, but he was adopted by Dr. and Mrs. Jacob Logan in Cheyenne nine years ago."

"How wonderful this is!" exclaimed Kitty, looking back and forth between her daughter and the young physician. "Oh, please excuse my lack of manners, Doctor!" With that she offered her hand.

While Dane was shaking Kitty's hand, Tharyn said, "Mama, let's you and I get supper on the table, then Dane can tell us all about the years between when I came West, and he was in prison."

"Oh yes! You and I will have supper on in no time, honey."

The men were told to wash up, and in less than ten minutes, they were sitting down to the table. When Kitty eased on to her chair, she smiled across the table at Dane. "Dr. Logan, I'll tell you right now — this girl hasn't lived a day since we adopted her without bringing up your name."

Dane smiled at Tharyn, who was blushing.

David prayed over the food and also thanked the Lord for bringing Dr. Dane to Denver so he and Tharyn could see each other after all this time.

The foursome enjoyed the meal together while Dane told his story to David and Kitty. At certain points Tharyn asked questions, wanting to get every detail.

When the meal was over, there was still more to tell. The men were sent to the parlor while the women did the dishes and cleaned up the kitchen. Later, Kitty and Tharyn joined the men and Dane picked up where he had left off at the table.

David and Kitty both noticed that as the story went on, Dane and Tharyn could hardly keep their eyes off each other.

Finally, when the story had been told, Dane looked at the grandfather clock in the corner of the parlor. "Well, Mr. Tabor, I guess I should have you run me back to the hospital. It's getting late, and I'm afraid I'm keeping you people up past your bedtime."

"Oh, it's not that late," said Tharyn. "Mama, how about you and I riding along as Papa takes Dane back to the hospital?"

Moments later, the Tabors and Dr. Dane

Logan were in the buggy as it rolled along the lantern-lit streets of Denver. Kitty was sitting on the front seat beside her husband, and Tharyn and Dane were sitting together on the backseat.

Along the way, Dane and Tharyn agreed to spend as much time together as possible when Dane was in and out of Denver with his Central City patients in the future.

Soon they arrived at the hospital, and as he moved out of the buggy, Dane thanked David and Kitty for the nice meal and the enjoyable evening.

He then put his attention on Tharyn in the backseat, who was looking at him with eager eyes. He moved up close to her. "Tharyn, could I hug you again?"

"Yes!" she replied with enthusiasm.

David and Kitty looked at each other furtively and smiled.

Dane leaned in and took Tharyn in his strong arms. She wrapped her own arms around him and they held on to each other for a long moment.

When the young couple released each other, Dane took a step back. "I'll see you again soon, Tharyn."

He bid David and Kitty good night, smiled at Tharyn, and headed toward the front door of the hospital. When he reached the door and opened it, he turned around and waved.

Tharyn and her parents waved back, and as they drove away, Kitty remarked, "What a fine, handsome young man he is."

Tharyn sighed. "That he is, Mama. That he is."

Tharyn lay in her bed, staring at the ceiling by the dim light that flowed through her bedroom window from a nearby street lamp.

"Thank You, Lord, for bringing Dane back into my life. Thank You for always knowing what is best for me. Just a short time ago I was so upset over Scott leaving me for his childhood sweetheart."

She chuckled softly. "All the time, Lord, You knew that today, You would let Dane and me be reunited. Please forgive me for doubting, and help me to remember that in Your time, You do all things well."

She lay there for several minutes, then knowing that sleep would be very elusive, she threw back the covers, picked up her warm robe and fleecy slippers from the small bench at the foot of the bed, put them on, and curled up in the soft over-stuffed chair by the window.

Her mind wandered back to that terrible

day when her parents and her aunt were killed, and the young lad who worked at the Clarkson Pharmacy bravely saved her life. A warmth stole over her as she relived the moment when Dane took her to the alley and gave her a home with the other street orphans. Dane was a hero to the others too, because he had become their protector.

Lying on his hard cot at Mile High Hospital, Dane was reliving those early days in the alley too, and thanking God for His goodness.

Every time he closed his eyes, willing sleep to come, a vision of beautiful Tharyn was there on the screen of his mind. No other girl had ever touched his heart like Tharyn did. It was so wonderful to see her, and to know she was all right. It was also comforting to know that she was not married.

As planned, the Tag Moran gang entered the bank in Vernal, Utah, and rode away, leaving one of the bank tellers lying dead on the floor. Though the gang members were disturbed that Tag had shot and killed the teller, they were elated to have so many stuffed money bags.

They were able to elude the posse that was quickly on their trail by using streams to cover their direction of escape.

Three days later, they robbed the bank in Evanston, Wyoming, and rode away with even more money than the Vernal robbery had yielded. Bart, Jason, Gib, and Tony were feeling queasy in their stomachs because Tag had shot down a customer in the Evanston bank who was pulling his gun in an attempt to stop them.

As Tag's four men put their minds on the money they had garnered in the Evanston robbery, the queasiness soon left them.

At the Brockman home outside of Denver, John, Breanna, Paul, and Ginny were eating breakfast together on Monday, October 11, while John and Breanna were talking about Tharyn Tabor's long-lost friend, Dr. Dane Logan, showing up in Denver a few days ago.

Breanna had worked at Mile High Hospital the day after Dr. Logan had done the hip replacement on Elsa Johnson, and had talked to Tharyn at church yesterday about Elsa. Tharyn had told her that Elsa was still doing quite well and would be going home in a few more days.

John swallowed a mouthful of pancake. "I'm glad to hear she's doing so well. And let me tell you, honey, it's a real blessing that young Dr. Logan is going to be taking over for Dr. Fraser. That poor old man is so tired. He desperately needs a rest. I'm sure he's going to want to jump in and help Dr. Logan once in a while, but he'll get that much needed rest."

"Yes," said Breanna. "And believe me, from what I learned about Dr. Dane Logan, he's going to be such a blessing in Central City *and* here at the hospital. Matt and Dr. Jess White are both singing his praises."

"I'm glad."

"And let me tell you, darling, I've never seen Tharyn so happy. She's a walking sunbeam."

John chuckled. "Maybe they'll get past the brother-sister thing and something more serious will develop."

Breanna smiled. "It wouldn't surprise me."

"Well, I'm looking forward to meeting this young Dr. Logan." He picked up his coffee cup, drained the last few drops, and set it down. "Well, this federal lawman had better get to his office. Lots of work to do."

That morning when John Brockman was at his desk in the U.S. marshal's office, Deputy Charlie Wesson tapped on the door, opened it, and stuck his head in. "Chief, I have a telegram here for you from the Uintah County sheriff in Evanston, Wyoming."

"Oh? Well, let's see what it's about. I'd sure be pleased if it's to inform me that the Tag Moran gang pulled a bank robbery there, and Sheriff Billington and a posse had caught them."

Wesson handed the chief the yellow envelope.

Brockman tore it open and began reading it silently. He frowned and stopped reading. "It's about the Tag Moran gang, all right, but they didn't catch them."

"Oh," said Wesson.

Brockman read on, and when he had finished it, he looked up at Wesson. "Charlie, the Moran gang robbed the bank in Vernal, Utah, five days ago, then three days ago, robbed the bank in Evanston. Tag shot a bank teller in Vernal and killed him. Then in Evanston, Tag shot and killed a bank customer who tried to stop them. Sheriff Billington chased them with a posse but lost them. He thinks I should bring some deputies and see if we can track them down."

"I'm all for it, Chief. You remember that I asked to be one of those deputies if it came to this."

"Yes."

"How about it?"

"You're on. Let's see, the deputies who are here in town right now are Tom Lewis, Steve Hagan, and Roger Thurston, right?"

"Right."

"Okay, I'll have Roger fill in for you here in the office, and Tom and Steve will go with us. I want you to wire Sheriff Billington that three deputies and I will leave by train today. I have a hunch that the Moran gang just might hit the bank in Green River next. Tell Billington we'll let him know how it goes in Green River. Then wire Sheriff Mike Randall in Rock Springs and tell him what's happened in Vernal and Evanston, and that we'll be there tomorrow. We'll rent horses in Rock Springs and be in the saddle to ride to Green River."

"Yes, sir."

"I'll find Tom, Steve, and Roger and set things up. Then I'll ride home and let Breanna know what I'm doing. We'll take the next train to Cheyenne, which leaves in two hours. Then we'll grab the next train out of Cheyenne heading west."

"I can't wait, Chief," said Charlie, showing his teeth. "We've got to bring that gang to justice."

Sixteen

In Rock Springs, Wyoming, Sweetwater County Sheriff Mike Randall sat behind his desk while the afternoon sun slanted through the office windows, and ran his gaze over the faces of his three deputies. "Yes, gentlemen, I fully believe the Moran gang will hit our bank next. I'm really glad that Chief U.S. Marshal John Brockman and his three deputies are coming. This could very well be the downfall of Tag Moran and his gang."

"Have you met Chief Brockman in person, Sheriff?" asked Deputy Ross Allen.

"Yes. When he first arrived in Denver to become chief U.S. marshal, I happened to be there. I went to his office, introduced myself to him, and we had a nice chat. Of course, I had heard a great deal about him when he was traveling the West as the mysterious John Stranger."

"Supposed to be faster'n greased lightning on the draw, isn't he?" said Deputy Corey Rapp.

Randall grinned. "That's putting it mildly. A lot of hotshot gunslingers have tried to outdraw him just to make a name for themselves. Most of them did make a name for themselves, all right — on tombstones or grave markers. A few lived through the ordeal, only because Brockman was able to put them down without killing them." He chuckled. "And the ones I know about who lived could never fast-draw again because Brockman purposely put a bullet in each one's gun arm."

"I'm really looking forward to meeting him, Sheriff," said Deputy Rick Lampton. "I know a family up in Lander who was down and out financially, and John Stranger came to their rescue. Gave them — I forget now, how much — but gave them quite a sizeable amount of money."

The sheriff started to comment, but his eye caught sight of four riders drawing up to the hitch rail outside the office. A grin split his face. "He's here."

Outside, as Chief U.S. Marshal John Brockman and his deputies were dismounting, they saw the sheriff and his deputies come out the door.

Brockman and Randall shook hands,

then introductions were made and the lawmen shook hands all around.

As they were filing inside, Brockman was walking next to the sheriff. "Mike, have you heard anything about the Moran gang since I wired you yesterday? Do you know if they're still in the area?"

"That they are, Chief. They robbed the bank in Green River about this time yesterday afternoon. Got away clean. I've got a powerful hunch that they'll lay low for a few days, then hit our bank right here in Rock Springs."

"I have the same powerful hunch, Mike. Let's sit down with our deputies and devise us a plan."

Two days later — Thursday, October 14 — Tag Moran and his gang rode out of a tree-lined gully just west of Rock Springs and headed across the rolling prairie toward the town.

"Boys," said Tag, "so far on this trip, we've done well for ourselves. We should have a pretty good haul at this bank too. Then we'll hightail it back into Colorado and find us a good place to hide for a few days. Once we're sure the coast is clear, we'll head back to the hideout."

Soon they rode into Rock Springs and

paused at Main Street, looking both ways.

Tony Chacone was first to spot the sign to their right a block away that read: Bank of Rock Springs. "There it is, Tag," he said, pointing. "Okay, boys. Let's go do it."

As they rode up to the front of the bank, the clock on the sign told them it was ten minutes before three o'clock.

Bart Moran grinned. "Should be plenty of cash in the tellers' drawers right now."

"Not to mention what they've got stashed in the vault," said Jason.

"Yeah," Gib Tully said. "More in the kitty for our future life in California!"

As the five outlaws were dismounting, Tag said, "Okay, boys. I'll lead in as usual and announce that we're holding the place up. Do your stuff."

Tag walked a couple steps ahead of the other four and ran his gaze around to see if anyone on the street was watching. He saw no one looking their way. He pulled his revolver from his holster just before he reached the door. The others drew their guns at the same time and followed their leader inside the bank.

Tag quickly counted three customers at the tellers' windows, but before he could announce loudly that they were there to hold up the bank, he froze in place when eight lawmen rose up promptly from behind desks and tables on every side and cocked guns pointed at him and his men. One tall, dark-haired lawman said, "Drop your guns and get those hands in the air!"

Sweat beaded on Tag's brow as he looked at his gang members. "Give it up, boys. We don't have a chance."

The others followed suit as Tag dropped his revolver and it clattered on the hardwood floor. Dismay was on their faces as they raised their hands above their heads.

"I'm Chief United States Marshal John Brockman!" boomed the dark-haired man. "Tag Moran, you and your henchmen are under arrest."

The gang members stood mute as the lawmen closed in, picked up their guns, and began handcuffing them with their hands behind their backs.

As the handcuffs made their clicking sounds, Tag looked at Brockman, his face twisted. "How do you know who I am? Ain't no lawmen got a picture of me."

"No photographs, Moran, but plenty of artists' sketches. That's how we know it was you who killed that bank employee in Vernal and the bank customer in Evanston."

Tag's face blanched and he licked his lips nervously.

"You and your cohorts are going to be locked up in Sheriff Randall's jail for right now," Brockman said levelly. "Bank robbery is a federal offense, as I'm sure you know. The closest federal judge is in Rawlins. My deputies and I will take you there tomorrow to face Judge George Yeager. It'll be quite convenient that way, since the Wyoming Territorial Prison is at Rawlins."

Tag drew a grating breath. A coldness washed over him that made his flesh crawl. He stared at Brockman, but his lips stayed pressed together in a thin line.

Sheriff Randall said, "Chief, I'll have Deputy Ross Allen drive one of our wagons. He will drive you, your deputies, and your prisoners to Rawlins. You can take your rented horses back to the stable."

Brockman smiled. "Thanks, Mike. If you'll have your deputies feed Tag and his bunch some supper, my boys and I will take you to one of Rock Springs' cafés and feed you."

Randall nodded. "It's a deal, Chief."

"Since it's a hundred miles from here to Rawlins, we'll head out right after supper, okay?"

"Sure," said Randall, looking at Deputy Ross Allen. "Okay with you, Ross?"

"Sure," said Allen. "The quicker we can get these low-down outlaws to Judge Yeager, the better."

In the Sweetwater County Jail, the Moran gang was split up into two adjacent cells. Tag and his two brothers were in one cell, and Gib and Tony were in the other.

When supper was brought to them by Deputies Corey Rapp and Rick Lampton, none of them had much appetite. The deputies left, and the gang members sat on their bunks and picked at their food.

After a while, Tag gave up on eating and laid his plate and coffee cup aside.

Bart did the same. "Tag, we should have listened to Kathryn. She was right. We should've taken what we had and gone to California. Now look at us."

Tag sat on his bunk, his face resting in his hands, and stared at the floor.

In the adjacent cell, Gib nodded, looking through the bars. "You're right, Bart. We should've followed my sweet wife's advice. Now we're gonna be locked up for years in that prison at Rawlins."

Jason's features were almost as pallid as those of his oldest brother. "What's bothering me is what that judge will do to Tag. He'll sentence him to hang as sure as anything for killing those men in Vernal and Evanston."

Tony peered through the bars at the sick-looking Tag Moran. "I wish there was some way we could break out of here."

Tag raised his head and set dismal eyes on him. "Me too, Tony, but there isn't. The best time would be when we're riding in that wagon toward Rawlins. But with Brockman and his three deputies escorting us, we ain't got a chance. It's thirty or forty years for you guys in that stinking prison, and the hangman's rope for me."

At nine-thirty the next morning Deputy Ross Allen pulled rein in front of the Carbon County courthouse in Rawlins, Wyoming. Chief U.S. Marshal John Brockman was on the seat next to Allen. The three federal deputies were in the bed of the wagon with the outlaws, who had their hands handcuffed behind their backs. All five faces were pictures of total gloom.

Brockman turned around on the seat and looked at his deputies. "I'll go in first and talk to Judge Yeager. Be back as soon as I can."

Judge George Yeager had met the chief

U.S. marshal on a couple of occasions in years gone by, and warmly welcomed him into his office when his secretary, Millie Warner, ushered him in. When Yeager heard how Brockman and his deputies had apprehended the Moran gang, he was elated. Yeager told Brockman he already knew about the recent robberies of the banks in Vernal, Evanston, and Green River, and was aware that Tag Moran had been identified as the one who killed the bank employee in Vernal and the bank customer in Evanston.

Yeager smiled from ear to ear. "Good work, John! Those no-goods have run rampant all over this part of the country. I guess you know they also robbed a stagecoach here in Wyoming not long ago. Got fifty thousand dollars."

"Yes. I know about it. I want you to know that Sheriff Mike Randall and his men found the money in the Moran gang's saddlebags that they had taken from the banks in Vernal, Evanston, and Green River. The money will be returned to the banks."

Yeager was a beefy man with a round face. He smiled again. "Great! I'm glad to hear it." He paused, then said, "John, I have court cases booked today, and through next Wednesday. I can have the trial for the Moran gang next Thursday, October 21."

Brockman nodded.

"Until then, I'll have the sheriff keep Tag and his bunch in jail here in town."

Brockman nodded again.

The judge then looked toward the open door that led to his secretary's office. "Millie! Would you come in here for a moment, please?"

Millie quickly appeared at the door. "Yes, your honor?"

"I need you to go across the street to the town's photographer and tell him I want him to go to the county jail yet today and take pictures of each man in the Moran gang. We've never had photographs of those outlaws, and we should have them."

"Yes, sir."

"And, Millie?"

"Yes, sir?"

"Will you go first to the *Rawlins Herald* office and have them send one of their reporters over here right away? I want to alert the paper of the Moran gang's capture and upcoming trial. I'll have the people at the *Herald* wire the news to newspapers all over Wyoming, Colorado, and Nebraska, and send them copies of the photographs by train and stagecoach. They should have those photographs so they can publish them in their papers along with this story and let people see exactly what each gang member looks like."

When Millie was gone on her errands, Yeager said, "John, I'm positive the gang members will be convicted in their trial. And I'm also positive that since Tag Moran killed those men in Vernal and Evanston during the robberies, he will get the death sentence. And because those other gang members were in on the robberies when people were killed, they will all be sentenced to life in prison."

"I have no doubt of it, Judge," said John, rising to his feet. "My men and I will go ahead and take the prisoners over to the jail so the sheriff can lock them up."

"All right," said Yeager, also standing up.

"Once we've got them behind bars, my men and I will head for the railroad station and catch the first train to Cheyenne, then we'll head for Denver on the next train south."

Yeager moved around his desk and shook Brockman's hand. "That was excellent work, John — trapping the Moran gang right there in the bank. And just think! The banks in Wyoming, Colorado, and Nebraska won't have to fear them any longer. You and your deputies will be heroes when this story hits the newspapers!"

Dr. Dane Logan was sitting in a coach on the afternoon train from Cheyenne to Denver. He was alone on the seat, and while looking through the window at the magnificent Rocky Mountains in the distance to the west, he let his mind wander back to the moment at the Cheyenne railroad station some thirty minutes ago when he went through the difficulty of saying good-bye to his parents. They were so special in his life. Because of them his dream of becoming a physician and surgeon had come to fruition.

"Bless them, Lord," he said in a whisper. "As I look back, I know in my heart that once I was released from prison, I would have eventually become a doctor. But knowing I had their love and support, not to mention the financial aid they gave me, made the road a lot easier and much more pleasant.

"Lord, thank You that Dad already has a new partner. That will make my new venture a lot more enjoyable. I must always make time for my parents, Lord, even though we'll be living some distance apart. Help me never to neglect writing to them and help me to make time to go see them as often as I can."

Dane's mind then jumped ahead to the future.

He smiled to himself. *My own practice. Wow! Who would ever have believed that a homeless street waif from New York City could achieve this in his life? Once again my heavenly Father has proven Himself faithful.* "I promise You, Lord, that I will do my very best in Central City to please You in all I do. I ask You to give me wisdom, and help me to use the skills with which You have blessed me."

Dr. Dane's line of sight focused once again on the beautiful Rockies as they gleamed in the autumn sunshine; then he took out his pocket watch. He glanced down at it, noted the time, and realized he would soon be in Denver.

His heartbeat quickened as he pictured Tharyn in his mind and knew he would see her soon. *Something is definitely happening in my heart,* he thought as a grin crossed his face. "Lord, have You really kept Tharyn and me for each other?"

The very thought made him catch his breath. *I think I'm beginning to feel more for her than just brotherly love.*

Dane felt elation at the thought.

Tharyn Tabor and Breanna Brockman were standing in front of the counter at the nurses' station in the surgical ward, talking, when Breanna looked down the corridor past Tharyn. "Here he comes!"

Tharyn pivoted around and let a smile light up her face. Dane smiled back. When he drew near, Tharyn was so glad to see him that she forgot there were people around and dashed to him.

Dane held her close and said, "Sorry I'm a couple days past a week, but it took longer to wrap things up than I thought. Certain patients needing my care after surgery, and that kind of thing."

"I understand, big brother. I got your wire."

"I had to wire Dr. Fraser too," he said as they let go of each other and Dane found himself looking at Breanna.

"Nice to see you again, Dr. Dane," said Breanna. "So are you heading for Central City immediately?"

"When I wired Dr. Fraser that it would be a little longer than a week before I could leave Cheyenne, I told him I thought I'd reach Denver today — Friday the fifteenth. I told him I would stay over in Denver, go to church with Tharyn on Sunday, then buy a horse on Monday and ride to Central City."

Tharyn sprang up and down on her tiptoes. "Oh, Dane, that's great! You'll love our pastor, his wife, and the church. There is especially one person at church that I want you to see. It's somebody you know."

Dane's brow furrowed. "Somebody I know? Who?"

Tharyn giggled, shaking her head. "I'm not telling. You'll find out on Sunday."

He laughed. "Okay, if that's the way you want it."

She took hold of his hand. "Oh, I'm so glad you'll be here over the weekend."

"Well, I wish I could stay longer, but I really need to get settled in my new home at the boardinghouse and get started in my new practice."

"I understand. It's just going to be so good to have you so close."

"Oh yes. I'll be back and forth between Central City and Denver a lot. Not only to bring patients here, but to see my little sis. The only thing that might slow me down will be heavy snows this winter."

A bright light showed in Dane's eyes. Tharyn and Breanna smiled at each other, seeing his happiness at finding his niche.

"Dr. Dane, my husband has been away with some of his deputies, chasing down a gang of bank robbers, but I got a wire telling me they had caught the gang and left them in jail in Rawlins where they will stand trial before a federal judge. John and his deputies were delayed a little in Cheyenne, but they will be home on the early train from Cheyenne tomorrow morning. He's been wanting to meet you. He'll get to do that at church on Sunday."

"I'll look forward to meeting him, ma'am."

Breanna smiled. "Well, I'd better get to work, or I'll get fired."

Tharyn laughed. "I can just see you getting fired, Breanna!"

Breanna gave her a quick hug, then hurried away.

Tharyn looked at the clock on the wall behind the counter. "It's almost time for shift change, Dane. Will you ride home with Papa and me and have supper at our house?"

"Sure will. I'll get a room at one of the hotels later."

David Tabor was glad to see Dane with Tharyn when he pulled up in front of the hospital.

At the supper table, the Tabors and Dane talked about his new practice.

Dane then changed the subject by saying, "Didn't the Ross family used to go to your church?"

"They sure did," said David. "It was really hard to see them move away. So many of us in the church got very close to Mike and Julie and those precious handicapped children they had adopted off the orphan trains." Suddenly David frowned. "How do you know the Rosses?"

"Well, when I was on the orphan train that ended up taking me to Cheyenne, I had a little friend named Kenny Atwood."

"Kenny!" exclaimed Tharyn. "You were on the same orphan train with him!"

"Yes. Mr. and Mrs. Ross came to Cheyenne to pick him up, because they had already arranged with Charles Loring Brace to pick him up there. Did Kenny do all right with his wooden leg?"

"He sure did," said Kitty. "The Rosses had a prearrangement like that with a blind girl named Leanne Ladd, only it was a train that was coming to Denver. Tharyn and Leanne were on the same orphan train. Even though Mike sold his law practice here in Denver and moved to Bozeman, Montana, to take over a practice there, Leanne and Tharyn still write to each other often."

Dane grinned. "Isn't that something? Kenny and I still write back and forth. It's hard to believe that he's eighteen now."

Dane noticed Tharyn grinning at him. "What's that grin about?"

"Oh, it's just because you're going to be so surprised when you see a certain person at church on Sunday."

"You mean somebody I know who came here on the orphan train with you?"

Tharyn closed her eyes and moved her head back and forth. "I'm saying no more. You will have to wait until Sunday to see who it is."

Dane chuckled. "Okay, smarty. I'll wait till Sunday."

Chief U.S. Marshal John Brockman and his three deputies arrived back in Denver at seven-thirty the next morning. At the office, John told the other deputies who were present about capturing the Tag Moran gang, and their upcoming trial next week. There were cheers.

At the Brockman place, Breanna was sweeping the front porch when she saw the big black horse with the tall man turn into the lane at the road and head for the house.

Although Breanna had learned over the years to always trust her lawman husband to God's protective care, and though she already knew he had safely captured the Moran gang, a sweet feeling of relief came over her as she watched him riding her direction.

She leaned the broom against the wall, tugged the shawl she wore up around her neck, and descended the steps.

John drew Ebony to a stop, slid from the saddle, and took her in his arms. He lifted her feet off the ground and swung her around in a circle. "I declare, Mrs. Brockman, you just get more beautiful all the time! I didn't think you could become more beautiful, but somehow God, in His marvelous handiwork, finds a way to do it."

Breanna laughed as he lowered her back to the earth. "You sure are good for a woman's ego, Chief United States Marshal John Brockman." She placed a hand on each side of his face, and while her own face glowed happily, she said, "Thank the Lord you're back home safe once more, my love."

She raised up on her tiptoes and kissed

the man who so long ago had captured her heart.

Suddenly they were interrupted by two squealing voices. "Papa! Papa!"

John let his arms fall from around Breanna, turned, and opened them to his children.

Later, over lunch, Breanna looked across the table and said, "John, darling, Dr. Dane Logan is back and will be going to Central City on Monday to take over Dr. Fraser's practice."

"That's good."

"He will be coming to church with the Tabors tomorrow. Since you're back now, I'd like to have the Tabors and Dr. Dane for Sunday dinner."

"Great idea! After all I've heard about this young physician, I can't wait to meet him."

Breanna smiled. "And I want to invite another family too. Dr. Dane is in for a surprise at church tomorrow, and I want to sort of add some icing on the cake."

John grinned. "Whatever you say, sweetheart."

Sunday morning was bright with a slight chill in the air. The church was on the west edge of town, almost in the country.

As the Tabor buggy pulled into the churchyard, other vehicles were being parked in the parking lot. People were moving in small groups toward the front of the white frame building. Tharyn pointed out the couple at the door who were shaking hands, telling Dane they were Pastor and Mrs. Nathan Blandford.

Dane noticed Tharyn looking around as they made their way to the porch. He wondered who this person was that she was so secretive about.

When they reached the door, David introduced Dr. Dane to the pastor and his wife, who welcomed him heartily.

When they stepped inside, Tharyn saw the Brockman family and hurried to show Dane to them. John Brockman warmly shook his hand, telling him how glad he was to meet him.

Tharyn then guided Dane to other people and introduced them to him.

All the while, her eyes were roaming over the auditorium. Suddenly she saw the person for whom she had been looking. She waved to her, then pointed at Dane. The young woman smiled and nodded. She said something to the people she was with and hurried toward Tharyn.

Dane happened to look at Tharyn at that

moment, then followed her line of sight to the young woman who was smiling at Tharyn as she wove her way through the crowd toward them.

He fixed his attention on her and blinked his eyes. "Tharyn! Is this your surprise?"

She looked up at him. "Uh-huh. Tell me who she is!"

"Why — why, it's Melinda Scott!"

Tharyn giggled. "It sure is. Only her last name is Kenyon now."

Melinda drew up and smiled at Dane. "Hello, Dr. Logan. Do you remember me?"

Dane was smiling broadly. "I sure do! You've grown up, Melinda, but I knew you the instant I saw you coming this way. Tharyn told me she had a surprise for me, that someone I knew would be here at church."

Melinda had tears in her eyes. "It's been a long time since those days in the Manhattan alley, but you were so good to me. And more than anything, it was your witness to me about Jesus that brought me to salvation."

As she spoke, she reached toward him and embraced him. Tharyn looked on and smiled.

Melinda used a hankie to dab at her eyes. "I've told my adoptive parents stories about you so many times, Dane, how you took such good care of the rest of us orphans in the alley. And then, of course, since we moved here from Topeka, Kansas, three years ago, Tharyn and I have talked much about you. I was so surprised when she told me you had shown up at the hospital and were now a doctor in partnership with your adoptive father in Cheyenne. Then just this past week, she told me that you are buying Dr. Robert Fraser's practice up in Central City."

Dane smiled. "Yes, and I'm looking forward to my new life there."

Melinda dabbed at the tears in her eyes with the hankie again. "I want you to meet my parents and my fiancé, Dane."

Tharyn and Dane followed her to the people she had been with moments before, and Melinda introduced him to her adoptive parents, Frank and Hattie Kenyon, then to her handsome young fiancé, Dr. Tim Braden. While the two doctors shook hands, Tim explained that he was a graduate of the Kansas City School of Medicine and was now doing his internship at Mile High Hospital.

"Oh, really?" said Dane.

"Yes. I'm just starting my second year. Melinda and I are planning to get married after I finish my internship and find a place to work in a practice wherever the Lord leads us."

"That's great, Dr. Tim. I wish you the very best."

"Thank you, Dr. Dane. Say, I heard about the marvelous job you did on Elsa Johnson's hip. It's the talk of the hospital."

Dane smiled. "So she's doing all right?"

"She sure is. Dr. Jess White was bragging about you in a staff meeting on Friday."

Dane chuckled. "Well, I'm flattered."

The organist started playing the pump organ, and people began finding places to sit in the pews. David and Kitty Tabor had just drawn up. Hattie Kenyon ran her gaze over the small group. "Frank and I would like to invite you to come to our place after the service this evening for a snack. Okay?"

The Tabors agreed, and everyone soon found their place just as the song leader called for everyone to stand. The Sunday school service was opened with a rousing gospel song.

John and Breanna Brockman sat in the same pew with the Tabors and Dr. Dane Logan. Just before the man who taught the auditorium class stood up to teach,

Tharyn whispered to Dane that he would enjoy the snack time at the Kenyons' after the service. She told him that the Kenyons lived in the country near the Brockman place.

Dane found the Sunday school lesson very interesting, and commented to Tharyn about it when Sunday school was over. The congregational singing in the morning service was uplifting. Dane was pleased when at announcement and offering time, he was introduced by the pastor, along with a man and wife who were newcomers to Denver and were also visiting for the first time.

Dane very much liked Pastor Nathan Blandford's preaching, and was glad to see the man and woman, who had been introduced at the same time he was, walk the aisle at invitation time and receive Jesus as their Saviour.

The fellowship was sweet at the Brockman home during the luscious meal Breanna had prepared — with Ginny's help, of course.

After dinner, Dane and Tharyn spent some time alone, walking around the six acres of the Brockman place. As they strolled leisurely across the pasture, they talked about how they missed each other all those years.

When Dane saw tears in Tharyn's eyes, he stopped. "Little sis, may I hug you?"

Tharyn reached for him, and he took her in his arms. They held on to each other for several minutes, then Dane took her hand as they walked on. Neither one voiced what they were feeling, but in their minds, they were both wondering if maybe the Lord had chosen them for each other.

Dane said, "You haven't mentioned a man in your life."

She looked up into his eyes. "There isn't one." She told him in brief about her relationship with Scott Hubbard, then followed by telling him about Pastor Blandford's talk to her about Isaac and Rebekah, and how it helped her to see that Scott was not the man God had chosen for her.

"That's really good," said Dane. "God's Word has answers for all of our questions, doesn't it?"

"It sure does. Dane?"

"Mm-hmm?"

"Is there a young woman in your life?"

He shook his head. "No. I'm just waiting for the Lord to send that right girl to me."

No more was said, but that part of the

conversation had them both thinking that possibly God was doing this very thing in their lives right now.

They returned to the house, and Tharyn and Dane went home with her parents.

After the evening service — which Dane enjoyed very much — the Tabors went to the Kenyon home in the country for the snack Hattie had prepared. Dr. Tim Braden was also invited, which didn't surprise anyone.

During the time of fellowship, Dane was told by the Kenyons how Frank and Hattie had chosen Melinda from among the orphans at the Topeka railroad station. Tharyn spoke up and told of the emotional parting she and Melinda experienced, and how hard it was for them to separate. The Kenyons gave Tharyn their address in Topeka so she would write to Melinda once she had been chosen farther down the line. As soon as Tharyn was chosen by the Tabors in Denver, she wrote to Melinda, and from that time on, they corresponded regularly by mail.

Frank then explained to Dane that he had been employed as assistant manager at the Denning Hardware Company store in Topeka. Then, in June 1877 he was approached by the owner and offered the manager's job at Denning Hardware Company's store in Denver. He accepted the offer, and he would never forget how happy it made Melinda when she learned that they were moving to Denver.

"We've had so many wonderful times together since they moved here, Dane," said Tharyn.

Dane grinned. "I can imagine."

Tharyn chuckled. "Melinda has become quite a horsewoman since they moved here. She's let me ride Abe many a time when I've come for a visit, but I can't compare to her when it comes to riding. She's really good. She rides Abe for an hour or better every morning, Monday through Saturday. Except in bad weather, of course."

Dane nodded, then looked at Melinda. "Your horse's name is Abe?"

"Uh-huh. He's a four-year-old bay gelding with white blaze and white stockings. I named him after my favorite president of the United States."

"Abraham Lincoln."

"Right."

"He was a great president, for sure."

At that point, Dr. Tim pressed Dr. Dane, wanting to know how he had learned to do an ivory ball hip replacement. Everyone else listened intently as Dane told his story.

Soon it was time to go. The Tabors and Dane thanked the Kenyons for having them as their guests. Frank Kenyon told Dr. Dane that he and his family would be praying for him as he took over the practice in Central City from Dr. Fraser.

Dane and Tharyn enjoyed the ride back into town, sitting side by side in the backseat of the buggy. When they arrived at the hotel where Dane would stay for the night, Dane bid David and Kitty goodnight, then kissed Tharyn's hand and told her he would come by the hospital in the morning and see her just before he headed for Central City.

The next morning, Dane went to a stable and bought a horse. Soon he was at the hospital, and found Tharyn at the nurses' station in the surgical wing. She explained that she had just finished assisting one of the doctors perform a surgery, and had a few minutes before she was to do another one.

"I'll walk with you to the door," she said.

"That would be great."

While they moved down the corridor

that led to the lobby, Dane said, "Tharyn, I'll be back to see you as soon as I can. I'm going to come to Denver as often as possible so we can have time together."

"I'll look forward to every minute we can be together."

"Me too."

They had now entered the lobby and were headed toward the double glass doors that led to the street and the parking lot. When they drew up to the doors, Dane noted that they had some privacy at the moment.

He moved close to her. "Could I hug you before I go?"

"You sure can!"

They enjoyed their brief embrace; then as Tharyn watched him pass through the doors and head for his newly purchased horse, she whispered, "I love you, Dane."

When Dane reached the horse, he looked back to see Tharyn watching him. She waved. He waved back, then mounted up.

As he put the horse in motion, he waved at her one more time. When he reached the street and put the animal to a trot, he said in a soft voice, "Tharyn, you do something to my heart that no other girl has ever done."

Seventeen

It was a cold, brisk cloudless day and the sun was at its apex in the azure sky when Dr. Dane Logan rode into Central City and dismounted in front of Dr. Robert Fraser's office on Monday, October 18.

He dismounted, tied the reins to the hitch rail, and patted the horse's neck. "Well, Pal, it's time for me to get the wheels rolling so I can buy the practice. There'll be a nice barn and corral for you at the boardinghouse, I'm sure."

Pal nickered softly and bobbed his head as if he understood.

Dane stroked the horse's long face. "You see why I named you Pal? You agree with everything I tell you."

Pal nickered again.

Dane started around one end of the hitch rail and spoke to two older men who were passing by on the boardwalk. He was about to step up on the boardwalk, but when he looked up at the sign by the door, he stopped. *Robert Fraser, M.D.*

A smile broke over his features. "Hmm. I'll have to have a new sign made. 'Dane Logan, M.D.' Wow, does that sound good!"

He glanced up and down the street, taking a moment to better familiarize himself with his new town. He patted his horse's neck again. "Welcome home, Pal. Welcome home."

Pal nickered once more.

When Dane opened the door and stepped into the office, Nadine Wahl smiled at him from behind her desk. "Hello, Dr. Logan. Welcome back."

He moved to the desk. "Thank you, Nadine. How are you today?"

"Just fine, thank you."

"Is Dr. Fraser in?"

"Mm-hmm. He's with a patient at the moment, but he should be through shortly. He received your wire, of course, so he has left his calendar open the rest of the day so the two of you can go to the attorney's office and finalize the sale of the practice."

At that moment, the door to the examining room opened, and Dr. Fraser emerged beside his patient. The man thanked him for his good care, paid Nadine, and left.

Dr. Fraser smiled warmly. "Well, Dr. Logan, it's lunchtime. How about I buy your lunch; then we'll go see my attorney and make everything legal on the sale of the practice."

"We'll do that, my friend," said Dane, "but I will buy *your* lunch."

Fraser winked at Nadine. "How do you like that? His name isn't even on the ownership papers yet, and he's already bossing me around."

Nadine laughed. "I guess you'd better let him pay for lunch, Doctor."

It was just past 2:30 that afternoon when Nadine looked up from her desk to see the two doctors coming through the door. She smiled. "Well, that's a pair o' docs if I ever saw a pair o' docs."

The doctors looked at each other and frowned.

Dane said, "Pardon me, Mrs. Wahl, but a paradox is a statement that seems contrary to common sense, yet is perhaps true. We haven't said anything yet."

"Yes," said the silver-haired Fraser. "What are you talking about?"

Nadine laughed. "Not P-A-R-A-D-O-X. Two doctors. Get it? A pair o' docs."

Both men laughed.

347

"Nadine," said Fraser, "you're a case; you know that?"

She smiled. "Guess I am."

"But I'll keep you around as long as I can," said Dr. Dane.

She smiled back. "That's something we need to talk about, Dr. Logan. But right now, I want to know if the official papers have been signed and the earnest money on the practice has been paid."

"The papers are all signed, and the earnest money has been paid," said Fraser. "In fact, because our young doctor did a hip replacement in Denver and was paid generously for it, I got more earnest money than I expected. If I hadn't promised Dr. Dane I'd stick around, I'd take Esther on a cruise to Europe."

Nadine snickered. "Sure you would!"

Fraser laughed, then looked at Dane. "In all seriousness, I will be at your side here at the office for the next several days just in case you need me. Even after that, as I already promised, I'll be available whenever I'm needed. And, of course, there will be times when you have to take patients to the hospital in Denver to perform surgery on them, and you'll need this old man to fill in for you."

Dane smiled. "This means more to me

than I can ever tell you, Doctor. I'm sure I will need you often."

"Well, while we're talking business," said Nadine, "what I'd like to talk about, Dr. Logan, is my future here."

"Yes?"

"Well, I'm putting some years on and I'll be wanting to retire within the next year or so. I'm telling you now so you will have time to find another nurse to take my job."

"That's fair enough, ma'am," said Dr. Dane. "I'd rather keep you on, but I can understand why you want to retire."

Nadine smiled. "Thank you, Doctor."

"Well," spoke up the older man, "guess I'd better take you to your boardinghouse."

The doctors walked down the street together with Dane leading Pal. At the next intersection, they turned and walked a half-block to a white frame building.

"This is it," said Fraser. "There's a nice barn and a small corral at the back for your horse."

"I figured so. I didn't realize the boardinghouse would be this close to the office."

"Well, I could have reserved you a room at one of the other two boardinghouses in town, but they are not as nice as this one and they are both farther from the office."

"You're a true gentleman, sir. You really are."

"I try," Fraser said, grinning. "The lady who owns this place is a widow. Her husband died four years ago."

"I see."

They entered the front door, and Dr. Fraser led Dane into a small office. He introduced him to the owner, Laura Sparks, whom Dane figured was in her late fifties.

Laura said, "I'm honored to have Central City's new doctor living in my boardinghouse, Dr. Logan. Let's go upstairs and I'll show you your room."

Dr. Fraser accompanied them as they climbed the stairs to the second floor, and Laura guided Dr. Dane to his room. When she opened the door and stepped in ahead of the men, Dane was pleasantly surprised at the size of the room. It was more like two rooms.

"Wow! Lots of space, Mrs. Sparks. I like it."

"This is my largest room, Dr. Logan. I was glad it was vacant when Dr. Fraser told me you were coming to town to take over his practice. I believe you will enjoy it."

"I know I will," Dane said, moving in a little farther and running his gaze around the room. "I'm very fortunate that it's available."

It was a corner room, with windows facing both south and west. The clean windows sparkled in the sunlight. They were adorned with dark green draperies that could be pulled closed when needed.

A large colorful rug lay in the center of the highly polished wooden floor. One end of the room was furnished with an upholstered sofa and matching chair. A mahogany desk and chair stood near one of the windows, and a small bookcase rested against the same wall.

In the adjacent space was a large four-poster bed, covered with a green, rust, and cream counterpane. Beside the bed was a bedside table, and a step away was a mahogany dresser. A small fireplace was in one wall, already supplied with kindling and logs.

"This is wonderful, Mrs. Sparks," said the young physician. "I couldn't ask for anything nicer than this."

"I'm glad you're happy with it."

"I sure am. And Dr. Fraser told me you have a place where I can keep my horse."

"Sure do. Right out back. I keep hay and grain in the barn and there's no extra charge. There's a water tank too."

Dane smiled and shook his head. "Great!"

"Breakfast is between six and eight each morning, and dinner is at six-thirty. Of course with your erratic schedule, Doctor, I'll be happy to keep a plate of dinner in the warming oven, and you can feel free to eat whenever you come home. The dining room is on the first floor, just down the hall from the office."

"Thank you, Mrs. Sparks. Well, I'm ready to move in!"

Lucinda Moran and Kathryn Tully were pulling into Fort Collins to purchase groceries and supplies.

Lucinda guided the team to a hitching post in front of Decker's Clothing Store, a short distance down the street from the general store. When they climbed out of the wagon, they saw a small group of people on the boardwalk, gathered around a man who was holding a newspaper up for them to see the front page. They heard a woman in the group say happily, "Oh, I'm so glad to know that Moran gang is behind bars!"

Lucinda and Kathryn looked at each other, eyes wide. They stepped up to the newspaper rack in front of the clothing store, which was stuffed with copies of the day's edition of the *Fort Collins Gazette*. The bold headlines announced: TAG MORAN GANG APPREHENDED IN WYOMING!

Lucinda quickly paid the attendant for a paper, and they moved down the boardwalk to look at it. Lucinda held the paper so they could both read it at the same time.

Their hearts pounded as they read the story of how the gang had recently held up the banks in Vernal, Utah, and in Evanston and Green River, Wyoming. The article was careful to point out that in Vernal, Tag Moran had shot and killed a bank employee, and that he had also shot and killed a bank customer during the robbery in Evanston.

The article went on to tell how on Tuesday, October 12, Chief U.S. Marshal John Brockman of Denver and three of his deputies — with the help of Sweetwater County Sheriff Mike Randall and his three deputies — got the drop on the Moran gang when they entered the Rock Springs bank to rob it. On page three, there were photographs of all five gang members.

Continuing on page three, the article explained that the gang was being held in the

Carbon County jail in Rawlins. Their trial was set for Thursday, October 21, over which federal judge George Yeager would preside. The article speculated that Tag Moran would hang for murder and that the rest of the gang would receive life sentences in the Wyoming Territorial Prison at Rawlins because they were in on robberies when people were killed.

Kathryn and Lucinda looked at each other, their faces pale.

With dry mouth, Lucinda said, "Kathryn, there's nothing we can do. I'm sure glad we have plenty of money at the cabin."

Misty-eyed, Kathryn nodded. "With Bart and Gib in prison for the rest of their lives, all we can do is visit them as much as possible."

"Yes. That's all we can do."

With heavy hearts, the two women bought groceries and supplies and headed back to the cabin.

On that same afternoon, Buck Cummons pulled the stagecoach to a halt in front of the Wells Fargo office in Casper, Wyoming. When he and Doke Veatch entered the office, the Fargo agent showed them the day's edition of the *Casper Daily*

Sentinel, which had the same headlines and the same articles as the other newspapers in Wyoming, Colorado, and western Nebraska.

As agent, driver, and shotgunner talked about the gang's capture and fate, Doke swallowed hard. "I . . . I know what Tag did was wrong. He shouldn't have killed those men, and he shouldn't have been an outlaw in the first place. But I still owe him for saving my life."

Both agent and driver looked at Doke in amazement.

Doke went on. "I'll watch the news close, and if Tag really is sentenced to hang, I will have to ask for enough time off so I can go to the prison and see him before they hang him. I owe him that much."

Buck chuckled. "Doke, ol' pal, you really are a true friend."

On Friday morning, October 22, Chief U.S. Marshal John Brockman was in his office talking to two of his deputies who had just returned from tracking down a man who had beaten his wife to death in Denver. The man was now in the Denver County Jail.

John smiled. "Boys, you did an excellent job, and I commend you for it."

At that moment, there was a tap on the door, and Deputy Charlie Wesson stuck his head in. "Chief, I have a telegram for you."

"Come on in," said Brockman. As Charlie entered the room, John noticed that his face was grim. "What's wrong?"

Charlie handed him the yellow envelope. "Well, Chief, the telegram is from Judge George Yeager in Rawlins. Since I was going to find out anyway, the Western Union messenger told me the contents of the telegram. It's bad news. Go ahead and read it for yourself."

John looked at him warily as he tore the envelope open. He took out the telegram and began reading. He was pleased to learn that the gang members had been convicted by the jury yesterday. Witnesses had come from Vernal and Evanston to point out Tag Moran as the gang member who had shot and killed the two men. Tag had been sentenced to hang, and the other four were sentenced to life in the Wyoming Territorial Prison at Rawlins.

John was stunned as he read what Charlie had referred to as bad news. Judge Yeager went on to tell him that when two of the Carbon county sheriff's deputies were taking the gang members from the courthouse with the intention of walking them to the prison at gunpoint, a gunfight broke out on the street between a group of cattlemen and a group of sheep men. Bullets were flying, and being caught in the crossfire, one of the deputies was hit.

The five gang members were wearing handcuffs, but the cuffs were in front of their bodies. In all of the confusion when the deputy went down, Tag Moran grabbed his gun and shot the other deputy, killing him. The gang quickly stole saddled horses at hitch rails on the street and escaped. The sheriff formed a posse and went after them, but they eluded the posse. The Tag Moran gang was now at large again.

The judge's wire went on to tell the chief U.S. marshal that since he now had photographs of the five gang members, he was having wanted posters printed up and would send them to law enforcement offices all over Wyoming, Colorado, and western Nebraska to be posted in conspicuous places in their towns.

Brockman dropped the lengthy telegram on his desktop and sighed. "I sure hate to hear that those no-goods are loose again. At this time, I don't have the manpower at my disposal to go after them. All the other deputies are out on assignments, and I already have pressing new assignments for you two fellas who just got back."

On Saturday afternoon, Dr. Dane Logan rode into Denver. It was cold and overcast, and it smelled like snow when he dismounted in the parking lot at Mile High Hospital. He had thought about writing to Tharyn earlier in the week to let her know that he was coming to see her on Saturday, but he didn't want to get her hopes up and then have something happen on Saturday to prevent his coming. In the doctoring business, nothing was ever certain, including his free time.

When Dr. Dane approached the nurses' station in the surgical wing, he was told that Nurse Tabor was assisting a doctor in surgery and would be for at least another half hour. He then headed for the doctor's lounge and poured himself a steaming mug of coffee.

He was just about to sit down when he saw Dr. Tim Braden enter the room. When Braden saw him, he smiled and said, "Well, hello, Dr. Logan! What brings you here?"

"I just rode down from Central City to spend some time with Tharyn. Right now, she's assisting in surgery."

Pouring coffee into two mugs, Tim smiled. "You and Tharyn are really good friends, aren't you?"

"Yes, we are. She's one fine young lady."

Tim started to say something else, but thought better of it. "Well, I've got to meet Dr. Carroll in his office, so I'm taking him a cup of coffee too. See you soon, I hope."

"Me too," replied Dane. "Tell Melinda hello for me, okay?"

"Sure will." With that, Dr. Tim was gone.

For some twenty-five minutes, Dr. Dane perused a medical book that lay on a small table, then returned to the nurses' station. Tharyn was just coming down the corridor from the surgical washroom when she spotted Dane and rushed toward him. He saw her coming and hurried to meet her.

Smiling, Tharyn took hold of both Dane's hands. "Oh, I'm so glad you could come!"

"Well, it's only because Dr. Fraser is kind enough to be on call if someone up there needs a doctor. May I take you out for supper?"

Her smile widened. "You sure can. Papa is coming from home to pick me up since the bank's not open on Saturday. He'll be here at five o'clock as usual. He can ride your horse back home and we'll use his buggy."

At precisely five o'clock, David Tabor arrived, and the switch was made.

The restaurant was crowded, as it usually was on Saturday nights, and light snow was blanketing the streets of Denver. When they moved inside, Tharyn rubbed her hands together. "Oh, it feels good in here!"

The hostess knew Tharyn, and even though the place was busy, she found a corner table by a bay window. Dane seated Tharyn, then sat down across the table so he could look at her. After they had given their orders to a waitress, Tharyn asked how his first week as Central City's physician had gone. While Dane told her some stories from the week's activity, they watched the lazy snowflakes falling from the leaden sky. They were so engrossed in each other and their conversation that they failed to notice the Brockman family sitting at a nearby table.

John and Breanna had seen them come in and sit down, but purposely waited until the young couple had given their order to the waitress. Leaving Paul and Ginny at the table, John and Breanna moved to the table where Dane and Tharyn were sitting. When they spotted the Brockmans, Dane rose to his feet and greeted them.

"How long have you been in Denver, Dr. Dane?" asked John.

"Just rode in a little while ago so I could spend the evening with Tharyn and go to church with her tomorrow. I can do this because Dr. Robert Fraser remains on call for me."

"I'm so glad you have him to help in this way," said Breanna.

"Me too," said Dane. "I read in the *Rocky Mountain News* — which is delivered daily to Central City — that the Tag Moran gang was convicted, then escaped while being escorted to the Rawlins prison, Chief."

John sighed. "Yeah. I'm very unhappy about that. That nefarious bunch are cunningly elusive. They got away from the posse that chased them, as you read."

"Yes. Too bad."

"Well, one of these days they'll make some kind of mistake and get caught again."

"I sure hope you're right about that, Chief."

"Where are you staying tonight, Doctor?" Breanna asked.

"I'll get a room at one of the hotels."

"No need for that," spoke up John. "We have a guest room at our house. Whenever you come to Denver, you can stay with us — starting tonight."

Tharyn smiled as Dane said, "I'll just take you up on that offer. Thank you very much. I'll be there later this evening then. Do you have room for my horse in your barn?"

"Sure do."

"Okay. I'll just ride him to church in the morning."

"Of course."

"And I'm planning on going to the evening service, so I'll need to stay with you again tomorrow night. I'll leave for Central City Monday morning. I really don't think this snowstorm is going to amount to much."

"That's fine," said Breanna.

John saw their waitress bringing the dessert they had ordered, and walked with Breanna toward their table, saying over his shoulder that they would be looking for Dr. Dane later this evening at their home.

Some twenty minutes later, the Brockmans passed by the table while Dane and Tharyn were eating, and Paul and Ginny took a moment to stop and hug Tharyn.

When Dane and Tharyn finished their

meal, they put their coats on and Dane went to the counter to pay the bill. When that was done, they went outside to the buggy. It had already stopped snowing.

Dane helped Tharyn onto the seat, then hurried around the rear of the buggy and climbed in beside her. Before he took the reins in hand, he turned. "Tharyn, could I hug you?"

"You sure can!"

After the brief embrace, Dane looked into her eyes by the light of a nearby street lamp. "Tharyn, there is something I need to tell you."

These words took her back to the night when Scott Hubbard broke her heart, and immediately she was on edge. "Y-yes, Dane?"

"I — just can't hold it in any longer. I am head over heels in love with you."

Tharyn felt her heart suddenly beat against her rib cage. Excess moisture was instantly in her eyes. "Oh, Dane!"

He cupped her face in his hands, looking deeply into her teary eyes. "I loved you like a sister when we were living in the alley with the other orphans. But as time passed and I grew older — having no idea where you were — my love changed, and when I thought about you, it was different. I was falling *in* love with your memory, though I thought I would never see you again. And — and now that I have found you, I know I am *in* love with you. It isn't big brother love, it's deep, romantic love. I'm head over heels in love with you."

The tears began to spill down Tharyn's cheeks. Holding his gaze, she said, "Oh, Dane, it was the same with me as the years passed. My heart yearned for you, though we were lost to each other. Since you hadn't replied to my letters, as I told you, I figured you didn't want to keep in touch because you would be in prison for the rest of your life. You remember Russell Mims."

"Yes. He had ideas about you one day belonging to him. It was easy to see."

"Well, since I had given up on ever seeing you again, I decided to let this happen between Russell and me. He was chosen by some people in California. We wrote back and forth for a while, then one day I got a letter telling me he had found the right girl for him and was going to marry her."

"And that broke your heart."

"Yes. Then, there was Scott Hubbard. I told you about him, and about Pastor Blandford's talk with me concerning Isaac and Rebekah."

"Yes."

She took a deep breath. "Dane, my love for you is beyond the little sister kind. I know without any doubt whatsoever that I am deeply in love with you. I know the Lord has been saving us for each other."

Thrilled at her words, Dane said, "Tharyn, could I kiss you?"

Tharyn nodded.

When they had enjoyed a sweet, tender kiss, Dane held her close and said, "Sweetheart, when we get to your house, I need to talk to your parents alone for a few minutes."

"Oh?"

"Uh-huh. Then afterward, I'll need to talk to you alone."

Looking puzzled, she said, "Of course, darling. That will be fine."

While they drove on down the street, heading for the Tabor home, Tharyn was thinking about Pastor Blandford's talk and how it helped her to see that God had the man of His choice ready to bring into her life. She never dreamed it would be her long-lost big brother. *Lord, I think he is going to ask me to marry him.* Her pulse was pounding as they arrived at the Tabor home.

Dane helped Tharyn out of the buggy and stole another kiss before walking her to the door. When they went inside, Kitty was on her way down the hall from the rear of the house, heading for the parlor. She smiled. "Did you two have a nice dinner?"

"We sure did, Mama," said Tharyn.

"Good. Come on into the parlor. Your papa's in there reading today's newspaper."

When they entered the parlor, David looked up from his paper. "Well, how was dinner?"

"It was just fine, sir," said Dane. "Ah . . . Mr. and Mrs. Tabor, could I have a private conversation with you?"

David laid down his paper. "Right now?"

"Yes, sir, if you don't mind."

"Well, of course."

"We can go into the kitchen," said Kitty.

Dane nodded. "All right. Tharyn, we'll be back in a few minutes."

Tharyn sat in silence in the parlor, her pulse pounding once again as she tried to imagine what was happening in the kitchen.

No more than twenty minutes had passed when Tharyn heard footsteps in the hall, and Dane Logan entered the parlor. He closed the door behind him, moved to the sofa where she was sitting, and looked down at her. "Sweetheart, I want to ask you something."

Tharyn's pulse was pounding harder than ever.

Eighteen

Tharyn Tabor, her heart throbbing, saw the love light gleaming in Dane Logan's eyes. Wondering if this meant what she thought it did, Tharyn was barely able to speak above a whisper. "Of course, my darling. What is it?"

Though Dane was quite sure of her answer, there was still some trepidation in his heart. Taking a deep breath and silently praying for guidance, he knelt down in front of her and took both her hands in his own.

Tharyn looked down at this man who long ago as a fifteen-year-old boy had captured her heart. A tremulous smile curved her lips.

He squeezed her hands. "Tharyn, I have loved you since the day I rescued you from those charging horses and the wagon they were pulling. We were like brother and sister for those few short months we spent together in the alley and on the streets of

Manhattan. I felt a need to protect you and to give you special care. When you came to the prison to let me know you were going west on the orphan train, and to tell me good-bye, I wasn't sure I would ever see you again.

"And, sweetheart, in all those years, never a day went by that I didn't think of you and pray for you. I didn't realize it then, but God was allowing my love for you to grow and to change from brotherly love to sweetheart love. Oh, how I prayed that I might find you again.

"And now, the Lord has answered my prayers and brought you back into my life. Since we have been together this short time, the Lord has made me understand that the love I feel for you is the sweetheart kind. I don't want to ever lose you again."

Tears misted her eyes. "I don't want to ever lose you again either, my darling Dane."

He took a deep breath. "Tharyn, I'm so in love with you. I love you with all of my heart. Will you please do me the honor of becoming my wife? Will you marry me?"

Dane's gaze seemed to be devouring her face. She could hardly breathe. "Dane, darling, nothing on earth would make me happier than to become your wife. I know

now that from the beginning of time, the Lord had chosen us for each other. Yes! Yes! I will marry you. Oh, I love you, I love you, I love you."

Tears misted Dane's eyes as well, and rising to his feet, he pulled Tharyn up and kissed her tenderly — once, twice, and a third time. Then holding her at arm's length, he said, "Sweetheart, your parents told me they were not surprised when I requested their permission to ask you to marry me. And they readily granted that permission."

Tharyn smiled and brushed the tears from her eyelashes. "I'm not surprised about that. They both love you already. And they certainly know how I feel about you."

"And at this moment, they are waiting eagerly in the kitchen to hear the outcome."

She smiled. "I'm sure they already know it, but let's go make it official."

"Before we do, we need to talk about a wedding date, so that will be official too."

"Okay. What do you think?"

"Well, to be proper, we need to make the engagement last a few months."

Tharyn nodded. "Mm-hmm."

"How about next spring?"

"All right. How about May?"

"That would be good. We'll discuss it with Pastor Blandford and set an exact date."

"Sounds superb to me, darling."

They kissed again, then holding hands, they made their way to the kitchen.

When they moved through the kitchen door, David and Kitty were sitting at the table. They both stood up just as their daughter announced happily, "Hear ye! Hear ye! In the year of 1881, in the merry month of May, Miss Tharyn Tabor is going to become Mrs. Dane Logan!"

Both parents were quickly in tears and rushed to embrace her. They also hugged Dane, then Tharyn said, "We will discuss the exact date of the wedding with Pastor Blandford."

Kitty wiped tears from her cheeks. "Oh, I'm just so happy for you, Tharyn!"

"Me too," put in David, his own cheeks shining with tears. "I keep thinking, Tharyn, of how much you talked about Dane all these years."

She took hold of Dane's hand. "Papa, I thought God had Russell Mims for me, then when it was evident that was not so, the day came when I thought Scott Hubbard was the one. I'm sure glad I was wrong about that too." She looked up at Dane. "This is the man the Lord had picked out for me all along!"

There were more tears and hugs, then Dane and Tharyn went out onto the front porch. They kissed once more, then Dane mounted Pal and rode out of town toward the Brockman place in the country.

The next morning in the preaching service, Pastor Nathan Blandford announced that he had asked Chief John Brockman to preach in the evening service. There were amens all over the congregation.

Tharyn whispered to Dane that John Brockman was an excellent preacher, and everybody loved to hear him preach.

After the service, Dane and Tharyn approached the pastor and asked if they could have a few minutes with him after the evening service. Blandford gladly granted their request.

That evening, John Brockman walked into the pulpit, Bible in hand, after being introduced by the pastor. Eager to hear him, Dane let his gaze go to the pew across the aisle where Breanna, Paul, and Ginny sat. Paul had an especially proud look on his face.

John had the congregation open their Bibles to Genesis 24.

A tingle went down Tharyn's spine at the mention of that particular chapter.

While John was preaching about how God had chosen Isaac and Rebekah for each other and how He brought them together, Dane leaned over and whispered, "Does John know about Pastor Blandford using this passage to help you when Scott dumped you?"

Tharyn shook her head. "No. The Lord is just using him to seal His act of bringing you back to me so I could become your wife!"

Dane took hold of her hand, squeezed it, then let go. She smiled at him.

Both Kitty and David had heard the exchange between Dane and Tharyn. David whispered to Kitty, "Isn't it great? John doesn't know it, but the Lord is using his sermon to clinch in Tharyn's mind exactly what Pastor Blandford said about the passage."

Kitty nodded and smiled at her husband.

After the service, Tharyn made it a point to go to John and tell him what a blessing his sermon was to her. She did not reveal why the sermon meant so much to her, but felt she should at least let him know that it indeed was a blessing.

Moments later, Dane and Tharyn sat down in front of Pastor Blandford's desk in his office. Looking at them across the desk, he said, "Well, what can I do for you?"

"We want to set a date to get married, Pastor," Dane said without hesitating.

The pastor's eyebrows arched. "Oh, really?"

"Yes, sir."

"You know a little about our past," said Tharyn. "You know that Dane once saved my life when we were teenagers in New York."

Blandford nodded. "I vividly recall your telling me that when you were explaining about becoming an orphan." He looked at Dane. "Tharyn brought your name up quite often over these years. I picked up that you really meant a lot to her. She seemed so sad that the two of you were no longer in contact."

"So was I, Pastor. We've talked it all out, and we both understand why we lost contact. The main thing is that we're back together now. The Lord's hand is quite evident in it all. The brother-sister feelings we had for each other have now become a deep romantic love. I proposed to Tharyn last night after obtaining her parents' permission to do so."

The pastor shook his head and chuckled. "Tharyn, isn't it something that John Brockman would preach from the very passage tonight that I used to comfort you when Scott had broken your heart? You have told Dane about Scott, I presume."

Tharyn nodded. "Yes, sir. And I told him about your talk with me about Isaac and Rebekah, and that you said when it was God's time to do so, He would send my Isaac to me."

"Well, young lady, you are now Dane's Rebekah, and he is your Isaac."

The couple looked at each other, smiling.

"Hello, Rebekah," said Dane.

She giggled. "Hello, Isaac."

"Well, young people, you certainly have my blessing. When do you want to have the wedding?"

Dane adjusted himself on the chair. "We have agreed that in order to be proper, we should be engaged at least a few months."

The pastor nodded. "Yes."

"So we want to get married next May."

Blandford smiled and opened a desk drawer. "I just happen to have an 1881 calendar here." He took out the small calendar, laid it on the desk top, and opened it to the month of May. "What day of the week would you like to have the wedding?"

"What would you suggest?" asked Tharyn.

"My favorite time to perform weddings is on Saturday afternoon."

Dane and Tharyn looked at each other.

"Sounds good to me," she said.

"Me too."

The pastor grinned. "Which week in May?"

"How about the third week?" asked Dane.

"Well, May next year begins on a Sunday, so the end of the third week is Saturday, the twenty-first."

The couple exchanged glances again.

"That sound all right to you, sweetheart?" asked Dane.

"Mm-hmm."

"All right," said the pastor, "how about two o'clock that afternoon?"

Dane and Tharyn looked at each other and nodded.

"Two o'clock it is, Pastor," said Dane.

"All right, I'll put it in my personal calendar. When the time grows closer, we can get down to details."

"That's fine," said Dane. "One other thing, Pastor . . ."

"Yes?"

"Even though there is a good Bible-believing church in Central City, I would like to have my membership in this church until Tharyn and I marry. I will be coming to Denver as many weekends as possible until then. When the weather is bad or my medical work keeps me from coming, I'll attend the church in Central City."

"Well, we'd love to have you as a member of our church until you marry this lovely young lady and take her away from us."

"All right, Pastor. If I'm able to make it to Denver next weekend, I'll join the church next Sunday morning."

On Monday, October 25, Lucinda Moran and Kathryn Tully went morosely about the cabin, sweeping and dusting. Since reading in the *Fort Collins Gazette* of the capture of the Moran gang, they lived in total grief.

When they had finished their housecleaning, they sat down in the parlor, both of them sighing.

Kathryn set her sad eyes on her friend. "Lucinda, what are we going to do? Right now, we have plenty of money here in the cabin. But since our husbands are going to spend the rest of their lives in prison, we'll use it up before we're ten years older. How will we survive then?"

Lucinda turned her face to Kathryn. "We'll have to get jobs. Of course, if we move to Rawlins so we can be close to Gib and Bart, and can visit them, we'll have to use a good portion of the money to buy a house. The money won't even last six or seven years. I hope we can find work right there in town."

"I was lying awake last night thinking about this," said Kathryn. "Won't we be taking a big chance on going to prison ourselves if the law finds out we're married to men who have been convicted like they have? What if they figure we were in league with the gang? Yes, Tag did the killing and is going to hang. But the other four members of the gang are in for life because they were committing robberies when innocent people were killed."

Lucinda shrugged. "I don't think the law could touch us since we were never actually in on the robberies or the killings. I'm not positive of that, but —"

"Oh, why did I ever get mixed up in this mess?" wailed Kathryn, jumping off the chair and moving to the large window. She hugged herself with shaky arms. "All these big dreams our husbands had about retiring in California and living like royalty! Look at us now. Doomed to a life of —"

Lucinda looked up to see Kathryn peering at something outside. "What is it?" She left her chair and headed toward the window.

Breathlessly, Kathryn said, "There are riders coming through the trees. They're heading directly toward us. Oh, Lucinda, do you suppose the law has found out where we are and —"

"Wait a minute, honey!" Lucinda moved closer to the window, squinting. "Kathryn, it looks like there are five of them and —" She gasped and pointed. "Look! That's Tag in the lead! I'm sure it is! And Bart's right behind him!"

Kathryn's eyes bulged and her hand went to her mouth. "Yes! And Gib is right behind Bart! Lucinda, how did they get out?"

Lucinda whirled and ran toward the door. "I don't know, but they're out! I just recognized Jason and Tony too!"

Kathryn blinked and dashed after her.

The two women bolted onto the front porch, the crisp air stinging their faces and hands. All five riders waved and put their horses to a trot. When they drew up to the porch, Gib and Bart were first to dismount.

Kathryn stumbled down the steps and dashed into Gib's arms, breaking into tears.

Lucinda descended the steps and sobbed as Bart folded her into his arms. While this was going on, the other three men dismounted.

While the two women clung to their husbands, Lucinda said to all the men, "A week ago today, Kathryn and I went to Fort Collins to buy groceries and supplies. We heard people talking about your being sentenced to life, and you, Tag, being sentenced to hang! We bought a copy of the *Fort Collins Gazette* and read every word about it. We were going to go to Rawlins as soon as possible to visit you! How . . . how did you get out?"

"Let's get inside," Tag said.

While the women wiped tears and clung to their husbands as they all entered the cabin, Tag explained about the gunfight breaking out on the street in Rawlins between the cattlemen and the sheep men when they were being taken from the county jail to the prison, and how the escape was made possible because one of the two deputies who were escorting them got hit and was killed by a stray bullet.

Everyone sat down, and Tag went on to

tell how he picked up the deputy's gun and shot the other deputy, killing him.

He took a deep breath and let it out slowly through his nostrils.

"There were lots of witnesses on the street. The law will want me more than ever now. You kill a lawman, and every man who wears a badge becomes a predator. We got away from the posse that came after us, so we're safe for now. The law has no idea where we're hiding out."

"But you can't hide here forever," said Kathryn.

Tag grinned. "Don't plan to. We'll lay low till early spring, then start robbing banks once more. We'll just have to be extra careful, especially me. The predators, you know. Of course the law confiscated all the money we had in our saddlebags from the robberies we pulled in Vernal, Evanston, and Green River. So we lost it. When we start in again, I especially want to rob those two Cheyenne banks simultaneously again. Both of them always have lots of cash on hand."

Kathryn felt as if a ball of cold lead had formed in her stomach.

On Sunday morning, October 31, Dr. Dane Logan and Tharyn Tabor sat to-

381

gether in the preaching service next to her parents, as usual.

During announcement and offering time, Pastor Nathan Blandford announced the engagement of Dane and Tharyn, and gave the proposed wedding date. There were smiles from the people, along with many exuberant amens.

When the sermon was finished and the invitation was given, Dr. Dane walked forward to present himself for church membership. Pastor Blandford explained why Dr. Logan wanted to put his membership in the church until he and Tharyn married. Afterward, they would join the church in Central City. A unanimous vote gave Dane a welcome into the church.

After the service was dismissed, the people crowded around the young couple and congratulated them on their engagement. John and Breanna Brockman were especially expressive in their words of congratulation, as were Melinda Kenyon and Dr. Tim Braden. Tharyn told Melinda she wanted her to be her maid of honor.

Melinda hugged her. "It will be *my* honor to be the maid of honor in your wedding."

The couple had dinner at the Tabor

home. When the meal was over and Tharyn had helped her mother do the dishes and clean up the kitchen while the men sat at the kitchen table and talked, Dane and Tharyn went to the parlor to have some private time.

As they talked excitedly about their future together, Dane said, "I know it's going to be hard for you to give up your job at Mile High Hospital, honey."

Tharyn smiled. "Darling, I love my medical work, but I will love being Mrs. Dane Logan more."

He grinned. "Well, I brought up the subject because there is something I want to discuss with you."

"All right."

"I've told you about Dr. Fraser's nurse and receptionist, Nadine Wahl."

"Yes. I'm sure you're happy to have her stay on and help you."

"Well, that's what I want to discuss with you. Just recently, Nadine told me that she wants to retire within a short time. We talked about it at length this past week, and she is willing to stay on until the end of next June. Would you like to have Nadine's job as my nurse and receptionist?"

Tharyn's face lit up. "Oh, Dane! Really?"

"Really."

"I'll take the job, Dr. Logan!"

"Good! You're hired!"

Tharyn put her hands together and closed her eyes for a moment. Then opening them, she blinked at the tears that had formed. "Oh, Dane, what a marvelous and wonderful God we have! Sometimes I'm just amazed when I look at His plan for our lives. You so desperately wanted to be a doctor, from your earliest years. Then came all the turmoil when you lost your family. On top of that was your being locked up in prison for a crime you did not commit. Then came God's wonderful way of allowing the law to find the real killer so you would be released.

"And then God allowed you to be adopted by the Logans. Just think of it! When you returned to Cheyenne after graduating from Northwestern, you were living just a hundred miles from me and neither of us knew it. And now here we are engaged to be married, and I just got hired to be your nurse and receptionist after we get married! I'm — I'm just so overwhelmed at how our heavenly Father cares for His own!"

Dane smiled. "You are so absolutely right, my love. It's just so wonderful to know that when you belong to Jesus —

when you're God's child — everything is in His control. Even though sometimes we can't see it, we can be assured by faith that He will always care for us and work everything out for His glory in our lives."

Tharyn leaned close to him, closed her eyes, and puckered her lips. When Dane had kissed her, she said, "Oh, I'm going to be so happy working with you, darling!"

"I'm glad to hear you say it. With both of us devoted to medicine, and caring for the sick and injured, I'm sure we'll make a great team. But . . ."

She blinked. "Yes?"

"Whenever you decide it's time for you to stay at home and for us to start a family, that will be fine too."

Tharyn caressed his cheek. "We'll leave that in God's hands, darling. Of course I want children. Our heavenly Father will guide us about that."

"Amen," said Dane, and leaned toward her for another kiss.

At that point, they prayed together, thanking the Lord for the marvelous way He had worked in their lives, and for the wonderful future they had ahead of them.

When they had finished praying, they discussed names for their children and thoroughly enjoyed arguing playfully over the names they each wanted.

After a while, the subject turned to the winter that was ahead of them, and the fact that there would be weekends when the mountain snowstorms would keep Dane from coming to Denver. They agreed that they would write letters to each other, and even if the United States mail couldn't get them over the mountains, they would give them to each other for mementos when Dane made it over the mountains for a weekend again.

Nineteen

During the winter months, things went just as Dr. Dane Logan and Tharyn Tabor had speculated. On many weekends in a row, Dane was unable to make it over the mountains because of the heavy snow, but he enjoyed visiting the church in Central City where one day he and Tharyn would have their membership when they were husband and wife.

As Dr. Dane and Nurse Nadine Wahl worked together day after day, Nadine talked about her retirement, and how good it would be for Dr. Logan to have his wife as his nurse and receptionist.

One cold, snowy day in late January, after she had assisted the doctor as he set a broken arm for a teenage boy, Nadine brought up again how nice it was going to be for Dr. Logan to have Tharyn at his side in his practice.

Dane smiled at her. "Nadine, I am looking forward to having Tharyn working with me here, but I am still going to miss you. I feel toward you just like Dr. Fraser does. You are one in a million."

The look on Nadine's face showed how much his words pleased her. "I appreciate your feeling this way, Doctor. It means a lot to me. And may I remind you, as I have told you before, since I'll still be living in Central City, I will be glad to fill in for Tharyn when she goes to Denver with you periodically so she can see her parents."

The young physician grinned and nodded. "Oh, you need not remind me. I am definitely planning on having you here in the office at other times too."

Nadine's eyes sparkled. "I'll look forward to every minute of it."

In Denver, the weeks between Dane's visits seemed long to Tharyn, so she kept herself as busy as possible, at the hospital and at home. Melinda Kenyon knew that Tharyn was lonely without Dr. Dane around and often spent time with her in the evenings and on Tharyn's days off from the hospital.

Tharyn and her mother spent many hours planning for the upcoming wedding. In the first week of February, Kitty took Tharyn to dressmaker Sarah McIntosh's shop, which was across the street from Mile High Hospital.

Sarah helped Tharyn choose her wedding dress from a book of patterns, then showed her several bolts of material. When the choice of pattern and material had been made, Sarah went to work on the dress. Tharyn dropped in regularly for fittings and was excited to see the progress Sarah was making on the dress.

Many nights at home, Tharyn and Kitty found themselves busily stitching on household items for Tharyn's future home.

One night in the second week of February, they were working together in the parlor while David was in the library, and Tharyn was having a difficult time with her emotions because it had last been Christmas week that Dane had been able to get to Denver.

Tharyn was trying to do some embroidery work on a pillowcase, and after a while, she dropped it in her lap. "Mama, you'd think I could do a better job with this pillowcase. At the hospital, I can make precise stitches in a patient's skin to satisfy the surgeons, but with this pillowcase, I'm all thumbs."

Kitty leaned over, picked up the pillowcase, and examined the embroidery work.

"Honey, you're doing fine. Don't give up. You'll be so proud to have it in your home."

Tharyn smiled at her mother. "I won't give up. I guess I'm just edgy because I'm missing Dane." She shook her head and blinked at the tears that were gathering in her eyes. "I miss Dane when he can't get here on the weekends, but there is joy in my heart, Mama. I went nine years without seeing him, then the Lord sent him back into my life. And now, I'm making things to go in our home when we're married. It's so wonderful! Sometimes I still can't believe all of this is really happening." As she spoke, Tharyn laid aside her sewing, left her chair, and walked to the parlor window.

"Oh my, it's really snowing hard now, Mama." A note of sadness crept into her voice. "I'm sure Dane won't be able to get here this weekend, either." She sighed, turned around, and let a smile light up her face. "Oh, well. Praise the Lord, He doeth all things well. Even the snow is a blessing because He sends it. It will just be all the more special when Dane does get to come."

Kitty looked up at her and smiled. "That's my girl. Just be thankful for *all* of your blessings, honey. Anyway, it will be spring soon. You can count on it."

Spring 1881 came, and in the first week of April, Tag Moran stood at the parlor window in the old cabin in the mountains and looked out at the sunshine and the melting snow. The others were seated behind him. He turned around. "Well, another week and Moran and Company will be back in the robbery business."

Bart, Jason, Gib, and Tony all smiled at him, as did Lucinda.

Kathryn was unable to create a smile, but kept the reservations she felt to herself. She wished with all her might that the robbing days were over, but tried not to show it.

Tag returned to his chair and ran his gaze over the faces of his men. "We'll go to Salt Lake City first and hit both banks at once, just like we did those two Cheyenne banks. We'll make a good haul in Salt Lake. Then we'll drop down into the western side of Colorado and rob the banks in Grand Junction, Delta, and Glenwood Springs. We'll be back here to the hideout late this month, then we'll lay low for a while again. On the next trip out after that, I want to hit those two Cheyenne banks again."

Exactly a week later, Lucinda and Kathryn kissed their husbands good-bye and watched them ride down the mountain with the other gang members, weaving among the trees.

When they had passed from view, Lucinda turned to see Kathryn wiping tears. She touched her arm. "Kathryn, nothing's going to happen to Gib. He'll be back, the same as my Bart and the rest of them."

Kathryn sniffled, but did not respond.

Lucinda patted the arm. "Look at it this way, Kathryn. The more robberies the gang pulls off, the quicker we'll have enough money to realize our dream and go to California and live like royalty the rest of our lives."

Kathryn stared at the last spot in the woods where she had seen Gib. Her voice quivered as she said, "But if Gib gets killed during a robbery or in a shootout with the law, the big dream will become a horrible nightmare."

Early in the third week of April, Chief U.S. Marshal John Brockman was at his desk, talking to two of his deputies who were about to leave in pursuit of a band of outlaws who had held up a stagecoach a few miles east of Denver.

"That bunch are known to be cold-blooded, boys," said John. "Be very careful."

"We will, Chief," said one as they rose from their chairs. "We'll get help from the local law once we locate them."

There was a tap at the door. It opened and Deputy Charlie Wesson said, "Chief, Mrs. Brockman is here. I told her I thought you were about through with Jack and Boris."

Brockman nodded. "Yes. They're about to leave. Tell Breanna to come in."

Charlie turned and looked into the hall. "The chief says for you to come on in, ma'am."

The lovely blonde stepped up to the door and smiled at the two deputies who were coming her way. "Go get them, Jack, Boris. My husband told me he was sending you after that gang who robbed the stagecoach yesterday."

"We'll do our best, ma'am," said Jack.

"Yes, we will," said Boris, and they hurried away with Charlie on their heels.

Breanna closed the door and headed toward her husband.

John rounded the desk, folded Breanna into his arms, and kissed her soundly. "To what do I owe this visit, sweetheart?"

She smiled up at him. "Oh, I was just lonesome for you, so I thought I'd try to get a few minutes with you."

"Well, come over here and sit down."

They sat down on the two chairs in front of his desk, and Breanna said, "I told you I was going to stop by the hospital this morning and talk to Matt about Dottie's upcoming birthday party. We'll really surprise her this time, doing it a day early."

"Good. That'll be fun."

"And I had a few minutes with Tharyn."

John smiled. "She's been a different girl since Dr. Dane has been making it down from the mountains on the weekends these past few weeks. And then there were those two days he was here last week when he did that hip replacement for Georgene Rogers."

"Mm-hmm. Getting to assist him on that surgery really thrilled her. The girl was walking three inches off the ground then, wasn't she?"

"That's for sure."

"Well, anyway, Tharyn just told me that Dr. Dane is going to Fort Collins next week to do a hip replacement at Larimer County Hospital."

John nodded. "He's becoming quite well

known for his successful hip replacements, isn't he?"

"Tharyn said more and more requests are coming to him from doctors, clinics, and hospitals to perform them on their patients. She reminded me that just since the first part of March, he has done hip replacements as far north as Casper, and as far south as Colorado Springs. He did two in Cheyenne day before yesterday, Tharyn told me. I'm glad for his expertise in this, and for the fact that Dr. Fraser so willingly fills in for him so he can be away to do it."

"Yes, that's good." John chuckled. "Did you hear me kidding Dr. Tim Braden at church Sunday?"

"Oh yes. The two of you were talking about how Dr. Tim had asked for permission to observe the hip replacement surgery Dr. Dane performed on Georgene Rogers. You ribbed him, saying he wanted to learn how to do hip replacements so he could *replace* Dr. Dane."

"Yes. Had to have a little fun with him. I'm glad to see Dr. Tim and Dr. Dane becoming such good friends. Maybe someday Dr. Dane's practice in Central City will grow so much he can take Dr. Tim in as partner."

Breanna smiled. "That would be good,

wouldn't it? I'm sure it would make Tharyn and Melinda happy."

"As close as they are, it would be like a dream come true."

"I'm sure it would. Well, darling, I guess I'd better head for home." As she spoke, Breanna arose from the chair.

John stood up, towering over her. "Oh, by the way, the Moran gang is back at it again."

"Oh? I was hoping they'd decided to quit the outlaw trail."

"Unfortunately, no. I just got a telegram from Sheriff Bob Gaston of Delta County, Colorado, informing me that the Moran gang robbed Delta's bank two days ago, and once again, got away clean."

"Oh no. Did they shoot anybody this time?"

"Not in Delta, but Sheriff Gaston also told me in his telegram that the gang has hit four banks in two weeks. They hit both banks in Salt Lake City, the bank in Grand Junction, and now the one in Delta. He said at Grand Junction, Tag Moran shot and killed a bank teller who pulled a gun out of a drawer and tried to thwart the robbery."

Breanna sighed. "I hope that gang makes some kind of mistake that will get them caught again."

Late in the third week of April, Lucinda Moran and Kathryn Tully left the old cabin and walked to the barn. They placed their purses in the wagon, and together, put bridles on the two draft horses, hoisted the harnesses onto their backs, and hitched them to the wagon.

Moments later they were on the wagon seat, and Lucinda took the reins and put the team in motion. She guided the team down the side of the mountain, weaving among the trees. At one point, a large limb from a birch tree lay in their path, having broken off the tree. Lucinda guided the wagon around the limb, but did not notice a hole in the ground to the right side of the wagon.

Suddenly, the right rear wheel dropped into the hole with the sound of wood splitting.

Lucinda pulled rein. "Oh no. Did you hear that?"

"I did. Sounded like something broke back there."

Both women hopped out of the wagon and walked to the rear. The wheel had broken off the axle and splinters of wood were scattered about.

Lucinda sighed dejectedly. "Well, we

won't be going to Fort Collins, now. Let's see if we can lift the wheel into the wagon bed. I'll just have to force the team to pull the wagon back up to the cabin with the rear corner dragging."

Four days later, clouds were gathering in the sky above the Rockies and a stiff wind was blowing. Lucinda and Kathryn had just finished breakfast and made their way to the parlor when Kathryn looked out the window and saw five riders winding their way up through the forest toward them. Focusing on Gib, she said with a lilt in her voice, "Lucinda! They're back!"

Both women dashed out onto the wide front porch and waved as the gang drew near. The wind plucked at their hair.

The first men out of their saddles were Gib Tully and Bart Moran. They dashed up the steps to their wives while the others were dismounting.

When Gib had hugged and kissed Kathryn and Bart had done the same with Lucinda, Tag led the group inside to get out of the wind and joyfully showed the women the money they had taken from the banks. The last one they had robbed was the bank in Glenwood Springs, Colorado. No one mentioned the bank teller Tag had killed in Grand Junction.

Bart's arm was around Lucinda as she looked at him and said, "I'm sure glad you didn't get captured again."

Bart laughed. "Never again, sweet stuff! We safely eluded capture after each one of the robberies, including the last one at Glenwood Springs, and we're dead sure there are no lawmen on the trail behind us."

"That's right," said Tony Chacone. "Having all these rivers and streams in the mountains makes it easy to lose those posses."

"Yeah!" said Jason. "We're the best posse losers in the business!"

The other men laughed.

Kathryn was clinging to Gib and looking at him with loving eyes.

Lucinda said, "I have one bit of bad news. Four days ago, we started out for Fort Collins to buy groceries and supplies, and I had to steer the wagon around a big limb that had fallen off a birch tree. The right rear wheel dropped into a hole and broke off the axle. So we're quite low on groceries and supplies. The wagon's out by the barn, with the wheel in the bed."

Tag frowned. "We'll have to repair it if possible, and if not, we'll have to steal us a wagon somewhere. Let's go take a look at it, boys."

Gib Tully said, "Tell you what, Tag. Even if it can be repaired, it's going to take a while. Since the ladies are so low on groceries and supplies, I'll ride into town right now and get enough to last a few days."

A frown creased Tag's brow. "I appreciate you volunteering, Gib, but since our pictures have been in all the newspapers, somebody's liable to recognize you."

Kathryn nodded, worry showing on her face.

"I'll be careful, boss," said Gib. "But we gotta eat."

Kathryn's brow furrowed. "I wish no one had to go, darling, but since it has to be — please be very, very careful."

Gib grinned at her. "I'll wear my hat down low over my face, honey. Don't fret yourself now. I'll be back before you know it."

In Fort Collins, dark clouds hung low and the wind was gusting through the town as one of Larimer County's deputy sheriffs named Doug Pritchard was coming out of the general store. He saw a rider draw up to the hitch rail in front of the store and dismount, his hat pulled low over his face.

Suddenly an extra powerful gust of wind tore the rider's hat off, and while he was chasing it along the edge of the boardwalk, Pritchard got a good look at his face. He bristled as he thought of the pictures of the Tag Moran gang that were on the wall at the sheriff's office, and whispered, "Gib Tully!"

The outlaw quickly picked up his hat and jammed it down on his head, making sure the brim was low over his face.

Unnoticed by Tully, Pritchard backed into the recessed doorway of the general store, hoping no customers would show up from inside or outside.

His mind set on getting the needed groceries and supplies quickly, Tully crossed the boardwalk toward the door. Suddenly he stopped, his body tensing. He was stunned to find a man with a badge on his chest holding a cocked revolver on him. Lines curved down from the lawman's lip corners into a squarely defined chin, creating an aspect of doggedness. The cast of jaw and mouth seemed almost brutal.

"Make a false move, Tully," Pritchard said, "and it'll be your last one."

Gib Tully was disarmed, while people on the boardwalk looked on, and taken to the sheriff's office where he was locked up in a cell.

Sheriff James Hoffman stood outside of the cell with Deputy Doug Pritchard at his side and peered through the bars. "All right, Tully. I want to know where the gang is holed up."

Gib shook his head. "You won't find out from me."

"It'll go a lot better for you if you tell me, Tully. We *will* catch the Moran gang sooner or later. You're going to face Judge Yeager again. When it comes time for your new sentencing, the judge will go a lot easier on you if I can tell him that you told us where we could find the rest of the gang."

Tully sneered. "What are you talking about? He already gave me a life sentence. Is he gonna have me hanged when I haven't killed anybody?"

"No, but he could sentence you to life in solitary confinement. If he does, you'll be locked up in a cell with no window, and you'll never see the light of day again. Is that what you want?"

Tully swallowed hard, but shook his head. "I'm not telling you where the gang is holed up."

Hoffman shook his head. "You'll wish you had when it's too late. Let's go, Doug."

Gib Tully stared after the lawmen with cold eyes as they left the cell block.

Sheriff James Hoffman went to the Western Union office and wired Chief U.S. Marshal John Brockman in Denver, informing him that they had Gib Tully in custody. He explained that Tully had refused to tell him where the Moran gang was holed up, and asked for word on what to do with him.

Brockman wired back immediately, saying he was sending one of his deputies, Clint Haymes, on the night train from Denver. He would have Haymes escort Tully to Cheyenne on a stagecoach in handcuffs, then take a stage to Rawlins and return him to Judge George Yeager and the Wyoming Territorial Prison.

The next day, just after noon, Deputy Clint Haymes had a sullen Gib Tully cuffed to his left wrist as they sat on a bench in the Wells Fargo office in Fort Collins, waiting for the stage to be brought from the Fargo barn and corral for the trip north.

Three other passengers were waiting, also: two men and an elderly woman. They were seated on wooden chairs close by. Obviously on edge, the woman kept staring at the handcuffs that linked the lawman and his prisoner together.

Soon the stagecoach pulled to a halt out front, and the agent saw driver Buck Cummons and shotgunner Doke Veatch leave the coach and head for the office.

The agent stood behind the counter. "Folks, the stage just pulled up. As you know, it's scheduled to leave at one o'clock. When it's time to go, I want you folks over here to let Deputy Haymes take his prisoner ahead of you so he can get him aboard first."

When driver and shotgunner came through the door, Doke Veatch saw Gib Tully sitting on the bench, handcuffed to the man with a badge on his chest. Doke and Gib exchanged secret glances, but neither let on that he knew the other.

The agent introduced Cummons and Veatch to Deputy U.S. Marshal Clint Haymes, explaining that he was out of the Denver office, and told them the man cuffed to him was Gib Tully, a member of the infamous Tag Moran gang.

Haymes then filled them in on how Tully was caught, and that he had been sent by Chief U.S. Marshal John Brockman to take Tully back to Rawlins where he would once again face Judge George Yeager, then be returned to the prison.

Standing there looking at Gib, Doke was wishing he could do something to help him escape — but knew he could not.

At nearby Larimer County Hospital, Dr. Dane Logan had just finished a hip replacement surgery, and leaving the patient in the care of her doctor, walked out of the hospital. As always, he carried his medical bag. He headed down the boardwalk on Main Street toward the depot to catch the train that would be leaving for Denver at 1:15.

As Dane neared the Wells Fargo office, he saw the passengers coming out the door of the office to board the Cheyenne-bound stagecoach. He noted that driver Buck Cummons was leading Deputy Clint Haymes and the prisoner who was cuffed to his left wrist ahead of the other passengers. A second glance at the prisoner's face told Dane he should know him. A second later, he knew he had seen that face in the newspaper as one of the Tag Moran gang, though he couldn't recall his name.

Dane recognized shotgunner Doke Veatch bringing up the rear and slowed his pace to watch the procession.

Just as Buck Cummons drew up to the

coach and reached out to open the door, he stumbled slightly.

Gib Tully was close to Cummons and saw the opportunity to grab the driver's revolver from its holster with his free hand.

It all happened in a few seconds.

Taking both Cummons and Haymes by surprise, Tully swung the gun on the deputy and fired, hitting him in the left side just above his belt. Haymes buckled, but already had his gun out. He fired it, shooting Tully in the chest. Both men fell to the ground, and while Doke Veatch froze in place and stared in disbelief, Buck Cummons yanked his gun from Tully's weakened grasp.

The elderly female passenger was screaming, and the two male passengers stood frozen in shock. People on the street were looking on wide-eyed as Dr. Dane Logan dashed up to the scene. The Fargo agent came charging out the door of the office.

Dr. Dane knelt beside the wounded men. His eyes met with those of Doke Veatch, who was searching the deputy's pockets.

"Hello, Doctor," said Doke. "I'm trying to find the key to the handcuffs so we can get these two men apart."

"Thanks, Doke," said Dane. He quickly

examined both men, then opened his medical bag and went to work on Haymes.

Doke produced the key and hastily unlocked the handcuffs, removing them from the wrists of both lawman and prisoner.

The sheriff was summoned by someone on the street and soon arrived, along with two of his deputies — one of them being Doug Pritchard.

Dr. Dane was working furiously on the wounded federal deputy.

People in the crowd recognized the wounded outlaw from pictures they had seen in the newspapers, at the post office, and at the sheriff's office. They were talking about him, agreeing that he was part of the Tag Moran gang. One man even called his name.

When Dr. Dane heard it, he then recalled it too.

A reporter from the *Fort Collins Gazette* was now on the scene, making notes.

The Fargo agent ushered the other passengers inside the office, apologizing for the incident. He asked them to sit down, telling them it would be a while before the stage could leave, then hurried back to the scene.

Noting that both wounded men were conscious, Sheriff James Hoffman bent down over the doctor. "Do you need help getting these men to the hospital?"

"I will a little later, Sheriff," said Dr. Dane, "but I have to do what I can first. Deputy Haymes has a big hole in his side where the bullet ripped through him, and I must stop the flow of blood before he bleeds to death."

Haymes looked up at the doctor with hazy eyes and whispered, "Thank you."

Buck Cummons and Doke Veatch were standing close, with the Fargo agent between them, watching the doctor work.

Doke was noting the blood bubbling from Gib's chest just as Gib looked up at Dr. Logan and wheezed weakly, "Y-you're . . . tending . . . to him first . . . because he's . . . the lawman, aren't you?"

Doke Veatch swung his gaze to the doctor's face, his mind flashing back to the day when Darryl Moran died while Dr. Dane Logan was tending to him in Cheyenne. He thought of Tag's words that day in Wheatland: *Maybe that doc let Darryl die because he was an outlaw.*

The shotgunner gritted his teeth and thought, *Tag, I told you that Dr. Logan didn't let Darryl die because he was an outlaw . . . but now, I'm wondering if you were right.*

Doke felt anger well up within him as Logan looked at Tully, but did not reply to his question.

Twenty

Dane Logan feverishly worked at getting Clint Haymes's bleeding stopped while the Fargo men, the sheriff and deputies, the reporter, and the crowd looked on.

Doke felt his rage toward the doctor growing. Gib Tully was bleeding too — from right around his heart. His shirt was soaked with blood.

Suddenly Gib stiffened, let out a low moan, and went limp, his eyes staring vacantly into space. Dr. Logan glanced at Gib, but quickly put his attention back on the bleeding wound on the deputy's left side.

Doke felt his own blood heat up. He took hold of Gib's wrist and felt for a pulse.

There was none.

Doke raked Dane Logan with a cold glance and said loud enough for all to hear, "This man's dead, Doctor!"

Dane looked at Doke, glanced at the vacant eyes of Gib Tully, nodded, and put his attention back on Haymes.

Outrage etched itself on Doke's features, but he quickly forced it away. Inside, he was raw with violence, wanting to grab the doctor and rub his nose in the blood on Gib's shirt. He sucked in his breath so hard it hollowed his cheeks.

Moments later, when Clint Haymes's bleeding had been stopped and a bandage had been securely applied to the wound, Dr. Dane looked up at the sheriff. "He can be transported to the hospital now, Sheriff."

A smile broke over Hoffman's rugged face. "Good, Doctor." He turned to his deputies. "See if you can borrow one of these wagons parked here on the street. We need to get this man to the hospital right away."

As the deputies hurried away, Dr. Dane said, "I want to go along with Deputy Haymes, Sheriff, so I can discuss the wound with whatever doctor is assigned to him. I was on my way to the depot when this incident happened, but I'll catch the late afternoon train to Denver."

At that instant, a man in the crowd said to Dane, "Doctor, I heard what that outlaw asked you — if you were tending to the deputy first because he was a lawman."

Dane nodded. "Yes?"

"Well, is it true? Did you work on the deputy first because he was the good guy?"

Clint Haymes ran his dull gaze to the doctor, wondering what answer he would give.

Doke's attention was riveted on the doctor's face.

Dane eyed the man steadily. "No, I did not. Upon examining both men, I saw that Tully's wound was lethal. The slug had definitely punctured his heart. He was not going to make it. So I concentrated my efforts on saving the deputy's life."

"Oh yeah?" pressed the man, his features stiff. "Then why didn't you answer the question when Tully asked it?"

Still meeting the man's hard gaze, Dane said, "I didn't answer Tully's question, sir, because I would have had to tell him he was going to die within a few minutes. If you were in my place, would you have told him that?"

The man bit his lips and shook his head. "No, I wouldn't. I'm sorry, Doctor." With that, he turned and walked away.

Doke Veatch clenched his jaw. *I don't believe you, Logan,* he thought. *You let Gib die because he was an outlaw, just like you let Darryl die that day at your office.*

The anger in him grew hotter. *I owe it to Tag to see that he knows the truth about it. Tag and Gib were very close. And besides that, Kathryn needs to know that her husband is dead.*

The borrowed wagon was drawn up close to the spot where Deputy U.S. Marshal Clint Haymes and the lifeless body of Gib Tully lay next to the stagecoach. Haymes was picked up by the deputies and placed in the wagon bed. Dr. Dane Logan grasped his medical bag and hopped in beside Haymes. The owner of the wagon waited for the deputies to climb up on the seat beside him, then snapped the reins and put the team to a gallop in the direction of Larimer County Hospital.

Moments later, the passengers were boarding the stage, with the Fargo agent apologizing to them for the delay in their departure.

Doke Veatch had one desire at the moment: to get to Tag Moran and Gib Tully's widow and let them know what had happened to Gib. He was aware that there was a retired older man named Clem Dobbins in town, who used to be a shotgunner with Wells Fargo. Clem still filled in now and then when needed.

Putting a sick look on his face and

placing a hand over his stomach, Doke said to the driver, "Buck, seeing all that blood on Tully's shirt has upset my stomach. I really don't feel good. Could you get Clem Dobbins to take my place on this run?"

Buck nodded. "Sure, Doke. You'd better go on home."

"I'll go get Clem," said the agent, and hurried down the street.

"Thanks, Buck," said Doke, and walked away as if he were very sick to his stomach.

As soon as Doke got to his boarding-house a few blocks from the Wells Fargo office, he saddled his horse and rode into the mountains.

The sun was lowering in the west as the Moran gang sat on the porch of the old cabin. A soft breeze brought the fragrance of pine across the porch.

"Well, boys," said Tag, "I'm glad we were able to repair the wagon. Saves us having to steal one." He glanced down the mountain to the east. "I'm really concerned about Gib. He should have been back by this time yesterday. I know we all agreed that he must have run into trouble, and had to hole up somewhere in these mountains for the night. But this has gone on too long."

Bart said, "Maybe we should take a ride toward town and see if we can find him. We can't go *into* town, but could be he's had a problem between there and here."

Tag rose from his chair. "I agree, Bart. Let's all take a ride. I'll go in and tell the gals."

While the other four waited on the porch, Tag opened the door and said to Lucinda and Kathryn, "We're gonna take a ride and see if we can find Gib."

Kathryn left her chair and headed toward him. She was wringing her hands, and worry was etched on her face. "We were just talking about Gib, Tag. I knew it wasn't safe for him to show his face in town. I should have talked him out of going!"

By this time, Lucinda was beside her.

Tag shook his head. "Kathryn, I'm sure he's all right. Gib's a resourceful guy. He's got to be getting close to home by now. The boys and I just decided to ride out and meet him. You and Lucinda go ahead and start supper. We'll be back with Gib before you know it."

"Hey, Tag!" came Bart's voice from the porch. "Gib's here now!"

Kathryn let out a sigh.

Tag hurried out the door with the

women on his heels.

A lone rider was making his way toward the cabin in the deep shadows of the forest.

Tony Chacone squinted at horse and rider. "Gib must have gotten another horse. That ain't his gray."

"Right," said Bart, his gaze fixed on them. "But that ain't Gib."

Kathryn's eyes widened and her hand went to her mouth, a sting of fear piercing her heart.

"Who can that be?" Tag said in a low voice, his brow furrowing.

"It's Doke Veatch!" exclaimed Bart.

Doke put his horse to a trot, and as he drew up seconds later, all could see the dismal look on his face.

While he was dismounting, Tag said, "What's wrong, Doke?"

Doke sighed as he started up the steps. "I've got bad news." His eyes went to Kathryn. "Gib's dead."

Kathryn's knees buckled, and Lucinda caught her before she fell. Kathryn's lips were moving, but she couldn't get any words to come out.

"Let's take her inside," said Doke. "I'll tell you all about it."

Lucinda kept a tight hold on Kathryn as

they moved into the parlor and helped her sit down on the sofa. She then sat down beside her and held both of her hands.

The men stood in a tight cluster close to the sofa as Doke told the story of Gib's arrest by Deputy Sheriff Doug Pritchard in Fort Collins yesterday, and of his attempt to escape this morning when he was about to be taken by stagecoach to Rawlins by Deputy U.S. Marshal Clint Haymes. He went on to give the details of how Gib tried to escape by grabbing Buck Cummons's gun, and how Gib shot Haymes in his side, but got shot in the chest by Haymes.

At this point, Kathryn wailed in anguish, tears flowing. She set her wild eyes on Tag and screamed, "I tried to get you to stop the robbing so we could all go to California with less money than you had planned! I told you something like this would happen! But you wouldn't listen to me! Now my Gib is dead!"

Tag bristled and met her teary glance with one as cold and hard as agate. "Shut up, Kathryn! Don't be giving me that 'I told you so' stuff!"

Kathryn drew in a ragged breath. "Well, I *did* tell you so! I begged you to —"

"I told you to shut up!"

Lucinda caressed Kathryn's tear-soaked face. "Honey, calm down now. You and Tag yelling at each other isn't going to make things any better."

Kathryn looked at Lucinda and buried her face against her shoulder, sniffling.

"Something else," said Doke. "Tag, you remember the doctor I took Darryl to in Cheyenne."

Tag's features hardened. "Yeah. Dane Logan. What about him?"

"Well, he happened to be in Fort Collins, walking right by the Fargo office when Gib and the deputy shot each other. It was him who dashed to them when they both went down."

A look of virulence leaped into Tag's eyes. His voice came out like the flick of a whip. "He saved the deputy's life, didn't he?"

Doke nodded silently, then told Tag about Gib's final words to Dr. Dane Logan, asking if he was tending to the deputy first because he was a lawman. "Tag, I think Logan purposely let Gib die when he might have been able to save him."

Tag's face was suddenly mottled with rage. He uttered a sound that sounded like a wild animal's growl. "You remember when Darryl was shot, Doke, I suspicioned that Logan had let him die because he was an outlaw."

Doke closed his eyes, then opened them. "Yeah. I told you it wasn't so. But now I believe you were right."

"Well, this confirms it! Logan did the same thing to Gib!" Wrath flamed in Tag's eyes. "I owe Logan double! I'll get him if it's the last thing I do! He's gonna die!"

Doke bit his lips.

Bart looked at Tag. "You gonna kill this doctor before or after we rob those two banks in Cheyenne?"

"After. We're gonna go ahead and leave for Cheyenne on Tuesday, May 10, as planned so we can hold up both those Cheyenne banks on Thursday afternoon, May 12."

Doke bit his lips again. "Uh, Tag . . ."

"Yeah?"

"Could I talk to you alone for a minute?"

Tag frowned. "I don't have to keep any secrets from my boys, here."

"Well, this is just something between you and me, as old friends."

"Oh, all right. Let's go outside."

Kathryn was sobbing heavily, soaking the shoulder of Lucinda's dress as Tag and

Doke moved out onto the front porch.

The old friends crossed the porch, moved down the steps, and walked slowly toward the dense forest.

"Okay, what is it?"

"Uh, I know Dr. Logan did wrong concerning Darryl and Gib, but — but —"

"But *what?*"

"Well, do you have to kill him? Couldn't you just find out where he lives and burn his house down, or something like that? I felt I should let you know what happened with Gib, but I don't want to be responsible for the doctor's death."

They drew up under a towering pine tree. Tag looked down and shoved a few pine cones around with the toe of his boot for a long moment, then looked at his old friend. "I appreciate you telling me about what the doc did with both Darryl and Gib, Doke. If it wasn't for you, I wouldn't know it. I really want vengeance on him. But since you're squeamish about being responsible for his death by what you've told me, I'll find a way to get even with Logan without killing him."

Doke started to say something, but before he could get it out, Tag said, "I *will* find a way, though, to make him suffer severely for what he did to Darryl and Gib."

Doke let out a shaky breath and touched Tag's arm. "Thank you. I couldn't stand to have the doctor's death on my conscience."

Tag nodded and smiled thinly. "Well, let's get back to the cabin. Lucinda will be fixing supper with whatever food is left. You want to stay the night with us, don't you?"

"Sure do," said Doke, feeling like a thousand pounds had been lifted from his chest.

When they drew near the cabin in the dying light of day, they saw Kathryn sitting in the old rocking chair near the door. The air was getting chilly, and Lucinda came out carrying a shawl. She was placing it on Kathryn's shoulders as the two men made their way up the steps.

Tag frowned. "What's this?"

"She wants some time alone," explained Lucinda. "I brought the shawl out to keep her warm. Supper's about ready. Go on in and get washed up. I'll be there shortly."

When Tag and Doke had gone inside, Lucinda leaned over and took both of Kathryn's hands in her own. Tears choked her voice. "I'm so sorry, Kathryn."

Kathryn raised her swollen eyes and looked at her friend. "Lucinda, I knew in my heart this was going to happen. From the very beginning of this outlaw life, something just told me it would end this way."

Lucinda didn't know what to say.

A fresh wave of bitter tears coursed down Kathryn's cheeks. "Go on in now and give the men their supper. I'll be all right here. I just need some time alone."

Lucinda gave Kathryn's hands a squeeze. "I'll check on you later."

With that, she headed toward the cabin door. When she stepped inside, she held the door open and looked back over her shoulder. She saw Kathryn lower her head and put her hands to her face. Tears were trickling between her fingers.

After giving way to her anguish, Kathryn wept for a long time. Then wiping her face and eyes, she rocked the chair slowly and stared out into the forest in the gathering twilight. "What will I do now? Will the gang give me the money that would have gone to Gib?"

She took a short breath and frowned. "Or do I even want it? It was taken at gunpoint. But — but if I don't take it, how will I live? Then again, if I do take it, I'll be just as guilty as these men are."

Her thoughts on the subject went round and round until darkness and a penetrating chill filled the night. Pulling the shawl up tight around her neck, Kathryn glanced toward the cabin windows. Lantern light shone through them and splashed a warm glow on the porch floor.

At that moment, footsteps were heard and the door came open.

Lucinda moved to Kathryn. "Honey, it's freezing out here. Come on in now and let me get some hot coffee and some potato soup in you. It'll help you feel better."

Kathryn nodded and let Lucinda help her out of the rocking chair.

A bit reluctantly, she allowed her friend to lead her into the warmth of the cabin and the presence of the gang.

At the federal building in Denver, Chief U.S. Marshal John Brockman was about to leave his office for the day when Deputy Charlie Wesson tapped on the door. "Chief, Dr. Dane Logan is here to see you."

John closed the desk drawer into which he had just placed some papers. "Send him in."

When Dr. Dane stepped into the office, he thanked Charlie, then moved to the desk while Charlie closed the door.

John stood up behind his desk and offered his hand. "Good to see you, Doc.

How'd it go in Fort Collins?"

"The hip replacement went fine, Chief, but something else happened while I was there that I need to tell you about. I just got in on the late afternoon train."

"Well, sit down and tell me."

When both men were seated, Dr. Dane told John about the shooting incident on the Wells Fargo property in Fort Collins earlier that day; that Deputy Clint Haymes was wounded; and that Gib Tully was killed.

Brockman called for Deputy Charlie Wesson and had him send another deputy immediately to both of Denver's newspapers with orders to bring reporters so Dr. Logan could tell the story of the Fort Collins shooting to them.

Very little time had passed when the deputy returned with a reporter from each paper. Both were very glad to see Dr. Logan, and they told him that just today they were given information on his upcoming marriage to bank president David Tabor's daughter on May 21. They congratulated him and assured him that both papers would carry the story of the forthcoming wedding in tomorrow's edition.

Dr. Dane thanked them, then gave them the details of the shooting in Fort Collins when outlaw Gib Tully was killed. He told them of treating the wounded Deputy Marshal Clint Haymes and assured them he would recover.

When the reporters were gone, John said, "Well, Doc, you've had quite a day. Are you heading for Central City right away?"

Dane grinned. "I plan to stay over and spend some time with Tharyn this evening. I'll ride to Central City in the morning."

"Good. May I remind you that you have a standing invitation to stay in our guest room?"

Dane nodded. "I'll take you up on it, sir. I'll show up at your place by ten o'clock, if that's all right."

"That will be fine."

"Okay. Well, I guess I'd better go get my horse at the stable and head for the Tabor house."

When Tharyn greeted Dane at the front door in response to his knock, she opened her arms and gave him her brightest smile. "Here's the man of my dreams!"

"Hello, sweetheart." He gathered her in his arms.

She cuddled close. "We saw you coming, so Mama and Papa went to the kitchen to give us a private moment together. Mama and I have supper cooking. We started it after I got home from work. You *will* eat with us, won't you?"

"Oh, of course!"

He kissed her soundly, then while he held her, Tharyn sensed a tenseness in him. When they let go of each other, she took his hand, and while leading him into the parlor, looked deeply into his eyes. "Darling, you seem a bit on edge. Is something wrong?"

Dane spied the flames dancing in the ornate fireplace. "Ah, the fire looks good on this chilly spring evening."

Tharyn batted her eyelids at him. "Darling, you are not quite yourself. What's wrong?"

Before Dane could answer, Kitty and David came in, smiling. Kitty was carrying a tray with cups of fragrant tea.

Both warmly greeted Dane, then as Kitty placed the tray on an inlaid oak table, she said, "I thought we could all use this on such a cool evening. Dane, you are going to have supper with us, aren't you?"

Dane smiled. "I wouldn't miss it. And this tea sure looks good to me, Mrs. Tabor. This has been quite a day."

Tharyn poured a cup for Dane and

handed it to him in a saucer. "So what happened today that has you not quite yourself?"

David and Kitty looked at each other, then at Dane.

"What happened, Dane?" asked David, accepting a cup and saucer from Kitty. "Anything you are at liberty to share with us?"

Dane took a sip of tea. "Oh yes, sir. I can tell you. It will be in both of Denver's newspapers tomorrow, anyway." He took another sip of tea. "You know, the British may have something here. A cup of this bracing brew really is therapeutic."

Kitty smiled. "Tell you what — supper will be ready in about twenty minutes. Let's all sit down here and Dane can tell us about his day."

When they were seated, Dane told them about the shooting incident in Fort Collins which left Deputy U.S. Marshal Clint Haymes wounded and in the Larimer County Hospital and resulted in the death of Gib Tully, a member of the Tag Moran gang.

David shook his head. "Well, my boy, indeed you have had quite a day. Praise the Lord you were able to save the deputy's life. Now how about some of Mrs. Tabor's good cooking?"

"Sounds wonderful to me! I didn't even have a bite of lunch today, and I am ravenous!"

During supper, Tharyn asked about the hip replacement Dane had done in Fort Collins that morning and was pleased to hear that it went well.

After supper, Dane and Tharyn spent some time alone, talking about their wedding and their future together.

The next morning, after Breanna Brockman had fed her family and their guest a good breakfast, Dr. Dane rode into the mountains, heading for Central City.

At the Moran gang's hideout in the mountains west of Fort Collins, Doke Veatch rode away after a slim breakfast while the men and women watched and waved.

When Doke vanished from view, Lucinda turned to the men. "Well, since the wagon has been repaired, Kathryn and I will head for Fort Collins to buy groceries and supplies as soon as we get the dishes done."

When the dishes were done and the kitchen was cleaned up, Kathryn told Lucinda she needed a few minutes in her room before they headed for Fort Collins.

Lucinda told her she would work on the grocery list and they would leave as soon as Kathryn was ready.

In her room, Kathryn quickly wrote a note on a piece of paper that she would slip to someone at the general store while they were in Fort Collins:

To Larimer County Sheriff
   James Hoffman —

Dear Sheriff Hoffman,
   The Tag Moran gang plans to hold up both banks in Cheyenne, Wyoming, on Thursday, May 12.
                    Sincerely,
                    Someone who knows

When Lucinda and Kathryn arrived in Fort Collins, they entered the general store, each carrying half the grocery and supply list so they could both pick up goods and place them in the handbaskets they carried.

Kathryn immediately made sure to go as far as possible in the store from where Lucinda was picking up goods, and began looking for just the right person. She quickly spotted a well-dressed middle-aged man in the hand tools section who appeared to be some kind of businessman.

Slipping up to him, she kept her voice low. "Good morning, sir. Are you a resident of Fort Collins?"

He smiled. "Yes, I am. I own the Spalding Furniture Store. My name is Howard Spalding. Is there something I can do for you?"

Kathryn moved a step closer, looked around to make sure Lucinda was nowhere in sight, then took out the folded slip of paper. "Mr. Spalding, will you please deliver this note to Sheriff James Hoffman as soon as possible? It is very, very important."

Spalding's brow furrowed, and a quizzical look captured his eyes.

"Sheriff Hoffman?"

"Yes, sir."

"I don't understand."

"There is no time to explain. Will you do it?"

"Why . . . ah . . . yes, of course."

Kathryn placed it in his hand. "Please, Mr. Spalding, don't let on to anyone but the sheriff that I am giving you this note, or I will be killed."

Spalding's face paled. "Really?"

"Yes, sir. Really. Now I must keep moving. And thank you, sir."

With that, Kathryn hurried away and moved into another aisle between rows of shelves.

Howard Spalding watched her disappear, then opened the note and read it. He gasped and hurried to the counter with his groceries.

A moment later, Kathryn caught sight of him at the counter. She observed as he paid for his groceries; then carrying two paper bags, he hurried out the door.

Biting her lower lip, she moved on through the store, picking up the items on her list. After a few minutes, she met up with Lucinda between two long rows of shelves. Lucinda rushed up to her with the day's edition of the *Rocky Mountain News* in her hand. "Look at this!" she said, flashing the front page at her. The headline read: MORAN GANG MEMBER KILLED.

Kathryn's lips trembled. "I — I don't want to read about Gib's death."

"I understand, honey, but Tag and the others will want to read it."

It was almost noon when the two women arrived at the hideout.

The men were glad to get their hands on the newspaper. While Lucinda and

Kathryn were in the kitchen putting the groceries and supplies in the pantry, the men sat down in the parlor, and Tag read the article to them, which related the interview the reporters had with Dr. Dane Logan.

The article told the reader that Dr. Dane Logan of Central City was engaged to be married to Miss Tharyn Tabor, daughter of First National Bank's president, David Tabor and his wife, Kitty. Further information about the wedding could be found on page 6.

While Tag was flipping back to the designated page, Lucinda and Kathryn entered the room.

Tag looked up at them. "This article on the front page says that no-good Dr. Dane Logan is getting married to the daughter of the president of the First National Bank of Denver. Page six is supposed to give more details about the wedding. I've got an idea. Let me read it."

Tag quickly found the aforesaid article and read it silently, then told the others about the wedding that would take place at the Denver church on Saturday, May 21, at 2:00 p.m.

Tag laid the paper down and grinned malevolently. "After you gals left for town this morning, I told the boys what Doke wanted to talk to me about alone yesterday. He asked me not to kill Logan because he couldn't live with himself if he was responsible for the doctor's death. I told him I would find another way to make the doctor suffer. It just came to me what we're gonna do."

Jason grinned. "Tell us about it, big brother."

Tag chuckled. "We're gonna break in on the wedding, snatch the bride at gunpoint saying we're gonna kill her, and ride away with her."

Lucinda's face pinched. "But if you kill her, Tag, Doke will still be responsible for *her* death. He'll know it."

Tag shook his head. "Aw, Lucinda, we won't really kill her. We'll keep her prisoner right here in the cabin and make Logan think we've killed her. That will cause him grief. When I figure he has suffered enough for what he did to Darryl and Gib, we'll let her go back to him."

"Well, that'll go better with Doke," put in Bart.

"Everybody agree?" asked Tag.

The other men, and Lucinda, nodded their agreement.

Kathryn conspicuously remained silent. *I*

*can only hope Howard Spalding has deliv-
ered my note to the sheriff. Tag isn't going
to let me go. I know too much. If the
lawmen don't catch them in Cheyenne
when they attempt to rob the banks, I
must find a way to escape from this place.
I'll have to plan carefully, and I'll need
some money to live on. I'll make my plans
and bide my time until I know if they are
captured in Cheyenne. Surely if my note
was given to Sheriff Hoffman, he will alert
the authorities in Cheyenne and have a
trap set for the gang at the banks on May
12.*

At that moment, Kathryn let out a little
sigh and looked up to see Tag looking at
her stonily.

"I didn't hear whether you agree with
my plan to kidnap the bride at the wedding, Kathryn."

Her throat constricted, and she couldn't
speak.

Tag shook his head. "Aw, I'm sorry,
Kathryn. You're too upset over losing Gib
to think about my plan." He ran his gaze
over the faces of the others. "We'll move
ahead as planned."

Twenty-one

For the rest of the day, Kathryn Tully was quiet and only spoke when spoken to. She helped Lucinda prepare supper that evening, but ate very little.

Later, when everyone was in the parlor discussing Tag's plan to abduct Dr. Dane Logan's bride at the wedding, Kathryn rose from her chair. "I'm really tired. I'm going to bed early."

Lucinda left the sofa where she was sitting beside Bart and put her arms around Kathryn. "I know you're hurting deeply over Gib's death, honey. You think you can get some sleep?"

Kathryn nodded. "I think so. See you in the morning."

Tony called to Kathryn as she was heading for the staircase. "Good night, Kathryn. Sleep well."

Kathryn smiled at him and nodded.

As she started up the stairs, Jason called out, "Good night, Kathryn."

Tag and Bart both called out the same words in unison. Kathryn reached the top of the stairs and turned. "Good night to all of you."

When Kathryn was out of sight, Tag looked at Lucinda. "I want you to keep a close watch on her. She could be dangerous for us if she wanted to. Her grief has her acting strange. Understand?"

Lucinda nodded. "Yes. I'll watch her. I don't think we would ever have had to worry about her if Gib had lived, but she is acting a bit strange now."

Upstairs in her room, Kathryn hung up her dress in the dark and slipped into her nightgown. When she climbed into bed, she thought about the horror Tag Moran had planned for Dr. Dane Logan and his bride. Her heart went out to them.

Soon she began sobbing over the loss of her husband, but after almost an hour, she finally cried herself to sleep.

On Tuesday morning May 10, a telegram was delivered to Chief U.S. Marshal John Brockman in Denver from Larimer County Sheriff James Hoffman in Fort Collins. Hoffman informed him of the note that was delivered to him by Howard

Spalding, declaring that the Tag Moran gang was going to hold up both Cheyenne banks on Thursday, May 12. Hoffman explained in the telegram about the young woman who had given the note to Spalding in the general store and the fear that was in her eyes when she asked that Spalding not let anyone but the sheriff know, lest the gang learn of it and kill her. Spalding had told Hoffman that he had never seen the young woman before and had no idea who she was.

Hoffman's telegram also informed Brockman that he had wired Laramie County Sheriff Jack Polson in Cheyenne about the note, and that he had advised Polson that he was also wiring Chief Brockman about it.

Brockman quickly wired Sheriff Polson that he received word from Sheriff Hoffman about the note, and that he and three deputies would arrive in Cheyenne on the evening train from Denver on Wednesday night. They would check into the Great Plains Hotel around nine o'clock, and Brockman asked that Polson meet them there so they could make plans to thwart the robberies and capture the gang.

Lucinda Moran and Kathryn Tully were

standing on the front porch of the old cabin, watching the gang ride away in the direction of Cheyenne.

Kathryn's hands were shaking. "Lucinda, why are they leaving so early? If they don't plan to camp near Cheyenne until tomorrow night, why didn't they wait and leave here this afternoon?"

"I asked Tag the same question, Kathryn. He said they will be moving slowly because the law may still have men riding these mountains, searching for them. They'll have to stay in the forests as much as possible and keep a sharp eye out for determined lawmen, who might just happen to be close by."

Kathryn nodded and placed shaky fingers to her temples. "Oh. I understand."

Lucinda noted Kathryn's nervousness. "Honey, what's wrong with you? You're as edgy as a long-tailed cat in a room full of rocking chairs. Nothing can happen to Gib, now. He isn't riding with them anymore."

Tears filmed Kathryn's eyes. "I know. I know." She stared off into space, knowing full well what was going to happen at the Cheyenne banks on Thursday if Howard Spalding delivered her note to Sheriff Hoffman — and she felt sure he had. Her heart went out to Lucinda. Bart was going to go back to prison for the rest of his life, or maybe even get killed when the lawmen surprised them at the banks.

Kathryn could not reveal to Lucinda what she had done. She turned and looked at her. "What's wrong with me, Lucinda, is that I'm worried about what's going to happen to me. I don't think Tag will ever let me go. I know too much. But — but I really do need to get away from the gang and this place and have a life of my own."

"Oh, Kathryn, if you can just hold on till we get to California, I'm sure Tag will give you Gib's share of the money. Then you'll be free to go and live wherever you want."

"Well, I hope you're right. But in the meantime, I'll feel like a captive."

Lucinda thought of Tag's uneasiness about Kathryn, and of his putting her on guard to keep an eye on her. She could only do as Tag had commanded. "It'll be all right, honey. Just hang on and let Tag and the others see that you are still a part of us."

Kathryn's stomach was jumpy and full of butterflies. She let her gaze trail down to the last spot where she had seen the gang as they rode away, knowing what lay ahead of them in Cheyenne.

Down below, the gang rode slowly and carefully through the dense forests, their eyes peeled for riders.

On Tuesday night, they made camp amid a stand of trees beside Creedmore Lake, some fifty miles southwest of Cheyenne, but did not build a fire. They traveled just as slowly and carefully on Wednesday as they left the mountains at midday and moved onto the Wyoming plains. They were relieved to arrive just outside of Cheyenne as the sun was going down and made camp in a deep draw about a mile from town. Still they had no campfire.

Wanting to let the banks have most of the day on Thursday to take in as many cash deposits as possible, Tag led his men into town just before two o'clock. First National Bank and the Bank of Cheyenne were at the town's main intersection across the street from each other. It had been agreed that Tag and Jason would enter First National at the same time Bart and Tony entered the Bank of Cheyenne.

Tag was excitedly talking about the big haul they were going to make when they drew up to the intersection. As he and Jason parted from the others, he said,

"Okay, boys, let's do it."

Tag and Jason drew up to the hitch rail in front of First National Bank and dismounted. When they looked across the street, Bart and Tony were out of their saddles, looking their way.

Tag nodded to them and headed for the bank's front door with Jason at his side. They both pulled their guns as they moved inside. They were barely in the door when four men wearing federal badges suddenly appeared, guns drawn and aimed at them.

Both outlaws froze in their tracks as they recognized Chief U.S. Marshal John Brockman behind one of the guns.

"Drop those weapons!" snapped Brockman. "Now!"

Moments later, when the handcuffed Moran brothers were ushered out the bank's front door, they looked across the street and saw Sheriff Jack Polson with three of his deputies, standing beside Bart and Tony, who were handcuffed.

Standing close by the sheriff was a reporter from the Cheyenne newspaper, making notes.

Polson and his men ushered the shackled outlaws across the street, and Bart and Tony looked sick as they set their disconsolate eyes on Tag and Jason. When they drew up, John Brockman turned to Tag Moran. "Well, Tag, you and what's left of your gang are going *inside* the Wyoming Territorial Prison this time. That is, after you face Judge Yeager again."

The reporter was making more notes while Tag and his men were looking at each other despairingly.

Brockman and his deputies used a wagon belonging to the sheriff's office in Cheyenne to take the Moran gang back to Rawlins with the reporter riding along so he could get the full story.

They drove all night and arrived in Rawlins just after nine o'clock the next morning. They went immediately to the county courthouse and found Judge George Yeager in his office. When Yeager learned from Chief Brockman that he had the Moran gang in custody outside the courthouse, he sent his secretary to fetch the Carbon County sheriff and his deputies. He also gave permission for the reporter from the Cheyenne newspaper to be present in his office as the Moran gang was brought in.

Once again, the outlaws faced a stern Judge Yeager, who already had the information on the bank robberies the gang had pulled since they had escaped and gone back to their old ways.

As the outlaws stood glumly before the judge with their hands shackled behind their backs and the federal marshals flanking them, Yeager said evenly, "Bart, Jason, Tony — your sentences will remain the same; life in prison with no chance of parole."

All three men hung their heads.

Yeager then put his cold gaze on Tag Moran. "And your sentence remains the same. You will hang. I am setting the time of the execution right now. Tag Moran, you will hang at sunrise next Wednesday, May 18. You have exactly five days to live. I could have you hanged before the sun sets today, but I'm setting it five days from now because I want you to have time to think about those people you have shot and killed during your robberies and the penalty you are facing for your wicked deeds."

With those words ringing in his ears, Tag seemed to cave in. His face went sheet white, his jaw slacked, and his knees buckled.

One of the federal deputies grasped him to keep him from falling.

The judge said thinly, "Mr. Moran, you

should have thought about your fear of dying before you became a killer."

Tag Moran's skin tingled with horror. His pulse pounded, his forehead dampened with perspiration, and his eyelids twitched nervously.

Yeager looked at the chief U.S. marshal. "Chief Brockman, you can take your prisoners outside now. The sheriff and his deputies will be here shortly to take them to the prison."

When the trembling Tag Moran and his three gang members were taken to the prison by the Carbon County sheriff and his three deputies, Chief Brockman went to the Western Union office and wired the news back to his office to be reported to both Denver newspapers. He also wired Sheriff James Hoffman in Fort Collins to advise him of the gang's capture and to give him the date that Judge George Yeager had set for Tag Moran's execution.

With this done, Brockman, his deputies, and the reporter headed back to Cheyenne in the wagon. Brockman and his deputies would catch the next train to Denver.

On Saturday, May 14, the stagecoach driven by Buck Cummons arrived in Fort

Collins on its regular run from Casper.

The Wells Fargo agent was quick to tell Buck and Doke the news, and showed them the story of the Moran gang's capture in Cheyenne on Thursday as reported in the *Fort Collins Gazette.*

Buck released a satisfied sigh. "This is great news! I'm so glad to hear that rotten gang is now locked up in the Wyoming Territorial Prison! They won't escape this time. And their leader won't escape the noose, either."

Doke's voice quivered. "I know Tag deserves to be hanged, but it's hard to think about it because it was him who saved my life years ago at the risk of his own life."

Buck nodded. "I can understand why it's hard for you, Doke."

"Yeah," said the agent. "I can understand too. The man who saved your life is about to lose his own."

Doke wiped a palm over his face. "Fellas, I'd like to go to the prison and see Tag before he's executed. Would you give me a few days off so I can do that?"

The agent nodded. "Sure, Doke. You all right about it, Buck?"

Buck nodded. "Of course. I'll get Clem Dobbins to fill in for him. When do you want to go, Doke?"

"Tomorrow, if it's all right. I'll ride to Rawlins. That way I can see him on Monday."

"Sure. See you when you get back."

On that same Saturday, May 14, Lucinda Moran and Kathryn Tully went into Fort Collins to buy groceries and supplies as usual.

As they hauled up in front of the general store and climbed out of the wagon seat, they heard people on the boardwalk talking about the Moran gang being apprehended again. This time it was in Cheyenne. They had been taken to the Wyoming Territorial Prison at Rawlins.

Kathryn felt relief wash through her body. Her note had done it.

Lucinda hurried to the nearby newsstand and bought the day's edition of the *Fort Collins Gazette.* She opened the front page so both could see it, and they silently read it together.

When they had finished, Lucinda blinked at her tears. "Oh, Kathryn, how am I going to stand it? Bart will be in that prison for the rest of his life. And — and next Wednesday, Tag will hang at sunrise."

Kathryn was secretly comforted, knowing the gang members were finally locked up. Now they wouldn't be abducting Dr.

Dane Logan's bride during the wedding next Saturday. As for Tag, he was getting what he deserved.

She hid a secret smile. *I don't want Lucinda to know that I'm the one who advised the law about the gang's plan to rob the Cheyenne banks. She would be furious. I can only hope that I never see Howard Spalding again. I'll have to be careful when I'm in Fort Collins.*

Kathryn met Lucinda's teary gaze. "I'm sorry for what this is doing to you, Lucinda, but at least your husband is still alive."

Lucinda sniffed. "Yes. Bart's still alive. And that is some comfort. But he's going to be in prison for the rest of his life. So what kind of life does that give me?"

Kathryn put her arms around her. "Honey, I'll stay with you until we can both make some plans."

"Thank you. Right now, I don't know what I'd do without you."

A pang of guilt struck Kathryn's heart, but she quickly dismissed it. *I did what I had to do. Those men had to be caught and put behind bars. But . . . I do feel sorry for Lucinda, even though she was all in favor of what the gang was doing.*

In Fort Collins, Doke Veatch entered his room at the boardinghouse and closed the door behind him. His mind was churning. He had been thinking about Tag Moran all the way to the boardinghouse, and had decided he could not just stand by and let the man who had saved his life die. If it weren't for Tag, he would have been dead a long time ago.

Doke crossed the room to his gun cabinet and took out a .41-caliber double-vertical-barreled Derringer pocket pistol. He opened a box of cartridges, loaded the gun, and put it in a paper bag.

Before dawn the next morning, he rode out of Fort Collins, heading northwest toward Rawlins, Wyoming, keeping his horse at a steady trot. He arrived in Rawlins as darkness was falling and took a room in the town's only hotel.

The next morning, under a clear, sunny sky, Doke rode out to the prison, wanting to look it over. As he rode around the twelve-foot-high stockade fence, he noticed the guards with rifles in the two towers that rose above the fence. At one point, he spied one of the guards watching him and waved at him, wanting to appear as a casual, curious rider. The guard nodded and waved back.

Soon he guided his horse to the top of a nearby grassy knoll, which was high enough to let him see into the prison yard. He noted that the gallows was visible in a corner of the yard close to the large stone building with the barred windows that housed the prisoners. A shiver ran down his spine as he thought of Tag dying on the somber gallows on Wednesday morning.

Doke observed the inmates milling about the fenced-in area, which he estimated would cover about half an acre. A few armed, uniformed guards were also moving about, keeping watch on the convicts.

Suddenly he saw Bart and Jason Moran and Tony Chacone standing aloof from the rest of the inmates, talking to each other. He told himself that since Tag was slated to be hanged, he no doubt was being kept in his cell.

Having taken it all in, Doke rode back into town and returned to his hotel room. That night after darkness fell, he rode back out to the prison to make the final move for the plan he had in mind. There was no moon, only the soft, faint glow of the stars to give him light.

On Tuesday morning, Doke drew near

449

the prison and guided his horse once more to the top of the grassy knoll. There he saw the inmates milling about the prison yard and soon picked out Bart, Jason, and Tony. Once again, the trio was aloof from the rest of the prisoners. The guards were there in the yard and in the towers.

Doke rode his horse up to the front gate and drew rein. One of the two guards in the tower next to the gate looked down and said, "What can we do for you, mister?"

"Sir, I'm a lifelong friend of one of your prisoners. His name is Tag Moran, and he is being hanged tomorrow morning. I would like to visit him if possible."

The guard nodded. "We know about Moran's appointment with the hangman tomorrow. You can see him. I'll be right down. Go ahead and dismount and tie your horse to one of those hitching posts."

Quickly descending the tower stairs, the guard opened the gate and escorted Doke inside the building. He told the guard at the desk who the young man wanted to see and left to return to the tower.

Moments later, after identifying himself as a shotgunner for Wells Fargo Stagelines and being frisked, Doke was escorted toward the visiting room while another guard went after Tag.

When Doke and the guard entered the visiting room, the guard guided him to a barred window and had him sit down in the wooden chair that was provided. Doke quickly noted that the window was covered with metal netting so nothing could be passed between convict and visitor.

A few minutes later, the door to the room on the other side of the barred window came open, and the guard who had gone after Tag had him at his side. He motioned toward the window where Doke sat and said, "You've got fifteen minutes, Moran."

Tag nodded glumly and headed toward the window. The guard stepped out, closed and locked the door. There were no other visitors at the moment.

When Tag sat down, he tried to smile. "Doke, ol' pal, I really am glad to see you."

Doke made a smile. "You too, Tag." Keeping his voice low, he said, "We don't have much time, so listen closely. I have devised a way of escape for you."

Tag's eyes brightened a bit. "Go on."

"I arrived in Rawlins Sunday night and took a room at the hotel. Yesterday, I rode out here to look the place over, then went back to the hotel. After dark last night, I came back out here. I sneaked up to the stockade fence and placed a paper bag containing a loaded double-barreled Derringer next to a fence post. With that four-inch space between the bottom log of the fence and the ground, it was easy to do."

Tag nodded.

"I'm gonna ask to see Bart next and I'll tell him where the gun is. It'll be up to him, Jason, and Tony to get you out of your cell, and all four of you out of this prison."

A smile spread over Tag's face. "Bart will handle it, I guarantee you." The smile drained away; then Tag said, "Doke, thanks for doing this."

"Hey, pal, you saved my life once. Now I'm doing what I can to save yours. Ah, just one thing."

"Yeah?"

"I know you still carry your hatred for Dr. Dane Logan."

"So?"

"I want your solemn promise that you will not kill him."

"Okay, you have my solemn promise that I won't kill him."

"Thank you. I'll give it a few days; then I'll come to your hideout in the mountains and see you."

"That'll be fine, Doke. You will be plenty welcome."

At that moment, the guard who had brought Doke into the visiting room came through the door. Moving up to him, he said, "Time's up, Mr. Veatch."

The lock in the door behind Tag rattled, the door came open, and the guard said, "Okay, Moran, let's go."

To make it look normal, Tag put on an act, shedding tears as if he were seeing Doke for the last time. He was still bawling when the guard pushed him out the door.

When the door clanked shut, Doke turned to the guard who was about to usher him out. "Sir, would it be possible for me to have a few minutes with Tag's brother, Bart?"

"Well, as long as you're here, I don't see why not. You sit tight."

Moments later, when Doke and Bart were alone, Doke told him of hiding the Derringer in the paper bag at the base of the third post from the southwest corner underneath the stockade fence, on the west side.

Bart grinned. "You really are a true friend, Doke."

"I owe Tag my life. If I can save his life and make it so you, Jason, and Tony can escape, I'm happy. I used a Derringer rather than a regular revolver because you can easily conceal it in a pocket or a boot. Tag said you can handle it from here, Bart."

Bart nodded. "You bet I can handle it. Once the Derringer is in my pocket, I'll casually make my way up to the captain of the guards. I'll grab him and put the gun to his head. I guarantee you, the warden and his guards will not jeopardize the captain's life. We'll make our escape, taking the captain with us as hostage. Once we're in the clear, we'll leave him tied up somewhere, steal some horses, and head for the hideout."

"Sounds good. See you soon at the hideout."

"You sure will."

Moments later, Doke was in the saddle riding toward Fort Collins, feeling confident he had saved Tag Moran's life.

Twenty-two

At the hideout on Wednesday morning some twenty minutes after sunrise, Lucinda Moran and Kathryn Tully stood at the parlor window looking northward, in the direction of Rawlins, Wyoming.

An emotional tide washed through Lucinda. She drew a shaky breath and looked at Kathryn. "Well, it's all over for Tag by now."

Kathryn nodded silently. After a few seconds, she said, "If only Tag had listened to me months ago, we would all be in California at this very moment. Gib would still be alive, and so would Tag. And you would still have Bart with you. Now our dream has turned into a nightmare."

It was Lucinda's turn to nod in silence.

Later in the day, the two women were sitting on the front porch of the cabin, both staring silently at the forests around them.

"Lucinda, we've both got to start thinking about our futures. I certainly don't want to stay here in this remote place, and I don't think you do either."

Lucinda moved her head back and forth. "No."

"Well, we have plenty of money in the kitty for the two of us. We can afford to move into a town and buy a house."

Without hesitation, Lucinda said, "I'd like to move to Rawlins so I'd be close to Bart and could visit him regularly. We could buy a house there."

Kathryn was feeling some guilt over the plight she had put Lucinda in by giving the note to Howard Spalding. For the time being though, she would go along with Lucinda's desire to make their home in Rawlins. She told herself that her time in this part of the country was limited. Not too long from now, she would take her share of the money and go to sunny California.

She was eager to get started in her new life: a life free from all that had to do with the gang, and from Lucinda, who was still a part of it because she had a husband she would be visiting in the Wyoming Territorial Prison. She smiled at Lucinda. "All right, let's plan to move to Rawlins."

Lucinda nodded and returned the smile.

"We'll do it. I'd like to wait a few days though, give my nerves a little time to settle down."

"Sure."

All was quiet around them, save the slight sound of the breeze in the surrounding trees and the periodic chirp of a bird.

Kathryn found herself daydreaming about California: the sunshine, the flowers in bloom year round, a place with a view of the blue Pacific Ocean, no snow or frigid temperatures.

She smiled to herself. *That sure does sound good! Maybe with my share of the money, I can open my own boutique. I'll live quietly and enjoy every day to the fullest!*

On Thursday, May 19, at Central City, Dr. Dane Logan was seated in the office of his medical practice with Dr. Robert Fraser and Nurse Nadine Wahl.

Running his gaze between them, Dane said, "I want to thank both of you for your great help in taking care of the practice when I've had to be away. And now, I want to thank you that you will do the same so I can marry Tharyn and we can have a three-day honeymoon in Colorado Springs."

Dr. Fraser smiled. "Esther and I would like to attend the wedding, and so would Nadine, but we can't do that and take care of the practice at the same time. But we certainly wish you well, and we're very much looking forward to having Tharyn living here in Central City."

"We sure are," said Nadine, her eyes bright. "And isn't she going to be surprised when you bring her here after the honeymoon and she finds out you bought that house over on Spruce Street?"

Dane laughed. "She sure *will* be surprised, Nadine. And since you and Esther looked it over and gave your opinions about the woman's touch already evident in the house, I'm so excited I can hardly contain myself!"

"She'll love it, Doctor; I guarantee it."

Moments later, Dr. Fraser and Nadine stood on the boardwalk in front of the office as Dr. Dane mounted his horse. As he settled in the saddle, he said, "See you in a few days, and I'll have my beautiful bride with me!"

Both of them waved as he rode away.

It was a glorious spring day in the Rocky Mountains, and as Dr. Dane guided Pal along the winding path that led eastward toward Denver, the sky was clear. Wild-flowers were poking their heads up through the soil, and green buds were evident in the aspen and birch trees.

Drawing in a deep breath of the pure mountain air, Dane spoke to the birds that were twittering in the trees around him. "Thank you for your congratulations! You are certainly right. I *am* going to marry the most wonderful and most beautiful woman in all the world!"

As he guided Pal down the steep path, Dane whistled a happy tune. It was a long arduous ride down the mountains to Denver, but it didn't bother Dane. His mind was focused on Tharyn, their wedding, and their future together.

"Just think," he said aloud, "the next time I make my journey to Central City, my bride will be by my side." He looked skyward. "Thank You, Lord, for Your abundant blessings. Truly, my cup runneth over."

On the same day at sundown, Lucinda Moran and Kathryn Tully were preparing supper for themselves in the kitchen of the old cabin when they heard horses blowing.

They looked at each other, eyes wide.

"Who in the world can that be?" whispered Lucinda.

Both women left the kitchen and rushed into the parlor. They hid themselves behind the drapes at one edge of the large window and peered out.

Lucinda felt her pulse leap and gasped. "Kathryn! It — it's T-Tag and the others!"

"How do you suppose they escaped?"

Lucinda was on her way to the door, and Kathryn caught up to her just as she plunged out on to the porch and down the steps. Kathryn paused on the porch, watching as Bart quickly dismounted and gathered Lucinda into his arms.

"What happened? How did you escape this time?" Kathryn asked the other men as they were leaving their saddles.

Tag started up the steps. "Let's go inside," he said, his voice void of emotion. "Then we'll tell you."

Suddenly Kathryn's heart lurched in her breast. *Could Tag possibly have found out about the note I gave Howard Spalding? If he knows, he will kill me. Maybe not immediately, but he will find a way to do it so the others don't know it was him.*

The fear that gripped her was building a pressure inside her head. Her neck muscles stiffened as she walked inside the cabin with the others.

When everyone had gathered in the

460

parlor, Bart and Lucinda sat on the sofa together, and the others took chairs. Kathryn's blood felt like it had turned to ice water, and a dagger of fear stabbed her heart.

Tag Moran told the women about Doke Veatch, having hidden the Derringer at the base of a fence post in the stockade fence at the prison, and how Bart used the gun to free them from the prison by holding the gun to the head of the captain of the guard. Tag warned the warden and the guards that if they followed, he would kill the captain. He also told them that once he and his gang members were a safe distance from the prison and were not being followed, they would leave the captain alive and tied to a tree where someone could find him.

Tag explained that when they were across the border into Colorado, they gagged the captain and tied him to a rancher's tree at night. They then entered the barn and stole four of the rancher's horses, along with bridles and saddles. They rode for the hideout, certain that no one had followed them.

Kathryn's fear suddenly grew more intense when Lucinda said, "Tag, how did the law know you were going to hold up the Cheyenne banks?"

Tag shrugged. "I have no idea. We asked them, but they refused to tell us."

Kathryn quickly averted her eyes from Tag's face for fear that her guilt would show.

"We figured since Tag was gonna hang and the rest of us were in for life," put in Bart "they could at least tell us how they found out. But not a peep from any of them."

The pressure Kathryn was feeling abruptly eased. But she was upset in another way at Tag's next words.

Vengeance was burning in his eyes as he said stiffly, "I'm still gonna get my revenge on that no-good Dr. Dane Logan. Since I promised Doke I wouldn't kill Logan, we're gonna go ahead with the plan to abduct his bride at the wedding. You gals can keep her here at the hideout until I'm satisfied Logan has suffered sufficiently thinking she's dead. Then we'll set her free."

Kathryn wanted to tell Tag he shouldn't make Dr. Logan's bride suffer for something the doctor did, but she knew better than to cross him.

"Anyway," Tag went on, "we'll pull several more bank robberies in Colorado and

Wyoming between now and September, then we'll hightail it for California. Even though we won't have the quarter of a million each that we had planned on, we'll live on what we've accumulated. No more of the outlaw trail after that."

Lucinda smiled at Kathryn, who was feeling some relief.

Kathryn told herself that one day she would rid herself of the gang and go on to live her own life.

On Friday morning, May 20, Dane and Tharyn stood in Denver's Union Station with John and Breanna and David and Kitty, waiting for the train from Cheyenne to come in.

They were talking excitedly about Dane's parents being on the train, as well as Dane's friend, Kenny Atwood Ross, and Tharyn's friend, Leanne Ladd Ross. Kenny and Leanne had taken a train from their home in Bozeman, Montana, to Cheyenne and met up with Dane's parents for the trip to Denver.

The Tabors and the Brockmans understood that Tharyn and Leanne — who was blind — had been on an orphan train together in late 1871; that Dane and Kenny — who had a wooden leg — had been on an orphan train together in early 1872, and that both Kenny and Leanne had been adopted by attorney Mike Ross and his wife, Julie, who lived in Denver at the time. Leanne was now twenty-two, and would be one of the bridesmaids in the wedding. Kenny, now eighteen, would be one of the groomsmen.

They also discussed the fact that Melinda Scott Kenyon was also a bridesmaid and Dr. Tim Braden was the other groomsman. Dane told John Brockman how happy he was that the chief had agreed to be his best man, and Tharyn told Breanna how honored she was that she had agreed to be her matron of honor. Both Dane and Tharyn told the Brockmans how glad they were that Paul would be the ring bearer and Ginny would be the flower girl.

At that moment, the sound of the train chugging into the station met their ears. The small group drew near the track on the platform.

Soon the train came to a stop and they saw Dr. Jacob Logan and Naomi coming out of the second coach, followed by Kenny leading Leanne.

Jacob and Naomi were thrilled to meet Tharyn, as well as the Brockmans and the Tabors. Leanne was thrilled to meet Dane.

It was a joy for the Tabors and the Brockmans to be with Leanne and Kenny again.

The Brockmans invited Kenny and Leanne to stay in their home, and the Tabors invited the Logans to stay in theirs. The four of them would catch a train for Cheyenne on Monday.

As the group was walking out of the railroad station, Dane and Tharyn were holding hands. He looked down at her and said, "So your wedding dress really turned out good, eh?"

"It sure did. I'm very pleased with it."

"Well, sweetheart, I can't wait to see you in it, walking down the aisle toward me on your daddy's arm."

That evening, the wedding practice was held at the church. The practice went well, with Pastor Nathan Blandford standing on the platform, watching David Tabor walking Tharyn down the aisle toward a nervous Dane Logan.

When the practice was over, and the wedding party was sitting in the fellowship hall enjoying a dinner provided by the women of the church, the men talked to Chief Brockman about the Tag Moran gang's escape from the Wyoming Territorial Prison, wondering how Bart Moran got his hands on the Derringer.

John told them he wished he knew. He explained the details of how the gang left the captain of the guards tied to a tree on a ranch just south of the Colorado-Wyoming border, and got away clean. It was anybody's guess where they were holed up. He and his deputies were ready to go after them once they made an appearance somewhere.

Later that evening, Dane and Tharyn were alone on the front porch swing at the Tabor house while both sets of parents were getting better acquainted in the parlor.

The stars in the black velvet sky were twinkling and seemed to be smiling down on the happy couple, who were holding hands.

The evening breeze ruffled Tharyn's auburn hair, blowing wisps across her forehead as Dane met her soft gaze.

"I still feel like I'm dreaming, like I'm going to wake up in the morning and find that none of this is real," Dane said.

A slow smile tugged at the corners of her mouth, then spread all the way to her starlit eyes. "I know what you mean, but it's real, all right. The Lord made it real. He has been so good to us. And speaking of waking up in the morning, just think, darling — one more sunrise and I'll be Mrs. Dane Logan!"

Dane felt as though his heart would explode with ecstasy. He pulled her close, kissed her softly, and said in a whisper, "You are so right, sweetheart. You sure will!"

They sat on the swing, holding hands for a few more minutes; then they prayed together, asking God to bless their marriage and their lives together.

Dane kissed her good night, saying he would be eagerly watching for her to come through those doors at the back of the auditorium on her father's arm. He then mounted Pal and rode away into the night, heading for the Brockman place in the country where he would spend the night as their third guest.

Dawn was painting the eastern horizon with a bright golden glow when Tharyn roused from sleep. Luxuriating for a few moments in her soft bed, a broad smile graced her face. She stretched, tossed the covers back, and sat up. Looking out the east window of her room, she saw the top rim of the sun mounting on the horizon.

She drew a short breath. "This is the day, Lord. There's that sunrise I've been expecting. It's the last one I'll see as Miss Tharyn Tabor. Today I will marry my best and dearest friend. How can I ever thank You for making this all possible? A few short months ago, I thought I'd never see Dane again on this earth. Now in just a few hours, I will be his wife!"

A familiar Scripture came to mind as she relished the day that lay before her: "For my thoughts are not your thoughts, neither are your ways my ways, saith the Lord. For as the heavens are higher than the earth, so are my ways higher than your ways, and my thoughts than your thoughts."

With her eyes still on the glorious sunrise, she said, "Yes! Isaiah 55:8 and 9. I'm so glad, heavenly Father, that I surrendered my thoughts to Your lofty thoughts and my ways to Your loving ways. How beautifully You have made the seemingly impossible become possible! Please take this day and grant us Your special blessings and may our lives be ever centered on You. I love You, Lord Jesus. Thank You for making this day possible."

Letting God's peace wash over her and knowing that the rest of the household was still asleep, Tharyn left the bed, put on her robe, and sat in her chair by the east window. Drawing her feet up under her, she watched the sun mount until it lifted off the horizon. Her heart beat fast as she contemplated the day that lay before her.

At noon that day, knowing the wedding was set for two o'clock in the afternoon, Tag Moran, his two brothers, and Tony Chacone tied their horses in a thick stand of trees some thirty yards to the west side of the white frame church building, which was on the west edge of Denver.

"Now let's go over the plan one more time," said Tag, facing his three gang members. "As I've pointed out already, I've attended enough church weddings to know that the bride and her father will enter the auditorium from the vestibule once everyone is seated. We'll have our horses ready at the front of the building, where Jason and Tony will be holding them.

"Bart and I will be on the porch, peeking through the windows beside the door. Just before the bride and her father leave the vestibule, we'll burst through the door, grab her at gunpoint, tell her father we're gonna kill her, then knock him cold with a gun barrel. I'll put my hand over her mouth, pick her up, carry her to my horse, and we'll all ride away in a hurry."

The gang talked it over for a while; then at 1:15, they peered through the trees and saw a buggy pull up to a door on the west side of the church building near the front. Three women got out of the buggy. One of them was carrying a white wedding dress on a hanger.

They moved into the side room through its door, closed it, and immediately pulled down the shades of the room's two windows.

"Well," said Tag, "it's obvious that those two women are going to help the bride get into her dress in that room."

At the same moment, they saw more vehicles coming.

In the Sunday school room, Kitty and Breanna began helping Tharyn get out of the dress she was wearing and into the wedding dress. Once the wedding dress was on, they lifted the shades on the two windows.

They could hear people entering the building at the front door, and knew this group would include the organist and soloist, Pastor and Mrs. Blandford, David,

John, Paul, Ginny, Leanne, Kenny, Melinda, Tim — and Dane.

In the stand of trees, the gang watched the small group enter the building through the front door, and shortly thereafter, the wedding guests began arriving. They stiffened a little when they saw that some of the male guests — though dressed nice for the wedding — wore badges on their suit coats and guns on their hips.

Tag said, "Boys, I've changed my mind about our tactics. With those lawmen among the guests, this could get dangerous. Instead of snatching Logan's bride when she and her father are about to walk down the aisle, we'll sneak up to the side of the building and take her from the room where she and the two women are right now. We'll gag and bind the two women and tell them we're gonna kill Logan's bride."

He pointed at the windows. "See? They're still in there. We'll go as soon as the coast is clear."

Minutes later, everyone else who was standing at the front of the building filed inside. Soon even the stragglers had entered the building.

With Tag in the lead, the gang members

led their horses to the rear of the building. They heard the organ begin playing in the auditorium and could hear a woman singing a solo.

They left their horses with Tony, and the Moran brothers ducked low as they hurried alongside the building to the door of the Sunday school room. Tag peeked through one of the windows and saw the bride in her wedding dress as the two women were adjusting her hair and the veil.

Tag burst through the door, his gun drawn, and hissed in a low voice as startled gasps flew from the mouths of all three women, "One peep and we'll kill all three of you!"

They stared in terror at the mean-looking trio.

While Kitty, Breanna, and Tharyn were being gagged and their wrists bound behind their backs, Tag said in a low voice, "I'm Tag Moran. I'm gonna kill Logan's bride because he let my brother Darryl and my good friend Gib Tully die because they were outlaws. He could have saved them! You tell him what I said, won't you?"

Wide-eyed and breathing hard, Kitty and Breanna were forced to lie down on the floor, and their ankles were tied together so it would be impossible for them to move quickly to the vestibule door.

Blood was pounding in Tharyn's head. Her face was a chalky mask as she looked at her mother and Breanna, making a whining sound through her gag while Tag hurried out the door with her in his arms.

In the church auditorium, while the organ was playing a hymn, Pastor Nathan Blandford, John Brockman, and the groom came out of a side room beside the platform and took their places.

Meanwhile, back in the vestibule, David Tabor waited with Leanne and Kenny, Melinda and Tim, and Paul and Ginny. He expected Kitty, Breanna, and the bride to come out of the Sunday school room.

David ran his gaze over the faces of the others and said, "I wonder what's keeping them. It's almost time to start down the aisle."

"They sure ought to be showing up here in a few seconds," said Kenny, adjusting himself on his wooden leg.

"Maybe I'd better tap on the door," said David, heading that way.

They all watched as David tapped on the door. When there was no response, David looked back at them and frowned. He turned the knob, opened the door, and was surprised to see Kitty and Breanna on the floor, bound and gagged.

As the others dashed into the room, David untied Kitty's gag first. While he was working on Breanna's gag, Kitty told him with a quivering voice what happened, who it was, and of Tag Moran's words about killing Tharyn and why.

David turned to the others. "Get those ropes off them. I'll go tell Pastor, Dane, and the others what's happened!"

David ran down the aisle and told Dane, the pastor, and John what had happened, and of Tag Moran's words about killing Tharyn because Dr. Dane Logan let his brother and friend die when he could have saved them.

Standing at the foot of the platform with his best man beside him, Dane looked at David in stunned disbelief as the words came off his tongue. *This can't be happening!* his numb mind repeated over and over.

When David had finished, Dane turned to John. "Tag Moran is already a killer! He'll have no qualms about killing again! After all, he can only hang once, no matter how many people he kills. We've got to trail those heartless outlaws and catch them before they kill Tharyn."

John looked toward his deputies who sat in the pews and told them he was forming a posse to go after the gang right now.

Some of the deputies had to borrow saddled horses from among the guests, rather than using their own wagons that were in the lot.

John checked on Breanna and Kitty to make sure they were all right, and in less than five minutes, the posse rode away from the church, heading westward. The chief U.S. marshal figured the outlaws would head into the mountains.

Among the deputies was a determined Dr. Dane Logan.

Twenty-three

Fear clutched Dr. Dane Logan's heart. They had found the gang's trail leading into the mountains, but soon came to a stream, where the hoofprints of the gang's horses led to its south bank. Brockman had two of the deputies cross the stream and ride the north bank, while he, the other two deputies, and Dr. Dane rode the south bank in hopes of finding evidence where they had emerged from the stream.

Dane knew right then that prayer was his only avenue of hope. Bouncing in the saddle, he whispered, "Oh, Lord, You know how long I prayed that You would let me see Tharyn again. And in Your loving kindness, You answered those prayers and brought us together. I beg of You, please don't let her be taken from me again. Lead this posse in the right direction. Tag Moran has said he would kill her. Only You can prevent that from happening, Lord. Let us catch up to them and find Tharyn unharmed."

As the posse continued on, Dane prayed over and over.

The hours passed, and the search became more complicated when the stream merged with a wide river. The chief sent the same two deputies across the river to ride the far bank while he and the others rode the bank before them.

This went on until darkness was falling and the posse had found no further trace of the gang. Brockman signaled for the deputies on the other side of the river to cross back. He turned to Dr. Dane. "I'm sorry, Doc. We've lost their trail. We'd better head back to town."

"But we *will* take up the search in the morning, won't we?"

"Of course. We need to go back to town and get ourselves some food and rest since we didn't come prepared to camp. We'll start out at dawn tomorrow. I don't want to discourage you, but we have to be realistic. These mountains have so many streams and rivers the gang can ride and leave no trail. Besides, this gang has eluded the law for years. They know all the tricks."

"Yes, but we can't give up."

"We're not giving up yet. Tomorrow,

we'll have our bedrolls and food enough to last several days. Maybe those outlaws will slip up or get careless. Let's take a few minutes here and pray together."

"I'd really appreciate that, Chief."

John gathered the deputies around and led in prayer, asking God to keep His mighty hand of protection on Tharyn and to spare her life. He also prayed that the Lord would deliver the gang into the hands of the posse.

As they started down the mountain toward Denver, Dane said, "First thing in the morning, I'll go to the Western Union office and wire Dr. Fraser, so he will know what's happened."

The Tag Moran gang — knowing there would be a posse after them — rode many a stream, working extremely hard to make sure they left no trail. They rode all night and arrived at the hideout at sunup the next morning. They had blindfolded Tharyn late in the afternoon the day before and removed the blindfold when they dismounted in front of the cabin.

Lucinda and Kathryn were in the kitchen preparing their breakfast when the gang came in with Dr. Dane Logan's bride, whose features were drawn, and her wedding dress was wrinkled and a bit soiled. Tag told them her name was Tharyn.

Bart folded Lucinda in his arms and kissed her.

While more places were being set at the table, Lucinda spoke gruffly to Tharyn, telling her she would be staying in Kathryn's room with her.

Tag looked at Kathryn and said levelly, "You keep a watch on her at all times. Don't let her out of your sight."

Kathryn nodded.

When they were sitting down to breakfast, Kathryn spoke to Tharyn kindly and sat beside her.

While picking at her food, a frightened and heartsick Tharyn prayed, *Lord, help me not to question why You have allowed this to happen to me, but to trust in You. There has been no more said about killing me. Help me to stay calm.*

Tharyn was fully aware of her heavenly Father's hand on her and felt a measure of peace.

When breakfast was over, Lucinda said, "Kathryn you go ahead and take Tharyn up to your room. Since both of you are about the same size, you can let her get out of that wedding dress and into one of your dresses, can't you?"

"Yes. I was planning to do that." Kathryn looked at Tharyn. "I'm sure you would like to put a brush to your hair too."

Tharyn managed a smile. "I would, thank you."

As Kathryn and Tharyn rose to their feet, Tag looked up at his captive. "No funny business, Tharyn. You try to escape, you'll be caught, and you'll be sorry. Got that?"

Tharyn nodded.

The others watched as Kathryn led the weary bride out of the kitchen.

As they climbed the stairs, Kathryn took hold of Tharyn's hand. "I have several dresses for you to choose from. You can take your pick."

Tharyn set soft eyes on her. "Thank you, Kathryn. You are very kind."

When they reached the second floor, Kathryn guided her down the hall to the very last room on the right. She opened the door and closed it behind them. "The closet is right over here."

It took Tharyn a moment to pick out a cotton dress.

When she had removed the wedding dress, Kathryn handed her a hanger. "Here, honey. Put it on this, and I'll hang it in the closet for you."

Tharyn fitted the hanger on the wedding dress, then caressed the soft fabric with tears in her eyes.

While Kathryn was hanging the wedding dress in the closet, Tharyn put on the cotton dress. Turning around, Kathryn looked her up and down. "You look better in that dress than I do."

Tharyn didn't know what to say.

"Come on," said Kathryn. "If we stay up here too long, Tag will be banging on that door."

"Thank you, again, for being so kind to me."

The rest of the day was spent with Tharyn in the presence of both young women, and at times, the gang too. Periodically, Tag made it a point to speak roughly to her, venting out on her the wrath he felt toward Dr. Dane Logan.

That night at bedtime when Kathryn and Tharyn entered their room, Kathryn sat down on the bed and motioned for Tharyn to sit beside her. Taking both of Tharyn's hands in her own, she said, "Honey, I'm sorry for the way Tag treats you, and for what he did in abducting you at your wedding. I've observed you all day, and I have to say that I see unusual strength in you. Most women would have fallen apart."

"Kathryn, it is the Lord who is giving me this strength. I know the Lord Jesus Christ as my personal Saviour, and when a person belongs to Him, He has a way of giving peace and strength beyond human understanding."

Kathryn stared at her for a brief moment. "I've heard other people talk like that. This knowing Jesus as your personal Saviour is the same thing as being born again, isn't it?"

"Yes."

Kathryn shook her head in wonderment. "There really must be something to it."

"There sure is. I'd like to tell you about it."

"Okay. Maybe tomorrow night. Right now you look very tired, and I think I feel just as tired as you look." She paused, then said, "I want to tell you something."

"Yes?"

"You know that Tag left word with those people in the wedding that he was going to kill you."

Tharyn nodded.

"Well, Tharyn, Tag just wanted to make that young doctor of yours suffer. He isn't planning to kill you."

Tharyn felt a wave of relief wash over her and thanked the Lord in her heart. "I appreciate your telling me this, Kathryn. Because I'm a born-again child of God, I'm not afraid to die, but it's only natural to want to live, and of course, to marry the most wonderful man in the world."

"Well, honey, if it's at all within my power, you will wear your wedding dress again when you marry your young doctor. It'll have to be washed and pressed, but I'm trying to come up with a way to see that you can make a successful escape."

Tharyn looked a bit puzzled by Kathryn's words, but somehow felt she could trust her.

At midmorning on Friday, May 27, a solemn-faced Dane Logan walked into his office and was greeted by Robert Fraser and Nadine Wahl. There were no patients in the office at the time, so they sat down and listened intently as Dr. Dane told them the story in full.

Dane gave them the details on Tharyn's abduction, then told them of how Chief U.S. Marshal John Brockman led the posse in a search of the mountains for six days without ever picking up the gang's trail.

Dane sighed. "I couldn't ask the chief to

spend any more time searching. It would be fruitless. There's just too much territory to cover. And for that matter, they could be clear out of the area by now."

Dr. Fraser set compassionate eyes on the distraught young physician. "Son, Esther and I have been praying, as has Nadine. The Lord knows where Tharyn is, and I believe she is still alive. By prayer, we can see her escape and be back in your arms."

Dane nodded. "We have a God who can do that, Doctor. And though my mind will be occupied with Tharyn and I will be praying continually, I must resume my medical work."

Early in the afternoon on that same day, the stagecoach driven by Buck Cummons arrived in Fort Collins. Doke Veatch was on the seat beside him.

After they had unloaded the baggage for the passengers, they entered the Wells Fargo office. There was no one waiting, for the stage would not depart until the following morning.

The Fargo agent looked across the counter. "Welcome back, boys. Did you hear about the Moran gang escaping again?"

Doke frowned, putting on an act. "What's that? They escaped after I was up there to see Tag for the last time?"

"We haven't heard anything about it," said Buck.

The agent picked up a copy of the *Fort Collins Gazette* off the counter. "Not only that, but they went to Denver and abducted Dr. Dane Logan's bride right at the wedding, before she walked the aisle. Tag told a couple of her female attendants to tell Logan he was gonna kill her. Here, read it for yourself."

Doke's blood was heating up as he and Buck stood at the counter and read the article. If he killed Tharyn Tabor, her death would be on Doke's hands.

Doke turned to Buck. "Listen, I've got to go to Denver immediately. I can't explain it now, but it's a matter of life and death."

The sun was setting over the Rocky Mountains west of Denver as John Brockman was getting ready to leave his office and head for home.

The deputy on the front desk tapped on the door. "Chief, there's a young man here who says he's shotgunner on the Wells Fargo stage that runs between Fort Collins and Casper. He says it is very important that he see you."

"Sure. Send him in."

Doke Veatch entered the office, told the chief his name, and as they shook hands, he said, "Chief Brockman, I know you have been deeply involved with the Tag Moran gang."

"That I have."

"Well, sir, I am a childhood friend of Tag Moran. He saved my life when we were in our teens, at the risk of his own life. But, well, having read in the *Fort Collins Gazette* about the bride's abduction at the wedding, and of Tag's intention to kill her, I must do what I can to keep it from happening, if it hasn't happened already. I know where the gang's hideout is, and I'll lead you there."

Thanking God in his heart for answered prayer, John Brockman said, "Great! I'll dash over to the Western Union office and wire Dr. Logan in Central City and tell him about you, that you are going to lead us to the gang's hideout. By the way — where is it?"

"In the mountains about thirty miles west of Fort Collins."

"Okay. You wait here, and I'll be back shortly. You can stay as a guest in our house tonight if you wish. I'll take four of my deputies with us, and we'll head out in the morning."

Doke smiled. "That will be fine, sir."

Half an hour later, Brockman returned and informed Doke that Dr. Logan wired him back only minutes after receiving his telegram, saying he would ride for Denver immediately. He wanted to go with them to the hideout and would arrive at the Brockman place by bedtime. "You can go home with me now and have supper with us."

"Sounds good to me, sir."

During supper at the Brockman home, Doke Veatch was witnessed to by John and Breanna while Paul and Ginny looked on. He was shaken by the Scriptures the Brockmans quoted and did his best to cover it, yet be polite. The wedding and the abduction were also discussed, and Doke learned that those in the wedding party from out of town, along with Dr. Dane Logan's parents, had gone back to their homes.

Dr. Dane arrived almost three hours after supper was over, and since there were two beds in the room Dane always stayed in, both he and Doke would stay in that room.

When the two men were in the room at bedtime, they talked about meeting each other at separate times when Darryl Moran and Gib Tully were shot and died.

Then they discussed the abduction of Tharyn by Tag Moran and his gang, and Tag's intention to kill her. Dr. Dane expressed his appreciation to Doke for being willing to lead the lawmen and himself to the hideout.

When both men were ready to retire for the night, Doke climbed in his bed and noticed Dane take a Bible out of his overnight bag. Dane saw immediately that the presence of the Bible made Doke uneasy. "I always read from this Book before going to sleep at night. It make you nervous, Doke?"

The shotgunner licked his lips. "Well, Doctor, I've heard preachers preach from it a few times in my life, and it always puts me on edge."

"Oh? How come?"

"Well . . . uh . . . because it scares me about dying and going to hell."

Dane grinned. "You don't have to be scared about dying. And you certainly don't have to go to hell. God's only begotten Son died on the cross to provide a way for all sinners to be saved, forgiven of their sins, and go to heaven when they die."

Doke frowned. "You make it sound so simple."

"God's plan of salvation for sinners is indeed simple, Doke. It's the religious crowd that makes it seem complicated."

"Oh."

"May I show you what I'm talking about?"

"All right."

The doctor moved to Doke's bed and sat down on the edge. Doke slipped out from under the covers and sat beside him.

Dane opened his Bible to Romans 3. Holding it so Doke could see it clearly, he said, "Read me verse 23, will you?"

Doke nodded. " 'For all have sinned and come short of the glory of God.' "

"Who is *all,* Doke?"

"Well, ah . . . everybody."

"So all humans are guilty sinners before a holy God."

"Yes."

"That includes me, and that includes you."

Doke nodded. "Yes, sir."

"But there is a difference between you and me, Doke. I am a sinner who has had all of his sins washed away and forgiven.

Therefore, when I die, I will go to heaven. You already indicated to me that when you die, you will go to hell."

Doke's features crimsoned. "Well, yes, sir."

"Do you want to go to hell?"

"No. Who would want to burn forever?"

"All right," said Dane, turning a couple of pages. "Now read me this verse." He was pointing to Romans 6:23.

Doke took a deep breath. " 'For the wages of sin is death; but the gift of God is eternal life through Jesus Christ our Lord.' "

"Now think about it. If you get what you earn by sinning against God, it's death, isn't it?"

"Yes."

"That's more than physical death, Doke. In the book of Revelation, we learn that hell in its final state is called the lake of fire. Repeatedly in that book, the lake of fire is called the second death. So if you die without being saved, the wages you receive for a lifetime of sin is to burn forever in the lake of fire. Understand?"

"I'm beginning to."

"Good. Now, look at this verse again. There is not only death mentioned, but life — *eternal* life. That means forever with

God in heaven, doesn't it?"

"It has to."

"All right, now notice the word *gift*. Eternal life — spending forever with God in heaven — can't be earned by good works and religious deeds. It is a gift. If you earn something, it is a wage, right?"

"Uh-huh."

"But if you receive it as a gift, is it earned?"

"No."

"Correct. It is by grace. In Ephesians 2:8 and 9, God says, 'For by grace are ye saved through faith; and that not of yourselves: it is the gift of God: Not of works, lest any man should boast.' Salvation, forgiveness of your sins, and a place in heaven forever does not come from human works, but by God's grace, which is a gift. It can't be earned by good works, which would include religious deeds. Understand?"

"Yes, sir. Like never before."

"Good. Now, look here at Romans 6:23 again. Look real close. 'But the gift of God is eternal life through Jesus Christ our Lord.' See that? Salvation — eternal life — does not come through anything we can accomplish, like being baptized, taking communion, or saying prayers. It only comes through the Lord Jesus Christ. He came into this world by the miraculous virgin birth, lived a perfectly sinless life, and purposely died on the cross of Calvary, shedding His sinless blood for our sins. Do you understand that?"

"It's making sense to me, Doctor, like it never has before."

"Now, let me ask you — did Jesus stay dead after He was crucified and buried?"

"Oh no. He came back to life."

"Right. Now that's the gospel, Doke. In Mark 1:15, Jesus said, 'Repent ye, and believe the gospel.' Repentance is a change of mind that results in a change of direction. When we repent of our sin, we turn from it unto the living Christ, acknowledging that we are indeed sorry for sinning against Him, and call on Him to forgive us and save us because we believe the gospel.

"Now let's go back to Romans 3. Look what it says in the verse after the one we read a few minutes ago. 'Being justified freely by his grace through the redemption that is in Christ Jesus.' To be justified is to stand before God just as if you had never sinned. Redemption is the same thing as salvation. Please notice that we are justified *freely*. We cannot earn it. It's by His grace."

"Yes, sir."

"And our redemption — our salvation — is where, Doke?"

"In Christ Jesus."

"Right. Not in our good works. Not in baptismal water, not in communion elements, or some mortal religious leader. Just in Jesus Christ. Scripture tells us that after we're saved, we are to be baptized and to take communion, but in neither of these is redemption found."

"That is so clear, Doctor. I've never seen this before."

"Do you want to be saved?"

"Yes, I do."

"Good! Now let me show you what the Bible says you have to do."

Dane flipped to Romans 10. "Read me verses 9 through 13, Doke."

Doke's heart was throbbing. " 'That if thou shalt confess with thy mouth the Lord Jesus, and shalt believe in thine heart that God hath raised him from the dead, thou shalt be saved. For with the heart man believeth unto righteousness; and with the mouth confession is made unto salvation. For the scripture saith, Whosoever believeth on him shall not be ashamed. For there is no difference between the Jew and the Greek: for the same Lord over all is rich unto all that call upon him. For whosoever shall call upon the name of the Lord shall be saved.' "

Dane looked him in the eye. "Notice the use of the word *heart*. In verse 9 it says you must believe in your *heart*. In verse 10 it says it is with the *heart* that a person believes unto righteousness. A person can believe about Jesus in their mind, Doke, but that doesn't save them. The heart is the very center of your soul. You must receive Jesus into your heart as your own personal Saviour. You do that by repenting of your sin and doing what it says here in Romans 10:13: *call* upon Him. Understand?"

Tears were misting Doke's eyes. "Yes, Doctor. I want to call on Him and ask Him to come into my heart, forgive me of my sins, and save me *right now!*"

Dane closed his Bible and put his arm around Doke's shoulders. "Let's bow our heads, and you do exactly as you just said."

When Kathryn Tully and Tharyn Tabor were in their room alone, Kathryn referred to the Scriptures on the subject of salvation that Tharyn had shared with her the past several nights. She told Tharyn she had not slept well since the first night. She wanted to be saved.

Tharyn had the joy of leading her to the Lord.

The next night, in their room — after Tag Moran had spoken roughly to Tharyn several times through the day — Kathryn took hold of Tharyn's hand, a worried look in her eyes. "Tharyn, I can't stand the way Tag is treating you. Of course it's because you represent Dr. Logan to him. I'm afraid one of these times he's going to harm you physically. He does have a vile temper, and he hates your young doctor with a passion. If you will agree to it, we'll escape out of the bedroom window later tonight, when all of them are asleep."

Tharyn's eyes widened. "Escape? The *two* of us? You will go with me?"

"Yes! I want to get away from here too. We'll go to the closest neighboring cabin in the forest. It's about five miles to the southeast. I've never met the people who live there, but their names are Will and Nora Darby. We'll explain the situation to the Darbys and ask if they will take us to the sheriff's office in Fort Collins."

"But — but —"

Kathryn frowned. "But what?"

"I'm afraid for you. If these outlaws would catch us, Tag would take it out on you!"

"They won't catch us, honey. We can make it. Okay?"

"Okay."

"Good. We'll wait till after midnight, to make sure they're all asleep. Then we'll climb out the window onto the roof of the back porch. It'll be easy to get down to the ground from there. We'll take your wedding dress with us."

Tears welled up in Tharyn's eyes. She hugged Kathryn, thanked her, then breathed softly, "Thank You, Lord! I know You are going to take care of us."

The next morning at dawn, John Brockman and his four deputies left their horses in the dense forest near the hideout, and approached the cabin on foot, guns drawn.

For safety's sake, Dr. Dane and Doke were ordered by Brockman to stay with the horses. While the two of them watched the lawmen close in on the cabin, Doke said, "Dr. Logan, it's just so good to be saved, to know that I'm going to heaven instead of hell. Thank you for leading me to the Lord."

Dr. Dane smiled. "It was my pleasure, Doke."

Inside the cabin, Lucinda had just discovered that Kathryn and Tharyn had gone out their bedroom window and run away. She ran down the stairs, announcing it to Tag and the others.

Filled with fury, Tag growled, "Breakfast will have to wait. Let's go after 'em!"

With Tag in the lead, the gang dashed out the front door onto the porch. "Kathryn and Tharyn will leave tracks, and we'll find 'em."

Suddenly he skidded to a halt on the porch floor, his face an instant gray mask of surprise as he looked down the barrels of the five guns that were trained on him and his gang. If fear had bounds, then Tag Moran considered he had reached the outer limits. Bart, Jason, and Tony were in the same condition.

"Take those guns out of their holsters and drop them!" said the chief U.S. marshal. "Now!"

Tag's legs went weak and his stomach felt like it was full of floating feathers. His arms were devoid of strength. Noting the determination on the faces of the five lawmen, he mumbled weakly, "Do as he says, boys. They mean business."

While Tag and the others were being handcuffed with their hands behind their backs, and John Brockman was questioning Tag about the two women running away, Dr. Dane and Doke drew up.

"Did I hear right, Chief?" asked Dane. "Tharyn and another woman have run away?"

John nodded. "Yes. Don't worry. We'll find them."

Tag looked at Doke. His eyes were fiery, and his cheeks were locked in a flushed state of anger. "You dirty traitor! You led 'em here! Some friend you are!"

Doke met his fiery gaze. "I'm still your friend, Tag, but when I found out you told those two women at the church that you were going to kill Tharyn, I had to try to stop you before you did it. I'm glad to hear that she and Kathryn have escaped."

Lucinda stood at the open door, tears in her eyes, as she looked at her handcuffed husband. Bart looked at her for a few seconds, then looked at his feet.

Chief Brockman said to his deputies, "Take these guys to Judge Yeager in Rawlins. I want him to know they are once again in custody. The judge can see to it that they are taken back to the prison. Dr. Logan and Doke will go with me. We'll trail Tharyn and the other woman and find them."

Having said thus, Brockman set his gaze

on Lucinda. "We'll leave you here, ma'am. No reason to take you to Rawlins."

Lucinda's lips were quivering, her face pinched. She avoided his gaze.

Brockman said to his deputies, "When you've seen to it that the gang has been put back in the prison, go on home. Once Dr. Logan, Doke, and I have found the women, we'll bring them to Denver."

The lawmen saddled and bridled the outlaws' horses and hoisted them into their saddles. Bart gave his wife a despairing look as the lawmen led the gang away. Tag looked back and looked accusingly at Doke.

In his saddle, Tag didn't show it, but he knew this time he would hang. He was terrorized at the thought of dying. As a youth, he had heard an evangelist preach twice. In both sermons, the evangelist warned of a burning hell for those who died without Christ. Chills slithered down his back.

Lucinda stood on the porch and wept as she watched the deputies and the gang members ride down the steep slope into the forest and vanish from sight.

Being an experienced tracker, John Brockman soon found tracks left by Tharyn and Kathryn in the woods, descending down the mountain to the southeast. Leading their own horses on foot, John, Dane, and Doke followed the tracks through the forest.

As they moved slowly among the trees, Dane looked at John with a smile. "I'm so relieved to know that Tharyn is alive. Praise the Lord!"

"Amen!" John said.

"Amen!" Doke echoed.

John grinned at Doke. "Not saved much more than a day, and you're already learning how to talk right, Doke."

Dane laughed. "He's learning fast, Chief."

As they continued down through the forest, following the tracks left by Tharyn and Kathryn, Doke's conscience was bothering him about his guilt in making it possible for Tag and the others to escape from prison. He finally confessed it to Dane and Chief Brockman.

John said, "Well, Doke, as an officer of the law, I must arrest you for what you did. But since you confessed it on your own and are truly sorry, I will take you to Judge Yeager in Rawlins and ask him for clemency on your behalf."

Dane said, "Doke, you're a child of God now. I'm sure that because you confessed this to Chief Brockman, the Lord will have mercy and make it so Judge Yeager doesn't have you put in prison."

"I feel the same way, Doke," said Brockman. "Don't worry about it."

It was almost noon when they found the women's tracks leading to a log cabin beside a stream.

Dane's heart leaped in his chest. Tharyn and Kathryn made it to safety! He ran ahead of the other two, jumped up on the porch, and knocked on the door.

John and Doke quickly followed and stepped up on the porch just as the door came open and an elderly woman appeared.

"Ma'am," said an excited Dane, "are Tharyn and Kathryn here?"

Her wrinkled brow furrowed. She glanced at the other two — noting the badge on the tall man's vest. "Well, just who might you be, young man?"

"Oh, I'm sorry, ma'am. My name is Dr. Dane Logan."

She looked at Brockman. "I don't have my spectacles on, but I think that badge says you are a United States marshal."

John smiled. "Yes, ma'am. I'm Chief U.S. Marshal John Brockman from Denver. Dr. Logan was to marry Miss Tharyn last week, but —"

"I know all about that." She chuckled. "Well, that's good enough for me. I jist didn't want to be passin' any information on about them two young ladies without knowin' for sure who was askin'. I'm Martha Darby. I live here with my son, Will, and his wife, Nora. Please come in."

"Are Tharyn and Kathryn here?" asked Dane, as she widened the door and they stepped inside.

"No, they're not," said Martha, closing the door behind them.

"Tharyn and Kathryn knocked on this door at four o'clock this mornin'. My son was already awake, though he was still in bed. He put on his robe and went to the door. Seein' how frightened the young ladies looked, Will invited 'em in. After he had dressed and awakened Nora and me, we went into the parlor together. Tharyn and Kathryn told us the story — about Tharyn's weddin', the abduction at the weddin' by those bad guys, and Tharyn bein' kept a captive at the cabin."

Martha looked at Brockman. "You're gonna go arrest them bad guys, ain'tcha?"

"Already did, ma'am. My deputies are taking them to prison right now."

"Good! Well let me explain now. Will and Nora have taken those two young ladies to the Larimer County sheriff's office in Fort Collins. They left about eight-thirty this mornin'."

Dane's eyes lit up. "Praise the Lord! Chief, let's head for Fort Collins!"

"We'll just do that," said John.

The three men thanked Martha Darby for the information. Elated to know that Tharyn and Kathryn were all right, they mounted up and rode for Fort Collins.

Twenty-four

When Dane Logan, John Brockman, and Doke Veatch arrived at the sheriff's office in Fort Collins and asked him about Tharyn Tabor and Kathryn Tully, Sheriff James Hoffman sat them down in front of his desk and said, "Well, gentlemen, I'll tell you what. Those two young ladies are now on the train that left here for Denver just over an hour ago."

John turned to Dane. "Looks like we missed them again."

Dane smiled. "That's all right, Chief. At least we know they're safe, and soon Tharyn will be home with her parents. Thank the dear Lord for His loving mercy."

"Amen!" said Doke.

"That's right," John said, nodding.

Hoffman grinned and leaned forward with his elbows on the desktop. "I took the young ladies to the depot myself. Tharyn asked me to send a wire to you at Central

City, Dr. Logan. She wanted to let you know that she had escaped the clutches of the gang, was all right, and what time the train would arrive in Denver. She also asked me to wire the same message to her parents, and to add that she had a friend with her who would need to stay at the Tabor home for a while. I sent the telegrams immediately after the train pulled out."

"Thank you for doing this for Tharyn, Sheriff," said Dr. Dane. "I really appreciate it."

The three men returned to their horses at the hitch rail in front of the office.

"Well, Doke," said Brockman, "let's ride for Rawlins. We've got to see Judge Yeager."

While Doke was untying the reins from the rail, John turned to Dr. Dane. "When you and Tharyn set the new wedding date, Breanna, the kids, and I will be ready to do our part."

Dane smiled. "It'll be soon, I can tell you that."

Dane started to say something else, but Doke spoke to Brockman: "Chief, do you think you can get me in to see Tag at the prison before he is hanged? I want to tell him about my getting saved and try to lead him to the Lord."

John smiled broadly. "As chief U.S. marshal, I'm sure I can arrange that for you."

John then turned to Dane. "You were going to say something a moment ago."

Dane grinned. "I was about to tell you that Tag is heavy on my heart, and that since I know Tharyn is safe now, I would ride with you and Doke to Rawlins, go to the prison, and ask to see Tag so I could try to lead him to the Lord before he is hanged."

Doke's eyes lit up. "Hey, that's great!"

"Let's go!" said John.

Before riding out of Fort Collins, they stopped at the Western Union office so both Dane and John could send telegrams.

Dane sent a wire to Dr. Robert Fraser in Central City, advising him that Tharyn was all right and on her way to Denver, and that he would be arriving home within three or four days. He also sent a wire to Tharyn in care of her parents, explaining that Chief Brockman and his deputies had arrested the gang at the hideout, and the deputies were escorting them back to the prison. He explained that he and the chief tracked her and Kathryn to the Darby cabin, and that Sheriff Hoffman explained that he had put both of them on the train to Denver this morning. Dane also wrote that he and the chief had to go to Rawlins, but they would be in Denver within two or three days. Dane added in the telegram that he loved her more than ever, and the wedding would be very soon.

John also wired Breanna and his office, explaining briefly about the capture of the gang, Tharyn being safely on her way to Denver, and he would be home soon.

While they were riding toward Rawlins, Doke said, "Dr. Logan, if Chief Brockman can get me permission, will you let me go to the prison with you so I can see Tag too?"

"Sure. I'd be glad to have you with me."

John then told Doke of a good church in Fort Collins he should go to and gave him the pastor's name. Doke said, "I most certainly will do that, sir."

The next day, after spending the night in Rawlins's only hotel, the three men went to the courthouse, and after a forty-five minute wait, were ushered into Judge George Yeager's office.

The judge told them that Tag Moran was scheduled to be hanged at sunrise the next morning, then sat quietly and listened as Chief Brockman told him Doke Veatch's story.

When Yeager had heard about Doke's having planted the Derringer at the prison's stockade fence, which resulted in the Tag Moran gang's escape, then heard Doke humbly ask for clemency, admitting how wrong he had been, he thought on it for a long moment.

Before the judge opened his mouth to comment, John Brockman spoke a good word for Doke.

Yeager then said, "Mr. Veatch, it tells me a lot about your character, that you owned up to your wrongdoing to Chief Brockman when you didn't have to. No one would have ever known. I'm going to mark your admission to this crime as forgiven. It will be sealed and locked away. However, should you ever commit another crime, this confession can be brought up and used against you. Do I make myself clear?"

"Oh yes, sir — I mean — your honor, sir. I just got saved a few days ago. I'm a born-again child of God. You don't have to worry about me. I'll never disobey the law again."

Yeager smiled. "Well, what do you know? I'm a born-again Christian myself, son. Tell you what, I'll say as the Lord Jesus did to that repentant woman in John 8 who was taken in adultery: 'Neither do I condemn thee: go, and sin no more.' "

While John and Dane looked on, Doke bowed his head for a moment, then looked up at the judge, a smile of deep gratitude on his face. Rising from his chair, Doke extended his hand and grasped the hand of the judge. "Thank you, your honor, from the bottom of this saved sinner's heart."

The three men headed immediately for the prison, and based on Chief Brockman's request, Doke was given permission by Warden Harold Quinn to go into a private room with Dr. Dane Logan to talk to Tag.

John Brockman waited in the warden's office.

In his cell, Tag Moran was pacing the floor, terrified of dying and going to hell. He thought of the sermons he had heard that evangelist preach so many years ago, but could not recall what he had to do to be saved.

Wringing his hands as he paced, he shook his head. "Even if I *could* remember, what good would it do? As wicked as I've been, God wouldn't forgive me anyhow. I'm doomed. There's no hope for me. I —"

"Moran," came the voice of a guard at the barred door, "you've got visitors."

Tag stopped pacing, turned, and looked at him. "Visitors?"

"That's right."

"Who?"

"I don't know them, but you do." He inserted the key into the lock. "Let's go."

The guard ushered Tag down the corridor to a small, private room and opened the door. Tag was shocked to see Dr. Dane Logan and Doke Veatch already seated at a table in the room. As he stepped through the door, the guard said, "Since you're gonna hang tomorrow, I'll give you an hour, Moran."

The door closed and a key turned in the lock.

As Tag sat on the third chair at the table, he noted that Dr. Logan had a Bible. Tag ran his gaze between the two men. "I — I'm, well I'm quite shocked to see you."

Dr. Dane smiled. "We thought you might be."

Tag blinked. "I'm glad you're both here because I can make my apologies to you before I die."

Dane and Doke looked at each other, both knowing what the other was thinking: *Tag is not his old self.*

While they listened, Tag told Doke he understood why he led the lawmen to the hideout, and that he did the right thing. He was only trying to save Tharyn's life.

Doke nodded. "I'm glad you understand, Tag."

Moran then set his gaze on the physician and apologized for the accusations he had made about his letting Darryl and Gib die because they were outlaws. "I was wrong, Doctor. I'm asking your forgiveness."

"You're forgiven, Tag," said Dane.

Tag cleared his throat. "And . . . uh . . . Doctor, I'm sorry for abducting your bride. Did — did you find her?"

"No, but she and Kathryn made it to Fort Collins. The sheriff told us he put them on a train to Denver."

"Oh. Well, I'm glad." Tag shook his head. "I've been so wicked! I'm so sorry that I killed those people when we were robbing the banks."

"We're both glad to hear that you're sorry, Tag," said Doke.

Moran wiped tears from the corners of his eyes and looked at the Bible that lay on the table in front of Dane. He raised his eyes to the doctor. "I'm scared, Doctor. I'm scared of dying tomorrow morning and going to hell. I haven't been in church much in my life, but when I was young, someone took me to a revival meeting. I heard an evangelist preach about dying in your sins and going to hell. They took me to two services in that revival meeting, and the evangelist preached about hell both nights. I've been thinking a lot about that lately."

"I can see why," said Dr. Dane.

Doke leaned close. "Tag, let me tell you a story."

Tag nodded. "All right."

Doke told him of Dr. Dane Logan leading him to the Lord and the peace he now had in his heart.

Tag was looking at him dumbfounded.

Doke grinned. "It's true, Tag. And because I am still your friend, I want you to be saved. If you will listen, Dr. Logan will show you from the Bible how to be saved, miss hell, and go to heaven."

Tag said eagerly, "Yes, I will listen!" His brow furrowed. "But —"

"But what?" asked Dr. Dane.

Tag's eyes were now filled with tears. "I'm a murderer, Doctor. God can't forgive me for that. Jesus doesn't save murderers."

Dane opened his Bible. "Let's see what the Bible says about this, Tag." He turned to 1 Timothy 1, then angled the Bible so Tag could see it. "Did you know that the apostle Paul had his hand in killing Christians before he got saved?"

Tag looked stunned. "No."

"Well, he did. Now I want you to see what the Spirit of God had the apostle Paul write here in verse 15. Read it to me."

Tag focused on the verse. " 'This is a faithful saying, and worthy of all acceptation, that Christ Jesus came into the world to save sinners; of whom I am chief.' "

Dane looked at Tag. "Paul called himself the chief of sinners because of the wicked life he had lived before he was saved, Tag. Now, what did he say Jesus came into the world to do?"

Tag swallowed hard. "To save sinners."

"Right. Are *you* a sinner?"

"Am I ever."

"Then did Jesus come into the world so he could save you?"

"Well, I — uh — but I'm a murderer."

"Jesus came into the world to save all kinds of sinners except murderers. Is that what it says?"

"Well, no."

"All murderers are sinners, aren't they?"

"Yes, sir."

"Does it say that Jesus came into the world to save sinners?"

"Yes."

"Then are you going to say that He can't save you and cleanse you of all your sins?"

Tag shook his head. "I can't say that, Doctor. Since Jesus came into the world to save sinners, then He can save me too."

Dane smiled at Doke, and Doke smiled back.

"Okay, Tag," said Dane, "let me show you about Jesus dying on the cross and shedding His precious blood for our sins."

Dane carefully took Tag through the Scriptures, showing him the gospel and God's plan of salvation clearly. With tears flowing, Tag called on the Lord to save him, and great peace flooded his heart and soul.

When Tag had dried his tears, Dr. Dane said, "Tag, let me tell you what Tharyn said to me on the night before we were supposed to get married. She said, " 'Just think, darling. One more sunrise and I'll be Mrs. Dane Logan!' "

Tag was watching the expression on the doctor's face.

"Tag, you prevented that from happening by abducting my bride. But listen to me. You will indeed hang tomorrow at sunrise. One more sunrise and you will be in heaven. But *nothing* can prevent that!"

At that moment, the guard opened the

door. "Time's up, gentlemen."

Dr. Dane and Doke rose from their chairs. So did Tag, while wiping tears. There were tender good-byes between Tag and Doke, and between Tag and the man who had just led him to the Lord.

When Dane and Doke returned to the warden's office and told John Brockman the story, John rejoiced in Tag's salvation.

They left the warden's office, went outside the prison gate to their horses, and swung into their saddles.

Dane looked at the other two. "Thank God for His grace. Tomorrow, Tag will be in heaven."

John and Doke chorused an amen.

Dr. Dane took a deep breath and looked southward. "Let's move out. My precious little bride is waiting for me!"

Dust clouds rose up from the horses' hooves as the three men galloped away.

About the Authors

Bestselling author **Al Lacy** has written more than one hundred historical and western novels, including those in the Angel of Mercy, Battles of Destiny, and Journeys of the Stranger series. **JoAnna Lacy** is his wife and longtime collaborator, as well as the coauthor of the Hannah of Fort Bridger, Mail Order Bride, Shadow of Liberty, and Orphan Trains series. The Lacys make their home in the Rocky Mountains of Colorado.

The employees of Thorndike Press hope you have enjoyed this Large Print book. All our Thorndike and Wheeler Large Print titles are designed for easy reading, and all our books are made to last. Other Thorndike Press Large Print books are available at your library, through selected bookstores, or directly from us.

For information about titles, please call:

(800) 223-1244

or visit our Web site at:

www.gale.com/thorndike
www.gale.com/wheeler

To share your comments, please write:

Publisher
Thorndike Press
295 Kennedy Memorial Drive
Waterville, ME   04901